Special EDITION

Believe in love. Overcome obstacles. Find happiness.

Her New York Minute
Darby Baham

A Deal With Mr Wrong
Anna James

MILLS & BOON

HER NEW YORK MINUTE
© 2024 by Darby Baham
Philippine Copyright 2024
Australian Copyright 2024
New Zealand Copyright 2024

First Published 2024
First Australian Paperback Edition 2024
ISBN 978 1 867 29999 8

A DEAL WITH MR. WRONG
© 2024 by Heidi Tanca
Philippine Copyright 2024
Australian Copyright 2024
New Zealand Copyright 2024

First Published 2024
First Australian Paperback Edition 2024
ISBN 978 1 867 29999 8

MIX
Paper | Supporting
responsible forestry
FSC® C001695

Published by
Harlequin Mills & Boon
An imprint of Harlequin Enterprises (Australia) Pty Limited
(ABN 47 001 180 918), a subsidiary of HarperCollins
Publishers Australia Pty Limited
(ABN 36 009 913 517)
Level 19, 201 Elizabeth Street
SYDNEY NSW 2000 AUSTRALIA

Cover art used by arrangement with Harlequin Books S.A.. All rights reserved.

Printed and bound in Australia by McPherson's Printing Group

Her New York Minute
Darby Baham

MILLS & BOON

Darby Baham is an author and storyteller on a mission to make women like herself feel seen and believe that love is possible for them, yes them. The former *Washington Post* contributor often uses her doubts, hopes and fears to connect with her readers and inform the themes in her Harlequin romance series, The Friendship Chronicles. This series is a love letter to female friendships and offers an intimate look into the dynamic love lives of Black women.

Dear Reader,

Growing up, I always bristled at the saying "Want to make God laugh? Tell him/her about your plans." Maybe that's because I love a good plan. It's something about the linear nature of it—if all goes right, it can be the simplest and most satisfying thing in the world. Yet when I look over my life, many of the best things that have happened to me have been entirely unplanned. Weird, right?

Well, this is exactly what Olivia Robinson is facing in *Her New York Minute*. In the fourth book of my Friendship Chronicles series, the British native goes to New York with one goal in mind: become the youngest head of her company's portfolio division. She never expects to also meet a charming attorney who shows her what it's like to be loved just as she is—and to be honest, she struggles with that disruption.

With the help of some of your faves from the rest of the series, however, Olivia eventually realises some of the best things—even the dreams she stopped believing could ever happen for her—come unexpected...out of the blue...and in a New York minute.

Hope you enjoy!

Darby

DEDICATION

To the unexpected blessing who came into my life
and knocked me off my feet—thank you.

Part 1

"There is no force more powerful than a woman determined to rise."

—Bosa Sebele

Chapter One

This is going to be my year.

That was all I kept thinking as my plane began descending into JFK International Airport, carrying hundreds of passengers and all my hopes and dreams of kicking ass and taking names in the most limitless city on Earth…plus my year's worth of luggage.

In just six months' time, I'd gone from being the portfolio manager of a team that had shocked our global investment company when we'd raised $500 million for a little social impact fund that no one but us had really believed in to being offered the opportunity to go to our New York office to duplicate my efforts in America. So, I bloody well knew the impact I could have in a short amount of time, and I was ready.

Like I said, this was going to be my year.

Never mind that I didn't really know what I was in store for—all that mattered was that I had a grand plan and I was going to execute it to perfection. On my agenda? Show up, flawlessly polished stilettos in tow, wow the US office with my ideas for taking what we'd learned so far and expanding on it, and prove to everyone that I was even more than the superstar they maybe imagined I might've been. I'd already started to establish myself in the UK office, having overseen multiple million-dollar portfolios since, but it still sometimes seemed as if people were waiting for me to take my next step up. And even if they weren't and it was all in my head, I'd certainly put enough pressure on myself to excel that it made up for at least ten people at once. Either way, I knew one thing to be true—I couldn't just succeed in London if I wanted to move up the ladder at my investment management group; I also needed the C-suite brass in America to see what I could do up close and personal before they, hopefully, eventually gave me the thing I really wanted: head of the portfolio division.

So, there I was, on a flight headed thousands of miles away from the only home I'd ever known, taking on a new position that they hadn't fully described to me other than saying, *New York needs you, and we think this can be a great opportunity.* Not exactly a detailed job description, but I had decided to bet on myself. And as long as everything went according to my plans, I expected that this time next year, I'd be flying right back to the UK, a year older, perfectly positioned for a promotion to senior portfolio manager at thirty-six and in line for my dream job soon after. What more could a girl from Brixton really ask for, yeah?

I closed my eyes and waited for the plane's wheels to hit the ground so that my new adventure could begin, allowing the smooth sounds of Tems's voice to calm my nerves as "Free Mind" played softly in my ears. About two songs and five or six minutes later, one of our flight attendants turned on her mic and announced what we'd all been waiting for after sitting around for eight hours on a plane.

"Ladies and gentlemen," she began. "Welcome to New York City, where the local time is 5:25 p.m. For your safety and the safety of those around you, please remain seated with your seat belt fastened and keep the aisles clear until we are parked at the gate. Be careful when opening overhead bins as items tend to move during flight… On behalf of all of us here at JetBlue, thanks again for choosing us. For those of you from New York City, we'd like to be the first to say welcome home. If you're visiting, we hope you enjoy your stay, and we look forward to seeing you again soon."

Welp, I thought as I readied myself for the eventual dash off the plane, *this is it.* And as my friend Robin would say, *Here goes nothing and everything all at once.*

Once I heard the familiar ding letting us know that we could unbuckle our seat belts, I began packing up all my items in an attempt to have my ducks in a row before I inevitably had to wrestle down my heavy luggage from the overhead bin. Down into my knapsack went my bottle of water, the snacks I'd been noshing on the whole flight, a book I'd ambitiously thought I would read and hadn't and, of course, my trusty earbuds only after I'd reluctantly turned off my playlist. Each item had its own place in the gray-and-teal backpack that served as both my carry-on and purse for the day, meticulously plotted out during the weeks prior to my trip to ensure I didn't leave anything I really needed in London. The plotting and planning also helped me to make sure I could magically fit everything I might need in a year into what I could only bring with me on the flight: my backpack, a carry-on and two checked pieces of luggage.

As soon as I saw the rest of my row begin to move, I dutifully slid out of my seat, stood up tall and turned to face my luggage nemesis that had already given me a struggle when I put it in the overhead bin. But I was also me, Olivia Robinson, a badass woman on a mission, so I wasn't about to let a bit of heavy luggage stop me from starting things off just right. Fully determined, and with a deep breath conjuring up all my strength, I resigned myself to the struggle I'd ultimately overcome and then reached my right arm up and pulled on the top handle with all my might, tugging it with proper force…only for it to not move even one tiny little spec.

"Okay, that's all right," I whispered to myself. "Even Beyoncé has to do things twice sometimes, yeah."

I prepared myself for my second attempt, this time rising onto my toes in my white low-top trainers and using both hands to try to wrestle the carry-on out of its home. I jiggled it. I tugged at it. I even grunted while I pulled. But again, no such luck. To make matters worse, the frustrated sighs I had been worried might come if I didn't stop holding up the progress in the aisle began loudly making their way to my ears, causing me to not only feel completely embarrassed but also wholly upset with myself that I couldn't just will this thing to work.

This was not how I'd planned my year to start. Not staring down a stupid little heavy carry-on trying to make me second-guess all my beliefs in a matter of a few minutes. The fact of the matter was that the way I'd lived my life for years now was pretty simple: you put your all into something, you believed in yourself fully and the results you desired would come. *Why didn't this carry-on understand basic physics or whatever?*

I was two seconds away from going down a nasty rabbit hole in my head when I heard a deep-toned voice behind me, offering what felt like the nicest gesture known to man.

"Can I help you out here?" he asked, startling me out of my thoughts.

With a heavy sigh of relief, I answered with the only thing I could utter in that moment: "Yes, please."

Then, swiftly, I came off my tippy toes, closing my eyes briefly in thanks, and turned toward my knight in shining armor.

"I would really appreciate that," I added, running my

hands down my dark blue skinny jeans as I laid my eyes on the kindest smile staring back at me.

It was one of those full smiles, where the joy permeated on every part of the person's face, showing up not only in the off-kilter upturn of his lips but also in the fullness of his cheeks and the glow in his eyes. His teeth, white like a Colgate ad, sparkled in contrast to the dark brown hue of his skin, set off perfectly by his low-cut beard and the goatee that traced along the indented curves of his mouth. But it wasn't just his smile that caught my attention. His chuckle—just as deep-toned as his voice and probably stemming from my less-than-stellar attempt at trying to compose myself in his presence—revealed a playful nature underneath the suaveness of his gentleman persona. And his beautifully sculpted arms, covered only by a long-sleeved white shirt that left nothing to the imagination, only served to add to my now very persistent desire to melt back into my seat so I could watch him work his magic in full view.

Resisting that particular urge, I simply stepped aside to give him full access to my luggage in hopes that he could quickly rescue me from being the embarrassed woman holding up an entire international flight of people from de-boarding their plane. With one hand and one full swing of his arm, my handsome knight snatched the luggage down from the overhead bin as if it were the lightest piece of paper on a table. Then, with his eyes stayed on mine, he delicately placed it on the ground, lifted the handle and put it right next to my hand so I could easily grab it and wheel myself off the flight.

"Wow," I uttered before I could stop myself. "Thank you, honestly."

"It's no problem at all," he replied with a wink and a gentle head nod toward the exit. "I was a little worried the eye daggers you were getting were going to turn into real ones, so I couldn't leave you to fend for yourself too much longer."

"Truthfully, I was, too."

Taking his cue, I turned toward the exit, gathered myself and tried my best to walk as fast as I could down the aisle. To my absolute horror, this only served to embolden the crowd behind me, which proceeded to give me a loud round of applause for finally moving out of their way. It wasn't exactly the first impression I'd planned, but I had my luggage, so I was back in swing mode. Plus, as recently as two days before, I'd experienced something far worse than a bunch of strangers mocking me—I'd maybe, kind of, sort of broken up with my boyfriend of two years, except it had gone about as well as my attempt to pick up my luggage, so I really wasn't quite sure.

All I did know was that despite any mishaps that had occurred between now and then, I was in New York. And so, if nothing else, I was going to hold my head as high as the top bun that my waist-length, brown-and-blond passion twists were tucked into as I walked off that plane. I also vowed to myself not to look back at anyone behind me until I got to baggage claim. The last thing I was going to do was let these strangers see me sweat. Not after I'd fought through all my fears to be right where I was.

My handsome knight, however, didn't seem to get my telepathic memo that I was avoiding anything and everyone from that plane experience—a fact I soon realized as I heard him calling from behind me as we stepped into the gate area of the airport.

"The clapping might have been a little unnecessary," he said, falling in step with me as he quickly caught up to my five-foot-four stride.

"Ha. Oh yes, a bit," I replied, a little flustered that he wanted to keep talking…to me.

"Though you were giving *'damsel in distress who refuses to ask for help'* vibes, so maybe they felt you needed some encouragement."

Ah, so he was a funny guy, too, I realized. *Just my luck.*

I paused my steps and turned to directly face him, wanting him to see clearly that while I'd appreciated his help, I wasn't exactly in the mood for his jokes. Unfortunately for me, as soon as we locked eyes, I completely lost my train of thought. The devious and kid-like smirk on his face somehow took hold of my very brain process, causing me to simply—and almost uncontrollably—smile back at him, which then led to us both tumbling into a series of giggles that only we understood.

"It wasn't that I refused," I replied, trying to contain my chuckles and suddenly feeling like I needed to plead my case. "No one offered until you did."

"Fair point."

He dipped his head slightly to the side in acknowledgment, all the while keeping his eyes trained on mine in some sort of hypnotic force that demanded I stare right back. The wild thing was I didn't even think he was actively trying to seduce me, but in the brief period of time that we'd stopped walking, I'd had to catch my breath on at least three different occasions in his presence. Maybe this captivating effect was something this guy was used to, I theorized. After all, the man had the makings of every picture-perfect model that my friends and I would cut out of our *Right On!* and *J-17* magazines to hang on our bedroom walls when we were preteens.

Standing at what looked to be about five foot ten, with gray eyes so deep they matched his baritone voice, he also had the kind of broad shoulders every heterosexual woman dreamed of holding tightly on to when she was in the throes of passion with her man. His hands were also impeccably manicured and looked like they were both soft and moisturized to perfection but also might have a slight gritty texture on the back side, as if he might have been a former athlete who now only used them to get someone's attention in a restaurant. And his body? Let's just say I imagined even Broderick Hunter would be envious.

I shook my head and all the arresting thoughts of this man who I didn't know out of it, reminding myself that I was barely single and not at all in New York to meet new men, let alone captivating ones in airports. Plus, I wasn't starring in anyone's romantic comedy film last I checked, so I quickly put aside any foolish notions of some sort of meet-cute where the slender, brown-skinned woman from London met the dashing American with an intoxicating smile, and brought myself back to our conversation at hand.

"Also, maybe if they had, the whole ordeal wouldn't have lasted as long as it did," I opined.

"Or…and don't try to tussle with me on this…you could have asked for what you clearly needed, and that also would have resolved your problem."

He tilted his head to the side again and held back what looked like another smirk, betraying how much he was enjoying our banter as the single dimple he had on his right cheek poked out from behind his beard.

"I guess I'm not used to asking for help," I admitted in a slight whisper—and then almost immediately regretted being that open with someone whose name I didn't even know.

"I gathered. Which is why I stepped in."

For a split second, he allowed himself to look at me sincerely, and the eyes that had once shown me kindness and then turned playful were suddenly relaying that he understood what I'd meant on a foundational level. That I didn't need to explain to him why everything in my body resisted asking anyone for help; he already knew. Thankfully for my weak knees, he just as quickly returned back to his jokes, because I was fully unprepared to have someone read me that well in a matter of seconds.

"You know, to rescue you from your damsel ways," he added, winking at me again before going back to his insanely hypnotic stare.

"Well, I do thank you kindly, sir," I replied, and then mockingly curtsied before him. "Whatever would I have done without you?"

"In my head? I imagine you would have eventually climbed onto the arm of one of those seats, grabbed that suitcase with all your might and forced it to bend to your will. It might have taken you another five to ten minutes, but you would have gotten it."

"I don't know if I should take that as a compliment or an insult," I said, still smiling.

"Definitely a compliment. You seem like a woman who doesn't back down from a fight and who usually gets what she wants. I like that."

Stuck standing in front of each other as if our feet couldn't move if we tried, it felt like he was waiting to see which route I would take our fairly innocuous conversation. As if he were silently asking me: Are you going to choose to be even more vulnerable with a perfect stranger in the airport, or should I keep up our surface-level teasing rapport until we part ways?

The answer seemed pretty obvious to me, of course, especially as more people piled off the airplane and rushed past us on their way to Passport Control. Door Number Two was what normal people chose in airport interactions. They went about their business, and if they actually spoke to anyone, it was surface-level chitchat that they'd forgotten by the time they jumped into their Uber and headed home.

As obvious as my choice should have been, there was something about this guy that made me want to choose Door Number One. I wasn't sure if it was the way I kept losing my breath every single time he hit me with one of his bloody intense stares or if it was the fact that he was quite literally stunning or if something behind his eyes just made me want to know more. Whatever it was (and maybe it was all three), the temptation was strong. Any normal woman would have already melted right into his arms, really, told him all her fears, hopes and dreams, and plotted out how their chance encounter would evolve into a marriage proposal within the year. But I…try as I might…had never once been accused of being normal, at least not by any of my exes. Of being a founding member of #TeamTooMuch? Sure. An incessant planner who didn't know how to let life come to her? Mmm-hmm. Unemotional, coldhearted and only focused on winning? Yes, yes and yes. But never normal. So, it was pretty clear what my choice was ultimately going to be.

"Well," I said, clearing my throat. "Once again, I find myself saying thank you to you, so th…thank you, genuinely."

I fumbled my way through my words as I started trying to walk away, hoping to end our impromptu conversation as soon as possible so that I could go on pretending like I didn't notice the little crinkle on his nose as his smile grew wider while watching me squirm.

"Is that a Brixton thing?" he asked, seamlessly matching his steps with mine as he once again caught up to me.

"Is what a Brixton thing?"

."Overly thanking people."

"Oh, well, I didn't know that you could thank someone too many times," I replied. "Plus, how do you know
I'm from Brixton?"

"It's hard to miss the accent, love. And I've spent
enough time in London that I'm starting to learn the dif-
ferences."

"Oh, well, good on you, babes."

I caught myself right before I winked at him in some
sort of instinctual effort to mimic his demeanor toward
me even as we continued walking in step.

"But...to answer your question, no, I wouldn't say we
are overly generous with our thank-yous. And to prove it,
I take mine back."

I lifted my eyebrows to show him that I could join in
on the teasing, too, when I wanted.

"Well, that's not how it works," he retorted with a big
smile on his face and that damn crinkle catching my attention again. "Once it's out there, you can't take back a
thank-you."

"Oy, you say that, but I believe I already have, innit.
Thankyouverymuch."

"And...you just thanked me again."

He burst out laughing, bending forward as he proudly
chuckled to himself and causing me to stop walking again
as I protested my point.

"That doesn't count! You know what I meant there."

"Doesn't matter what you meant, love. It's what you
said."

I sighed loudly.

"Fine. Well, now that you've added to my embarrassment from the plane, th—"

This time, I caught myself before finishing my sarcastic

thank-you in response. The grin on his face showed me I didn't catch it soon enough, however.

Ugh. How had my knight in shining armor so quickly turned into someone who I wanted to shake—and maybe kiss, but mostly shake—that fast?

Really, it didn't matter. I just knew, as I'd known all along, that I needed to get out of his presence as fast as I could before I succumbed to whatever chemistry we seemed to have that had me equally intrigued and frustrated since it was more than I'd ever once had with the man I'd been dating for the past two years.

"You know what?" I asked rhetorically. "I think it's time for me to head to Passport Control. I assume we're going in different directions, yeah?"

His once bright smile faded upon maybe, finally, realizing that I really was trying to end our airport banter.

"Wait, wait, I'm sorry," he replied sincerely. "I'm not trying to embarrass you further, I promise. I was just having a little fun."

"At my expense?"

"I'd like to think not, but if I really have offended you, please let me know."

The look on his face was genuine and probing as he waited for my reply, almost as endearing as the first time he'd slipped his cool and had shown how caring he could be. So, as much as I wanted to play coy and get him back for all his teasing, those deep gray, thoughtful eyes wouldn't dare allow me to let him think he'd actually hurt my feelings. He'd pulled me in yet again.

"No, you definitely didn't offend me," I admitted with a smile. "Though it certainly has been an interesting welcome to a new country. I'd been told that New Yorkers weren't this talkative, so already you've managed to throw everything I believed out of the window."

"Hmm," he said, stepping in closer to me. "Well, that might be because I'm not originally from New York."

"No?"

"Uh-uh. I mean, I've lived here for almost a decade, so it is home. But I'm actually from Philly."

"Philadelphia, Pennsylvania?" I asked to clarify.

"Yep, born and raised."

"On the playground is where you spent most of your days?" I joked, using the follow-up iconic line from *The Fresh Prince of Bel-Air*'s opening theme song.

"Hold up. Y'all were watching Will Smith in London, too?"

"Don't do that. London's not on an entirely different planet, you know."

"No, I know. But to be honest, it's not like we grew up thinking about what anyone outside of America watched or listened to, so that's kinda interesting. Makes me want to know more."

He shrugged casually as he said his last statement but also drew his eyes back up to mine with that familiar probing look that had almost made me choose Door Number One before.

"We had our own stuff, too, yeah," I replied. "But especially among us Black Brits, we definitely paid attention to what Black Americans were doing. You know, diaspora and all. Beyond that, however, *The Fresh Prince of Bel-Air* was just bloody popular in the UK. It shaped a lot of what I thought about America when I was a little girl."

"You are aware now that it's very different, though, right?"

"Ha ha, yeah. I've seen a lot more shows since…oh and rap videos, too. Very important," I teased, and watched him stare at me wide-eyed in horror.

Finally, I had *him* on his toes, which I took great pleasure in, biting my lower lip and playfully raising my eyebrows before I continued.

"I also have actual American friends now, too…so that's probably helped the most."

"Oh, good," he said, breathing a sigh of relief. "For a moment I thought I was going to have to give you a breakdown of Black American culture, complete with my top ten movies you have to see, a nineties-music playlist and at least one full-season watch of *A Different World*."

"Just not the first season!" we said in unison, laughing like we'd known each other for ages.

Locking eyes with me once more, he moved in a few steps closer so that I could just barely make out the cologne that seemed to perfectly complement his entire essence. Again, a different woman, a normal woman, might have inhaled deeply to take in his full scent, but I resisted. I didn't have the luxury to get caught up in some fairy tale with a guy who was likely just a big flirt.

Remember, Liv, I reprimanded myself, *we're only here in America to improve our chances at a promotion. Handsome, charming, irresistibly sexy men are not in our plans.*

"How long are you in town, by the way?" he asked, wrestling me out of my thoughts again.

"A year," I said with a wistful sigh.

"Wow, okay, that is not what I expected you to say."

"Not even with my heavy luggage?"

"Oh, true, that could have been a giveaway. Or you could just be a bad packer."

"I think maybe quite the opposite, or at least I hope. I've had to pack up a year's worth of luggage for this flight, so fingers crossed I got it right."

"Something tells me you made damn sure you did," he replied, sending chills down my spine again as he caught my attention with yet another bloody intense gaze. "Can I ask—what are you doing for the next year?"

"Well," I said, clearing my throat again, "my job is interested in seeing if I can pull off some more big portfolio wins for them, this time in the States. And I'm using it as a chance to kick ass and take names, so that they have to give me the promotion I want."

"Well, all right, Ms. London. Welcome to America, then."

I smiled as I recognized his admiration for my ambition. It was a nice change from what I'd been dealing with in my relationship with David, where it felt like any big win that I'd had at work made him more and more resentful of me.

"Ha ha, thanks," I replied sheepishly, realizing I'd done it again but hoping he didn't take the bait and call me out. "What brought *you* to New York, by the way?"

"So, actually, I came here after law school, but I didn't always know that I wanted to be a lawyer. Before that, I worked in tech sales for a little while, stacked some money, and then decided to try something new—law. After that, everything just fell into place—I knew where I wanted to work and that I loved to travel. New York law firms offered me the best chance to practice law in the US and overseas, so it was kind of a no-brainer for me. Once I passed the bar, I started working for my current firm, and now here we are."

"Wow, that's really cool," I said, genuinely impressed by him and, frankly, myself for correctly assessing that his current job wasn't one that was physically labor intensive. I could totally understand why he wasn't intimidated by my ambition, too; he had his own with some to spare, it seemed.

"Yeah, guess we're both doing our thing, right?"

He raised his right hand up toward mine and stared into

my eyes as he waited for me to meet his hand in return. After a short hesitation, I lifted mine as well, meeting him for a high five as I also realized that my cheeks were starting to get heavy from cheesing so much. Then, the two of us stood in front of each other, not knowing what else to say but simultaneously not quite ready to leave…our right hands falling down together and moving into something of a handshake that neither of us wanted to end.

In truth, I probably could have stood there forever now that I finally experienced what it was like to feel the touch of his skin, but that would not have been a smart move on my part. Just as I'd presumed, the texture of his skin was soft with just a hint of roughness underneath; what I hadn't counted on was the electricity that had flown through us as soon as our hands collided.

With another quick breath, I slowly began to untangle my fingers away before I lost myself and never wanted to let him go.

For better or worse, he took the hint.

"Well, it's been nice meeting you," he said as he took a step back from me.

"And I *thiiiink* it's been lovely meeting you, too," I replied, still smiling but inside realizing this was definitely goodbye. "At the very least, us meeting helped me get my luggage off the plane."

"At the very least, yeah."

My shining knight took another step away from me, and with one final wink, he turned to his left and walked out of my life. Well, it was to go to the American Passport Control entrance, but for my purposes, that was the same thing. I grabbed my earbuds again and started my playlist back up, falling right into the achingly apropos "Yebba's Heartbreak."

Chapter Two

There's something about waiting for my luggage at baggage claim that gives me the deepest of anxiety. It's like waiting for my food to finish being warmed up in a microwave and watching it go around in a circle as my stomach grumbles beneath me. Switch out a TV dinner with the most important clothes, shoes and accessories I chose to pack for my trip and you could quickly see how I could find myself starting to freak out (at least internally). Absentmindedly, I tugged at the sleeves of my mustard-colored sweater as I waited for my luggage to pop up while person after person walked away with theirs gleefully.

The wait time had another nasty side effect. It gave my mind just enough space to wander back to the days right before my flight, when my excitement for this new opportunity had almost been squelched by *the breakup that wasn't* with my boyfriend, David. What I'd thought was going to be a dramatic affair, with him making a last-ditch effort to ask me to stay, instead had ended with the two of us agreeing to a pause until my return with not one tear shed about my departure. For most, this might have symbolized a sense of maturity in their relationship. But for me and David, it really just magnified the lack of passion we'd had all along—something even my annoying but lovable younger brother had noted to me on several occasions.

Olivia, if it's what you want, who am I to stop you? David had asked me rather ironically, sitting in my flat just days before my flight. What I suppose he hadn't realized was that if anyone could have been the person to stop me, it would have, in fact, been him—which was something I hated to admit even now. Or maybe he had known, and that simply wasn't what he wanted.

Part of me had thought, or rather hoped, that he was going to at least throw me the kind of going-away bash I would have for him—complete with decadent foods and tokens from our moments together, perhaps some bubbly and a surprise final shag to remember me by. But, perhaps unsurprisingly to my friends who hadn't ever been really big fans of his, David had done nothing of the sort. He'd just shrugged off the moment as if the last two years had meant nothing to him. And when he'd left my flat for the last time, he hadn't even kissed me goodbye.

So much for including love and a happy, healthy relationship in my plans for my thirties, I thought. *I won't make that mistake again.*

Really, when I thought about it, David had taught me a good lesson. When we'd started dating, my family had been so happy that finally, in my thirties, I'd brought home a man who'd seemed respectable and ready to settle down. And for a while, I'd been happy, too! Never mind that, together, we'd had the passion of a toad on a log; I'd had an attractive and successful man who liked me, and for most of my family members that was all that mattered. There was just one problem: when I was truly honest with myself, whenever I stopped to think about what I really craved from my partner, I had to admit that there had always been something off about us despite how much we'd tried to make it work.

I mean, I was a woman who liked over-the-top everything, and David had really never appreciated that. He'd loved me—I thought he still did—but in his heart of hearts,

I also believed he'd always thought *it just doesn't take all that* whenever he'd look at me and how I operated in my life. But that place where it seemed like an extra step might be too much? Well, that was where I thrived! It was why simple girls' nights in with my friends included sparkly decorations, balloons and champagne. And why I'd made my company millions of dollars in less than a year. Because when someone else thought they'd done enough, I was just getting started. Maybe in relationships that could be too much for some people to deal with—there was a reason I was staring down thirty-six and single again, yeah—but it had always served me well in my career...so the lesson I'd learned from him was clear: my career was bloody well where my focus needed to be.

On the bright side, my brother and Robin had made up for everything David hadn't done. The two lovebirds, who quite literally owed me for putting them together after serendipitously meeting at my flat, had pulled out all the stops and showed up to my flat the next day with three bottles of bubbly (one for each of us) and plans for a farewell tour throughout London. For a full day, we'd traipsed our way through the city, drunkenly giggling at all my old haunts and finishing off in Brixton with a surprise dinner hosted by my family. Craig, who was an accomplished photographer, had even taken a ton of photos while we'd been out—one of which I'd posted on Instagram with a *Goodbye, London* caption right before boarding my flight.

Now that's how you send someone off like a boss, David. Tuh!

Right as I could feel myself getting upset again, I saw out of the corner of my eye the first of my matching gray-and-teal luggage pop out of the carousel shooter and make its way toward me.

"Yes," I whispered under my breath, and ran toward my

bag, catching it by the side handle and dragging it toward the rest of my things.

What a relief. I double-checked the tag to be sure my name was on it and then lifted it onto the cart that held all my luggage together so that I could easily wheel them out when I was ready.

Now there was just one more to go.

I fixed my eyes back toward the carousel in anticipation of seeing my next one come around the corner.

"Now, what's in *this* bag? The UK army?"

As soon as I heard that unmistakably deep voice to the left of me, another smile I couldn't control instantly grew on my face. If I was going to keep running into him, I would need to work on that for sure.

"We really must stop meeting like this," I said, turning toward him. "One might begin to think it's on purpose or something."

"To be fair, it's not a huge leap that we would see each other again at baggage claim," he said, correcting me slightly with that same smirk he'd had when he'd called me out about not asking for help.

I guess he'd had a point both times.

"But also," he continued as he snaked his fingers through his luggage handle for safekeeping, "I was kind of hoping I'd run into you again."

"Oh?"

His words caused my heart to skip just a beat faster than normal, but I steadied myself in time to not let him in on that little secret.

"Yeah, well, I realized after we parted ways that I never got your name. And I…"

Before he could finish his thought, I saw my last piece of luggage come bouncing around the bend from the corner of my eye. Without hesitation, I dived toward it in a feeble attempt to catch it before it went back around, and then I'd be stuck waiting for it again for God knew how long. Unfortunately, because of my impromptu dive, I caught ahold of my luggage in a weird position and once again found myself struggling to wrestle it down—that was until I felt my kind, handsome stranger's hands on the left side, helping to pull it off with me.

Together, we yanked it down from the carousel and then stood the twenty-three-kilogram bag up onto its wheels, the dynamic duo having once again conquered what felt like my ongoing luggage wars.

"Apologies," I whispered, catching his eyes. "I didn't mean to interrupt you, but…"

"Please. There's no need to explain. It's important you get your suitcase. I get it."

"Thank you," I said with a chuckle, knowing full well that would make him smile.

I wheeled my last bag over to my cart to add it to my ever-growing pile before turning to him again.

"You were saying?" I asked once I'd connected my bag with the others.

"Oh right, I was just going to finally ask you your name."

"Oh, of course," I replied, raising my hand to meet his again. "It's Olivia. Well, Liv is what most people call me."

"Okay, well, hi, Liv. I'm Thomas."

The way he grabbed my hand, keeping his eyes fixed on mine, if I'd been a betting woman, I might have actually thought the man *was* trying to seduce me this time around. But I knew better; in London, I'd hardly ever had anyone approach me out of the blue. So, while I'd dated my fair share—mostly men who I'd met at get-togethers—I'd long realized that I wasn't the meet-cute kind of girl. And yet second after second passed by with our fingers intertwined before Thomas and I let go, only prompted by the sleeve on my mid-thigh-length sweater falling down to my wrist and breaking my attention from his gaze. Finally, I did us both a favor and loosened my grip, similar to our last handshake, eliciting the ripple effect of him parting from me again.

"Hi, Thomas," I said, stepping back from him just a tad. "I feel like I already said this, but it's lovely meeting you."

"Technically, the last time you didn't seem all too sure."

"That's true. But now you've helped me twice with my luggage. I can't deny it anymore."

He chuckled to himself, turning his head slightly away from mine in what seemed like an attempt to regain his composure.

"Duly noted," he replied, shifting his intensity as he returned his eyes to mine.

"You know," I said, looking back at him, desperately holding on to the last remaining bit of willpower I had to not "accidentally" fall into his arms so he'd have to put his hands on me again, "I could actually use your help with one more thing."

Thomas raised his thick eyebrows at me as he waited for me to continue.

"You mentioned you've lived here for a fairly long time, yeah?"

"Yes."

I could see his smile growing again, betraying whatever cool pretense he was trying to give off.

"Well, I'd love any recommendations on anything I should do or see while I pretend to be a New Yorker for the next year."

"Recommendations, huh? Hmm."

He stepped back and looked at me quizzically, very obviously trying to read me. Unfortunately for him, I couldn't afford to let him see how much he'd captured my attention in just our three short interactions, so I wasn't exactly making it easy. And to his credit, he didn't try to push me to give more than I was comfortable divulging, either. He just simply…observed.

"Where are you staying?" he finally asked.

"My company put me up in a flat… I'm sorry, apartment—I have to get used to saying that—in the East Village."

"Okay, okay. Nice area, but can I be honest with you?"

"Please do."

"Actually, first let me ask you something else. Where did you last live in London? Was it Brixton?"

I laughed, having a thought of where his line of questioning was going.

"Uh, no. I was born and raised there, but my last flat was in the City. It was easier to live in London's financial centre when I started working for investment firms."

"Sure, that makes sense."

Thomas paused and looked at me again before proceeding forward, almost as if he was still trying to determine how honest *he* would now be with me.

"So, I'll say this… The East Village has a lot of character, so I don't think you'll ever be bored there," he began. "But it's not exactly known for being a bastion of Black cultural experiences, if you get my drift."

"I sort of expected that, yes. Hence my question to you."

Once again enjoying my rare position of being the one to slightly tease him, I finally let my wink fly and laid it on thick so he knew it was my version of "get back" toward him. My clumsy attempt at teasing, however, only seemed to embolden Thomas instead of embarrass, as it had done for me. For all at once, his eyes lit up, and I could almost see a streak of joy run across his face, even as we both began walking toward the doors to leave the airport.

"Well, then my recommendation for you, Liv, if you want to find something in New York that's a little different…you gotta check out this Everyday People day party happening in Brooklyn next Saturday. The music's going to be lit, they'll have all kinds of food vendors—everything from Jamaican to Dominican to soul food from Mississippi—the people are going to be cool as hell, just trying to dance and have a Black-ass good time before the weather turns too cold here, and…"

Thomas paused and let his lips curl up slightly in that now signature smirk of his.

"I'll be there, too, of course."

What woman could resist all of that, normal or not, right? Especially the way his eyes twinkled as the last part of his argument floated out of his mouth.

Okay, I thought, *maybe I'm not being ridiculous and he is actually flirting with me.*

"Is this your way of telling me you want to see me again, babes?" I asked, hoping for some clarity and, even more than that, a simple yes.

He licked his lips before responding, which only served to draw my attention to how kissable they seemed.

"I'm a little more straightforward than that, Liv. If I wanted to ask you on a date, and I'm assuming that's what your question really meant, I would."

He never took his eyes away from mine even as he shattered the little dream I'd begun to let sprout up. Served me right. I knew better than to think this guy, of all guys, was into me and not just being a genuinely nice person who just so happened to have a proper dangerous smirk.

"Don't get me wrong—you're very beautiful," he continued. "But you just moved to a new country, so I'm not under any mistaken impression you're looking for anything more than what you already told me…"

"To kick ass and take names," we said in unison, eliciting another round of laughter from us both.

"Exactly," he continued. "And I don't want to get in the way of that. You really just seem like cool people, so I think you'd have a good time there. Plus, it wouldn't be a bad thing to run into you again without having to help with your bags."

"You're right," I replied, feeling some sense of relief that once again this stranger got me in a way no one else had seemed to do so before. But also a little sadness because in understanding me, he somehow intrinsically knew he wasn't part of my plotted-out story. And yet he appeared content to be a fun witness on the sidelines, which I kind of really appreciated.

"And that's not a bad proposition," I continued. "I'll be sure to tell my girl about the party, and maybe we'll see you there."

"Oh, so you have friends here already? The American ones you mentioned earlier?"

I couldn't tell if he was shocked that I knew other people in the city or disappointed to not be the sole source of my New York recommendations, but there was a bit of a curious tone in his voice. I shrugged it off so I wouldn't start overthinking it.

"One. And sort of," I explained. "She's a friend of my friend who moved to the UK earlier this year, but she's already been very kind to me. She and her boyfriend are even picking me up from the airport today."

"Ahh, well, that's great, Liv. I'm glad to know you won't be alone in the city."

Thomas's eyes dipped between my eyes and lips as he stared back at me. It seemed like there was so much more

he wanted to say, but from our brief interactions, I understood something about him, too—he was used to thinking everything out so that he always presented as cool,
calm and collected. That meant he certainly wasn't going
to allow himself to come across flustered in any way, at
least not in some feeble attempt to, what, woo *me*? Doubt-
ful. After all, he'd already said if he wanted to ask me on
a date that he would, and he hadn't. I guess he'd chosen
Door Number Two as well.

"I hope I see you both there," Thomas continued. "And
I can guarantee you one thing—you won't regret going."

"Well, you certainly make a compelling argument. So,
chances are good."

"I'd rather the chances be great, but I'll take it."

I stood in front of him for just a few seconds more,
cheesing like I had a high-school crush, until I eventually gathered myself again, took in one last breath and
said my goodbye.

"Until we meet again, dear Liv," he replied, holding
my attention until I stepped back and made the left turn
to walk away from him this time, maneuvering with all
my bags on my cart.

Before I walked through the exit doors, I glanced behind me once more and saw him heading to the Uber/Lyft
pickup area, carrying only a small duffel bag and rolling
a piece of luggage that could have been a carry-on if he'd
desired. We couldn't have been more different, and yet
there was something about him that felt oddly familiar...
like home. I'd have to unpack that on another day.

For now, I had a friend to find in the pickup area. And
maybe thanks to Thomas, I had one piece of clarity about
my big adventure to the Big Apple—nothing about this
trip was going to be boring or go as I expected. But I was
ready for every minute of whatever it was going to be.

Chapter Three

"Liv, oh my God, I'm so glad you made it, *cher*!"

As soon as I walked outside, I saw Reagan and her boy-friend, Jake, standing next to their car, waiting for me to arrive. Reagan, whose friends called her Rae, was, as I'd said to Thomas, actually one of Robin's close besties, so not even really someone who I'd had a direct relationship with for very long. And yet as soon as she'd heard I was moving to New York, she'd graciously offered to be my city buddy. She'd only just moved to New York herself within the past year, having grown up in New Orleans and lived in Washington, DC, since college. So I think she was intimately aware of what it felt like to move here after having lived somewhere else very comfortably for so long. Plus, as she'd said to me at the time: "New York can be magical, yes, but it can also be a place where a lot of lonely people lose their way because of its vastness and the millions of people often looking out for themselves."

I hadn't realized back then that she'd meant even show-ing up to pick me up from the airport and shepherding me to my new flat. But in the eight weeks since I'd said yes to my interim new job, I'd learned that Reagan's kind of at-tentive friendship was not just reserved for Robin and her other best friends—it had been for me, too.

All of this was some kind of fated connection, really. Robin, who everyone at work had told me about before we'd met but who'd happened upon me in the kitchen of our office just a few days after she'd moved to London for *her* new promotion, had become one of my closest friends in less than a year's time…and not for nothing, my brother's girlfriend. And because of that friendship, I now had someone in New York waiting for me at the airport as I embarked on what I hoped to be the trip that would put me on a direct path for *my* next promotion. If that wasn't kismet, I wasn't sure what was!

"Oh," I exclaimed, enjoying the friendly embrace of Reagan's arms. After *the breakup that wasn't* and all my anxious thoughts about whether I was making the right decision, it was nice to have someone excited to see me, no strings attached. "Reagan, babes, you are a sight for sore eyes."

"Liv, please. I think we've long moved past the formalities of full names. Call me Rae, *cher.*"

The remnants of her Louisiana Creole accent dipped in and out as she spoke, especially when she used colloquial nicknames like *"cher"* that were common French derivatives down there. Mixed with what I considered to be a typical American accent employed by journalists and TV hosts alike, Reagan's interesting tone to her voice was equally soothing and could be used to cut someone down if necessary. That said, if it was possible, I maybe appreciated this statement from her, laced with her dual accents, even more than her hug, because Robin's friend group— amazing as they all were—hadn't exactly been easy to penetrate at first. That was never more evident than with their nicknames.

I could remember like it was yesterday, meeting Robin's friends for the first time at our favorite pub, Dirty Martini, and making the grave mistake of calling her by the nickname they'd endowed her with, "Rob." She hadn't let me in on the fact that only three people in the world called her by that name (Reagan, Jennifer and Rebecca, to be exact). So I'd walked right into an incredibly awkward situation as they'd all looked around to see where I'd purchased my audacity from when I'd casually used it. I'd later learned that there had been one other friend who'd used that nickname—Christine—who they'd all been close with and who had passed away after fighting a long health battle. That had helped me better understand their instinct to close ranks and want to make sure some random stranger wasn't encroaching on something they all considered fairly sacred.

Thankfully, we'd recovered from that mishap and they'd each, in their own way, proven to be incredibly helpful as I'd prepared for my new adventure. Still, I'd never dared to use any of their nicknames since—Rae, Jenn and Becs, respectively—for fear of the death stares I'd received the first time around. Reagan's explicit permission—no, encouragement—to do so felt like a big step toward me actually being her friend and not just Robin's workmate who she'd agreed to show around.

Reagan shook me in her embrace one last time. Holding her hands still on my forearms, she then positioned me an arm's length away so she could see me in full and smiled. "You look good, girl. I'm especially loving the new hair!"

"Thanks, Rae," I replied, and then chuckled to myself, thinking of how Thomas would have almost certainly made fun of me just then if he were with us. "You know how it is—I wasn't quite sure how long it would take me to find a new hairstylist here, so I thought it better and easier to get my hair braided for the time being."

"Oh, I totally get it. That's my go-to for any extended trip—that or a cute wig I can plop on and off as needed."

"Mmm, I didn't think wig, but that's a good idea, too."

"No, but I love these passion twists you have going on.

Keep that," she replied, swinging her head around my shoulders so that she could get a full look even as she held me tightly. "And when you're ready to take them out, I'll bring you to my girl uptown. She does a mean silk press. Don't worry—I got you."

"You are the best, truly."

"Please, I wouldn't be a good friend if I held out on you like that. How was your flight, by the way?"

Reagan dropped her hands from my arms and motioned to Jake to begin off-loading my luggage into his trunk. Without any protest, he winked at her, mouthed a quick *Welcome* to me and pulled my cart toward his car. I was curious to see how he planned to get everything in there, but he didn't look at all concerned, easily grabbing the largest of the luggage first and sliding it into the left side of his trunk.

"Honestly, the flight was pretty unremarkable, which is just what I needed," I said as I followed her to the right side of the car. "My anxiety has been on high alert, really wanting to make sure I do everything right while I'm here. I can't afford for this to be a waste of time, you know? So it was nice to have several hours to zone out, listen to my tunes and be still for a bit…give my mind a short break from all my plans."

"Liv, that's great. I'm genuinely happy you took that opportunity on your flight over here. I can't express enough how necessary that was, especially coming here, where life can be so *go, go, go* if you're not careful. But what am I saying? I'm sure London is no different, right?"

"Time will tell, I guess. London can be pretty fast paced, but it's also home, and my guess is that there will still be some adjustments I have to make."

Reagan stared back at me with one of her signature smiles that started at her eyes and somehow permeated throughout her whole face. It was yet another comforting thing I'd grown to love about her as she and Robin had both turned into my risk gurus, delivering various reminders, exactly when I needed them most, that change could be scary but was worth it.

"Oh, of course," she said, seamlessly jumping into her latest "you got this" spiel. "But the main thing to remember when you're questioning if you made the right decision—and you will question it, that's just kind of the nature of taking risks—or when you're wondering if you're doing things quote, unquote 'right' is that we get to decide what's right for us and what's wrong for us. So, if you're here in the middle of it, doing your thing like I know you will be, then already, it's right. At least for now. And that's all you need to know in the moment, okay?"

I took in a deep breath while listening to Reagan speak, hoping to somehow soak up everything she was saying and have it ready in my arsenal during those quiet moments when I'd inevitably be wondering what the heck I was doing. I'd had more than a few of those already before arriving, but I'd managed each time to remind myself that I wasn't going to get what I wanted by playing safe. Hearing Reagan's reminder that I wasn't going to get it by worrying whether I was doing things the right way or not, either, was also important because I knew what it meant for her to be saying it, especially as she used her fingers to emphasize her belief that there was no such thing as "right" by putting it in fake air quotations.

For years, Reagan had been the one stuck in a job she hadn't wanted, dating men she hadn't wanted and living her life by a bunch of strange notions of what she'd thought perfect success looked like. But two years ago, she'd admirably decided to stop waiting for everything to be perfect before she'd gone after what she'd wanted. Since then, she'd quit her coveted online political-journalism job, started a vertical at a women's magazine, taken a chance on her ex-boyfriend from college who at the time hadn't lived in her city, and moved to New York after convincing her new job that they needed a New York office and that she was the best one to make it happen. If anyone understood my internal struggle of wanting to always get things "right" but also secretly just wanting to be okay taking a risk that was worth being wrong, she did.

"You're totally right, babes. I'll use that as my reminder over the course of the next year. I'm sure I'll need it a few times."

She winked at me as Jake closed the trunk, having finished putting all my bags inside with zero problems. The three of us then climbed into his black BMW 7 Series and headed to the East Village—my new home away from home.

"So, tell us, Liv, what are you most excited about?" Jake asked as he drove us through the streets of Queens to get onto the motorway.

"Mostly I'm just thrilled to have the chance to shine in a new country. I know what I can do for our investment firm, and I know what I have done, yeah? This is my chance to show *them* it wasn't a one-, two-or three-time fluke."

"I know that's right," Reagan chimed in, snapping her fingers in agreement.

"But also, I just met this guy when I was deboarding the plane and…"

"Oh, a new guy? Already?" Reagan interrupted.

"Yes." I chuckled. "But it's not like that, and that's not the point of the story. Yes, he was quite dreamy, but he also made it bloody clear he wasn't interested in anything. He did, however, pique my interest in learning more about New York and even mentioned that there's this day party happening on Saturday in Brooklyn. So I am slightly curious and excited about that. Have you heard of it?"

"Oh, the Everyday People party?" Reagan asked.

"Yes, I believe that is precisely what he called it."

"Yeah, of course, we know that one well," Jake chimed in. "We've been to it a few times, right, Rae? Good vibes."

"Definitely good vibes and great people," she replied. "Are you trying to go?"

Reagan contorted her body so that she was looking directly at me from the front passenger seat, waiting for my response.

"I was considering it, maybe. But I also don't want to lose focus while I'm here. I feel like by next weekend, I'll probably need to be studying whatever first set of portfolios I'm going to be handed when I get to the office this week, so…"

"Say less," she interrupted again. "We're totally going. But I think this needs to be a girls' outing. That all right with you, hon?"

Jake threw his right hand up briefly to show his relief in being let off the hook. I imagined that the last thing he had in mind was taking a perfect stranger to her very first American dance party, so I didn't blame him at all. Of course, Reagan was the exact opposite—all too excited to make it a thing.

"Perfectly fine with me, Rae. You all go and have your fun."

She delicately kissed him on the cheek in appreciation and then turned her body back toward me.

"Then that's settled. I'm going to invite my girls Keish and Gigi. We'll make a day of it and still get you home in time that if you want to do some investment work on Sunday, you won't be so exhausted that you can't," she continued. "Deal?"

"I don't know, Rae."

Her enthusiasm was intoxicating, and there was a little part of me that wanted to maybe run into Thomas again, but I still wasn't sure if it was the best decision given all I wanted to accomplish in such a short amount of time. Did I have time to play around and day drink and dance all day when I had really important work to do?

Reagan certainly seemed to think so.

"Listen, Liv, I get it. You came here for a very specific reason, and we're totally going to support that. I'm never going to be that woman that isn't here for another Black woman and all her ambitions. But girl, you're in New York for the next year, so you might as well *liiiive* while you're here. I promise you that you can do both."

She paused her speech and stared me down, refusing to turn her body back toward the front windshield until I'd acquiesced to her.

"And besides, I'm not taking no for an answer," she finished.

"Okay, okay," I replied. "I guess we're going to a day party next weekend."

"Yes! Ugh, Liv, you're going to have so much fun. I think this will be your real welcome to the city."

I smiled in the back seat and resigned myself to the fact that I'd definitely met my match in Reagan, even though she was four years younger than me. Where I'd been accused of being #TeamTooMuch by people in my past, known for planning and plotting out everything meticulously and had worried maybe they were right, Reagan didn't seem to care. In fact, before I ever moved to New York, she'd warned me that she had made good with herself about her little quirks, like being the friend who had no qualms telling her friends what to do. She hadn't been lying.

"Now, tell us more about this guy who you met," she said as she finally positioned herself comfortably in her seat, facing forward. "You said he was dreamy?"

"I don't think Jake wants to hear about this kind of stuff," I demurred.

"Oh, please, men love this kind of stuff," she said, laughing. "Don't you, Jake?"

She took her left hand and cupped his chin in a joking manner, causing him to roll his eyes and chuckle a bit.

"We don't like to admit it," he said, his eyes still on the road. "But yeah, I do enjoy hearing all of Reagan's friends' dating stories. If nothing else, they're never boring."

"See?" she asked me rhetorically. "So go ahead. Spill the beans."

Damn, I just knew Jake would have been on my side on this one, but I'd forgotten one hard and fast rule: healthy couples actually did tell each other a lot, so he was likely quite used to hearing about all her friends' escapades. That was something David and I had never done now that I thought about it.

"Well," I began hesitantly, "we're not dating, so this won't be a fun dating story for you, but yes, he was quite dreamy. And funny, too, actually."

I sat back into my seat and remembered the way Thomas had me giggling even when he'd been making fun of me. Also, the way he'd shown up twice and helped me out of a jam without ever having to be asked.

"But he had multiple opportunities and never even asked for my phone number," I added.

"Hmm," Reagan moaned aloud, betraying the fact that she was pondering the information she was receiving. "But he did invite you to this party. So, maybe he's shy?"

"No, I didn't get *shy* from him at all. In fact, he seemed pretty confident and aware of himself."

Reagan paused again as she took in the latest bit of information.

"I guess we'll just have to see what happens at the party, then," she finally responded.

To my left, I heard Jake laughing to himself and caught his eyes in the rearview mirror.

"I hope you know that means she's plotting, right?"

"Yeah, I'm picking that up right now," I said.

Reagan twisted herself around so that we could both see her raised eyebrows and her face filled with glee. Then, without missing a beat, she turned to face the windshield again and declared, "Make fun of me all you two want, but this is going to be really good!"

She turned around to face me once more. "You know, dear Olivia, everything can change here in a New York minute."

"Is that so?" I asked.

"Yep. That's part of what makes this city so magical. Just you wait and see."

Reagan turned back to face the front of the car, leaving me in the back seat alone with my thoughts to ponder the future. In the quiet of the moment, as we zipped through the motorway, I felt my heart beat just a smidge faster than normal. Something about what she said had me excited, a prospect that was both scary as hell and exhilarating all at the same time.

Chapter Four

A couple days later, I found myself walking into my firm's building in New York's iconic Financial District, clad in my deep chocolate-brown trousers and matching blouse with my favorite pair of Christian Louboutin heels—the medium camel-brown So Kate 120 mm leather pumps. From outside, the building mirrored many of the others around it: towering skyscrapers either adorned with tons of glass or aluminum or art-deco remnants from the 1920s.

Inside, however, it was an arborist's dream sight to behold, featuring almost a maze of rows and quadrants of stone and wooden benches flanked by the greenest, most plush bushes and potted trees I'd ever seen not in an actual park. In an area of town that surely leaned into the mystique of the concrete jungle, this green oasis was a stark disruption from the sidewalks filled with more people than plants.

Finally, set off to the back of the atrium and flanked by a row of lifts was the concierge desk, there for any guests who needed to be checked in or, in my case, employees who had yet to receive their entry badges. With a quick glance at my watch to check the time, I sauntered my way to the back, received my guest pass and walked to the nearest lift that would carry me to my new office. By the time I arrived on the twenty-second floor, I'd steadied my breathing enough to walk through the doors of our firm with my head held high and ready to meet all the top players in America.

I stepped toward the receptionist's desk and noticed that the clock had just struck 7:30 a.m. *Good job, Liv*, I thought, patting myself on the back in my head. *Way to start this new adventure off right.*

One thing I had vowed when I'd said yes to New York was that these new people I'd be working with would never be able to say they saw me slacking off, ever. Showing up just as the sun rose in the sky, even as I was still trying to adjust to the time difference, was step one in my plans. Now I just needed to meet the man who would hand me my first American portfolio, set up shop in my new office and hopefully find my own version of Robin when I inevitably made my way to the kitchen for some coffee.

"Cheers," I said, walking up to the receptionist, a young woman who looked to be in her early twenties and rocking the cutest little short bob of red hair. "I'm Olivia Robinson, and I'm here to meet with Walter Cody."

"Oh, hi, Olivia! It's very nice to meet you," she greeted me in return. "Walter just walked in as well, so let me call him back here for you. It'll probably just be a minute."

"Sure, thank you!"

I watched as she dialed Walter on the phone, waited for him to pick up and then politely explained I was waiting at the front desk for him. I could only barely make out his end of the conversation, but it sounded like he was a bit floored and hadn't expected me to get there around the same time as he did. Little did he know this was the very least of the surprises I had in store.

"He's coming now," she said, hanging up the phone and turning her attention back to me.

"Thanks! I guess he wasn't expecting me?"

"To be honest, it's usually just me and him here for the next hour," she replied with a shrug.

"Hmm. Well, go ahead and count me as number three. I might be here with coffee, but I'll be here."

"Ha ha, good to know. We have tea in the kitchen, too, if you prefer?"

"I do enjoy a cuppa tea," I replied with a wink, letting her know that I caught her attempt at trying to make the new British woman feel comfortable. "But not for early mornings. That requires French roast, dark, with a few teaspoons of sugar."

"Noted," she said, laughing. "For what it's worth, I agree."

"I can see we'll get along swell. What's your name, by the way? I apologize for not asking before."

"Oh, that's okay. It's Wendy!"

She paused and watched me gather myself as I was sure my face completely gave away my very tickled reaction. Then, after a beat, she shrugged her shoulders, patted the bottom of her bright red hair and said, "I know, it's funny."

"There are worse ways to make an impression," I replied.

"I'll remember that the next time some weird guy on one of the dating apps makes a joke about loving their four-for-four deal with a junior bacon cheeseburger."

"Oh, no, Wendy. No."

Why are some men on dating apps so weird? I wondered. *Ugh.* If nothing else, I was glad at least to not be worrying about that at all. No need for dating apps when you weren't planning to date.

"Oh, yes," she replied. "And I wish that was the worst joke I've heard."

"Wendyyyy!"

I moved closer to the front desk and grabbed her hands

in horror for what else she could have possibly endured simply because her parents must have seen her red hair and thought, *Wouldn't it be cute or funny to name her after the little fast-food girl?*

"I know, I know. Commiserate with me!"

She held my hands tightly and dropped her head onto the desk, inciting one of those guttural laughs from us both that helps to fully wake you up in the morning. Since the floor was so quiet, with no one else around to mask them with the natural noise that came from a bustling office, our outcries reverberated through the walls of the lobby just in time to practically slap Walter in the face as he walked up on us.

"I see you've met Wendy," he said with a straight face and his hand outstretched to meet mine. "I'm Walter."

I dropped my hands from Wendy's and turned around slowly to properly greet my new boss. "Hello, Walter. It's nice to meet you."

"Likewise," he replied, straightening out his posture even as he spoke. "I apologize—I didn't realize you'd be getting here at this time, or I would have had everything ready for you."

I watched Walter closely as he ran his hands through his blond hair in what seemed like a sort of nervous fidget. He was certainly dressed in what Reagan had warned me was the typical New York–finance guy's uniform—dark blue suit, light blue button-down shirt underneath and camel-brown hard sole shoes—but I wasn't getting the arrogance from him that she'd said usually came with it. Straitlaced demeanor that indicated he would never be caught dead laughing with Wendy in the lobby? Yes. But outside of that, he seemed, well, fairly normal.

"Do you need more time? I'm in no rush," I said, deciding to give him an out and to let him know I wasn't judging him. Technically, he was my supervisor, so if anything, I should have been the one looking nervous while meeting him. "It's just that when we spoke, you said that you normally arrive around this time, so I figured I should, too."

"No, you're fine. I appreciate the initiative, I do. And we're all very excited to have you with us. We've heard some pretty amazing things, haven't we, Wendy?"

It was the first time he'd acknowledged her since walking up to us, which seemed to catch her off guard as much as it did me.

"Hmm," she said, looking up and trying to restrain a small giggle. "Oh, yes. Lots of great things."

Walter ran his hands through his hair some more, his now telltale sign that things weren't going according to his plans.

"Right," he said, looking off to the side. "Why don't I show you where your office is, let you get settled and then I can come by a little later and give you the full tour. I think you'll find that the layout is pretty similar to what you're used to in London. We have four floors in this building— a trading floor, C-suite floor, this one's for us in portfolio management and then, of course, there's a floor for the RFP and marketing teams."

"Perfect—I'm looking forward to learning my way around," I replied. "Just one small request? Can you also point out the kitchen to me? I'd love a French roast sooner than later."

"Oh, of course. Not a problem."

Walter paused as if he was waiting for me to ask him something else. When I didn't, the look of relief on his face was palpable.

"Well, shall we?" he asked, pointing me in the direction away from the lobby.

"Sure."

I turned to Wendy once more and waved. It was obvious Walter seemed concerned that he hadn't been waiting for me in the lobby when I'd arrived, but truthfully, I was thankful she'd been the first of the two I'd met. She wasn't going to be the Robin to my Liv, but I had a feeling we were going to get along a lot better than stiff ol' Walter.

I'll meet you in the kitchen in ten minutes, she mouthed.

"Deal," I whispered before turning back around and nodding my readiness to Walter.

Step-by-step, I followed him as he walked me into the rest of the floor, past the sea of tall cubicles for the junior staff and over to the surrounding walls of glass offices reserved for senior employees. As we turned to our right, I caught a glimpse at what looked to be his office in the corner, immaculately bland except for the multiple stacks of papers on his desk. That seemed about right.

We walked by another four offices before we finally got to mine: pristine, empty and cold.

"And here we are," he said, motioning toward it like my own Vanna White.

I stepped into the space and scanned it quickly, immediately contemplating how I could give it my own flair and make it more *me*. I'd need to get a painting for the main wall at least—something vibrant that reminded me of home—or maybe I could even convince my brother to send me a canvas of one of his photos. Then, I might also bring in some framed pictures of friends and family and even a plant I'd try to keep alive for at least a month.

As I strode in further, I noticed a coat hanger in the corner and a double-screen monitor and MacBook on my desk, plus a sticky note with a few predetermined passwords I could use and then tailor to my own. The tech items were each positioned so that, while seated, the window facing outside would be on my right and the glass doors looking back into the rest of the floor would be on my left. I'd need to see if that worked for me once I got a little more settled, but for now, it would do. No need to really freak Walter out and start moving furniture on my first day in the office. He already clearly didn't quite know how to be a normal human being around me.

"So, this is it?" I turned back to him, wondering if he had more information that he wanted to detail for me.

"This is it," he replied with a shrug. "But I can still show you the kitchen and where the women's restroom is, of course."

"That would be great—thanks."

"And then we'll have our first meeting in the main conference room at eight thirty, so I can introduce you to everyone there and give you the full tour afterward. Maybe, if you're comfortable, you can talk about some of the lessons you and Frank learned from such a successful fundraising effort with your social impact fund. I think our teams are eager to see how we can use what you both did as a model."

"I'd love that," I replied, realizing this had been the most words Walter had used with me yet. "And I'm totally comfortable talking about our experience launching that fund and the multiple others that have been successful since."

The last part of my statement was a small addition to his, but I needed Walter to understand he wasn't getting a one-trick pony here. The recognition on his face as he took in my words let me know that he understood what I was saying—we'd done so much more than that first social impact fund, and I was prepared to talk about it all. Before we stepped back out of the office, I hung up my cherry-red coat with its wide, turned-down collar and belt at the waist, placed my workbag onto my desk and grabbed my mobile phone. As we made our way to the kitchen, I took my opportunity to quickly text Reagan.

Me: Hey, Rae! I know I was on the fence about it before, but on second thought, let's definitely go to that party this weekend.

She responded before I had time to even black out my screen. Thankfully, Walter wasn't exactly what one would call a Chatty Patty, so I was able to read her response and text back without him even noticing that my attention wasn't solely on him.

Reagan: Well, we were always going, but I'm glad you came around instead of me having to drag you out there, ha ha. What made you change your mind, though?

Well... I replied hesitantly. I just got to my job, and girl, I don't think I'm going to find my Robin here. I did meet one young lady who seems nice, but I get the feeling I'm going to have to really connect with my people outside of the office.

Reagan: I hear you, sis, loud and clear. And don't worry, I got you. Just one question: What size shoe do you wear?

I looked up from my phone just in time to catch Walter silently pointing out the women's bathroom and mouthed a quick thank-you in reply. A few moments later, however, he finally perked up as we made our way into the kitchen, looking at me with an awkward but distinct grin on his face. I hadn't had a chance to respond to Reagan yet, but I had a feeling that I'd have plenty of time to do so once I was back in my office. I locked my phone and slid it into my pants pocket just as Walter realized he needed to say words to me again.

"And here we are…at the kitchen."

He was nothing if not succinct. Walter outstretched his arm and waved it around to emphasize where we were, which all came off just as clumsily as when he showed me my new office. Off to the side, I peeped that Wendy was also in the kitchen, standing near the single-serve coffee machine and trying to hold back her giggles from our interaction. That only made it harder to keep a straight face, but I knew I needed to try. After all, *he* was my new boss, not Wendy.

"Thanks again, Walter. You've been incredibly gracious this morning," I said. "I know you weren't expecting me here so early, so if you want to head back to your office, you can. I think I can take it from here now."

"Thanks, Olivia," he replied.

I wasn't sure whether it was relief that shone on his face or if he was genuinely touched by my response, but something about what I'd said produced the first relaxed smile from him I'd seen all morning. Either way, I was going to happily take the win.

"Great. Then I'll see you at 8:30 a.m."

And with that, Walter turned on the heels of his brown shoes and quickly disappeared out of the shared kitchen. It took Wendy just about thirty seconds—enough time to make sure he was out of earshot—before she burst out laughing.

"God, he's so weird," she said, passing me one of the office mugs from the cupboard. "I often have to remind myself that just because you can make a company a lot of money, that doesn't mean you're not a super self-conscious nerd."

"Well, I'm hoping that it's just jitters about meeting me

for the first time. I need this next year to be a lot less stiff than the past ten minutes."

"Don't worry, sis. You got this."

For some reason, Wendy's "don't worry" didn't give me the same confidence that Reagan's had. In fact, I kind of bristled at her use of the term "sis" so soon after meeting me, but I *had* just been joking around with her, so I shook away any thoughts of her being a bit too familiar, rinsed the mug in the sink and turned to my newfound, much younger friend and asked her possibly my most important question of the morning.

"So, Wendy, how do I make coffee in this contraption you all have?"

"Oh, it's super easy," she said as I watched wide-eyed while she pressed what looked like eighteen buttons before the steaming-hot liquid began to pour into my cup. That would be something I would need a greater tutorial on eventually, but for today, I was just happy to see coffee coming my way soon.

"You need anything else?" she asked.

"No, but thank you. This right here, when it's done, will be more than enough for now."

Another twenty minutes later, I'd changed what felt like fifty passwords, made sure that my email and files were all synced from the UK and onto my new laptop, and desperately tried not to second-guess my decision to leave the job I'd only started less than a year ago to come to America as part of some foolish plan to wow a bunch of people in a country I'd never been to and convince everyone I deserved a senior-level position. If my interactions so far were any indication, I was going to have my work cut out for me. While Wendy wanted to be my best friend before she even knew my middle name, Walter could barely look me in my eyes, and I'd yet to see anyone else even show up in the office yet. *Bang-up job so far, Liv.*

After some slight pouting, I took in a deep breath and refocused myself, determined to do what I set out to do. Kicking ass and taking names wasn't always going to be awkward-interaction free, I reminded myself, but it was still the ultimate goal. I also recalled that I'd yet to text Reagan back, so I scooped up my phone and quickly tried to rectify at least that one mistake.

Sorry, sorry! I typed as fast as I could. I didn't mean to go that long without responding to you.

Once again, she texted back immediately.

Reagan: Please, there's no need to apologize. You are at work.

And so are you, I responded. That's no excuse.

Reagan: Negative. I never get to work this early. It'll probably be another hour and a half before I stroll into my office. But also, give yourself a break, Liv. Again, I know you're at work, so I'm not stressing over here like why didn't she respond to me? That would be ridiculous.

Me: Wow, must be nice...and okay, thanks for that reminder.

Reagan's comments reminded me of my brother's, who was always saying that I put a lot of pressure on myself to show up perfectly for everyone all the time. I was sure he would have agreed with her in this moment.

Reagan: Well, on the flip side, you all make far more money than us writers, so I think it evens out lol

Me: Fair!

Reagan: Back to the important topic, though. Shoe size, please.

Me: Oh, I wear a size 6.

Reagan: Wow, really?! I didn't realize you had such small feet! lol

Me: Wait, shoot, I forgot it's different here. Umm...

I paused to remember the conversion in my head.

Me: I think it's an 8 in the US.

Reagan: Okay, Liv, you just won over my heart. I, too, am a size 8. This is going to be so good!

Right after Reagan's text, she also sent over a GIF of Steve Harvey as a judge on his daytime TV show repeating her last words, which made me laugh a lot louder than I'd expected it to. And because my luck was what it was that morning, I finally saw a few people walk toward their desks just as I realized they probably heard my outburst. I quickly stood up, went to close my door and sat back down before replying.

Me: Okay, well now I'm excited, too lol

Reagan: Oh, you should be. This means you totally have to come over to shop in my shoe closet before we go to the party.

Me: Wait, you have a shoe wardrobe…in New York City?

Reagan: Well, I have something I made into one. Don't worry, you'll get to see it.

Me: Of course you do. And okay, I'm looking forward to it.

I looked up again and noticed it was a few minutes to eight thirty and I should start heading to the conference room. I already had my spiel ready to go in my head. Now it was time to do all the wowing I'd been planning on when I'd first arrived.

Me: All right, babes, I need to head to this meeting. But thanks again for everything! Talk soon.

Reagan: Have a great day, girl. And btw, has anyone ever mentioned you thank people a whole lot? Don't answer. Just think about it.

Ha. Well, Reagan didn't know it, but she was the second person who'd said as much in a few days' time. Maybe they were both onto something, but remembering the first person to call it out only served to bring back flashbacks of Thomas's deviously dangerous and dimpled smirk. And there was no way that I needed that kind of distraction on my mind.

I took in another deep breath, stood up, straightened out my back and gave myself one last internal pep talk before grabbing my laptop and heading toward my glass office door.

This was it.

My moment.

And I wasn't letting Walter's awkwardness, Wendy's

overfamiliarity, Reagan's incredible shoe wardrobe or visions of Thomas's grin get me off my game.

With my renewed sense of confidence, I stepped out of the office and strode past the gaggle of cubicles that lined the walkway to the main conference room on our floor. To my left, I heard people as they began shuffling their belongings around their desks, as they greeted their colleagues "Good morning," and even as they click-clacked away on their computers. I could see a few of them also begin to gather their laptops and pens and paper, presumably preparing to head to the same meeting I was off to.

By the time I arrived at the glass-enclosed office space, decorated with only a large cedarwood conference table in the middle and rows of ergonomic office chairs flanking it plus one lonely side table with a plant on top, only two other people were seated. I casually glanced at my watch to see if I'd had the time wrong before greeting them. Nope—according to my clock, at least, it was 8:28 a.m.

"Oh, you'll see everyone pile in here in a few," the first woman said, likely noticing the concerned look on my face. "Most people here believe in being on time but not necessarily early."

"Good to know," I replied, and immediately realized how that correlated with Walter's consternation about my early arrival this morning. "I'm Olivia Robinson, by the way."

I stuck out my hand to shake hers as she returned the favor.

"Julie," she said, gripping my hand firmly. "It's nice to meet you, Olivia. Walter has told us a lot about you."

"Really?" I asked, perplexed.

For someone who'd barely spoken more than a hundred words to me this morning, I had a hard time grasping that he'd been over here extolling my efforts prior to my arrival. And yet Julie was the second person who'd said as much. There seemed to be plenty I needed to better understand in America. For example, in my very Jamaican family, if you were just on time, you were late. Basically, the exact opposite of what seemed to be the culture in our New York office. Then again, my parents and their siblings were trying to combat decades of stereotypes about Black people in the UK as part of the Windrush generation. No one in this office, from what I'd seen thus far, came from anything close to a similar background or understanding.

True to Julie's word, people began strolling into the office less than a minute later. So, with no real guidance about hierarchy, I made a quick decision to sit in the chair that seemed the least likely to cause any issues—definitely not at the head of either side of the table, but also not too far away from at least one of them. The one I chose—third on the left from what I guessed was Walter's seat, the head of the table on the right side of the conference room—was a gamble, but I figured it was better than sitting smack-dab in the middle or off to the side in the chairs that were the stepchildren of the room.

Luckily for me, my gamble paid off. Because just a few moments later, Walter also arrived and plopped down right into the seat I'd guessed was his. Once he settled in, opening his laptop and adjusting into his seat, he looked around to make sure everyone else was seated, scanning the room until he landed on me. And then, in yet another surprise, he smiled, nodded his head and mouthed *Welcome* to me once again.

It was as if the person I'd met an hour earlier had been some sort of off-brand clone and this was the real Walter Cody, commanding all the attention in the room, not seeming to be at all awkward and, oddest of all, helping to welcome me into the office among a room full of strangers when he barely even looked me in my eyes while we were by ourselves. Maybe he was just really good at rising to the occasion when he absolutely needed to, I thought. I certainly hoped I had that in me as well—but without the opposite-clone part.

"Good morning, everyone, and happy Monday," Walter began, quieting the room without raising his voice. "I know we have a lot to cover today, but first I want to introduce you to the star of the UK, the person I've been telling you about for weeks, Ms. Olivia Robinson. Olivia, as you know, will be joining us for the next year, and while she'll probably start off with one or two portfolios at first, I want to have her eyes on all of them by the time she leaves. I think we'll all be able to benefit from her perspective and her expertise, and if we can't convince her to stay—because that is also a goal of mine, Olivia—then we can at least send her off in the best way possible, with several millions of dollars raised under her watch."

Walter's break in the middle of his speech, wherein he spoke directly to me, completely threw me off and, just for a second, threatened to distract me from what I'd been planning to say. But he had on his best "command of the room" mask, so come hell or high water, I was going to as well.

"Hi, everyone," I said after clearing my throat just a bit. "I'm really so excited to be here. And thank you, Walter, for such a gracious introduction. I hope to live up to those lofty words."

"You will," he replied with a nod. "Olivia, I know we talked about this earlier, but I'd love it if everyone could hear from you on how you have grown multiple funds in the UK from ones that were pretty niche to multimillion-dollar investments."

"Sure. I'd love to," I said, adjusting myself in my seat

to make sure that everyone around the table could see and hear me clearly. I noted that he'd changed his language from just being that I'd succeeded with the one investment fund, so at the very least, he was really good at listening and taking notes.

"Before I dig in, however, let me just start by acknowledging that nothing Frank and I have done this past year is revolutionary, really. What you are going to hear me talk about, and what you'll hear me preach every day that I'm here, is that we listened to our clients, we worked very hard to identify the pieces they didn't realize they were missing and we executed on that with creative ideas. Nothing more, nothing less. For one portfolio, that amounted to us getting one hundred thirty percent of the investors we were expecting and exceeding our fundraising goal by one hundred fifteen percent. I'm here today with you all, however, not because we did that once but because we have reached at least those metrics eight times since."

I paused and looked around the room to get a gauge of my audience and saw that, to a person, they were each staring at me wide-eyed and eager to learn more. Maybe I'd misjudged how things were going to go this morning after all because what I now knew to be true was that as much as I was looking forward to making a name for myself this year, they all needed me here, too. And that wasn't exactly a bad position for this expat to be in.

"So, let's jump in to talk about how we did that."

For the next fifteen minutes, I explained my approach to life and how it had seemingly resonated in our investment world: I always went the extra step, yes, but more importantly, I studied my clients, my friends, my colleagues... and learned them to a T. I had literal folders upon folders of background information on each client, which I painstakingly pored through before I ever offered even a morsel of advice. It was how I'd known that first social impact fund had needed high-quality photos and a dynamic website to really resonate with our target audience. And it was what I wanted everyone in my new office to commit to do at least while I was there.

When I paused to see if anyone had questions, I looked around the room and saw each person taking notes, even Walter—whether on their laptop or in their notepad— meticulously jotting down all that I was saying so they wouldn't lose any of it.

Maybe these were my people after all, I thought. Things were certainly trending in a better direction— that was for sure.

Chapter Five

"Reagan Lorraine Doucet, when you said you'd created a shoe closet in your apartment, I could never have imagined this is what you meant."

My eyes scanned her bedroom with equal wonder and glee as I processed what I was seeing before me: a meticulously decorated bedroom split in half to where she had her queen-size bed, rug, dresser, nightstand, full-length mirror and bedroom bench on one side, and the other side was lined with what looked to be custom floor-to-ceiling shelves, a second complementary rug and an ottoman chair in the middle. Separating the two sides of the room were a decent-size window on the wall that faced her bedroom door and a natural walkway on the floor between the two rugs. Finally, in the corner when you first walked in was the most elegant pearl-white ladder I'd ever seen not in someone's bookstore, presumably for Reagan to reach the shoes that were positioned beyond what her five-foot-three stature could muster with outstretched arms.

To say I was in shock would have been an understatement, but really, I shouldn't have been. The reason we'd gotten along so well thus far was because we were both the good kind of extra…planners who were going to make sure that what we wanted was executed perfectly. So, honestly, the more accurate phrasing would be to say that I was in awe, not that I was at all surprised.

"You thought it was just going to be, like, a second

room turned into a closet, right?" she asked, her eyes betraying her excitement.

"Maybe! To be honest, I didn't bloody know, but whatever I thought it was going to be, this is beyond that."

I stepped my bare feet closer to her shelves, noticing how the shoes were organized by not only color but shoe style, too, ranging from red stiletto heels on one side to faux-snakeskin mules on the other. It was almost like being at a shoe-store showcase but tucked away in a flat uptown.

"Now that you mention it," I said, turning back to face her, "why didn't you just rent a two-bedroom and convert one of the rooms into a wardrobe? This is gorgeous, but I'm sure that would have been a lot easier."

"Easier, but not cheaper. We may be uptown, but the rent is still expensive. The only difference is if you're lucky like me, you can find a place up here that's more than six hundred square feet and has enough room in the bedroom for me to get creative."

She paused and chuckled before spitting out the rest of her words.

"Well, that and it's slightly more Black people uptown, but don't get it twisted—that's not what it used to be, either."

"Still, I'd wager a lot more than what I see in my East Village neighborhood."

"Oh yes, that's not even a question," she replied, laughing again. "Okay, enough of all that, though. Let's get into the good stuff. We have to find you some shoes for today."

Reagan jumped up and down like a little kid who'd just been told she could have some candy and let out a tiny squeal before her face turned dead serious. Raising her right hand to her chin, she circled me, checking out the outfit I'd chosen for the day party we were going to attend in Brooklyn that day: a loose-fitting denim long-sleeved shirt, unbuttoned to right above the small amount of cleavage my 32B breasts could form and tucked into my ripped and distressed fitted jeans of the same color. Both my sleeves and jeans were rolled up, with the sleeves stopping halfway to my elbows and my jeans hitting right above my ankles. To tie it all together, I'd pulled my passion twists into a half-up, half-down look with a loose topknot so that my big gold hoop earrings could be seen.

"Hmm," she said finally, as if she were a doctor assessing the scene before giving a diagnosis to a patient. "I think I have the perfect pair of shoes for this."

"Wait, really?" I asked, completely caught off guard.

I'd guessed when she'd said I could come over and shop through her wardrobe that we were going to be pulling out a ton of shoes until finally, after partially destroying her room, one emerged as the winner, the exact right one for the occasion. That was what happened in all the films, yeah?

"Oh, did you want to pick out something yourself? Because you totally can. I just have a feeling that these will be perfect."

"No, I mean, it's your shoes, babes. We can do whatever makes you feel comfortable."

I spoke with some hesitation, not wanting things to get awkward with the one friend I had in America—and especially not over a favor she was offering me.

"Are you kidding me right now?" she asked incredulously. "Liv, I wouldn't have invited you over here if I was worried about my comfort level. When are you going to believe we're actually friends?"

She stared me down and waited for a reply, but I was too busy processing how quickly she'd read my reluctance for what it truly was—a mistrust in our friendship—but deeper than that, a mistrust that anyone really wanted to be connected to me who wasn't obligated to like family or indebted to me like my colleagues.

"Sorry," I responded sheepishly. "I guess you can only be told so many times that you're 'too much' before you start to believe everyone thinks the same thing."

"Olivia, look at my bedroom. How could I ever think anyone else is 'too much'?"

I panned my eyes across her room again and began to chuckle from some place deep inside my belly. She was right. I might have been over-the-top for some, but at the very least, I'd met my #TeamTooMuch crew through Robin and her friends.

"Better question, though—who is the jerk that made you think you were too much?" she asked as she pointed for me to sit down on the ottoman and grabbed her ladder from the corner.

"Jerks, plural, you mean?"

"Ugh, okay. Well, yes, jerks, plural."

"Well, David certainly thought so…"

"David—your ex David?"

"We're not exactly exes…actually I don't know what we are right now."

"Wait, how are you not?" Reagan turned back toward me, interrupting me and sliding her ladder to the shelves at the same time. "Y'all aren't doing the long-distance thing, right, *cher*? Because that might change my plans for you and ol' boy at this party today."

"Plans?" I asked, narrowing my eyes at her.

"Never mind all that," she said, waving off my suspicious looks. "Tell me what's the deal with you and David."

"There's no deal."

Reagan was mid-climb on her ladder when she looked back at me again as if to say *Girl, please*.

"There's no deal!" I protested. "We just didn't end

things on a great note before I left. But we talked later and decided to press pause while I'm over here, and then we'll see where things are when I get back."

"Pause. As in the relationship?"

"Mmm-hmm."

"With a man who said you were too much? On what sounds like multiple occasions?"

"To be fair, he may never have said those exact words, but..."

"Okay, give me an example of his words. I know you remember them vividly."

She wasn't wrong about that. I remembered every bloody word David had ever said that had made me feel small, whether he'd meant to or not. I also had an uncanny ability to play them over in my head late at night when I should have been sleeping.

"All right, so for example, on our last night together, we got into a little tiff because I wanted him to show me that he was going to bloody miss me. It was like he had no emotion about me leaving whatsoever, despite the fact that we'd just spent the last two years together. So I asked him, 'Do you even care that I'm going away for a whole year? Like, has any of this meant anything to you at all?' And his response was very classically David. He said to me, 'I should have known you would blow this out of proportion. It's not like you're dying, Liv, so what do I need to be sad about? Plus, you made the choice to take this job, to choose your ambition over us. You didn't *have* to, so don't get upset with me for being okay with your choice. And I mean, really, Olivia, if it's what you want, who am I to stop you? I could never stop you even if I wanted to. I learned that a long time ago.'"

"Wow, I hate him," Reagan replied as she stepped down her ladder with a clear container in her hand.

"It wasn't great, that's for sure."

"And you're on a *break* with this guy?"

"I… I know it probably sounds dumb, but we have been together for a while, so… I don't know. There's a part of me that thinks we've never been a great fit, and then the other part doesn't want to end a two-year relationship because of one bad conversation, especially when I probably wasn't being very fair questioning his feelings for me in the first place."

"But you said it was *classically* David, right? That would mean it's been more than one bad conversation."

I didn't know what to say in response. David and I weren't always compatible, to be sure. Where I was the hopeless romantic, he just wanted simple. And where I believed in dotting every *i* and crossing every *t* at all times, he would rather me just have been more chill and go with the flow. But that didn't mean there hadn't been good times between us. And I wasn't sure I was ready to give all that up on the chance I might meet someone new who fit me better. I was also afraid that if I kept trying to explain myself, my eyes would start watering and I'd have to redo my makeup soon. Thankfully, Reagan understood my silent response and pivoted slightly as she handed me the clear container.

"You know what? It's okay—you don't have to answer that. I'll just say this—I don't believe in breaks. As Monica said on *Friends*, a break is a *breakup*."

"Haven't you and Jake been on a few breaks yourselves?"

"Absolutely not." She chuckled. "We've totally and completely and fully broken up more times than I can count, yes. But there was no mistaking when we weren't together what the deal was. I was single AF when Jake and I were off, and I enjoyed every moment of it, you hear me?"

"I hear you," I said, joining in with her in a round of giggles.

"Luckily for him, though, no one in this world gets me like he does. So, despite all our messiness and our actual breakups, I wouldn't trade my worst days with him for my best days with anyone else. Can you say the same about David?"

This question elicited my second silent reply mixed with only a heavy sigh this time, a response that was probably all Reagan needed to hear to know that my answer was *no* yet again.

"Then, no offense but screw David," she replied. "I'm Team Thomas anyway."

"You haven't even met Thomas yet." I laughed in response, rolling my eyes at her.

"And I don't need to! I've seen the way you can't control your cheeks when I mention his name, *cher*. That's enough for me!"

"He is a very attractive man," I said, agreeing partially.

"Mmm-hmm, and you like him."

"I don't know him."

"You *want* to know him."

"I want to…pick out a pair of shoes and have a great time with you and your girls today. Honestly, that's all I can focus on wanting right now."

"Lies! But I'mma let you have it because we don't have much longer before we need to meet up with Keish and Gigi, and I might need time to revive you after you see these shoes."

With one last bashful giggle and another playful roll of my eyes, I finally opened the container in my hand and saw before me a pair of velvet dark olive green pointed-toe mules with a big faux-fur pom-pom situated on the top of each. I'd never seen anything like it before and was quite possibly in love.

"Reagan," I whispered.

"Oh, I know."

"These are…"

"Too much?" she asked with a wink.

"Ha! I was going to say 'exquisite,' but yes, that works, too."

"Well, I think they're perfect for you, your outfit and your time here in New York—where we don't believe in 'too much,' okay?"

"Okay," I replied, failing at holding in a huge smile yet again. "I really do love them."

"I knew you would," she said smugly. "Now, try them on and make sure they fit so we can get on out of here. We've got a cute boy to find… I mean, fun party to get to."

About an hour later, the four of us walked into the Everyday People party like we were the original members of Destiny's Child. Alongside my Canadian-tuxedo 'fit and Reagan's beloved olive green mules, stood Rae herself, with gray distressed jeans that had a slight fringe at the ankle and a long-sleeved white textured blouse, which she hadn't buttoned at all but simply tied at her natural waist. Miraculously, she managed to keep her double-D breasts lifted up and tucked inside of this blouse but had also strategically used her long, barrel-curled hair as a second barrier, draping her tresses just inside the boundaries of the shirt. She then paired her outfit with scarlet-red pointed-toe slides from Anthropologie that included three rows of tassels on the top. Standing next to her was Keisha Edwards, who often simply went by Keish—a five-five beauty with thick thighs and bee-sting boobs. She had on a pair of ripped, acid-washed jeans with a white fitted

T-shirt tied at the front, some white Chuck Taylor trainers and her signature leopard-print glasses that set off her
short hair that was slicked to the side just right. And finally, Giselle Lewis, aka Gigi, was rocking quite possibly
my favorite outfit of the bunch—a pair of royal blue jeans
with rips at the knees, a yellow-and-black crop top that
said *Girl Power*, black lace-up oxfords and her shoulder-
length jet-black twists practically glistening under the sun.

One might have easily thought we'd coordinated our
outfits so that they perfectly complemented each other
without matching, but they would have been wrong. In
fact, Reagan and I hadn't even seen Keisha and Giselle
until a few minutes before when we'd joined them in line
to show our tickets to the bouncers. And yet I was very
happy to say that just like our clothes, the connection between myself and the other ladies was almost immediate.
This was something I should have assumed being that I'd
yet to meet anyone even tangentially related to Robin who
I didn't get along with, although I continued to be pleas-
antly surprised by it. I made a mental note to tell her this
the next time we caught up on WhatsApp.

"Liv, I hope you are ready for some good drinks and
dancing," screamed out Giselle as we walked in. "This is
one of my favorite parties to go to."

Once inside the venue, which was actually mostly an
outdoor spot with a covered vendor area surrounding it, the
volume increased exponentially, so our voices had to match
the intensity to hear each other. Not only were we trying to
speak over the sounds of '90s music blasting through all
the speakers but we were also competing with the laughs
and conversations of at least a thousand other beautiful,
golden-brown Black people all around us.

After a full week of being the only Black woman on my
team, this felt like heaven. So much so that I found myself

gazing, starry-eyed for a bit, completely missing my cue to respond to Giselle.

"Oh, she is," Reagan replied for me with a wink.

"Do you have a drink preference?" Giselle followed up quickly, thankfully not giving me enough time to wander back into my thoughts.

"I'm guessing a martini is a long shot here, yeah?" I asked.

"I think that's a good assumption. I would stick with something more typical, like a liquor plus a chaser."

"In that case, I'll get something with gin…maybe a Tom Collins?"

All three women stared at me blankly so long that, at first, I thought they hadn't heard me over the music and the crowd, so I repeated myself but louder.

"No, no, we heard you," Keisha chimed in. "We just have no idea what the heck a Tom Collins is. Is that the British version of a gin and tonic?"

"Oh." I laughed. "Sorry! It's just basically gin, lemon juice, soda water and simple syrup."

Giselle chuckled to herself before responding to me. "All right, well, I think that will work—they should definitely be able to make that. I'm just so not saying the name!"

"Fair," I said, shrugging my shoulders.

She turned to the other two ladies and confirmed their drinks with them as well.

"I already know whiskey ginger for you, Rae. And, Keisha, do you want a vodka tonic today?"

"Sure do," Keisha replied enthusiastically.

"Okay, great."

I watched as Giselle then swung herself around and squeezed through the crowd gathered at one of the vendor bars, the three of us following close behind her so that we could be there to grab the drinks as she passed them back to us. I was also fascinated that she'd barely even had to ask what the other women had wanted; she'd just known. That alone wasn't shocking—friends tended to know what their friends liked to drink—but Reagan had only moved to New York earlier in the year, so I hadn't assumed she'd connected with Keisha and Giselle so quickly. Plus, I always associated her with Robin's crew, so it was pretty cool to see she'd formed a close bond with another group of friends in her short time in the city and hadn't lost the closeness with her original friend group. That was definitely inspiration for me—I wanted to make sure I kept my friends and family back in the UK close but certainly wanted to take this time away to branch out, meet new people and make even more friends along the way.

"How long have you all known each other?" I asked, turning to Reagan while we waited for Giselle to send the drinks backward from the bar.

"I went to high school with Keish, so we've known each other a pretty long time. Back then, it was me, her and Christine that were unstoppable, but then she went to the University of Southern California for undergrad while Chrissy and I went to Howard, and we didn't stay as in touch with each other as we should have. We reconnected at Christine's funeral, though, and I found out then that she lived in New York, which, you know, definitely came in handy some months later."

"So she was your Reagan when you moved here, essentially?"

"Kinda, yeah. I mean, I had Jake here, too, of course. But it was good to have someone else I knew here other than him, so I wasn't just relying on him and his friends for any sort of connection outside of work."

"Totally," I replied, not really knowing but presuming

sort of what she'd meant. I'd never experienced anything like what I was doing now—moving thousands of miles away on my own and knowing just a couple people who I could call if I needed them. I'd traveled around the world, but in the thirty-five years I'd been alive, I'd never lived more than thirty minutes from home.

"And Gigi, she is a friend of Keisha's from college," Reagan continued. "They both moved here about six years ago and were roommates until they could afford their own places. When I got to town, Giselle and I clicked super quickly, too. It was like I'd known her just as long as I'd known Keish."

"That's awesome," I said, trying to hold back my face from showing how much I was gushing about their connection. "I hope this year is like that for me."

"There's no hoping about it, *cher*. I already know it's going to be."

Just then, Giselle caught our attention as she began passing the drinks back to us one by one, sending the overflowing plastic cups our way. By the time we received the third one, she was making her way toward us with her own drink as well, dancing through the crowd like a woman on a mission.

"Y'all ready to really get this party started now?" she asked, staring directly at me.

"Oh, yes, very much so," I replied, this time making sure I did so myself.

"Then let's get it!"

Giselle dragged out her last word in glee as she grabbed my waist. Then the four of us strutted our way onto the outdoor dance floor just as the DJ started spinning the iconic remix to Brandy's "I Wanna Be Down." That was just the cue I needed to truly let my hair down as I proceeded to rap every bar like I was onstage, seamlessly flowing through each verse from MC Lyte to Yo-Yo to Queen Latifah and using my cup as the perfect fake microphone. The girls could hardly contain their glee as they joined in, singing Brandy's chorus and egging me on as I continued on my one-woman show.

"Okay, Liv, let me find out we need to give you a rapper nickname!" Reagan screamed out as she bounced along to the '90s beat.

"No, for real—you didn't tell us you knew nineties hip-hop like this," Keisha chimed in, agreeing. "You betta get it!"

I shrugged my shoulders playfully and kept rapping, not wanting to mess up the flow on my favorite verse from the Queen just to explain that we often listened to the same songs in the UK as they did; we simply had some extras they probably didn't know.

Just as the song was ending, I realized I needed to capture this moment as our first real bonding experience, so I pulled my phone out and started snapping photos of the three ladies singing Brandy's last notes like their lives depended on it. One by one, I clicked the camera app on my phone, snapping them in various positions and capturing all the fun we were having in our own little pocket inside of this massive venue. It wasn't until they each started making googly eyes, nodding their heads in rhythm to the beat and pointing at me that I realized something else was happening, too.

"What's going on?" I asked, laughing and confused.

It took maybe another few seconds for it to dawn on me that they weren't pointing *at* me, they were directing me to turn around and look behind me. As I swung around to see what they were staring at, everything came into focus all at once. Because there, in all his charming and handsome glory, was Thomas and those extremely dangerous dimples acting as if he was also posing for my camera. Maybe the ladies had figured out it was him without me ever having to even tell them what he looked like. Or maybe, like me, they were just drawn in by the orange aura he seemed to carry around with him wherever he went.

"Thomas!" I screamed out before I could contain my excitement. Luckily, I caught myself before I acted on the sudden urge to throw my arms around him.

"Heyyy!" he replied, revealing his excitement and maybe, I dare say, a tiny bit of embarrassment. "My bad—I thought you were taking a selfie at first, so I was trying to photobomb you until I realized you were actually taking pics of your girls."

"Oh, ha ha, so that's what was going on behind me. All I saw were their giggles and figured I needed to turn around."

I paused awkwardly, not knowing what else to say just yet, and then let my mouth simply blurt out the next thing that came to mind.

"But yeah, it was just of them…not me."

Honestly, I could have kept that inside.

It was hard to think straight with him suddenly standing in front of me, however—clad in an all-black outfit that accentuated his beautiful skin tone under the brightness of the warm October sun. He wore a crisp black T-shirt that looked as if he'd steamed it to perfection for at least ten minutes before putting it on, matching joggers and a simple gold chain that landed at the top of his chest moving in sync with him as he breathed in and out while staring at me. Truthfully, it was less about the clothes and more about the way they fit on him as if they'd been constructed simply to entice poor souls like mine, dipping in and out in concert with his muscles and showcasing all the ways that his body was molded over time. It was also his deep gray eyes that I could never turn away from whenever he set them on me. And that smile—the same one that had lured me in on the airplane and the same one that was now trying to take me out in front of a crowd full of people.

It was enough to make a woman swoon right there, out in the open, with no shame at all. Somehow I resisted, but what I couldn't avoid was the annoyingly enticing thought running through my head that with all the people crowded into this venue, he'd still found me.

"You know what? It's good to see you," I said, trying to start over.

"Same, Liv. I'm glad you actually came."

"Well, you did make a very compelling argument in the airport."

"Oh yeah?" he asked, drawing closer to me, presumably so we wouldn't have to scream as loud to hear each other.

His new proximity to me had a dual effect, however; while I could hear him more clearly, I was also perfectly positioned to catch the faintest scent of Le Labo Santal wafting off his body.

"What part was most persuasive?"

"Umm, I think it was the 'Black-ass good time' part," I replied with a smirk, desperate not to take in a deep breath so my knees didn't buckle in his presence.

"Ohhhh, okay."

Thomas nodded his head in understanding, and yet the look on his face was one of playful suspicion as he stepped even closer to me, barely leaving enough room for air between us.

"Well, it does look like you and your friends are having exactly that," he replied.

"Yeah, we are! So I absolutely have to thank you for the recommendation."

"Seeing you this happy is good enough for me, love."

I felt the smile on my face growing exponentially. Then, despite my best avoidance efforts, Thomas's eyes caught mine in a deep and penetrating stare before he expertly dragged them down to my lips, subtly licking his at the same time.

Yeah, that certainly isn't going to help me not feel all swoony around him.

Thankfully, the DJ became my saving grace as he switched up the tunes and began playing yet another one of my all-time favorite songs, "Creep" by TLC. He was most definitely in a '90s-music zone, and I loved it. So much so that my legs began bouncing to the music even as Thomas and I fixed our eyes on each other. To keep the little bit of composure I had remaining, I took the playful tone of the song as my chance to change the vibe between us and began mouthing the lyrics as I started my two-step.

"Oh, so this is your jam, huh?" he asked, bouncing his limbs in step with mine.

"Yesss! I mean, how can you not love TLC, yeah?"

"You're not wrong. All-time classic female group right there."

"Exactly!"

I continued swaying my body to the beat as we talked, inciting more and more smiles from Thomas—a fact that I didn't exactly mind as a side effect to my love for the song.

"Well, don't let me stop you," he said, nodding in the direction of my friends as if he was reluctantly giving me permission to go back toward them.

I had another thought in mind, however. I didn't know if it was the swagger of Left Eye creeping into my bones or the idea of him walking away again that propelled me to push past my fears, but before I could second-guess myself, I grabbed Thomas's hand and pulled him back toward me. As soon as his body was close enough that I could practically feel his heart beating, I turned around so that my back now faced his chest, wining my butt and torso in a circle as T-Boz's raspy vocals intermixed with the trumpet and drums on the song. To his credit, Thomas barely skipped a beat, pressing his frame into mine and mimicking my dancing style in a perfect rhythm.

It was almost as if we were created to melt into each other, the way our limbs seamlessly moved together, his hips meeting mine in a move that felt so sinfully amazing.

"So you're sure I had *nothing* to do with you choosing to come here today?" he asked, whispering into my ear as we continued grinding to the song. "It was just for a good time?"

I leaned my body into his and turned my head slightly backward so that I could see his eyes in my periphery as I replied, "Well, you know, in London, we have a right to silence, yeah, if a person is on trial and thinks that their answer may incriminate them. Sort of like your Fifth Amendment."

"I'm aware," he responded with a deep chuckle in my ear.

"Good. Then you'll understand when I choose not to respond to this line of questioning."

"And you can certainly do that, Liv. But just know that means I'm exercising my right to assume it was all me."

I didn't respond; there really was no need to because he knew—and I knew that he knew—he was right. Instead, I continued dancing to the sounds of TLC as the DJ began blending in the melody for "Red Light Special," automatically grinding our moves down to a sultry wine. Thomas took the opportunity and wrapped me in his arms, forcing our bodies to move as one in a rhythm likely only intended for dance floors with no lights, or private bedrooms. Instead, there we were, out under the illumination of a 3:00

p.m. sun, slowly letting our bodies do all the talking we'd had difficulty accomplishing with our mouths. Exposed for anyone and everyone to see if they wanted, including Reagan and her girls, who I'd yet to return to.

I didn't care, though. In that moment, and with that man, I'd managed to forget all my rules. And instead of continuing to fight it, I finally closed my eyes, took in the deepest breath and let him and his Le Labo cologne sweep me away.

Chapter Six

*B*un-bun! Bun!

Phew. One verse and chorus into TLC's "Red Light Special," the DJ let off the definitive horn sound that always signaled to the crowd that the vibe was getting ready to change. This time around, it also literally saved me from descending into a mush of a woman whose body was ready to be at Thomas's beck and call.

I snapped my eyes open as the horn reverberated in our ears.

"Nah, nah, nah—y'all not quite ready to go there just yet," the DJ shouted into the microphone in response to the round of awws drawing loudly from the crowd.

"Don't worry, I got you. But it's too early! It's too early," he continued protesting. "So let's pick this vibe back up, all right. You're rocking with the best of the best today, baby. So let's gooooooo!"

With that, he jumped us from 1994 to 2019 as he dropped the staccato beat of City Girls' "Act Up," immediately getting the crowd back on his good side. All around me, the women soon became their own personal rap stars, joining in on JT's classic first verse and informing all the men that they didn't care about them unless they were doling out Birkin bags on a regular.

For my part, I took the opportunity to loosen my body from Thomas's grip and showcase my skills again, jumping into Yung Miami's superfast rap flow with ease.

"Oh, it's like that now?" Thomas asked as I playfully pushed him off me so I could have the space I needed to wave my hands and bounce my body to the new beat.

He watched in awe as I continued, the both of us staring each other down but unwilling to let either win in our unspoken game of chicken. Two more seconds of TLC and I might have lost, but with the City Girls? Tuh! I was up again.

Reagan, Keish and Gigi must have realized this, too, because just as Yung Miami started flowing on the second verse, they bounced right up to us, rapping alongside me with all the fervor that part of the song required.

"Ayeeee," I shouted out, excited to have my girls around me.

Now that they were there, I could see clearly again, too, and very quickly reminded myself of what I'd known to be true since the moment Thomas had helped me lift my luggage off the plane: yes, he was cute and could charm my pants off without trying, but I didn't have time to be falling for him or his dimples, despite what the parts of my brain and body inspired by Left Eye might've thought.

"Oh, so y'all are like a crew of female rappers, huh?" Thomas asked jokingly.

"Nah, that distinction is only for our little London fairy Liv, here," Reagan chimed in, raising her voice so we could all hear her over the music. "But who can resist a verse by Caresha, right?"

"I could see how that might be difficult, especially when you've got your own version of Monie Love in the building," he replied with a wink toward me.

"Ugh, I stan her!" I shouted back.

"I had a feeling you did."

I took in a deep breath and shook off the sensation that quickly ran down my spine. It was an incredibly small detail, but the fact that he'd assumed my love for her just added onto the *He Gets Me* pile of examples building up between us, and that was sexier than I wanted to admit.

"By the way, these are my friends, Reagan, Keisha and Giselle," I shouted out, pointing to each one as I called their name.

"Nice to meet you! I'm Thomas."

He raised his hand to shake each of theirs, and I watched in horror as they gleefully made it known he'd been the topic of previous conversations.

"Oh, we know who you are," Reagan replied through a fit of giggles.

"Yes," added in Giselle. "In fact, we heard you recommended the party to our girl, right?"

"I did. I did," Thomas replied, nodding and simultaneously raising his eyebrows toward me. "None of you have been before?"

"No, we all have…plenty of times actually. Liv is the only newbie," said Keisha.

"Ahh. Okay, well, I'm glad she's in good hands, then."

"Meaning yours?" Reagan asked, quickly boomeranging the conversation to what they'd all been obviously thinking as they'd watched us a few steps away. "Because, I mean, we weren't trying to interrupt earlier, but…"

"Ahh." Thomas grinned bashfully. "You know, it's easy to get a little carried away around this one."

He absentmindedly scratched an itch on his right ear and then bumped the side of my torso playfully, giving me a knowing look that told me I was going to hear about this discussion later.

"But no, I actually meant with you all. That way you can navigate her through the ins and outs of the whole party since you've been before."

"Oh yeah, that's a given. We got our girl's back, ain't

that right?" Reagan replied, soliciting a round of "mmm-hmms" and "yeps" from Keisha and Giselle.

She also nodded her head toward me with a similar knowing look. Clearly, everyone had intentions of replaying this conversation with me afterward.

"Well, that's real good to hear, Reagan. Real good. Because this lil' dangerous ass twerk that she seems to have could get her into trouble, you know."

Thomas laughed out loud, bumping me in my side again as he talked *about* me to my new friends but was clearly directing his comments with the intention of riling me up.

"One might argue you're the dangerous one," I chimed in, unable to resist the need to defend myself.

"Who, me? Nah, I'm a literal angel when I'm not around you, love. You can ask anyone."

Thomas punctuated his sentence with his now patented smirk that threatened to snap the very feeling out of my knees. It also managed to miraculously quiet down my City Girl squad, who simply watched in awe as he lured me into another concentrated stare. Powerless to his desires, all I could do was stand there, biting the inside of my mouth to keep from responding or smiling back too hard…a fact that he clearly noticed and replied to with another wink.

"Now, tell me again how you came here just for a Black-ass good time and not for me," he whispered, bending his torso and neck toward me so that his lips were perilously close to the nape of my neck.

"It may have been a combination," I admitted.

"Mmm."

"But to be fair, you did tell me you weren't interested in me. So…"

"That's definitely not what I said."

"I'm bloody sure that's not something a girl forgets, yeah."

"Well, Olivia, I'm pretty intentional with my words. So, trust me, I know that's not what I said."

His eyes kept mine in a trance as he awaited my next reply, somehow admonishing me and encouraging me to be a better spar partner all at the same time. When I didn't say anything in return, his eyes lit back up, like he was a man who knew he'd finally won our game of chicken.

With his symbolic championship belt in hand, Thomas turned his head back around to the other girls and offered up his hand again for a goodbye shake.

"Ladies, it has truly been a pleasure meeting you," he said. "I know you probably came out here to have a good time with your friends, so I'm going to leave you to that. My apologies for monopolizing Monie Love's time for a while, but she seems to have some kind of an invisible hold over me where that just happens."

They each stared back at him, clearly charmed as much as I had been when we'd first met (and still was, despite my best efforts). I also recognized that he was once again using a conversation with them to speak to me indirectly.

"Do me a favor, though?" he asked playfully. "Don't let her in on that secret, okay? I told you she's dangerous—she might try to take advantage of me."

"Don't worry," Keisha replied, now fully hypnotized by the dimples and the charm as well. "We got you."

"Umm, I thought it was 'we got Liv,' remember?" I interrupted.

"Of course," Reagan replied, playing cleanup man. "We got you, too, girl. Always."

Too. Tuh!

Thomas finished shaking each of their hands and turned back to me, with now four championship chicken-game belts under his wing. He'd somehow silenced me and impressed my friends, and I could see in his face that he knew it and was quite pleased with himself.

"Are you happy now?" I asked.

"I told you earlier I was happy just seeing you happy."

"But you're even happier now. I can tell."

He tilted his head to the side and gazed at me with a mischievous grin that made me want to jump up and kiss it off of his face. I shook away the thought and instead attempted to pivot the conversation once more before he said his final goodbye. It was all I had left to help me keep some kind of composure.

"By the way, before you leave, we should still take that picture from before," I offered.

"What was that?" he asked, slightly perplexed.

"The picture! You know, the one you were initially going to photobomb? I was thinking we could just take it together instead."

"Oh! Yeah, we should definitely do that. You're right."

Without another word, Thomas reached out his left arm and wrapped it around my waist as he expertly maneuvered my body next to his, positioning me right into the nook of his five-ten frame, our bodies sinking into each other like magnetic forces we couldn't control. In response, I focused my attention on the mechanics of the photo. I unlocked my phone, turned the camera to selfie mode and raised my right arm high, trying to get us the perfect angle. And it would have been—perfect, that is—if not for the fact that I was six inches shorter than him and thus was not doing a very good job of getting us both in the picture.

"Why don't you let me do that," he asked, gently taking the phone out of my hand and lifting it into the sky before I could reply. "This is your side, right?"

"Ha ha, it is, yeah."

"Good. Then let's do this, shall we?"

Thomas held my attention with his eyes until he received the silent yes that he was waiting for: a simple nod from me. Then he pulled me into him even closer and, with the flick of his thumb, snapped seven photos in succession as the two of us stared into the camera with the widest smiles ever on our faces. When he was done, he promptly returned my phone back to me and waited patiently as I looked through my gallery to see if he'd done a good job or not.

"There's got to be at least one cute one in there that you'll like," he said, drawing my eyes to his again.

"Oh, I'm sure! I mean, look at us. How could there not be?"

"Exactly. When the woman's not wrong, she's not wrong, ladies and gentlemen."

Leaning toward each other, we both fell into a fit of giggles. I even had to grab his arm to steady myself, a mistake I soon realized once I felt another powerful shiver crawl down my spine as our bodies connected again. I quickly removed my hand and cleared my throat.

"You should, uhh…take my number," he said with a slight stammer that made me wonder if he'd felt the electricity that had flowed between us, too. "So that you can send me whichever one you like best, you know. It's not fair if you get to just have it, right?"

"That's very true," I replied, maybe a little too eagerly, at once happy for the logical excuse he'd given us both as for why I needed his number but then instantly wanting him to betray that reasoning and tell me something else. "Is that the only reason you want me to have your number, though? So I can send you a picture of us?"

He smiled in response, clearly enjoying the fact that I'd rejoined our banter game better late than never.

"No, it's not," he admitted. "But I wasn't lying in the

airport, either, Liv. I get that you probably have a lot going on just having moved here and everything, so I'm not trying to jump in and be that guy who asks you on a date before you've even finished unpacking. Plus, I remember what it was like when I moved here. I want you to take the time to enjoy all that the city has to offer before you go back to the UK."

"That's fair, and I appreciate you understanding my priorities."

And the thing was, I really did; the fact that he wasn't trying to get me to choose him over my plans for the year was not only refreshing, it was also comforting. I hadn't realized how nice it would feel to be around someone who didn't seem as if he needed me to be less than myself to like me. At the same time, it was still a little disappointing to hear that same person once again say he didn't want to date me. Try as I might, I was sure it showed on my face.

"Of course. I'm a man with my own as well. That said, I wouldn't mind us spending some time together," he added, looking at me earnestly, his head tilted to the side again. "Whenever you're ready."

"Soooo…a date but not a date?"

Thomas smiled at me again and moved in closer. "How about we just say I'll let you decide what it is. That work?"

"Okay. We can do that."

I handed him my phone again, feeling as if I was getting sucked into a vortex that I wasn't sure I wanted but also wasn't sure I didn't want. It was the strangest feeling I'd ever had.

Is this what American women have to deal with on a regular basis? I wondered. *Because it isn't for the faint of heart.* I made a mental note to talk about this with Reagan and Robin later. My girls Nneka and Tracy—my besties since primary school—were certainly going to want to hear the play-by-play, too, but I needed my American friends to tell me if I was losing my mind or not.

Thomas dutifully typed his number into my phone and then, just as he had before, gently handed it back to me, our fingers grazing slightly as we made the exchange.

"I look forward to seeing you again, Liv," he said before leaning in and planting the softest, sexiest and quickest kiss on my forehead.

It was like the man was determined to make me squirm with a thousand people as his witnesses.

"Same here, Thomas."

He winked at me once more and then slipped away into the thick of the crowd. By the time my legs gave from under me, he'd disappeared into a sea of dancing people, all bouncing and rapping along with Saweetie and Doja talking about riding with their best friends in a Tesla. Thankfully, Reagan was there to catch me as my knees literally buckled from the weight of the swoon pulsing through my body.

"Damn, girl!" she shouted out. "I'd say Mr.— Wait, what's his last name?"

I straightened myself up and took in a deep breath before responding to her, scoping the area to make sure he wasn't still snooping around as Keisha and Giselle joined us. The last thing I needed was for him to hear what I was sure was about to be a discussion all about him.

"I don't know it yet," I replied, cringing at the implication.

"He's got you sprung like that, and you don't even know his full name?" Keisha asked. "That's some powerful juju right there."

"He does not—well, he might—but don't worry, it's not going to be like that going forward. He already knows my plans for this year, and falling for him is just not in the cards."

I looked around wistfully, suddenly remembering how incredible his lips had felt on my forehead. What an inconvenient flashback to have while I was protesting my case.

"Please," Giselle chimed in. "Don't let Keish make you feel bad about anything here. The way that man was looking at you the whole time he was with you… Shoot, if he's not in your plans, you need to reevaluate those plans!"

I laughed and took a big gulp of what was left of the drink in my hand.

"In other news, does anyone else need a refill?" I asked, waving my empty cup in the air. "Because I could surely use one right now."

"I bet you could!" joked Keisha. "But I'm definitely down."

"Me, too," added Reagan.

"Same here," Giselle said, lifting her cup in solidarity, too.

"Okay, great. I'll get this round at the bar. Does everyone want the same thing?"

"Yep," they replied in unison.

"And I'll come with," said Reagan. "It's a big difference between carrying three drinks and trying to maneuver through the crowd with four."

"Oh, true. Thanks—I appreciate it."

"You bet. Plus," she said, her voice turning to a whisper as we began walking toward the bar, "I need to hear more about what all just happened."

"Well, first, can you tell me how you knew it was him behind me?"

"Oh, that's easy. The look he had on his face was so obviously that of a man drawn to you—and not just because he thought you were cute. Like, you could see there was more there. And then the way he was awkwardly trying to pose behind you…it just was no question. That was a man excited to see the woman he'd invited show up."

I laughed, trying to envision exactly what they'd all seen. I could only imagine the spectacle from their perspective—going from that awkward exchange to me damn near falling over as he'd left. What a show we'd put on!

"If it's any consolation," she added, "the way things went down were even better than the devious plans I had cooked up. So maybe that should tell you something right there."

"Tell me something? Like what, that the best things can happen outside of your plans?"

"You said it, not me."

"Hmm. I get that, but it's just really not how I live my life, Rae."

"Oh, I know."

We squeezed ourselves through the crowd in front of the bar and, within a few seconds, got the bartender's attention to order our drinks.

"I'd like one whiskey ginger, a vodka tonic…oh, do you know how to make a Tom Collins?"

"I sure do," he replied.

"Okay, so a Tom Collins, and wait…" I turned to Reagan as I realized I didn't know what Giselle had been drinking. "Do you know what Gigi would want?"

"Oh yeah, get her a gin and orange juice."

"What? You're kidding me, right?"

In my head, I immediately started hearing the chords to the chorus of one of Snoop Dogg's most known rap songs. That was not what I would have expected from the friend with the *Girl Power* tank top on.

"I know. You can take the girl out of Southern Cali but not the Southern Cali out of the girl."

"Okay," I replied with a chuckle, and turned back to the bartender. "And lastly, a gin and orange juice."

"All right—coming up. Anything else?"

"No, that's it. Thanks!"

I turned back to Reagan and saw the glimmer in her eyes as she stood there waiting for me to speak again.

"Okay, now that that's done, give me the tea! How was it seeing him, dancing with him, everything? You've had me waiting far too long for this."

"Oh, Rae, it was…" I sighed "…far too dreamy and confusing and exhilarating for me to even put into words."

"Don't I know it, *cher*. We could see that from where we stood just a few steps away," she said with sympathetic eyes. "But try."

Chapter Seven

Thomas: I never said I didn't like the episode. Just that I think it's mad wild Dwayne Wayne waited until Whitley was in her dress, down the aisle and getting ready to marry another man before he finally stepped up and said something.

I laughed to myself after reading Thomas's text message. Since the party, we'd been having just these kinds of debates on almost a daily basis, covering everything from sibling-order personality traits to the benefits of registering as a Democrat or Republican and not Independent, plus our ongoing '90s-versus-2000s R&B battle. In each, I learned something new about him, not the least of which was that he was the oldest of three boys; a voracious reader, especially of politics and economics; and willing to die on the hill that the 2000s had been as important to R&B even though that era didn't get the same hype as the '90s. I'd even finally learned his last name: Wright.

Today's conversation was on whether or not the most iconic episode of *A Different World* was as romantic as it was remembered or a massive display of reckless intentions and selfish behaviors. This was something we'd been going back and forth on for at least twenty minutes while I played double duty, shopping with Reagan and Jake to make my flat feel a little more like home.

That's true. It was bloody late on his part. But ultimately, he fought for his girl, I texted back. That's where the romance comes in.

Thomas replied a couple minutes later, just as I was wheeling my trolley out of the cashier line.

But at what cost? he asked. You're telling me that this incredibly intelligent man—with an engineering degree, at that—didn't recognize he might actually be losing the woman he loves until right at the moment Whitley's about to say I do? He didn't know while she was dating Byron, or even once she got engaged?

Oy, you're right. But I think it's less about him not realizing it until the wedding date and more that his need to fight for her became extremely urgent, I retorted. He did go to her the night before, remember?

Thomas: And stopped short of saying what he really wanted to, which was I love you. Don't choose him. Pick me.

Me: He did.

Thomas: I just don't think that's romantic. Now, I'm no one's expert on love—I haven't even really been interested in a serious relationship for a while now. But I know that if I were in love with someone, I'm not waiting until they are walking down the aisle to marry someone else to tell them that. That's an incredibly high risk, low reward way of doing things. Not to mention, it's rooted in everything being about him. If it was about her, there were plenty of other, better opportunities to achieve the same result.

I paused and reread his latest text, not knowing exactly where to start with my response since he'd sufficiently packed a lot into one message. Most intriguing, of course, was his admission that he hadn't been looking for a relationship for a while. But that felt like a trap I should stay far away from. After all, I had yet to take him up on his "non-date" date anyway, so what did it matter to me?

The only problem was the gulp in my throat I immediately felt upon reading that admission. I breathed in deeply to release the tightness that had suddenly developed in my chest and decided to simply address the main topic at hand. Just call me Olivia "Avoidance Queen" Robinson.

What's the alternative then? I asked. He doesn't fight for her at all, and she marries Byron? That would have made for an awful outcome.

Thomas replied back almost immediately, but I blacked out my screen before I could read it, suddenly realizing that I'd been texting with him nonstop even while shopping with Reagan. And although I never wanted to be that person who spent all day on their phone while out with friends, I'd found myself caught up, too fascinated by the workings of his brain to disengage. It was Reagan's voice as she called for Jake to join us at the store exit that provided the interruption I'd needed to jolt me out of my trance.

"Did you find everything?" Jake asked as he strode up to us wearing an all-royal-blue casual-wear ensemble from Polo combined with a pair of white-and-blue Nike Air Maxes.

"Oh yes. I think we've done enough damage in T.J. Maxx for the day," she replied, pointing to the shopping trolley full of rose-gold and silver knickknacks and necessities.

"Okay. Well, let's drop these bags off at the car so we can keep the party going."

I watched them with interest as I rolled my trolley

behind them and out onto the sidewalk. Reagan gently grabbed Jake's hand and pulled him close to her, then melted into the side pocket of his eager and awaiting torso. It was a small gesture, but as an outside observer, I could tell she was clearly letting him know she didn't take him being with us today for granted. Jake might not have been directly by our sides the entire time—vacillating between strolling three or four aisles away to give us uninterrupted girl time and joining us right when we needed him to help pick up the heaviest of the items—but my girl hadn't forgotten he was there by any means. The smile on Jake's face as he bent his body slightly to meet hers revealed that he appreciated the act and all debts had been paid.

Reagan and Jake were a marvel, really. The stories I'd heard about their breakups (and makeups) would put Carrie and Big to shame. But in person, all I ever saw were two people who cared deeply for each other and showed it through simple acts of kindness—a far cry from Jake's previous reputation as a selfish, manipulative man who'd broken her heart too many times to count and Reagan's as a woman on a mission to do everything by the book, perfectly, and never let a man get too close to hurt her again. I was bloody sure, for example, that Jake had plenty he could have been doing on a Saturday afternoon besides hanging with us, and yet there he was—shopping the likes of Target, HomeGoods and T.J. Maxx on the Upper West Side just in case we needed his help. That had not been on my bingo card.

I briefly looked down at my phone and noticed that Thomas had now sent me three messages back-to-back, definitely igniting my curiosity to read his replies. But I was also determined to try to stay in the moment with Reagan and Jake as we walked to his car just a block away. In the time we'd spent in T.J. Maxx, the temperature had dropped significantly—New York's way of reminding us that it could still get chilly in the fall—so, I was immediately thankful we'd found a place to park nearby as we walked out into the cool air. And while the wind tried its best, it didn't make it past my black-and-tan ankle-length coat and light mauve sweatpants set. That, plus the hoodie on my top, which had a satin interior made to protect Black women's hair, was all the coverage I needed in case the November breeze grew to be too prickly once the sun set on our shopping spree.

Jake began expertly unloading my shopping bags into his trunk as soon as we arrived at his car, making sure to leave room for whatever we bought in the remaining stores. To help, I grabbed the next largest bag on top of my trolley, momentarily forgetting that it was packed with a box of champagne flutes, two extra-large coffee mugs, a small rug to lay next to my bed and a hair dryer to replace the one I'd blown out despite the power adapter I'd tried to use my first week in the city.

"Oh God," I cried out, trying to get my bearings so that I didn't drop the bag onto the ground.

"You okay?" Jake asked, immediately springing to action and trying to wrestle the heavy bag out of my hands.

"Mmm-hmm," I said, doing my best to tighten my grip on the bag, walk the few steps from the trolley to the trunk and drop it off quickly but gently. "'I am woman, hear more roar' or something like that."

"'Or something like that' is right," Reagan chimed in, laughing from where she was perched beside the passenger door of the car with her gray full-length jacket and its turned-down collar casually blowing in the wind.

"Wait, why are you laughing?" I turned to ask her.

"Because literally the whole point of Jake being here is to do what you just did. And you know this but still couldn't stop yourself from picking up the second-heaviest thing in that cart and almost falling on your face with it."

"I know, but—"

I stopped myself before I could continue protesting. It didn't seem like my rationale about not wanting him to feel used or as if he was always my butler when we were together was going to be received well...or at least not without another round of laughter.

"But what?" she asked with a smile, gently egging me on.

"Nothing. You're right," I admitted. "It wasn't the smartest idea."

"It's not about it being smart, Liv," Reagan replied, finally leaving her spot by the passenger door and bouncing her way up to me with her white scoop-necked T-shirt and gray skinny jeans showing underneath her coat.

When she was close enough to me so that she could whisper, she finished her thought. "It's about not feeling the need to jump in and grab the first thing you see so that you don't feel helpless or as if you're not always in control, you know?"

"You got all of that from me picking up a shopping bag of items *I* purchased?"

"You didn't?"

She gave me a wink and turned her attention back to Jake, who had successfully finished packing everything else from the trolley into his trunk while the two of us had debated about my contribution to the effort. As he closed the trunk door, she planted a soft kiss onto his cheek and then grabbed the trolley to bring it back to the entrance of T.J. Maxx. Another small gesture between the two of them. Clearly, they'd gotten something right that I hadn't quite figured out. It made me think of my debate with

Thomas and how desperately I wanted to see what else he'd had to say.

"You all right?" Jake asked as he pressed the lock on his keys to secure his car.

"Yeah—nothing a good stretch won't cure."

"Well, it's a good thing Rae has at least two more stops on deck for you today. That should help."

I chuckled that Jake thought of shopping as stretching. Then again, the app on my phone said we'd already walked five thousand steps, so maybe he was onto something.

"We're going to HomeGoods next, right?" he asked while checking his watch.

"I think so, yeah."

"Okay, good. You should definitely be able to find the pillows and the kinds of mirrors you were looking for there. T.J. Maxx has some of those, but HomeGoods will have more options you can choose from."

"Wait, how do you know this?" I asked, amused at the thought of his extensive decor knowledge. "Are you frequenting HomeGoods on random Saturdays or something when Reagan thinks you're at the gym?"

"Don't put me in a box, Liv. I'm an evolved man," he joked back with me. "Plus, who do you think helped Rae gather all that stuff for her customized bedroom? She couldn't stay out of that store, so that meant I didn't, either."

"You know what? I didn't even think of that. I guess you're a 'Jake of all trades,' hee-hee."

"Cute," he said with a playful roll of his eyes. "But honestly, I'm no one's handyman. I'm just good at picking up on things, you know, like the fact that you've been dying to check your phone since we walked out of the store."

"Huh?" I asked, completely caught off guard that he'd noticed that small of a detail even while I'd thought he'd only been focused on my bags and Reagan's ass. "I don't think that's true…"

With nothing else to say in protest and probably the worst poker face known to man, I closed my mouth shut before I could finish my sentence and simply nodded that he was right.

Jake smiled in response and shrugged his shoulders. "Like I said, I'm good at picking up on things."

He paused to see if I'd take the hint and unlock my phone to respond to whoever he assumed was on the other end waiting for me.

"It won't bother me if you check it, you know. Reagan, either."

"I know."

"Okay," he said with another shrug.

Reagan soon came bouncing back up to us, buoyed by her crisp white Nike Air Force 1s and her zeal for more shopping. The look on her face showed that she could sense she'd missed something important, but instead of probing either of us about the details, she playfully squinted her eyes at us and then grabbed our arms to lead us to our next destination.

"All right, Liv," Reagan said as we stepped into the interior of HomeGoods, with its white tile floors, wood-laminate walkways and rows and rows of everything from dinnerware to actual furniture. "Jake will attest that I've gotten so much of my decor from this store alone, not those fancy boutiques down in SoHo that your coworkers wanted you to go to. I mean, yes, they have great stuff, too, if you like spending your entire paycheck on a rug, but *this* is the real golden goose."

"Ha ha, he may have mentioned this was your go-to spot," I replied.

"Oh, did he?"

Her previous suspicions now at least somewhat confirmed, Reagan turned to her boyfriend and squinted her
eyes at him again, waiting to see if he'd spill any further
details.

"In a good way!" I offered with a laugh.

"Mmm-hmm. I just bet it was."

I stepped back to grab a new shopping trolley while I
watched the two lovebirds as they jokingly argued about
whether Jake had ratted her out to me. Their playful dynamic as an expression of love was almost enough to make
even the most measured person smile from a place that
they didn't know existed at first. At the very least, it inspired me to stop being stubborn and finally check my
texts from Thomas, even as we began scoping the store for
the decorative throw pillows I'd been promised.

Of course not, he'd replied in the first of four texts I'd
missed.

Thomas: He should definitely have fought for her, but
months before.

Thomas: To me, the wedding just showed his emotional
immaturity. And ultimately, it put the woman he loved in
a horrible position—run to him and humiliate the other
man she was in the midst of pledging to spend the rest
of her life with, or say no to him, the man she loves, begging for her at the other end of the aisle.

Thomas: You think that was fair?

Damn. It was easy to see how he'd made such a name
for himself at his law firm. I couldn't exactly argue against
him advocating for honest communication as the more ro-

mantic of the options. That said, I felt there had to be some nuance in between his all-or-nothing reasoning.

You're right. It wasn't fair to Whitley, I texted back. But surely you understand that everything isn't always black-and-white. I think we can agree that he should have fought for her earlier, but in the absence of doing that, he had to take drastic measures to make sure he didn't lose her before it was too late.

Thomas: Yes, exactly! And that's why it's an example of poor planning more than anything else. It shouldn't have ever even gotten to that point.

Wow, how had he managed to flip this back to his side of the discussion? I wasn't going down without a fight, however. Quickly, I typed back, hoping to get in one more reply before Reagan and Jake noticed my attention wasn't on them.

Me: But then we'd never have gotten the cultural zeit-geist of Dwayne begging her to come to him. You'd take that away from all of us just so he can be...logical? Tuh!

Touché, he replied with a wink emoji. I can't argue with that.

"Yes," I whispered to myself, proud that I'd finally stumped the charming attorney who had been beating me at our debate game all week.

My victory was short-lived, however, as I looked up and saw Reagan standing in front of me with yet another suspicious look on her face.

"And just who have you been texting all day, Olivia?"

She stood with one hand on her hip as she awaited my response, but I was like a deer caught in headlights. I'd barely had enough wherewithal to blacken out my screen before she tried to swipe my phone out of my hand.

"You know who she's texting," Jake interjected.

"Oh, of course I know, but I want to hear her say it."

My cheeks grew hot as I hesitated to confirm their assumptions but ultimately knew there was no use in trying to cover it up.

"Just Thomas," I said, trying to at least make it sound as casual as I could.

"Oh, *juuust* Thomas, huh?" Reagan asked, raising her eyebrows at me.

"Yes." I laughed.

"And how long have you been 'just texting Thomas?'"

She punctuated her last three words with air quotation marks, as if I didn't already know that she wasn't going to believe a word I said in protest.

"Since the party, I guess."

I shrugged my shoulders to suggest this wasn't that big of a deal and we could all very much move on to the next conversation. Neither of them took the hint, however.

"Wait, that was weeks ago, right?" Jake asked.

He was clearly enjoying what he thought might be turning into another one of Reagan's friends' dating stories.

"Yes." I laughed again in return. "I suppose it has been weeks."

"Hmm. And have you taken him up on his offer for— what was it you called it—a non-date?"

I wasn't quite prepared for the two of them to be tag teaming me in their questioning, but I continued brushing it off in an attempt to assure them (and maybe myself, too) that nothing had dramatically changed since we'd seen each other at the party. A bunch of texts really and truly didn't amount to much.

"No, definitely not," I replied. "I've been so busy at

work, and he's been very respectful of that. Plus, his job keeps him pretty active, too."

"Uh-huh. Do you know what this sounds like to me, Jake?" Reagan asked, turning to face him. "Excuses."

"Mmm, yeah, we know them well."

"Don't we? Ugh. But why is Olivia making them, do you think?"

I was apparently in yet another situation where the people around me were having a conversation about me as if I wasn't there but also clearly directing their comments toward me. I enjoyed this one about as much as I had the instance at the day party—which was to say, not at all.

"Guys." I stepped in to try to stick up for myself.

"Oh yes, hi, Liv," Reagan said, turning her body back toward me. "Would you like to respond as to why you're making excuses?"

"I'm not making excuses. I promise," I said, chuckling at how ridiculous this conversation had become. "If you recall, the man said I could take him up on his offer whenever I was ready..."

"I'm fairly certain he didn't expect weeks to go by," Jake replied.

"Especially not if y'all have been texting the whole time!" Reagan added.

"You don't even know how much we've been texting," I said, my voice raising slightly as I continued to protest my case.

"Olivia, look at me," Reagan replied, her once playful expression turning very serious toward me. "Do you really think I don't know? The smile on your face as you talk about him tells me everything I need to know."

I sighed heavily. Maybe Reagan was right and Thomas hadn't thought he would be texting me daily for this period of time without me bringing up our non-date again.

But everyone seemed to be forgetting one thing: despite appearances to the contrary, Thomas was also the man who'd now told me on multiple occasions that he didn't want to date me. *What am I supposed to do other than take him at his word?*

"You know what? Hold whatever thought is going through your mind right now," Reagan added as she pulled out her phone and smugly began pressing a few buttons before I heard a familiar voice on the other end.

Robin.

"Hey, Rae! What's up?"

I could hear her booming voice through the phone almost immediately.

"Hey, Rob, you busy?" Reagan asked.

"Not really—just getting dressed to meet up with Craig for dinner."

"Oh, good. Well, we won't keep you long. I just needed your help real quick with the other Robinson sibling."

"Wait, with Liv? Why—what's going on?"

"Nothing too crazy. She's just over here denying her feelings for this guy who clearly likes her—I saw it for myself, Rob. He couldn't control himself even if he wanted to—and who she can't stop grinning about to the point that I think her cheeks should be tired by now."

"Oliviaaaaa!" Robin screamed out loud, admonishing me from thousands of miles away.

Reagan swung her phone around so that Robin could lay her eyes on me as she continued to speak. It was almost as if she'd called my mum on me, except for the fact that even though she was my good girlfriend, Robin was also four years younger and dating my brother. So maybe the more accurate feeling was that she'd called my little sister to have her chastise me. *I think I might have preferred my mum.*

"That's not exactly the whole story," I replied.

"It kind of is," Jake chimed in softly from the sidelines. *Now all three of them are ganging up on me!*

"It really isn't," I said calmly, flashing him and Reagan looks of fire before turning my attention back to Robin.

"Wait, is this the airport guy?" she asked.

"It is," we replied in unison.

"I didn't realize he was still around! Good for him."

"Except that Liv seems intent on stopping herself from seeing what things could be with him because he wasn't part of her grand New York plans."

I stared at Reagan, tears threatening to fall from my eyes because I didn't see how I could make them understand that they were right and wrong at the same time. Yes, meeting Thomas hadn't been in my plans, but beyond that, I just didn't have the time or energy to put myself out there for yet another person. Time and time again, I'd been disappointed by men who'd either wanted me to be less ambitious for them or who'd stopped liking me once they'd gotten to know the real me. So, it was easier to just be his friend—that way I knew I couldn't end up hurt again. And that was the last thing I needed when, yes, I had big plans for my time in New York.

"Is that true, Liv?" Robin asked.

"Partly, Rob," I said with a sigh. "But it's so much more than that. Honestly."

"Okay, well, I'll just say this—you were the voice I needed to calm me down right before my first date with your brother. So, should you decide to go on a date with—What's his name again? I don't want to just call him Airport Boy."

"Thomas." I laughed.

"Right. So, if you decide to ever go on a date with

Thomas, I'm here. And if you don't, you might have to hear from Rae for a bit, but that'll be okay, too."

"Thanks, Rob," I replied, passing the phone back to Reagan.

After we all said our phone goodbyes, Rae grabbed me and wrapped her arms around me, squeezing me tightly.

"I just don't want you to miss out on something that could be amazing because you're scared you didn't plan for it so you can't control it," she said.

"I know," I said, leaning into her embrace. "And I'm not trying to. I just—"

"Need some more time?"

"I think so, yeah."

"Okay. I get it. No more pressure from me, then."

As the two of us unwrapped ourselves from each other, we saw Jake coming down the pillow aisle carrying a six-foot-tall mirror wrapped with a wooden frame that had a gold metallic finish. I hadn't even noticed that he'd walked away while Reagan and Robin had been talking, but clearly he'd thought he could be more useful elsewhere.

"Jake, OMG."

I watched in awe as he drew closer to us.

"I know, right?" he said, gently placing it down.

Immediately we noticed it was one of those mirrors that was able to stand on its own at an angle if you wanted it to. I stepped up to it and looked at myself in the mirror, already starting to imagine where it could go in my flat.

"This is beautiful," I said, still marveling at the craftsmanship of the mirror but also that he'd found it so quickly and known it would be the one I'd like. I guess he was right after all—he was good at picking up on things.

Reagan stepped up behind me and put her head on my shoulder as we looked into the mirror, both admiring the women we saw before us, who had in different ways taken on a new adventure, coming to New York with hopes for the future. A few seconds later, my phone began vibrating in my hand, jolting us out of our moment of reflection.

I knew who it was without even needing to look.

"Tell Thomas I said hi," Reagan said with a wink before she left me to walk over to where Jake was standing.

Once she was gone, I unlocked my phone and beamed from ear to ear.

In other news, have you heard this new song by H.E.R.? he'd texted with a link to "Come Through."

Clearly he wasn't content with our conversation ending for the day, and neither was I.

That's not new! I replied. It's been out for a while now.

Thomas: Oh damn. Well, I guess it's just new to me.

Me: Ha ha, I guess so! But it is fire. I'll give you that.

Thomas: And maybe also instructive?

Me: Hmm. Maybe.

I blackened out my screen before I got caught smiling too much again and ran back up to Reagan and Jake to keep our shopping spree going.

"Well, I think we have the mirror," I said. "It's just the pillows left, yeah?"

"Yep," they replied, now both giving me Reagan's signature suspicious look.

"So you're not going to tell us anything more about whatever has you grinning right now?" Reagan asked.

"Nope," I replied quickly. "But I will say, I think there's more to come."

"Okay," she said, jokingly throwing up her hands. "I'll take that for now."

Part 2

"Always go with the choice that scares you the most, because that's the one that is going to require the most from you."

—Caroline Myss

Chapter Eight

Bryant Park in the winter was even more enchanting than any photos I'd ever seen of it, especially as small snow flurries crisscrossed in the night sky, lightly dusting the Christmas decor all around us. It wasn't just the village of shops and snow that made it special, however; Bryant Park was also beautifully designed to give its patrons both a clear view of iconic New York structures like the Empire State Building, statuesque even from afar, and a feeling that they were in a small sanctuary away from all the chaos of the city. At least that was how I felt as I waited for Thomas to return with our drinks as we officially made good on our first non-date. It was in that moment of silence that I had a chance to marvel at my surroundings and really take in the beauty before me, up to and including the giant Christmas tree that towered over the entire area, lighting up the open space with hints of purple, red and silver everywhere you looked.

"Okay, I promise you're going to love this," Thomas said as he walked back up to me and handed me a glass mug of hot chocolate topped with whipped cream and a giant red, green and white funfetti–covered marshmallow.

His presence quickly jolted me out of my thoughts, and I smiled in return—happy to have him near me again so we could experience the magic of the evening together. Looking down at my mug, I noticed that the color of the funfetti perfectly complemented the emerald green scarf

I'd chosen as the accent to my outfit for the evening—a black knee-length wool coat, patent-leather black oxfords and a black Yves Saint Laurent cross-body purse. Thomas, who had his own mug of hot cocoa but topped with an Oreo-covered marshmallow, stood in front of me just as handsome as the first time I'd seen him, dangerous dimples and flawlessly coiffed beard intact. This time around, he wore a tan winter coat that popped off his gorgeous skin tone and a light blue jean shirt with dark blue jeans underneath. It was almost as if we'd purposely switched our outfits from the day party, just with some winter clothing added to the mix.

"It looks amazing," I replied, still in awe as I clutched the warm mug with both hands.

"It tastes even better."

Thomas waited for me to take my first sip as the sun set on the beginnings of what he'd promised would be a fun-filled Christmas mini tour through the city, starting in Bryant Park, where the winter treats included a free ice-skating rink, a festive market filled with more than one hundred seventy shops and an après-themed area called The Lodge that offered specialty cocktails and remarkable views. But while the decorations and the Christmas lights twinkling the sky above the park were stunning, one thing was clear as soon as the first taste of it touched my lips— the hot chocolate was the star of this show.

"Wow, this is incredible," I said, savoring the warmth as it flowed throughout my body on the chilly early December evening.

Thomas winked in reply, instantly sending a shiver down my spine that even the hot drink couldn't cure.

"And we're only just getting started," he added. "Come with me."

Before I could respond, he grabbed me by the waist and

gently pulled me toward him, leaving barely any space between our bodies as we started walking through the winter village. With anyone else, that would have seemed like a harmless move, but with Thomas—the man I was desperately trying to just be friends with—it was the kiss of death to my resolve. He'd effectively put me right into the best position to snuggle into his frame if I wanted to, allowing his arm to wrap me in his embrace as we continued on our tour.

I took in a deep breath and did my best to maintain my composure, hoping that as we continued walking in and out of the dozens of glass-encased shops filled with handmade jewelry, purses and more, we'd inevitably find our friend groove and the tension between us would lessen. In the meantime, however, I knew I had to do something to bring down the heat factor ASAP.

"Tell me something about you that most people don't know," I asked him as I took a few tiny steps to the side and then filled my mouth with another steamy sip of the hot cocoa.

"Oh, all right, Ariana Grande. You want to know all my creep shit, too?"

"I mean…" I shrugged an implied yes and laughed at the fact that, of course, Thomas knew the reference to her song "Imagine."

He'd yet to stop surprising me since the very moment we met.

"Listen, she's got the right idea. The best way to get to know someone is by divulging some things between the two of you. So…spill."

I playfully bumped the side of his torso and bit my lip when he looked back at me as if he was ready to devour me and my hot drink all at once.

"You think we don't know each other yet?" he asked.

"I think we're still getting to know each other."

I looked back at him, my eyes wide, waiting for him to play my new game. It was my best shot at getting the two of us to loosen up since we'd met up forty minutes before. In that time, there'd been nothing but deep and longing stares, unconscious lip bites, and undeniable sparks any time we even slightly grazed the other. That would have been fine if this were a normal date, but it wasn't, and I missed the ease in which we connected as friends—who maybe flirted more than they should have.

"Okay, okay," Thomas said, resigning himself to the fact that I probably wasn't going to let up. "Definitely none of my boys know this, so don't laugh. But when I've had an especially long day at work or one of the clients is getting on my last nerve…"

He stopped before he could finish his sentence and looked me in my eyes again, almost as if he were trying to see how much he could trust me with his truth. That deeply intense look had almost ruined me previously, but this time, I didn't back down or let the butterflies in my stomach stop me from staring right back at him and making it known that it was time to give me the goods.

"Yesss," I said, egging him on. "Come on with it."

Prolonging the inevitable, he sighed deeply and then sipped a long gulp of his hot chocolate before continuing on. "So, the best way for me to decompress after that kind of day is to blast Rihanna in my headphones and go out for a run."

Thomas said the last few words in his sentence incredibly fast, so fast that I might have missed it if I hadn't been paying as close attention as I was. But I'd heard every word and absolutely loved his very sweet and innocent admission.

"Wait, what?" I said, unable to control the glee spilling

out of me. "That's your deep, dark secret? That you listen to Rihanna when you run?"

"Now, hold on. I don't think you're supposed to laugh when someone reveals something to you that they've never told anyone else. Not too many grown, heterosexual Black men are out here bumping Rihanna on their own, Liv."

"You're right," I said, pressing my lips together to try to contain my giggles. "I'm sorry… But I mean, she's Rihanna! Who doesn't love her music?"

"Don't get me wrong, most men absolutely respect her, and we'll be the first to say she's got some undeniable hits, but it's not the same for you as it is for me. I'm supposed to gravitate to Moneybagg Yo or any of the other popular rappers out right now when I need to de-stress—that way no one can question my masculinity."

"Well, Bagg is cool, too, but he doesn't have 'Pour It Up' in his catalog," I offered as a concession for my previous unrestrained laughter.

"Exactly. Or 'Loveeeeeee Song.' 'Talk That Talk.' The list goes on. All I'm saying is when I need to zone out, I either want joyful dance music or trash talk that has been backed up in real life—and in both areas, not too many people are besting her."

"Okay! Let me find out you're literally in the Navy!"

"I'm telling you," Thomas said, letting out a chuckle as he nodded his head to the side.

I clutched my mug tighter and smiled as I listened to him gush over his secret Rihanna fandom. I could understand what he was saying now and was actually bloody grateful he'd chosen to open up to me about something he thought made him seem less cool. That was a lot coming from the smooth-talking attorney who'd charmed me into my first-ever non-date. He may have started off embarrassed to tell me, but as he kept talking, I could see the joy flowing all over his face. And I was suddenly really happy I'd asked the question and he'd engaged me in it, even despite his initial reluctance. In truth, Thomas's love for Rihanna had only served to endear me to him even more—something he was becoming all too good at despite our attempts to stay just friends.

"Well, now I need to put this to the test. Are you telling me that I could begin singing any Rihanna song and you'd know all the words?"

"Every single one," he replied confidently, almost daring me to try.

"Tuh! Well, challenge accepted, Mr. Wright."

I thought about it for two seconds, and then, once again using my cup as my microphone, started rapping the first few bars of her verse in "Lemon." With my love for hip-hop, it only made sense that I'd choose a song she actually rapped on. Plus, I kinda wanted to stump him and figured only her biggest fans would know all the lyrics to that verse.

To my continued unsurprising shock, Thomas didn't miss a beat, jumping right in as if we were duet partners. Before I could even finish the second line, he grabbed my hand so he could rap into my mug as well and then expertly finished off the entire verse without skipping a word.

I stood beside him, impressed and in awe as he pretended to drop an invisible mic and raised his eyebrows to me with pride. I wondered if that was how he'd felt watching me in my zone at the day party. If it was, I could understand exactly what had drawn him to me because I felt like I was getting a sneak peek into a part of him that most people didn't get to see, and I was sure that the sparkle in his eyes could have rivaled that of the Christmas tree behind us.

"Okay, that…was…fantastic," I said, trying to find

my words as I described the feeling of watching him in his element.

It was more than just fantastic, though. It had also been exhilarating, tons of fun and oh so swoony, being let into this inner circle of his brain that few could ever dare reach. Fantastic felt like the safer description, though.

"So you believe me now?" he asked, staring deeply into my eyes again.

"Yeah, that's kind of hard to deny."

"Good, good. Well, now that that's settled, it's your turn, love."

Thomas took my free hand in his and spun me around in the middle of the village walkway, landing me right in front of his face after two twirls—once again, whether he'd intended to or not, removing any space between us. Standing before him, suddenly without motion and giggles distracting us, I could see his chest rise and fall as we locked eyes and desperately tried not to lean in for a kiss.

"What's something most people don't know about *you*, Liv?" he asked, his breath so close to me that I felt it on my forehead.

I thought long and hard before responding, looking up at all the festive surroundings while I pondered just how real I was going to be and whether I would choose Door Number Two again?

"Honestly?" I started and then hesitated a bit, trying to get my bearings before I divulged my own deep, dark secret.

"Always," he replied, waiting for me to proceed.

It was something about the way that he looked at me that truly made me believe him, as if there was nothing that I could say that would affect his opinion of me. And maybe it was also the fact that he'd been so vulnerable with me, but whatever the reason, suddenly the choice became as obvious as it had been before, just with a different conclusion this time.

Mimicking his move from earlier, I took in a deep breath, closed my eyes and let my lips move before I could stop them.

"Probably...how scared I am that I'm going to fail this year," I admitted.

"You? Fail?"

"Yeah," I replied, opening my eyes again and linking them with his. "Literally every time I walk through the atrium of my office building, I feel this deep sense of fear. Like everyone's waiting for me to either soar or fall on my face and they'd be perfectly fine with either because at least they'd get the show out of it, you know? And there I am, the little Black woman from London, all dressed up, trying to act like I know what I'm doing when, truthfully, I'm deathly afraid of disappointing everyone around me all the time."

I held my breath and dropped my chin after divulging my secret, waiting to see how he would react to it.

"Liv, wow. First of all, thank you for being honest with me," Thomas replied, lifting his free hand to my chin so that he could raise my head to look at him.

The motion upward permeated through my body so that before I knew it, I was also standing on my toes just so I could be closer to his face.

"I hate that you've put that kind of pressure on yourself, though. Especially because you're already doing things that probably astound everyone around you. The fact that you could ever disappoint..."

He stopped himself before finishing his thought, leaving me to wonder what he was holding back, even as I tried to stop the tears from falling out of my eyes just from the relief of sharing something so intimate with him and not having it used against me.

"Listen, I can't tell you how you should feel. All I know is I am amazed daily by you," he added.

"Thomas…"

"No, I'm serious, Liv. You're a boss. Anybody who's around you for more than two minutes knows that. Hell, I saw it from the moment we met on the airplane."

"When I couldn't even bring my own luggage down from the overhead bin?"

"Yes!"

I thought about that first interaction of ours, recalling how helpless I'd felt, which had only been reinforced by Thomas swooping in to save me. Not my finest hour, by any account. And that could have been the end of our story—the damsel in distress saved by the handsome knight—except he hadn't let it. For some reason, he'd kept popping up by my side, wanting to know more. And now, here we were, rapping to Rihanna together in the middle of a Christmas-shop village. Life was so interesting because who could have predicted that? Certainly not me.

"You did say that you believed I could do anything," I said with a nervous giggle.

"Exactly. And the only way that's changed is that my belief is even stronger now. You are the smartest, most capable and most beautiful woman I've ever met, Olivia."

Well, that's it. There's no way to get around just how swoon worthy that was.

I stepped down from my tippy toes and closed my mouth that was now desperate for his lips.

"Thank you, Thomas, truly…for listening to me and seeing me," I said, nibbling on my lower lip, which had an annoying mind of its own and was trying to propel me toward him.

"There you go with the thank-yous again."

"I know, I know. But really, I'm grateful for our friend-ship."

"Me, too," he replied, and then bumped me on the side of my hip again.

It happened so quickly, but I could have sworn I saw just a flash of disappointment appear on his face before he replaced it with his signature grin.

"Shall we continue our holiday tour?" he asked. "We still have to go to Lillie's so you can experience what it's like to have every single Christmas decoration known to man strown throughout a bar, then there's the Union Square holiday village, too, and finally we have to get you some dumplings from The Bao, though that part isn't about Christmas—it's just a great spot for the winter, and we're going to be starving by then."

"Wow, you've really thought tonight out!"

"Yeah, I had to. I can't half step when it comes to you."

"Duly noted," I said, biting my lip again to keep her from doing things I might regret in the morning.

"Just one thing before we leave…" he said with a bit of hesitation and then a huge smile.

"Yes?"

"You have a wad of whipped cream on your right cheek. You might want to get that before we hit up the next spot."

"Wait, what?"

I swiped at my cheek and stared in horror at the large dollop of cream on my fingers. It was massive, like a big freaking cloud burst onto my hand.

"Oh my God. How long has that been there?"

"Well…"

"And you're just now saying something?"

"I mean, I thought you could feel it. It was so big!"

Thomas curled his body over in glee, laughing so hard I could see tears starting to well up in his eyes.

"Wow! I've just lost all trust in you," I said through my own set of giggles. "That quickly. Our friendship's now over."

Thomas stood up swiftly, and with the silliest grin still on his face, he looked me dead in my eyes, once again holding me in that sort of trance he had when he wanted to.

"That's not possible, Liv. I'm sorry to have to be the one to tell you, but you're stuck with me now."

Three hours later, I'd learned more than I'd ever thought I could about Thomas Wright in such a short span of time. First, he liked to dabble in a little photography, often joining up with a walking photog group uptown to capture various parts of the city when he wasn't in the UK for work. He also thoroughly enjoyed linking up with his friends in what he called "Black NYC," hopping around to events like the day party he'd invited me to. On that list was everything from Trap Karaoke parties to rooftop get-togethers in Brooklyn, but no matter where the spot, according to him, it was always a "Black-ass good time." One other crucial detail I learned was that, if nothing else, he was not a liar. In fact, everything he'd hyped up before our non-date had actually exceeded my expectations, including the massive display of Christmas decor at Lillie's and the best dumplings I'd ever had at The Bao.

By the time we rolled ourselves out of there at around 9:30 p.m., I was stuffed to the brim with every kind of dumpling known to man—crab, shrimp, wasabi, chicken, even chocolate, to name a few—and I could barely think past climbing into my bed and curling up to get the best sleep of my life. The tricky part, however, was that as much as I wanted to get home, I wasn't quite ready to end our outing yet. That was one other thing I'd learned actually. I could probably spend all day with Thomas and not be knackered.

That realization didn't exactly bode well for all my "focus on your career during this year abroad" plans.

"You know, your place is only about a fifteen-minute walk from here," Thomas said, once again jolting me out of my thoughts as we re-bundled ourselves up in the cold night air. "I could walk you home…if you wanted."

It was like he could read my mind, which was both a good and a bad thing.

"Oh," I replied with just the slightest hesitation. "You're not too full to walk? Because I might be!"

"Nah, this is exactly when you should walk. Get that food moving in your digestive system."

"Okayyy," I replied with a forced smile. "Let's do it, then. But only if I get to ask you some more questions."

"Damn, woman, are you an undercover reporter?" Thomas laughed and stepped closer to me so that I could see him playfully eyeing me suspiciously. I also noticed that crinkle growing on his nose again.

"Nooo, I just like getting to know you," I admitted softly.

I felt my cheeks rising on their own accord and desperately tried to stop them from making a fool of me. It was of no use, however. I was sure that my face beamed as bright as a traffic light when I looked at him.

"Well, that smile of yours might just be my kryptonite, so I guess we've got a deal."

Thomas bumped the tip of my nose with his pointer finger and then grabbed my arm to swing me around to what I presumed was the direction toward my flat. Clearly he'd noticed said mortifying smile, but ultimately it had convinced him to let me keep quizzing him, so I was going to take the win.

"You know how to get to my flat?" I asked before we started walking.

"Oh yeah, I know the East Village well—so don't worry, I got you."

I wanted to tell him that that was the least of my concerns, but I shut my mouth before I did or said anything else embarrassing.

"Okay, then great. I guess I'm following you."

Arm in arm, we began walking down St. Mark's Place toward Second Avenue. Under the night sky, the tree-lined street and rows of different-colored brick buildings interspersed with various shops, restaurants and bars almost looked majestic and unreal—like I was on a film set version of New York City. I could see how people came here and instantly chose to make this city their home. It was just something about the energy that flowed out from the concrete and the people that made you want to throw caution to the wind and just try anything you'd ever wanted to go after.

"What's your favorite British TV show?" I asked Thomas as we neared the end of the block and suddenly reached the bright openness of Second Avenue.

"What makes you think I have one?"

"Oh, I know you have at least one. You travel to London multiple times a year at this point. And you're too calculated of a person not to think of immersing yourself in some of the language and traditions. What better way to do that than through media, yeah?"

"Fair, except we already discussed how some shows don't always present the real-life experience of living in America. I assume it's the same for you all."

I stopped walking and stared at him with a quizzical look. Was he serious or avoiding the question again? I wondered.

"Is this another Rihanna situation?" I asked. "Are you embarrassed to tell me?"

"No." He laughed sheepishly. "I just don't want you to think you know me already. I'm a mysterious guy, Liv. People always tell me that I keep them on their toes about my moves, my interests, etcetera. And I generally like that, except now there's you—"

"Ohhh, okay," I interrupted, playfully rolling my eyes at his foolishness. "I'll try to remember this next time. Now, will you stop avoiding the question, please?"

"*Starstruck*," he answered quickly, and then started walking again, forcing me to catch up to his long stride.

It was reminiscent of when he'd given his Rihanna reply, except this time his feet were moving fast instead of his lips.

"Wait—I'm sorry, did you say… *Starstruck*?"

"I did."

"The BBC One show?"

"Yes. Well, I saw it on HBO Max, but yes."

"The one where the main character isn't even British?"

"See, this is why I didn't want to tell you."

"No, I just…didn't expect that to be your answer!"

"You don't like the show?"

"I love it, actually. Jessie and Tom forever," I said, laughing. "But the main character is from New Zealand!"

"Yes, but she's in London and everyone around her is British."

"So, if someone were to make a show about my life right now, you'd call that an American TV show?"

"I certainly wouldn't call it a British one."

"Wow, wow, wow. Okay. Now I see that *I'm* actually the one who needs to have you over for a British TV marathon.

I mean of all the shows—not *Fleabag*, *I May Destroy You*, *The Crown*, even bloody *Peaky Blinders*!"

"All I'm hearing you say is how much you want me to come over to your place," he said, flashing that insanely gorgeous grin of his to distract me.

"Ugh. You're insufferable, you know that?"

"So I've been told."

Thomas swung his left arm around my shoulders as we passed by a mural featuring purple, green, yellow and blue galaxies floating in a black sky with a woman's blue lipstick–covered lips as the focal point. *What a New York thing to casually walk past*, I thought as I once again found myself resisting a strong desire to snuggle into his five-ten frame, especially as the intoxicating mixture of his body scent and his Le Labo cologne wafted into my nose. In some ways, the whole scene kind of reminded me of home since Brixton was filled with murals randomly scattered all around the neighborhood. Maybe Thomas did, too.

"So what else does Monie Love want to know?" he asked as we turned the corner and began walking down First Avenue, just a few more blocks before we arrived at my flat.

"I think only one more thing for tonight."

"Oh, okay. Now I'm really intrigued. Seems like you saved the best for last, so hit me with it."

I smiled at his excitement and burrowed my face closer to his torso while simultaneously looking up at him so he could hear my next question.

"What's one thing you *think* I already know about you?" I asked.

"Huh. Like something I haven't explicitly said but should be obvious by now?"

"Yeah, or at least you think it should be obvious."

Thomas took in a deep inaudible breath. If I'd been farther away from him, I probably wouldn't have even noticed it, but as I was so close to his body, I literally felt his chest rise and fall as he contemplated his response. I pondered what he was thinking of in that moment. Was he having his own door-number-one-or-two dilemma? Or maybe he was wondering what the heck kind of question this was that I'd just asked of him?

"Honestly? Probably…how irresistible I find you and how much I can't stop picturing what things would be like if we were together," he finally replied.

Whatever I'd thought he was going to say, it definitely wasn't that.

Instinctually, I jumped almost an arm's length away from him, creating space between us while I processed the grenade he'd thrown into our happy little friend-like non-date.

"I'm sorry, what?"

"Are you telling me that hasn't been obvious? We're literally on a date right now."

"You called it a non-date! That's what we agreed to. That's what—"

"C'mon, Liv, don't be that obtuse," he interjected.

"I—I mean…" I stammered my way through my words, unsure of exactly what to say. "I'm not going to lie and say I haven't felt anything between us. Of course I have. We talk every day, and let's not even get into *that* dance at the party. But you…you've been adamant from the beginning that you didn't want to date me."

"I haven't wanted to date *anyone*…for a while now. But that had nothing to do with you. It's just that I like the life I've built for myself. My career is where I want it to be, I don't have any obligations outside of work, the partners at my firm entrust me with high-value clients here and overseas, so when I need to travel to the UK for work sometimes, I don't have to worry about missing anyone or checking in. It's the life, actually."

"Exactly. So how does that translate to—"

"To me wanting to be with you?" he asked, interrupting me again.

"Yes."

"Well, I guess I realized both things can be true. I haven't been interested in a relationship, but I also never expected to meet you, an incredibly tenacious and driven woman whose opinion I want on basically everything and who makes up the best part of my day every day. You just hopped into my world and disrupted everything I thought I wanted."

I listened to Thomas speak, stunned silent as we continued walking and running every interaction back in my head, trying to see where I'd missed the clues. I wasn't dumb, so obviously I'd felt that we were drawn to each other, but I also got the sense that he was a man who once he made his mind up about something, rarely changed it. I could relate to that, in fact, and it made things less complicated. Indeed, it was all bloody black-and-white. Neither of us wanted a relationship, so, despite any flirting or lingering looks that might have occurred, we were never going to be anything more, I'd assessed. And at the end of the year, I'd go back home with a cute story to tell about the American boy who I had a slight crush on. He was ruining all of this with his latest admission.

"That said," he continued, "I genuinely haven't wanted to be the guy who makes the precious time you have in the city about me. It's just that…well, you've messed me up in the head quite a lot… I can't believe all this hasn't been obvious?"

"Well, I don't know, Thomas," I replied, finally regaining my voice. "I'm not exactly used to men telling me that they don't want to date me but expecting me to know that they really do."

"That's fair. And all of this is new to me, too, to be honest. Even up to just now, when you asked me that question, I wasn't sure if I was going to say something because I didn't…"

"Because you didn't want to ruin what we have?" I offered, again understanding him more than I cared to admit.

"Yeah. Exactly."

We turned the corner onto my block, and Thomas stepped toward me, closing the gap in between us once again.

"So, now that you know how I feel, are you really going to tell me it's just me?"

I watched as his face, genuine and sincere, waited to see if I was going to crush his heart or make it flutter. His eyes, kind as the day we'd first met, looked back at mine, relaying a sense of urgency I hadn't yet seen in them before…and damn me, combined, it all worked to conjure up a sensation in my spine that threatened to have me laid prostrate on the ground if I couldn't muster up some strength in my calves and knees.

"It's not just you," I admitted. "But—"

Before I could finish that thought, Thomas's lips were on mine, soft and tender at first but then filled with a passion I'd never experienced. With his right hand now on my back, we clung to each other, our lips and tongues intertwining like our very breaths counted on it, like we'd been waiting for this release for years. I instinctively arched my back and stood on my toes to get closer to his face, never wanting to let his mouth go even as he alternated between tracing soft bites along my lower lip and sucking it in whole, a combination that sent continuous shivers throughout my body.

His lips, somehow soft and gritty at the same time, tasted like the sweet chocolatiness of the last dumpling we'd eaten mixed with the mint he'd slipped into his mouth right as we'd walked outside. I did my best to hold my own, standing tall as wave after wave of a pending orgasm crashed over my body as we licked, sucked, bit and pulled at each other's lips for minutes. When we finally came up for air, the softest moan escaped from my mouth, betraying just how putty I was in his hands.

"I told you the first day we met I was a pretty straightforward guy," he said, locking eyes with me once again.

"That you did."

"I don't know if I can be more honest than that, Liv."

I took in a deep breath and contemplated everything that had just happened in the past twenty minutes or so. Somehow, we'd gone from our fun playdate to Thomas blowing up everything I'd thought I knew to be true, even though he'd claimed that was what I'd done to him. And yet that kiss… Oy—if I could lock myself in a chamber of his kisses for hours, I probably would. I didn't know what to do. I didn't know what I wanted. I just knew I didn't want him to leave…not yet.

"Do…do you want to come upstairs?" I asked, stammering through my words, completely overtaken by the moment.

"No," he said, still holding me close to him. "I interrupted you—and I'm sorry about that, by the way—but I heard you. You were getting ready to say, 'But something,' am I right?"

I stared at Thomas in disbelief again. *What the hell kind of roller coaster is this?* He was right, of course. Once again. But God help me, I was more confused than ever now.

"And that's fine. Really," he continued. "But the thing

is, when I do come upstairs, I don't want there to be any hesitation in your mind that you want me. That you want to be with me and you want me to please you—mind, body and soul. So, I'll wait."

"Wait?" I asked softly.

"Yeah, wait," he replied with a sly grin. "You know, that thing where you delay an action—even when you're eagerly anticipating it—until the time is right."

"Oh, right, that."

I tasted just a tiny bit of blood as I nibbled on my lower lip again and stepped down onto my heels. This man was literally trying to drive me crazy; that was the only conclusion I could realistically come up with.

"I guess waiting can be good," I said.

He laughed heartily as I tried not to squirm in front of him.

"But you should head up," he replied. "Because I really want to kiss you again, and if that leads to you asking me to come up once more, I don't think I'd have the willpower to say no next time."

"Okay," I sighed, untangling myself from his grasp and slowly turning toward my front door. "I'll talk to you later?"

I looked back at him over my shoulder as I unlocked the door to enter my building.

"Of course. I already told you, you can't get rid of me now."

I turned my head back toward my building and walked through my front doors, desperately trying not to let him see the ocean-wide smile on my face. *Damn*, I thought as I closed the door behind me and watched him slowly walk away. *What the hell did I just get myself into?*

Chapter Nine

"Whoa. How did you stop yourself from melting right into his arms?"

Robin was mid-throw as she tossed a new set of clothes into her overnight bag when she paused to stare into the FaceTime camera, stunned by my recount of the night before. Technically, she and I were on a five-person video chat to talk about Jennifer's upcoming bachelorette weekend in Palm Springs, but when each of the women had noticed and pointed out a particular glow on my face fifteen minutes in, the conversation had suddenly become about the night before.

Try as I might, I hadn't been able to convince Reagan, Robin, Jenn or Rebecca that they were seeing things, probably because my stupid cheeks wouldn't fall down. So, after much consternation, I broke down and told them everything—word for word, from the lingering looks and laughs to the inevitable kiss that had literally taken my breath away. Well, not everything—one thing I didn't include in my story, and never would, was how I'd been playing H.E.R. and Daniel Caesar's "Best Part" on repeat since I'd fallen onto my bed last night.

"Honestly, I literally don't know," I replied.

"Well, I'd like to just throw out there that I told you there was no such thing as a damn non-date," Reagan chimed in.

"Oy! Guess who doesn't need I-told-you-sos right now?" I asked her.

"You're right. My bad."

Jennifer, who had always been the more sensitive one out of their friend group, giggled off to the side as she kindly let the news of my non-date that actually was a date take over her scheduled call. I was grateful she didn't consider it rude, but in truth, I probably didn't have that to worry about. Ever since I'd announced I was moving to the States for a year, all of Robin's friends had taken me under their wing in different ways. Jenn immediately started sending me inspirational messages every morning, almost as if she was my own personal Rev Run—this despite the fact that I was moving to New York and she lived in the District. And while that might've sounded funny on its surface, somehow each time she'd sent one, it had been at the very moment I'd needed a reminder that what I was doing wasn't crazy and I had it in me to succeed. I thought it was some kind of intuition she must have possessed and then perfected as a dean of students at an elementary school. As our friendship had quickly bloomed, she'd also graciously invited me to her bachelorette weekend, knowing, of course, that I was going to be in America anyway and it might be fun for me to come out and have a girls' weekend in Palm Springs. That was the kind of person Jenn was—never selfish and always down to support her friends no matter what.

"Have you heard from him since then?" she asked.

"Yeah, he let me know when he got home."

"Okay, that's good," Robin interjected.

"And I woke up this morning to my normal set of Sunday morning texts from him."

"Wait, you all have texts that are typical for the days of the week?" Rebecca asked.

"Okay, when you say it like that, it sounds cheesy. But on Sundays, he usually gets up pretty early and reads different newspapers online, so by the time I wake up, he's already sent me a bunch of links to stories that he wants my opinion on. That's all."

"Wow," they all replied in unison.

"He's a keeper," Jenn added. "And you know, engaged lady over here should know."

She flashed her ring into the camera with a big grin in a cute attempt to win me over, but I was still too out of it from all that had transpired in the past twenty-four hours to join them in their pure glee. Yes, this super charming, incredibly handsome man had just told me that he thought about us being together, but I didn't get the sense that any of them understood just how much that had blown up everything I'd considered safe about him.

"Well, he's not mine to keep just yet," I replied.

"Oh my gosh. Reagan, why aren't you two in the same location right now so we could ask you to either hand her a drink or shake her silly?" Rebecca asked. "Because clearly she needs something to remind her that all of this is a good thing. Do you hear that, Liv, a good thing?"

"Honestly, I was wondering the same thing myself just now," Reagan replied. "I should have taken the trip downtown."

I chuckled at Rebecca and Rae's interaction, mostly because Becs was almost eight months pregnant, so all her solutions had become alcohol based lately. Needed to decompress? Have a glass of wine. Just came back from a run? Quench your thirst with some bourbon. Had your new best friend admit that he found you irresistible? Wash that realization down with a nice cocktail! It was almost as if she needed us all to be perpetually tipsy for her since

she still had another few more months before she could
partake in any spirits on her own.

Also, I'd learned a lot about her since their first trip to
London in April. Rebecca and I had initially bonded over
the four (me) and five (her) years we had on the other ladies, plus the fact that we were the two who hadn't gone
to college with them, but our shared love of all things
Housewives with no judgment whatsoever truly made our
friendship something I'd come to cherish. Her no-nonsense
takes on those shows lined right up with her input today.

"I have a martini right beside me," I said, still laughing.
"That doesn't make up for the fact that this has changed
everything."

"Okay, okay, we hear you," Robin chimed in.

"But what are you so scared of, *cher*?" Reagan asked.

"Right, because I've never seen you look this happy
about anyone. Not even when you told me about David
that night that we went out for our first drinks. And definitely not during the times when we were all hanging out
together."

"And that's what makes this so scary, Rob," I said,
clutching my almost-empty martini glass out of sight of
the camera.

*Maybe Becs has the right idea after all. I might need
more drinks to truly keep having this conversation.*

"I was with David for two years and never felt like this
about him. But that was okay because I knew if we ever
broke up, it wouldn't hurt as much. And I was right. For
whatever break or breakup David and I are on right now,
I've been relatively okay about it. With Thomas, it's only
been a few months and yet I'm scared that if I let myself
like him as much as I could, I'm just setting myself up
for failure."

I blinked my eyes a few times to stop the tears trying

to fall out of them and took the last gulp of my drink before I carried on.

"You're all in relationships now, so maybe you can't relate, but my track record with men hasn't been that great. The few times when I've actually liked them and dared to open up and let them get a taste of the real Olivia Robinson—not just the perfect image of a girlfriend that I know how to play when I want to—they've run away so fast they could have battled Usain Bolt. Even David…he stuck around for a while, sure, but he found a way to let me know I was a lot of everything he didn't want in a partner. I don't know if I have it in me to go through that again, especially not with Thomas. It just…it would be too hard of a thing to come back from. Besides the fact that even if none of that were true, I'm leaving in less than a year. How many international romances do you all know that have worked out?"

Robin zipped up her overnight bag and plopped down onto the lavender tufted trunk in front of her bed just as I got up to walk to my kitchen so I could make myself another martini.

"Can I jump in since my relationship is less than a year in?" she asked, and briefly paused until she received my silent head nod to continue.

I'd just put my glass on the counter and grabbed the jar of olives out of the fridge when I heard the break after her question and realized it wasn't exactly rhetorical. She didn't need much beyond the head nod, however, because she quickly jumped right back in as I began pouring the gin into my jigger to measure out the right amount for my mixture.

"You know I get how scary it is to open yourself up to someone when you've experienced nothing but disappointment in your past. But Thomas is a new person, first of all, so I encourage you to do what you asked of me when Craig and I first started dating—give him a chance without putting all the pain from others onto him. You've already acknowledged how different it's been with him, where the two of you have gotten a chance to really learn each other before jumping into anything super fast. Annnd he's not rushing you! I'm still amazed that you both stopped your-selves last night. Craig and I were on each other like white on rice the night of our first date!"

"Rob, eww, that's her brother. C'mon!" Jenn screamed out, interrupting Robin's giggles down memory lane.

"Sorry! I'm just saying…the fact that *he* was the one to say no last night because he could tell you still had your reservations tells me how much he cares about you. And maybe, just maybe, the man likes you precisely for all the reasons those other guys haven't. It's kind of hard to keep everything that makes you special under wraps as much as you all have been communicating nonstop."

"Now, Rob is right about that," Jenn added. "I know we're all thankful we've gotten to know you as more than just Robin's friend. Maybe give the guy some credit that he knows what he's getting into and he likes it?"

"Oy, I'm great with friends," I said, sitting back down in my drawing room, my new martini in hand. "That's where I shine. And what I thought he and I were."

Reagan pursed her lips and eyed me suspiciously through the camera. "Did you, though? Because from the moment you told me and Jake about him, you couldn't stop grinning. I don't look like that about any of my friends."

"Rude!" Rebecca jumped in. "You better glow when talking about us."

"Well, y'all are different. You know what I mean, and she does, too!"

"Okay, so friends who find each other attractive," I admitted.

"Mmm-hmm. That ain't friends, *cher*. That's denial with a splash of fear. And if Chrissy were on this call, she'd tell you, *mana*, we don't do *vidas cautelosas* around here."

"Yeah, she would!" Robin shouted out, punctuating her statement with a loud clap.

"And then she'd use that booming, raspy voice of hers and force Reagan to get down to the East Village ASAP and bring some tequila and nachos with her," added Jennifer.

"No lie," Reagan admitted. "That is definitely what she would have suggested."

We all laughed in unison, and I watched them as they remembered their friend fondly. I had no idea what it was like to mourn a close friend and wasn't looking forward to learning it anytime soon. But I was amazed at how they kept her alive in their conversation and their interactions regularly. Indeed, while I'd been spending more one-on-one time with each of the ladies lately, any time we were collectively together, Chrissy's name inevitably came up— and always in a good way. It was as if their union wasn't complete without her. This reminded me that I owed Nneka and Tracy some returned calls, too. *I might do that later when I order some food for the evening*, I thought.

"Okay," I said, throwing up my hands. "I will certainly take all your points into consideration. Now, I don't want to take up much more of this call for my drama. Can we get back to talking about Palm Springs? We've only got a week before we all see each other, and I've never been to California, so I need to know what to plan for ahead of time."

"Oh, that's easy," Reagan said, chiming in. "Think casual chic. Pack light. Basically bring bathing suits and club attire—wait, do you have that with you, or do we need to go shopping?"

"Lord, Rae—you're always looking for a reason to go shopping." Jenn laughed.

"What? I'm just offering my services if they are needed."

"I actually could use a small shopping trip," I said meekly. "I brought one swimsuit with me from London, but it sounds like I need more."

"See?"

Reagan stuck her tongue out at Jenn, who rolled her eyes off to the side in response.

"Reagan never misses a shopping trip, but she is right about packing light," Robin added. "We're having all the bachelorette decorations and other little treats shipped there, so no one has to worry about that. And you know, we already purchased the tables for when we go out on the town. So there's not much else to prepare for, really."

"Well, it's California, so prepare yourself for the cultural difference," Becs chimed in. "Palm Springs is nothing like the UK. But other than that, you should be good."

"Okay, all very good to know! I'm actually really excited for this trip," I said, turning my attention back to Jenn. "I can't thank you enough for inviting me."

"Please," she replied. "I couldn't have you in America and not be there with us. What kind of monster would that make me? Plus, I already know we're going to have such a good time, and you being there with us is just going to be the icing on the cake. It also sounds like we'll need some real face time, and not the virtual kind, to make sure you're not messing things up with our new best friend Thomas."

"Wait, how did we get back onto him?" I asked.

"Get used to it, *cher*," Reagan interjected, laughing. "This is how things go in this friend group. Once they know fear is the only thing stopping you from going after what you want, they will wear you down until you give in. Ask me how I know."

"And you're living the life with your man and your fancy job that was made just for you, so no complaining, missy," Robin replied.

"Yeah, yeah. I'm just saying. They are relentless."

"I think you should be using the word 'we' here," I said, amused at how they'd all effectively flipped the conversation back to Thomas despite my best efforts to re-center Jenn and her trip. And of all people, it had started with the bachelorette herself!

"Who, me? You think I'm relentless?"

"You made a plan to get us together after only hearing about our first interaction in the airport," I replied.

"Oh, well that's just being a good friend, no?"

I stared back at her with a *girl, now you know what that means* look on my face, and she giggled in return.

"Well, whatever, I guess I stand with my girls, then. We…firmly believe in 'what's the best that could happen,' and *we*…make no apologies about that."

"Say it!" Robin chimed in.

"Are you going to see him again before Palm Springs?" Jenn asked.

"I think so. This morning when we were texting, we started talking about meeting up after work one day this week."

"Wow, way to bury the lede!" Reagan screamed out.

"It's not in stone," I protested. "It's just an idea we floated."

"Mmm-hmm."

"Well, I, for one, am very excited about our next round of story time," said Rebecca. "Let's make sure we have time in the schedule in Palm Springs for that, please."

"Done and done," Robin replied.

I drank another sip of my martini, shaking my head at the women who I'd come to all call "friend." Robin had warned me just how much this group was always at the ready to cheer their people on. That had been a warm welcome when I'd needed the boost of confidence to say yes to my year in New York. But now that it was about something that didn't have to do with work or my career, I had to admit, I was a lot more uncomfortable with it. Still, I could appreciate a friend group filled with lots of strong opinions and love, and it seemed like I was stuck with them in the same way Thomas kept saying I was stuck with him.

"All right, ladies, before we sign off, can we make a toast to the fiancée of the group and this banging-ass trip we've got planned for her?" Robin chimed in, interrupting me out of my thoughts.

"Yes, yes. A perfect idea," Rebecca replied as she lifted her cranberry-spritzer mocktail into the camera.

One by one, each of us did the same, until all you could see in the chat were glasses filled with different colored drinks and some faces melting into the background.

"To an amazing upcoming weekend in Palm Springs," Robin began. "We're all so so happy for you and Nick, Jenny. And while we can't wait to stand up with you to celebrate your love on your wedding day, this weekend is our chance to cheer on the incredible woman Nick is soon going to get the privilege of calling his wife."

"And let me tell you, he's got a baaaaad mama jama on his hands, okay!" added Reagan.

"She's right," Robin continued. "So, here's to a real one. To the heartbeat of our friend group and the woman who taught us all how to bloom where we're planted. Palm Springs is going to be so litty!"

Chapter Ten

Even though I was head down on the latest portfolio proposal that needed my review, I knew it was on or about 5:30 p.m. as soon as I heard the all-too-familiar hustle and bustle from the cubicles near my office. Over the past couple months, in fact, I'd learned all the telltale signs of various hours in the day at my job, never even needing to look at the gold, sunburst-style wall clock that hung near the canvas image of me symbolically waving goodbye to London.

Around 8:30 a.m., I'd normally hear the rush of people walking onto the floor, telling stories about their evenings and sighing about all the work they still needed to accomplish. At about 10:00 a.m., the floor would seem eerily quiet, but only because most of the staff had inevitably either started congregating in the kitchen area for their morning coffee breaks or were in various meetings throughout the building. No later than about 1:00 p.m., I usually heard puttering footsteps as groups of people decided if they were going to eat lunch somewhere in the neighborhood or simply heat up whatever they'd brought from home. And somewhere around 5:30 p.m. usually signaled the time for the mass exodus, leaving only the few masochists like me and Walter to close down the floor each day.

Every once in a while, I stepped out of my office during these daily interactions to partake in the activities with the rest of the teams—feel like I was actually part of the portfolio crew. But more often than I'd like to admit, I spent my time like a working Sleeping Beauty, enclosed in my glass office until someone (usually Wendy or Julie) burst in and forced me to take a sanity break.

The last of the telltale signs was the sound of Walter's feet as he stomped down the hallway toward my office anytime between 6:00 and 6:30 p.m.—something that had become a sort of regular routine for him, especially in the last couple weeks. The first time I'd heard him clobbering around, I'd thought it to be an indication of his anger, but no. He just seemed to have a heavy walk, which was quite interesting considering he was maybe one hundred sixty-five pounds wet and probably no taller than five foot nine. But Walter did almost everything big—commanded the room when he walked in, paced up and down in his office during calls and stomped throughout the floor when he was simply walking from one office to the next. It was a far cry from the meek and mild man I'd met on day one, but then again, I'd also learned by now that our first interaction had been more of an anomaly than the norm. Walter was the man in this office, and he knew it.

Since that first day, he and I had actually formed a pretty great thought partnership. Not to say we were the best of friends—he was still my boss, obviously—but he'd meant it when he'd said that he wanted my hands on and ideas represented in most of the proposals and strategy briefs by the time I left New York. And because Walter expected mountains to move when he said so, he'd really only given everyone about two or three weeks after my start date before he'd begun consistently asking anyone who'd sent him something to approve if I'd seen it first.

"Did Olivia see this?" he'd ask, straight-faced with serious eyes and hands tucked into his pockets until he received a yes.

If he got a no, his answer was simple: "She sees it before I do."

Within a week, he never had to say those six words again.

It was a great testament to his trust in me. It also meant I had a lot of work on my plate all the time.

Just like clockwork, I heard Walter's feet coming toward me. *Must be about 6:00 p.m.*, I theorized, looking up just in time to see him standing at my door with a big grin on his face. That usually amounted to one thing—at least a few more hours of work for us both. Instinctually, I grabbed my phone to get ready to text Thomas that I might have to cancel our date.

"Olivia, my favorite," Walter said, sauntering in and plopping down into one of the chairs facing my desk.

"No, Walter, you can't butter me up today," I replied. "I have plans. I know it's hard to believe, but I really can't be here with you until nine o'clock tonight."

"Oh, perfect—this is exactly what I came in here to talk about."

"My plans?"

"No, Olivia, do I look like Wendy to you?" he asked, clearly taken aback by my suggestion.

I laughed at his confusion, but he wasn't alone. I was equally curious about where this conversation was going.

"Of course not," I replied, trying to hold back my chuckles while a quick vision of Walter with bright red hair flashed before my eyes. "Please continue."

"Thank you," he said, leaning back into the chair so that he could sit in a wide stance comfortably.

It was something I noticed a lot of American men did—white, Black and otherwise. I could only guess that it made them feel powerful somehow.

"You know, I've been loving the work coming across

my desk lately, and I attribute that all to you. I think you've been challenging our teams to listen to their clients and not just deliver proposals and updates that seem tried and true, but ones that are tailored to their unique needs and have proven results in other spaces."

"Thanks, Walter. I really appreciate that—"

"But that's not what I came in here to talk to you about," he said, interrupting my interruption of him. "I wanted to talk to you today about work-life balance."

"Excuse me?" I asked, now even more confused about what he was blubbering on about.

Still seated in the chair across from me, Walter leaned toward me so that his elbows were almost to his knees. I wasn't sure if this was his way of trying to indicate closeness without being *too close*, but it was an odd thing to look at, mostly because he didn't exactly seem like the kind of person one would want to have this conversation with. Data. Numbers. Winning. That was Walter's MO. But work-life balance?

It felt far-fetched, and even he seemed uncomfortable bringing it up. I also suddenly noticed that he'd rolled up his sleeves to about halfway up his forearms before coming to my office in some sort of odd attempt at trying to portray an "everyday man."

What is going on?

"Work-life balance," he repeated.

"What about it?"

"Well, my fiancée reminded me this morning that I needed to be doing a better job at it, and I realized when I didn't see you leaving with the rest of the office, you probably do, too."

"To be fair, Walter—"

"I know, I'm usually the reason for your late-night stays,

but not tonight. Tonight, I want you to go home, or I guess to whatever plans you have on a Wednesday night."

"It's a date," I replied, laughing at how uncomfortable even the littlest bit of gossip made him.

I could tell he was holding back another quip about not being Wendy, and it made me laugh that much more.

"Well, good for you," he said awkwardly. "So, this is me…telling you to go, you know, do that."

I eyed him as he squirmed in his seat, clearly ready for this conversation to end now that I'd taken it from just big, bold Walter giving me permission to take some time for myself. I also knew he was waiting for my silent head nod before he would inevitably jump out of the chair and go plodding back to his office, but I had one last question before I gave him what he wanted.

"Okay, Walter," I said. "I'm curious, though. Fiancée? How do you have time for that kind of commitment?"

I half expected him to fall out of the chair when he processed my question. Instead, I saw a fire in Walter's eyes that I usually only caught when he received confirmation that someone had exceeded their fundraising goal.

"Oh, that's easy," he said, perking up in his seat. "I got lucky and found someone who has no desire to change me or lessen my ambitions. She gets that some nights I'm going to be working late, and she doesn't judge me for it or question whether I love her because of it. And to make sure she knows I appreciate her, every once in a while, I actually leave the office before 6:30 p.m. and surprise her with something special. Tonight, it's tickets to her favorite Broadway play. She's watched it probably eight times now, with multiple different people. And yet she cries like it's her first time any time she sees it."

"Wow," I said, listening to Walter in awe. "That's special. And rare."

"Maybe. But I think people like me—and you—need someone like a Sarah in our lives. She keeps me balanced and challenges me in all the best ways."

Walter paused and nodded his head toward me.

"Do you think the person you're going on a date with tonight has the same potential?"

"Hard to know, really," I replied with a deep sigh. "It's only our second date, or really first—I don't know. But if precedent has anything to do with it, my chances aren't good."

"Well, if you'd told me a year ago that I would be talking to my senior consultant about work-life balance, I would have laughed in your face. Things change sometimes. Unexpectedly."

"That they do. You're very right."

"I'm always right, Olivia," Walter said with a wink, finally rising out of his chair. "Now, close that computer down and get to your date. I insist."

"Aye, Captain," I joked as he walked out of my door, stomping his way back down the hallway.

I turned my phone onto its back and unlocked the screen, noting to myself that it was now 6:10 p.m. If I hurried, I could make a quick outfit change in the bathroom and still make it to Thomas before our 7:00 p.m. class began. All I really had to do was freshen up and change into the dark blue jeans I'd brought with me, along with my classic Tommy Hilfiger shirt. I'd purposely chosen my double-breasted plaid oversize women's blazer to wear to work, figuring that it would make for a great work-to-date transition—same with my green velvet Taro Ishida slingback heels that were adorned with gold metal studs plus a gold ring and gold leaf embellishment on the pointed toes.

Hi! See you at 7, still? I typed as quickly as I could while walking to the restroom.

Thomas instantly replied.

Thomas: Yep. You'll know it's me because I'll be the guy with the smile that won't go away when you walk up.

Me: Please! I'll know it's you because of the way I can't stop smiling when I see you.

That, too, he replied.

I'll see you soon, I texted back, unsure of what else to say and in a desperate crunch for time anyway.

Thomas must not have known what to say, either, as he simply liked my reply with the thumbs-up reaction, letting me know he received it in the most millennial way possible.

As soon as I walked into the ladies' restroom, I practically threw my phone onto the counter, rushing to make my switchover happen in less than ten to fifteen minutes.

You got this, I said to myself while looking in the mirror. *Or something like that.*

Exactly forty minutes later, my Uber pulled up to the Great Jones Distilling Co. at 6:53 p.m. The first thing I noticed was how regal the exterior of the building looked with its three and a half stories of all-black paint and gold fixtures. Flanked by two grayish-tan skyscraper buildings, the facade stood out immediately, making for the kind of grand appearance that Manhattan's first whiskey distillery since Prohibition would necessarily demand. The second thing that caught my attention was Thomas, already standing outside, waiting on me with his matching all-black outfit and a fifty-thousand-watt smile.

"You look amazing," he said as he gently took my hand and helped me step out of the car.

I was instantly struck by the fact that I could somehow still see the muscles in his forearms underneath the thick black wool coat he was wearing. These were the kind of forearms that were made for scooping a ready-and-willing woman up and carrying her to his bed. That, of course, sent flashbacks running through my head of how crazy good it had felt when he'd gripped me tightly while we kissed under the moonlight just days before, and I instantly felt myself grow wet.

In truth, I hadn't stopped thinking about how Thomas's lips had felt as they'd enveloped mine since then. So I knew I was going to have to work hard to keep my composure on this date. Focusing on things like his perfectly sculpted forearms and how my hand seemed to fit in his, like they were made to seamlessly cup each other, wasn't going to make that easy.

"You look pretty dapper yourself, eh," I replied as I stepped fully out of the car.

"Well, it is our first date, so…"

Thomas's one lone but incredibly intoxicating dimple peeked out as he looked back at me and waited for my reply.

"Is it?" I asked. "So, the Christmas tour through the city didn't count?"

"No, definitely not."

"I feel like if it ends with the kind of kiss that you left me to ponder over all night, that automatically qualifies as a date, no?"

"Ha ha, well, you might be onto something there," he replied, chuckling off to the side. "But to be fair, we had specifically called that a non-date. I want you to be very clear that this is a real one."

Thomas stared at me intensely, holding my attention until I found myself squirming under his gaze. I could

barely breathe sometimes when he looked at me because
everything in my body felt like it was being tethered to
him, and so my lungs were waiting on his to even say *go*
before they moved on their own. This was one of those occasions. It just so happened that the last time, I was almost
ready to give myself to him in the middle of the street in
front of my flat.

"Okay," I said softly, releasing the tension in my body
with short, slow and steady breaths. "I am crystal clear."

"Good," he replied. "Now, let's go inside so we don't
miss the start of the class. I've been wanting to check this
out for a while now."

"Oh, I see! So, I just gave you a good excuse, then?" I
joked as we walked through the gold revolving-door entrance.

"Yep, sure did. The best excuse."

We quickly joined the rest of the evening's mixology
class as we all oohed and ahhed our way through a guided
tour of the distillery, followed by a four-part tasting of their
signature bourbon. By the time that was done, we were
treated to a few bites from a premade charcuterie board,
which included smoked almonds, marinated olives, dark-
chocolate pieces and some of the best cheese and prosciutto
I'd ever tasted. If that wasn't enough, they also gave us a
smoked old-fashioned to sip on while our mixologist for
the night led us in a hands-on course on how to make two
of Great Jones's house-made cocktails—the Saratoga Julep
and the Great Jones Rye Manhattan.

As the kick from the old-fashioned began warming up
my insides, I realized I'd worked through my lunch hour
earlier, so I was officially surviving off two cups of coffee,
a granola bar and the few bites to eat from the charcuterie board. *Maybe that's why the cheese tastes so good?* I
wondered. Either way, I knew I was going to eventually

need more than that to coat my stomach if I wanted to show up to work at 7:30 a.m. like normal—and without a massive headache.

I finished my first drink and looked toward Thomas so we could toast with the juleps we'd made, giving my best attempt at making flirty eyes at him. To my surprise, however, the next sound I heard was him bursting into laughter and curling over with tears threatening to fall from his eyes.

"What?" I asked. "Did I miss something?"

"Your eyes are so glassy right now," he said. "You never told me you were a lightweight."

"I'm not." I laughed, suddenly understanding what he found so funny.

"The eyes don't lie, love."

"No, really. It's not that. I actually just realized that I didn't eat much today, so, you know, the liquor doesn't have anything to soak it up."

"Mmmm, okay, see now that's good information to know. We'll have to make sure we get you a chopped cheese before you go home tonight. In the meantime, let's try to make sure your eyes focus on one thing at a time so they don't get stuck crossing over."

"OMG, it's not that bad!" I said, playfully slapping him on his broad shoulders.

"I don't know. I wish you could see what I see."

"Oh, really?" I asked. "Well, tell me, what do you see?"

"The most beautiful woman I've ever laid eyes on…"

"Thomas," I interrupted.

"Barely keeping her eyes open while she desperately tries to stay awake to make her next cocktail," he continued, laughing even harder.

"I'm so glad you're enjoying this," I replied. "It feels great to be the entertainment tonight."

"Nah, I just enjoy spending time with you, so the laughs come easy, that's all."

Damn it, there goes those swoony, spine-chilling feelings again. What is it that's holding me back from giving in to them again? I asked myself.

Oh right, I remembered as I took another sip of my drink. I didn't see how he fit into all my plans. That pesky little fact. But I really did enjoy our time together.

"Same actually," I admitted. "Which is why I'm so mad at myself for not eating earlier. I do kinda wish things were a little less hazy right now, to be honest."

"See? I'm glad you're finally telling the truth. I told you the eyes don't lie."

We both laughed as I bumped the side of his hip and licked my bottom lip to keep from biting it—something I was all too aware I did whenever I wanted mine to be on his. Then, just as quickly, we fell back into the rhythm of the class, following along as our mixologist walked us step-by-step through our final cocktail.

"Tell me more about this butchered-cheese thing you mentioned earlier?" I asked as we neared the end of the class.

"A chopped cheese," he said chuckling.

"Right, that."

"Wait, this isn't your first time hearing of a chopped cheese, is it?"

"Is it, like, an American delicacy or something?"

"I mean, kinda!" he said, stepping back shocked with a smirk on his face. "I would argue it's at least a New York delicacy and the best, classic late-night food option in the city. I'm surprised no one's brought you to get one yet."

"Well, that makes sense because I don't often find myself out late at night. You know my bed starts calling my name around 11:00 p.m."

"No, I know. I just figured that you and your girls would have partaken in it by now, especially with Reagan living uptown."

"Nope. We have had a late-night slice of pizza!" I replied, probably a little too enthusiastically.

"Okay, I mean, that's New Yorker 101. But once you've had a chopped cheese, I think you'll find it to be even better."

"All right. Well, I trust you, so I'm down."

The growing smile on Thomas's face after my reply could have lit up the night sky if we were outside, and I made a note to myself just how much I enjoyed being the cause of it.

"It's a good thing I'm here to help you dig in a little deeper," he said.

I smiled back, probably just as glassy-eyed as before, while I watched him down his last drink and call us a car for our next location.

A few minutes later, we were all bundled up again to brave the cold, December air and waving goodbye to all the temporary friends we'd made during the class as we rushed to catch our Uber before the car pulled off. Together, we climbed in, with Thomas right behind me, once again shooting chills up my spine as he lightly grazed the small of my back to guide me in. Once we were both settled into our seats, I leaned my head back and attempted to calm down the anticipation building within my body— of both Thomas's continued touch and this food he'd been bragging about for the past twenty minutes.

"I know this is very out of the way, and you can get a chopped cheese from almost any bodega now," he said, turning toward me as our car curved onto First Avenue and then FDR to make our way to East Harlem. "But if you're going to have your first one with me, it's gotta be from the OG."

Thomas was already right about one thing. We were taking a major detour for this thing, so I hoped it was worth it for us to travel twenty minutes away when we probably could have taken a long walk from the distillery back to my apartment.

"It's okay," I replied, facing him in the back seat of the car, my head still relying on the mounting anticipation to keep me awake. "At this point, you've talked it up so much, I wouldn't want it from anywhere else. I do have to know, though, what makes it so special?"

"To me? Or to New York?"

"I guess both."

"Well, for me, I equate my first chopped cheese with the day I knew I'd make it here," Thomas said, sitting up straight and turning his entire body toward mine. "You know, I came here so fresh and green and got a very quick awakening that life wasn't going to be a straight shot to the top. After about a few months, I'd started questioning whether I had what it took to be a 'New York lawyer,' whatever that meant. The job was stressing me out, I was struggling to make any kind of headway with the few clients the firm had entrusted me with, and I just was feeling really down. But thankfully, a few of my boys noticed, said, 'Bruh, let's go out for some drinks,' and by the end of the night, they had reminded me I wasn't alone trying to navigate this new world on my own. We were also very drunk, though, so they took me to Hajji's. We got some chopped cheese sandwiches—with grilled onions, lettuce, tomato, ketchup and mayonnaise, like you're supposed to—and I swear, every bite felt like it was changing my life."

"Wow," I replied, in awe of everything he'd just divulged—the connection with his friends, the vulnerability he'd shown in telling me this story, the way he made the food sound…

"I'm kind of at a loss for words."

"That's because you're drunk." He laughed.

"Maybe a little tipsy, but you know that's not why."

"No, I know."

We looked at each other with that unsaid understanding we'd had since our first conversation in the airport. That had been the moment I'd realized Thomas got me in a fundamental way that was both scary and refreshing. Now it was my turn. I'd had almost every single emotion he'd expressed (and the ones he hadn't) since moving here, too, so I knew how important that night must have been for him. After all, he was still in the city years later, thriving beyond, what I was sure, was even his wildest imagination. I also knew he probably still secretly had those moments where he questioned if he deserved it all.

"Do you still have moments like that at your firm?" I asked, bracing myself for an inevitable shutdown in his vulnerability tank. That was what every other man did whenever they dared to try to be open with me before.

"Yeah—of course," he said, drawing me toward him. "I psych myself out all the time, thinking today's going to be the day I don't do everything perfectly and it'll give them a reason to elevate the next guy before me. Or sometimes, I'll deal with those kinda gray situations where I wonder if they only put me on a specific file because they needed a Black man on it, or if a client requests a different attorney, there's that small voice in my head that makes me question if it's because they aren't the Black man from Philly, you know. But at the end of the day, it all just makes me go harder. I get to prove all of those doubts in my head wrong every time I show up and excel."

"Yeah, I know."

I leaned into him, snuggling myself into the nook under Thomas's arm and next to his torso. As he wrapped his left arm around me, I took in the deepest, most calming breath, preparing myself to enjoy the security of his embrace as we rode the next fifteen minutes up the motorway. In a perfect world, this could be my existence every night—just basking in the comfort of his presence without any worry for the future. Openly talking about the good and bad parts of our jobs; pushing each other to be the best and to find balance, just like Walter and Sarah. *If only*, I thought, momentarily stopping myself from even thinking the rest of that idea…but eventually, it came to me anyway. *If only women like me got to have that kind of joy, maybe I'd trust this more.*

"I wish you could see yourself through my eyes, too, you know," I whispered as they slowly drifted shut.

"The glassy ones that can barely stay open?"

"Yeah." I chuckled. "And the ones who see just how amazing you are."

Chapter Eleven

"You guys finally made it!"

A couple days later and after several hours of flying across the United States, Reagan and I pulled up to the villa we'd all booked for Jenn's bachelorette weekend in Palm Springs. To our great delight, Jenn, Becs and Robin came running out of the front door—drinks in hand—to greet us just as our cab swung into the driveway.

"We're heeeeeere!" Reagan screamed out in response, practically hopping out of the car without any concern that she would trip in her tan three-inch sandals that criss-crossed at her ankles. *"Laissez les bons temps rouler!"*

In awe, I watched as she grabbed her matching tan tote and took off in a short sprint to grab and hug on each one of them. It was like watching an Olympic track racer come off the starting block—if they had chunky heels and cutoff shorts on. Meanwhile, I stayed behind to tip the driver after he'd pulled our luggage out of the trunk to let the original close-knit crew have a moment before I intruded as the person who was still building a friendship with most of them. Sure, I'd been invited on their special trip, but I understood the friendship hierarchy in play and respected it.

If Reagan's all-out run toward them hadn't told me that, then the fact that I'd clearly missed the memo on what they'd all meant by "casual chic" certainly did. To a person, they each looked incredibly elegant, somehow complementing each other's style without any of them dressing fully alike, and there I was—dressed cute, yes, but nothing like them. Reagan, who had paired her cutoff jean shorts and heels with a tan button-down blouse that she'd let casually flow into a one-corner tuck into her shorts was also "casually" rocking a bunch of gold accessories—multiple-sized bracelets, two slender necklaces that dropped down her chest and slightly grazed the only two buttons she'd closed on the blouse, sunglasses that also matched her skin tone and a black-and-gold belt that pulled it all together. To top off the 'fit, she wore a red-and-tan headband, which pulled her long, wavy curls off her face, and matching red nail polish on her hands and feet. But I'd been traveling all day with her, so that wasn't surprising.

It was the way the others matched her *Housewives* swag that let me know I was going to need to step my game up the rest of the weekend. This was why I'd asked about attire when we'd FaceTimed the other night, but I also should have remembered that Robin was the same person who'd shown up to my flat for a girls' night in with a matching two-piece nude-pink lounge set complete with knit joggers and a crop top. So I should have guessed that her best friends would have a similar idea of "casual." True to that realization, the Palm Springs version of Destiny's Child was dressed far more appropriately for a fancy brunch than a day of travel. Like Reagan, Robin was also wearing jean shorts, in more of an acid-washed color that fell around mid-thigh on her, but that was about where the casualness ended. She paired hers with a dark coral blouse that tied in the front but hung loose in the back so that the bottom of it fell past her shorts, along with some gold slip-on kitten-heel sandals that any older Hollywood diva would have absolutely adored.

Rebecca was giving *pregnant holiday chic* with a black satin slip dress that fell about mid-calf on her and showed off her ginormous baby bump in all the best ways. With it, she wore a light jean jacket, bedazzled flat sandals and a tan fedora that actually really worked on her—despite the fact that no one had looked good in fedoras since the early 2000s.

And of course, the lady of the weekend stood out the most, with her flowy full-length white halter dress that literally grazed the ground as she moved and somehow didn't seem to pick up any dirt. The high-necked sleeveless halter cut looked amazing with her dark brown pixie-cut hair, statement earrings and crystal clear heels that had a striking gold stiletto that looked like it could be a dagger if you weren't careful.

Meanwhile, I'd at least got the jeans memo—wearing shorts that were not quite cutoffs but shorter than Rob's, paired with a short-sleeved scooped-neck black blouse and gladiator sandals that wrapped around my calves— but I clearly needed more *oomph* to fit in with these girls. I made a note to myself to do better tomorrow.

As the driver pulled off, leaving me with our bags, Robin came bouncing toward me with two glasses in her hands, followed by Reagan, who presumably finally remembered that she didn't have hers with her.

"So sorry, Liv," Reagan said as she jumped in front of Robin and grabbed her medium-sized luggage with the rollers on it. "I didn't mean to leave you with the bags—I just got so excited to see my girls."

"It's okay—I get it."

"No, it's not," she replied sincerely. "Definitely let me know how much you tipped him, and I got you on half, okay?"

As Reagan began rolling her luggage to the front door, Robin stepped in and wrapped her arms around me tightly, squeezing and rocking me for what felt like a few minutes.

"Livvieeeee," she said, dragging the nickname she had for me out into two long syllables.

After a few more shakes within the hug, she loosened her grip and handed me one of the drinks. "It's so good to see you, friend. London hasn't been the same without you."

"I know this is going to sound bad, but I'm really happy to hear that," I admitted somewhat shamelessly. "I miss it and you so very much."

"Doesn't sound bad to me at all! I'm the one who's been hoping you enjoy your time in New York but not so much that you decide to stay. You know I hear all the rumblings in the office. You're killing it, which I knew you would, but still, I get so worried they are going to make you an offer you can't refuse and convince you to stay."

"Ha! Thanks, sis," I replied. "But you don't have to worry about that. I'm loving my time in the States so far, but London is home. Brixton is home, you know? I don't want to be too far from there for too long."

"Okayyy, I hear you. I also know what it's like to move to a place and realize it might be your *new* home. Don't forget you're saying this to the woman who moved from America, fell in love with your brother and now can't see herself living anywhere else anytime soon."

"Your situation was very different. You wanted to find love in London—that's not in my plans."

"And yet…that little sparkle that shines on your face when anyone says Thomas's name… I'm not saying it's love," she said, throwing up her hands in defense before I could counter her. "But it looks familiar, that's all."

I chuckled awkwardly and sniffed the glass to try to move us to a different conversation. I hadn't yet told any-one how much I'd loved everything about the date he and I had gone on just two days before and how safe I'd felt in his arms as we'd ridden to and from East Harlem that night, mostly because I wasn't ready to think about what that meant for me going forward. But I knew if I engaged Rob any further, it was going to come up, and I certainly wasn't ready to dissect it with her before I even knew what I wanted.

"Enough about all that," I said. "More importantly, what's in this drink you just gave me?"

"Oooh! So, it's a new concoction I made just for our trip called Jenn's Sweet Treats. It's pineapple and mango juice mixed with white rum and tequila with just a splash of champagne to cut the sweetness."

"Robin! Are you trying to kill us?"

"I promise, no, but just try it! It tastes so good."

She raised the glass to my lips, and as I sampled it, I knew just how dangerous it was going to be. You could barely tell it had any liquor in it despite the fact that she'd just told me three were in it—a sure setup for failure. With the conversation successfully veered, the two of us began walking toward the rest of the ladies, who were still amazingly waiting outside of the villa's front door.

"Okay, I hope you have lots of food inside," I replied, taking another sip as we neared the others.

"Yes, of course—there's a whole spread waiting on the counter. I don't need anyone getting sick on the first day. I've got too many things planned for this weekend for that to happen."

"Ohhh nooo," Reagan cried out as we came within earshot. "Did I hear Rob just say the dreaded 'plans' word?"

"Don't start with me, Rae." She laughed in response.

"No, c'mon, we all know you can go a teensy bit overboard with trip planning if you're not careful."

"That's true," added Rebecca as she carefully but lovingly grabbed my arms and pulled me into a baby-filled embrace, whispering how good I looked before she continued her comments to Robin. "Do we need to remind you of the itinerary you made when we first came to visit you in London? It was at least fifteen items on your list. I swear, the only reason we convinced you to narrow it down was because I was pregnant. Otherwise you would have had us on a very strict schedule."

"No, you don't need to remind me," Robin replied, rolling her eyes. "And this one isn't as extensive. But we needed *something*, or I know us—we'd just end up sitting around the villa all day, lounging by the pool."

"From my perspective, there's absolutely nothing wrong with that," Jenn chimed in, peeking her head into the discussion before giving me a long hug as well. "I could use a relaxing break from the students and all their drama."

"All right, everyone, calm down," Robin began in protest. "Of course we're going to do that, too. But it's not a bachelorette weekend if we don't end up dancing on someone's table by the end of the night at least once."

"Okay, now that's true," Jenn admitted. "I do want that, too."

"Of course you do!" Robin replied.

The five of us continued laughing and joking about Robin's tendency to overplan trips as we finally stepped into the villa that was surrounded by the most fantastic mountain views I'd ever seen and yet really only took my breath away once I walked inside. With walls made of floor-to-ceiling windows covering at least three-fourths of the house, it was like our own private oasis complete with pearl-white and light wooden furnishings, a pool big enough to take laps in it and multiple lounging opportunities throughout. There was even a firepit surrounded by five white and wooden lounge chairs and a second dining table located by the pool, perfect for eating at sunset or sunrise.

"I'm down to hear your plans, babes," I interjected, admiring the scene before me while also wanting to stand up for all the overplanners everywhere. That had been one of the reasons Robin and I had bonded in the first place, so while it was fun to laugh with the crew about it, if anyone understood her need to organize the chaos in her mind, I did.

"Thanks, Liv," she said with a smile, and then quickly took the opportunity to run to her room to grab the stapled set of papers she had at the ready.

"Yes, thanks, Liv," the other ladies repeated sarcastically.

I shrugged my shoulders in reply and waited for her return.

"Okay, it's not as bad as you all think. Just listen," Robin began as she walked back into the sitting room, clearing her throat before she proceeded. "Today, of course, we're all getting settled. I figured we could chill for a bit and have a sunset dinner outside before maybe doing some in-home karaoke to cap off the evening."

"All right, Rob," Reagan chimed in. "That sounds nice and not over-the-top at all. Maybe we were being a bit too judgy."

Robin looked back at her with an *mmm-hmm, I told you so* look and then continued reading.

"So then tomorrow, I thought we could have an early breakfast. If anyone wants to come with me to Joshua Tree, I was thinking we could leave here around 7:00 a.m. That way we're back about ten or eleven o'clock for prime pool time. Then, I figured we could go to one of the resorts that the villa is associated with. They have a bunch of different restaurants, a water park, a spa, even a swim-up bar, so we could hang there for a few hours. Note—if we want to make a spa appointment, we probably need to do that today, though. And then, we come back here and get dressed for our night out on the town, where we have table reservations at two different clubs."

As Robin took a break from reading her list, the rest of us eyed each other, stunned into silence. Now, I was all for planning, but this was even too much for me.

"Uh-uh, see? Now this is what we mean! That's too much!" Reagan cried out.

Her protest was followed by a round of mmm-hmms throughout the room.

"She's right, Rob," Jennifer added. "You know we love you, and I sooo appreciate you wanting to make my bachelorette weekend as epic as it can be, but, like, yes, there's twenty-four hours in a day, but we don't need to use them all. You know that, right?"

"What?" she asked innocently. "I didn't say we had to do *all* these things. I just threw out some suggestions for options!"

"*Cher*, the only things I want to do out of that whole list you just read are the pool time, the spa and the dancing on tables. All the rest of that can go." Reagan laughed. "And honestly, I don't even need the spa as long as we keep drinking these cocktails you made."

"No shade, but I agree with what she said," Jennifer added.

"Same here," Rebecca chimed in after having spent the last few minutes trying to hold back tears of laughter. "I mean, did you hear yourself when you said you were leaving the house at 7:00 a.m....while on vacation?"

"Well, that's just because I didn't want it to eat into the pool time! Tell me, how often are any of us going to be this close to Joshua Tree again anytime soon?" Robin asked in her defense.

She turned to me as her one last hope, but this time I

couldn't help her out. While she was absolutely my connection to the group, I fully agreed with the rest of the ladies this time and was happy to see I wasn't the only one hoping this holiday would be more relaxing than anything else. I put my head down in my response before Robin could even direct her question my way, hoping it would curtail some of the sting.

"You, too, Liv?"

"Sorry, Rob," I replied softly.

"No, no, don't do that to her," Reagan said, sauntering up beside me and putting her arm around my shoulder. "You can't try to get Liv on your side because y'all met first. She's part of the whole crew now, so she gets to tell you when you're being ridiculous just like the rest of us."

Robin rolled her eyes and sighed deeply before plopping her papers onto the counter in defeat. Meanwhile, I was happy to hear Reagan say explicitly that I was legit part of their crew and have everyone agree. I hadn't realized until being around them all again in person that I'd still needed that validation, but I guessed I had and could breathe a little lighter now.

"You know what?" Rebecca asked as she walked up to Robin with the drink pitcher in her hand. "How about I take that itinerary and you take another pour of what I'm sure is an amazing drink that you've made, huh?"

Robin laughed at Rebecca's continued drinking solutions to everyone's problems in lieu of her being able to partake and grabbed the pitcher from her before complying.

"Fine!" she replied. "But you all are going to regret not going hiking two months from now when you're back home and someone randomly mentions our national parks. Mark my words."

"In what world is that happening, Robin?" Reagan asked, continuing the chorus of laughter in the room.

"Certainly not in any of ours," Jennifer interjected.

"Whatever," she replied, playfully rolling her eyes again as she filled up her glass. "Mark my words."

Robin paused momentarily and looked around the room before raising her glass high into the sky. "I guess now that I have a full glass again, we should at least toast to the start of a great weekend. Is that an okay plan for everyone?" she asked.

"Now that's a plan we can all get down with," Reagan responded.

The four of us gathered around Robin, near the grazing counter, and lifted our glasses high into the air as well.

"To Jenny," she began. "We all love you more than we could ever fully say, and we want nothing but the best for you. I hope this bachelorette weekend shows you even a snippet of that love and also brings us all even closer together."

"Cheers!" we replied in unison, and clanked our glasses together before everyone but Becs took a healthy swig of Robin's homemade concoction.

As Reagan struck up a conversation with Rebecca about what her mocktail consisted of—hulled strawberries, lemon ginger beer and a lemon slice for garnish, from what I could hear—I started making my way through the villa to find one of the remaining empty rooms to settle into. After rolling past two that were occupied, I came upon one that looked like it hadn't been touched yet and had everything I needed—a king-size bed with a white comforter, a sliding glass door that took up the whole back wall and led to the pool, and a soaking tub.

This is going to do just fine, I thought as I rolled my luggage in and sat down for a breather, taking my phone out of my back jean shorts pocket at the same time. Without overthinking myself out of it, I snapped a photo of the view from my bedroom and sent it to Thomas, letting him know that I'd made it safely.

Glad to hear, he replied just a few minutes later. I hope you have a lot of fun with your friends. But don't do anything I wouldn't do. I know how y'all like to get down on bachelorette trips.

Well, I texted back, there do seem to be plans for table dancing at some point.

And what makes you think that's something I haven't done? he asked.

Oh, I'm sorry, let me not put you in a box lol, I replied.

Thomas: Yes, you really shouldn't. I've still got a lot of surprises up my sleeve.

I smiled reading Thomas's messages and thought back to Robin's comment about how my face lit up when someone mentioned his name. If they could see it now, I was sure I'd be getting clowned. I texted back, trying my hand at flirting.

Me: Now, see, if there's one thing I fully believe, it's that. I already told you that you never cease to surprise me.

Good, he answered. And I don't plan on stopping anytime soon.

I clutched my phone in my hand and fell backward onto the bed, my cheeks burning from a grin that wouldn't disappear. *What am I going to do about this man?* I wondered. I guessed time would tell.

Chapter Twelve

The next day, to no one's shock, not a single soul woke up by 7:00 a.m. to join Robin on her hiking excursion. What *was* surprising, however, was when we all crawled out of bed, slightly hungover from hours of karaoke the night before, and learned that she hadn't gone, either. Seated around the grazing counter, we were passing around coffee mugs when Robin walked into the sitting room, still in her pajamas, at 9:00 a.m.

"Robin?" Jennifer asked, stopping in her tracks as if she'd just seen a ghost.

"In the flesh," she deadpanned, rubbing her eyes with one hand while putting out the other so that someone could pass her a coffee mug as well.

"But what happened to Joshua Tree?" Reagan asked.

"Well," she hesitated. "You guys might have been right about me going overboard with that one. Plus, I didn't want to be all the way out there while you all were here. I want to be where you are."

"Awwww, that's sooo sweet," Jenn replied, forming her hands into the shape of a heart and covering her chest to show how much love she was feeling in the moment.

"And the time difference probably got real this morning, too, right?" Reagan interjected with a smirk.

"That, too."

Robin shrugged her shoulders as she clutched her large

white coffee mug and walked to the Keurig machine in hopes that it would help to bring her back to life.

"Aaaaand someone might have been overcompensating because she misses her man?" Rebecca interjected.

It was one of those questions that was really more of a statement, but her voice rose up an octave or two higher at the end to make it sound like she maybe didn't mean it definitively. We all knew she did, however.

"Okay, don't push it." Robin laughed. "But maybe a little of that, too."

"Well, whatever the reason, I'm glad you stayed," I said, chiming in after taking a big gulp of coffee. "I've been looking forward to this girls' trip since I touched down in America. And our time in the pool wouldn't have been the same without you. I need as much time as I can get with you before you go back to London and I don't see you again for several months—probably not until Jenn's wedding, right?"

Robin put her hands over her heart to show how touched she was by my admission and then quickly jumped to attention when the Keurig machine alerted her that her coffee was ready.

"Liv is a big mush ball," Reagan chimed in. "I see why she fits in with us so well. But she *is* right. We would have missed you. Though—paraphrasing the famous poet Future—I do believe it's better to cry in the jacuzzi, so I guess that would have been my plight."

Unable to hold back her laughter from her own joke, Reagan giggled uncontrollably even as she tried drinking some coffee to contain herself.

"Get out of here!" Robin replied, before playfully tossing a big bag of chips at her. "I know you didn't just use the 'You gon' cry in this Phantom or dat Nissan' line on me!"

"Now, don't take your frustrations out on the tortillas,

cher. These are some prime nacho-making chips. We have plans for these tomorrow, and you know how you feel about plans!"

The five of us continued the morning just like that, giggling and carrying on as if there weren't normally thousands of miles in between us and we saw each other every day, the conversation covering everything from career plans to worst dates ever and always ending with someone curled over in tears from laughing too hard. As coffee mugs turned into champagne flutes and glasses full of Jenn's Sweet Treats, bathrobes turned into bathing suits, and then eventually, by the evening—all of our best outfits for a night out on the town.

Once again, without planning it, they'd all chosen 'fits that complemented each other but still let each woman shine on her own. The difference this time was that I did, too. My black mini crop top and gold-mesh high-waisted skirt with a slit on my right thigh were similar enough to Reagan's white one-shoulder crop top with her burnt-orange floor-length skirt that opened in the front due to her high split, but distinct enough that we could both stand high in our stilettos and command our own attention. The same went for Rebecca and Robin, who each had on a low V-neck top but in vastly different ways, and Jenn, who helped blend us all together with the high slit in her mini skirt and her low V-neck top. Rob wore a dark green, purple, hot-pink, yellow and blue striped blouse with a V-neck that went all the way down to her belly and only snapped closed with the help of the black belt that was attached to it. Her shirt then flared out, the hem landing a few notches above her knees—which made it the perfect complement to her cutoff jean shorts and heels. And Becs, who might have been the flyest pregnant woman I'd ever seen, made

quite the statement with her tan bandage skirt and cham-
pagne-colored V-neck blouse tucked inside.

By 10:30 p.m., we were all standing around, hyping
Jenn up as she climbed onto the table we'd reserved at the
first club. Robin had just convinced the DJ to play "Ladies Night" by Angie Martinez, Lil' Kim, Missy Elliott,
Da Brat and Left Eye, when Jenn—in all her bachelorette
glory—finally decided it was time for her moment in the
sun. I was particularly impressed at the fact that she managed to get up there without showing all her goodies to the
club, considering just how high the split was in her gorgeous black-and-white mini skirt. She'd paired that with
an off-shoulder white satin V-neck, long-sleeved crop top
and all the confidence in the world.

"Speech! Speech! Speech!" we all implored as she
quickly got her bearings in her clear chunky backless heels.

"Oh!" she said, feigning innocence while scooping up
a bottle of champagne out of the bucket on the table. "You
all want a speech? From me?"

"You already know we do, Miss Thang!" Robin replied.

"Yeah, give it to us," Rebecca added.

"Well, if you insist," Jennifer said, grinning from ear
to ear and holding her bottle high.

She cleared her throat once before proceeding.

"Ladiesssss!" she screamed out.

"Yessss!" we replied in unison.

"I said, my laaaaadies!"

"Yesss!"

"I love all y'all so freakin' much. This has truly been
one of the best days ever. I can't begin to thank you
enough."

I watched in fear as Jenn's abounding joy quickly turned
to sentimental tears, wondering how I could get her back
to her fun place. In a matter of seconds, she'd gone from

a '90s hip-hop star onstage to someone with supremely wet eyes, and I knew if I didn't stop her, she was going to have all of us joining in, crying in the club. We could not let that happen.

"Wait, wait!" I shouted. "This speech isn't supposed to be about us. It's supposed to be about you. Try again, Jennifer!"

"Welp, Liv's right," Reagan said with a shrug, and then shot me a quick, silent *Thank you* off to the side.

"Okay! Okay!"

Jenn threw her arms into the air and took in a deep breath before going at it again, literally swallowing her tears up as we all stared her down.

"All day has been amazing! And I know, I know, it's not done yet—but this has been one of the best days ever for me. And when I think about why I'm here, why we're all here tonight," she began. "I have to say that I'm so happy. A lot of that is because of the work I've done over the past year in therapy…and with you all…to get myself to the point where I love me, and my man, and my girls, for who everyone is, all on their own. No comparisons. No fear. Just love."

"I hear that," Reagan interjected, raising her glass up to Jenn, who clinked it with the bottle she still had in her hand.

"And listen, I know this might be controversial," Jennifer continued. "But Nick has literally changed my life, y'all. I'm so grateful for this man. I used to think that was an unfeminist way to think, but screw that—I have a partner who supports me, challenges me, loves me and is even willing to let me throw some pink plush handcuffs on him when I'm trying out something new."

"Yeah, he did!" Rebecca chimed in, holding her belly as she and the rest of us cracked up laughing at the memory of when she'd given Jenn those very handcuffs and learned later just how shocked Nick was when Jennifer had slapped them onto his wrists.

Confused at first, he'd tried it out because that was his girl. I didn't know much about Nick, but I knew one thing—he wasn't perfect, but there wasn't much he wouldn't do for Jennifer Pritchett. I could see why she was so happy with him.

"If you know, you know!" Jenn continued, laughing and pointing at Becs with her bottle. "But seriously, that kind of day in and day out partnership is so clutch. I know how blessed I am to have him, and you girls, in my life."

"Amen!" Robin added, now raising her glass in the air as well.

"Aaaaand," Jenn continued on, "I know Liv said this isn't about you guys, but…it's my speech, so I can add this part if I want."

She stuck her tongue out at me before proceeding forward.

"I'm so incredibly thankful that every single one of you has someone in your life just like that, too—who has shown up time and time again, and whether it's been years or its super new, you can just tell he's the one. So, shout-out to us, and shout-out to Nick, Jake, Oliver, Craig—"

"Ahem, excuse me," I interjected, raising my hand in defiance.

"I was getting ready to say Thomas!" she replied.

"No, no, but you shouldn't. He's not my man! I don't have a man," I protested.

"Girl." Jennifer paused her speech and looked directly at me. "If you don't stop playing around, acting like we haven't seen you texting this man the whole time you've been here."

"Mmm-hmm," Reagan chimed in. "She does that when she's with me, too."

"Of course she does—because she likes him," Robin added.

"And he's good for her," Reagan continued. "Sometimes unexpected things are good, *cher*." She turned toward me, lifting her glass in my direction.

"I do really like him," I admitted. "I don't know how to explain it—just when I'm with him, it feels like finally, I met someone who doesn't need me to change to be the partner for him. Like, he gets me, and he's supportive, and his kisses are what heaven probably feels like…"

I shook my head quickly to stop myself from spiraling down a rabbit hole.

"That's what we've been saying for the longest, *cher*! This is great. I'm just happy you're acknowledging it now," Reagan replied.

"Yeah, but he's also the same man who told me he wasn't looking for a relationship—"

"Until he met *you*, right?" Reagan asked.

I stared back at her in response, simply folding my lips onto each other to keep my mouth closed once again.

"Exactly," she added. "You're focused too much on what's the worst that can happen, *cher*, when what you should be focused on is the way you two look at each other when you're in the other's presence. I've seen it with my own eyes. That mess is seductive! I wanted to get home to my own man after being around y'all."

Jenn, Rebecca and Robin laughed and *mmm-hmm*-ed throughout Reagan's soliloquy, leaving me to just stand there and take my medicine as Robin had the day before.

"Not to mention, I've never seen you this googly-eyed about someone before," Robin added. "When you were in

London, you barely mentioned David's name unless some-one else brought him up."

"Boo, down with David," Reagan interjected.

"Agreed. I'm just saying," Robin continued. "No one's saying Thomas is endgame—"

"Actually, I did," Jennifer interrupted, still standing high on the table before us.

"Okay, well, Jenn is our sentimental bestie, so she's saying he's endgame. I'm just saying, and I think the rest of us are just saying, that it might be time to stop fighting it and actually give this guy a chance. You never know what could happen..."

"And what would Chrissy ask in a situation like this?" Reagan asked, interrupting Robin's speech.

"What's the best that could happen, *mana*, if you just tried?" Robin replied.

I smiled and rolled my eyes, grateful for the kind of friends who loved me enough to challenge me but an-noyed at the same time—because, like, who wanted to be challenged? I'd heard someone once say that you knew someone was your best friend when you could go months without seeing each other and pick right back up where you'd left off when you did. This night made me want to take that a step further. I'd learned someone was your best friend when they told you things you didn't want to hear with love and care and in a way where you could receive it as such. Being around these ladies, I definitely under-stood exactly what that felt like.

"Okay," I responded. "I hear everyone, loud and clear."

"Oh! That reminds me!" Jenn chimed in. "Before we take another sip, we have to pour out a little something for the homie Christine!"

"Oh my God. Of course," Robin replied as we all jumped to attention and rejoined our focus back toward the center table, where Jenn had begun tipping her champagne bottle ever so slightly to the side to let a few drops fall onto the floor.

After she blessed the floor, we all raised our glasses high in the sky and clanked them with Jenn's bottle, thanking God for this moment and our friendships. And just like magic, the DJ started playing "Friends" by The Carters, almost like it was fate—or more of Robin's perfect planning. Either way, we were all good with the win.

Chapter Thirteen

"So, Julie, I have some exciting news. I just learned that we're launching a new investment fund in the American market, and I want your team to put together a presentation outlining how many clients would be interested in the fund and what the long-term plan for attracting new investors looks like."

Julie sat across from me, wide-eyed and probably more than a little scared, as I gave her the news that she—one of the management group's youngest portfolio managers—was getting the chance to put together a proposal for this new fund. But she deserved it. From my first day in the office, I'd watched her step up and buy-in to the changes that Walter and I were implementing without hesitation. Her team's investment strategy briefs and proposals always had the most research in them, and I saw how she really took to heart the challenge I made to everyone to come up with ideas that would wow our clients. Whether it was an update to the investors about how to think about their overall portfolio, what factors might affect it or how to protect it, I was consistently impressed with the work she developed.

I'd also been in her position before, excited and nervous, not wanting to let the person down who stood before me, offering me this kind of opportunity. So her stunned silence, while slightly comical, was understandable.

"And of course, I want you to work with marketing to

build out materials and develop a launch proposal that's
going to set this new investment up for success," I continued as I watched her gather herself and slowly come
back to Earth.

"Of course, Olivia," she finally replied. "Thank you
for the opportunity."

"No need to thank me. You've earned this. And before
your brain starts wondering, you didn't earn it because
you and I have lunch together sometimes with Wendy.
You earned it because of the work you've put in. Walter
wouldn't have agreed to this if he felt any differently."

I looked at her from behind my desk and visibly noticed
her jaw loosen a bit and her shoulders fall from where
they'd been sitting high up toward her ears. She'd needed
that reassurance, and I understood that, too.

"Thanks for the vote of confidence, Olivia. Honestly.
I won't let you down."

"This I already know," I explained. "Or I wouldn't have
picked you to run point here. You got this."

She stood up from the chair in front of my desk and
walked toward my door, a smile building on her face that
told me just how amped she was. I could still remember the
first investment-fund launch I'd had a chance to develop
and the way I'd run to the ladies' room right after learning I'd be lead so I could silently shout and dance without anyone seeing. This was the kind of thing I wanted to
do more of—empowering the younger portfolio managers around me who deserved it and who needed to know
their senior manager believed in them more than anything.
Sure, I loved meeting and exceeding fundraising goals,
but I was steadily learning this was what really brought
me joy. It was why I didn't mind staying up late to offer
feedback on anywhere from five to fifteen proposals and
investment strategy briefs in a week. If they were going

to show up and put in the work, I was going to meet them with that same passion and dedication—sleep be damned.

Out the corner of my eye, I saw the notebook I'd brought with me from London that had all my goals for the year written out in it. It was a simple blue-and-white notebook, unassuming to most but containing some of my biggest hopes and dreams (and by virtue of all that, also my biggest fears) in it. I glanced at my clock and saw that I had another thirty minutes before my next meeting, so I scooped it up and quickly flipped to the pages where the blue ink had outlined everything that I'd set out to do once I got here.

What do I mean when I say this will be my year? I'd written across the top of the page.

I mean the following:

—I am walking into this new office confident and believing I deserve to be there. From the very beginning, they will quickly understand my value as a senior manager.

—I am building a rapport with the portfolio teams so they respect my input and are inspired to develop more creative proposals and more in-depth and researched strategy briefs.

—I am helping to change the culture, even slightly, to one where people take time to think outside the box, even if only by 1 percent, so that they can present tried-and-true ideas but also ones that aren't stale and get their clients and investors excited again.

—I am heading back to the UK after this year ends with a promotion to senior portfolio manager and well on my way to head of the division.

I hadn't looked at that list since my first day in the office, and yet I could already see myself checking off many of my goals. That felt really, really good. But I didn't want to stop at many. I wanted it all.

I closed my notebook with a renewed sense of energy

and turned back to the thirty unread messages in my Outlook folder. *No time like the present to keep moving toward my dreams*, I thought.

Just as I opened the first one, however, I heard my phone vibrating in my purse and picked it up to see who it was. Robin probably could have seen the smile on my face all the way in London when I finally unlocked it.

It was Thomas.

Thomas: Hey, I know we didn't have plans tonight, but it's been a pretty stressful day at work so far, and I'd love to see you. Are you free this evening?

I looked at my phone and at the virtual stack of work waiting for me to get to it. It had been days since I'd come back from Palm Springs, and I'd yet to see him, so everything in me wanted to say yes. I also knew that if I spent the night running around the city with him, I was going to regret it the next morning when my backlog of work to get through had doubled.

I'd love to see you, too, I typed back. But I have a lot of work to do tonight. What do you think about coming over to my place? Maybe we can do both. Spend some time together while I get some work done?

Thomas: I think that's a great idea. With one condition. You give me full reign in your kitchen, and I'll cook us dinner while you work. Then, you give me just a couple hours of your time during dinner, and we can call it a night from there if you want.

Me: You just said work has been stressful today lol. The last thing I want is for you to cook for me after a long day. We can order in.

Thomas: Actually, cooking helps me de-stress. And it's not for you. It would be for us. I have to eat, too, you know.

Me: Okay. Then you have a deal, as long as I get to see you in your Rihanna element, too. You did tell me that was part of your decompressing routine.

Thomas: We'll have to see about that, love. You already caught me slipping by getting me to even divulge that one to you.

Me: And it's a top five thing I like about you…and it's not five. So, c'mon! You know you want to sing some more bangers with me lol

Thomas: We'll see, we'll see lol. Don't forget, you'll be working while I'm cooking anyway.

Me: That's true. But I always have time for a little Rihanna.

Thomas: Ha! I'll keep that in mind.

Thomas: So, what time works best for you?

I looked back at my clock again and saw that it was close to 3:30 p.m. *At the rate I'm going, I'll be lucky to leave here by seven o'clock tonight*, I thought, and that was if Walter didn't come stomping his way over to my office. But he was the one who'd talked about work-life balance, so I was going to do my best to model that, starting with tonight.

Me: How about 7:30? I should be able to get home by then.

Thomas: Okay, great. I'll be the guy with the groceries waiting on you.

Me: And I'll be the one who can't stop smiling when she sees you.

Before I could get too caught up in all things Thomas, I locked my phone again and placed it back into my workbag. With only a few minutes left before my next meeting, I had a feeling I was going to need every second of it to pull myself back together from the pure joy I experienced while texting with him. The truth was I was happiest when I was with him—and the girls had been right; it was high time I stopped fighting that.

I walked up to my flat at just about 7:30 p.m. that night, and true to his word, Thomas was standing there with a bag of groceries on his shoulder.

"How long have you been waiting here?" I asked, once again unable to control the smile on my face that formed as soon as I saw him.

One of the many things I'd been learning in the time we'd spent together was that Thomas was a man of his word. If he said he was going to be somewhere at 7:30 p.m., you didn't have to wonder if he was going to show up. You just knew. I hadn't realized how important that was to me until he consistently did it, whether it was the simple things like calling when he said he would or the way he always seemed to arrive just a few minutes before me whenever we met up.

"Not too long. Maybe a couple minutes," he replied.

"You should have texted me. I could have been running late or already inside."

I grabbed my keys out of my workbag so that I could unlock the building door for us.

"I did actually," he replied, following behind me.

Once I opened the door and let him inside, I scooped my phone out of my bag, too, and saw that he was right. There it was, a missed text from Thomas that read, I'm here. Let me know if you're nearby.

I must have missed it while walking from the train.

"Oy, I'm sorry," I said, walking before him so that I could guide him up the one flight of steps leading to my place.

"It's all good. You said you'd be home by 7:30 p.m., and you were. No harm, no foul."

"Thanks."

We moved in step with each other as Thomas entered my flat for the first time, taking his shoes off at the front door as soon as he saw me slip my favorite camel-brown So Kate leather pumps off as well. Without a word, he gently placed the grocery bag on the floor as I began unbuttoning my coat, grabbing the back side of it so that he could slide it off my shoulders, revealing the navy blue blazer, white bodysuit and tan trousers I had on underneath. As I hung my coat on the rack in the hallway, he then took his off as well, which I grabbed from him right before he picked the groceries up once more to follow me toward the rest of the flat. It was like we were dancing a delicate tango—no words needed, but perfectly in sync.

Past the entryway, my flat ballooned into an open floor plan with my kitchen on the right and sitting room on the left, complete with a charcoal-gray sofa-and-chaise set, a glass coffee table and the TV I barely had time to turn on most days. As was the case in many a New York apartment, I didn't have a dining table—however, I did have a reading nook next to the window that lit up the entire area during the day. That was a compromise I'd happily make any day. As it was, my coffee table sufficed just fine as a dining table for one on most nights. Just beyond all that were my bedroom and bathroom, my two places of sanctuary—one with the huge tub I often found myself soaking in at night and the other decorated with the rug, full-length mirror and string lights I'd purchased while out with Reagan and Jake.

Thomas and I walked straight to the kitchen, where he began pulling everything out of the bag as I searched for cooking utensils for him to use.

"Can I ask what you're cooking, or is it secret?" I inquired, watching him pile bell peppers, an onion, celery, garlic, chicken, sausage, tomatoes, rice and more onto my kitchen counter.

"No secret. I'm making my dad's famous jambalaya recipe. It's what he would cook for us any time my mom had a long day and needed a break from feeding three very hungry young boys."

"Wow, I'm sure that required a lot of food all the time."

"Yeah, to say the least."

"So, what makes it so famous?"

"Well, famous in my home, I should say. It was always a hit with us. A Louisiana rice dish made with chicken, sausage and shrimp? Some things you just can't go wrong with."

"Okay," I replied, suddenly excited to try his dad's version of what my mum would have called jollof rice. "Let me pull out some pots for you, yeah?"

"How about…you leave me to find my way around the kitchen, and you go work," he replied, placing his hands on my shoulders and guiding me into the sitting room.

"Are you sure?"

"Very. I think I'm capable enough to find some pots.

And plus, the whole point of this arrangement was for you to get your work in while I cooked. You can't do that if you're in here helping me."

He smiled back at me, that dimple peeking out again and very much helping to convince me back into his plan.

"Okay, you're right," I said before pulling off my blazer and grabbing my laptop out of my workbag.

"That's what I like to hear."

I plopped down onto my couch and watched Thomas briefly as he walked back to the kitchen, peeled himself out of his own suit jacket and began maneuvering his way around my kitchen like a pro. It was the way he undid his tie right before he started slicing into the bell peppers that almost made me change my mind about working, eating, everything…but after a couple more seconds of silent ogling, I finally forced myself to turn my attention to the work waiting for me on my laptop, opening up the latest investment strategy brief that needed my sign off.

"Stay strong, Liv," I whispered to myself. It was harder than I'd expected to have Thomas mere steps away from me, with a clear view of the way his back arched as he sliced and diced the food he was preparing. But I really did need to finish up some work…and, importantly, he was making it possible for me to do so while still spending time with him. Maybe Walter was onto something about finding the person who got you, ambitions, hopes, dreams, fears, flaws and all.

An hour and a half later, and only maybe twenty or so glances from behind my laptop to see Thomas's body in motion, I turned down my screen and immediately reveled in the intoxicating smells coming from my kitchen.

"Wow, I hope this meal is going to be as good as it smells," I said, stretching my arms wide to make up for the time I'd just spent hunched over my computer.

Thomas turned around in response, his face revealing that he'd likely only caught some of what I'd said, a fact that was proven true when I saw him slide his earbud out.

"What was that you said, love?"

"Just that the food smells delicious… Wait, were you listening to Rihanna…without me?"

I squinted my eyes and awaited his reply.

"Well, I mean, I had to occupy myself while you worked. Plus, it is part of my decompressing routine, as you know."

"I know," I said softly. "I'm just mad I had to miss joining in with you on the fun. I feel like that happens with work more often than I'd like sometimes."

"You know what the good thing is? It's my playlist, so I can always go back to the last song and we can hear it together."

"It's that simple, innit?" I asked with a smile.

"It really is, love."

He picked up his phone and turned off the Bluetooth so that the tunes would play out loud for us both. Then, with a few more clicks, Rihanna's voice poured out of his phone, syncing up seamlessly with Calvin Harris's beats on "This Is What You Came For."

"The best part is…food's ready, too. So you finished your work at the perfect time."

Thomas began moving his arms to the beat as I got up from my couch and joined him, rocking my shoulders and hips from side to side.

"I wouldn't say finished, but I did enough for tonight."

"I'll take it. Besides, I didn't know how much longer I could go on pretending not to notice you sneaking glances while you worked," he added, briefly looking back at me with a devious smirk as he began scooping spoonfuls of jambalaya onto our plates, still dancing perfectly in rhythm with the music.

"Ha! Was it that obvious?"

"Only because I was checking you out, too."

Thomas turned back toward me with both of his hands full, our plates overflowing with the colorful rice dish packed with meats, and I about lost my footing when his eyes connected with mine.

"Good. At least I wasn't alone, then," I replied, quickly averting my eyes before I lost my breath control as well.

Chuckling under his breath, Thomas danced toward the couch and placed our plates onto the coffee table while I pulled out cutlery for us to eat with and poured two glasses of water.

"Would you like something else to drink besides water?" I asked.

"What do you have?"

"All that time in my kitchen and you don't know?"

"I tried not to dig around more than I needed to," he admitted.

"All right, well, I have some Riesling in the fridge."

"That works. Let's do it."

I grabbed the chilled bottle and two wineglasses and walked toward the couch, sitting down dangerously close to Thomas so that our thighs barely had any space between each other. It was thrilling, feeling the heat radiate from off our skin. But also, I was starving and desperately wanted to try the food he'd cooked before giving in to any other kind of temptation. Before either of us could make another move, I stuffed a big forkful of food into my mouth, delighting in all the amazing spices and how they blended together to form quite possibly one of the best things I'd ever tasted.

"Wow," I said, barely having finished chewing. "Now I see why you say this is famous."

"I'm glad you like it. My dad will be proud to hear that the tradition continues."

"It most certainly does. Does he have any other famous dinners that you want to cook for us one day?"

Thomas let out a big laugh before stuffing his own face with a forkful of rice. "You're already making me a househusband, huh?"

"Not quite. This is just…really nice," I admitted. "I'm glad you suggested it."

"To be fair, it was kind of a team-effort suggestion," he replied.

"That's true. I guess it's a good thing that I have a job that sometimes requires long hours," I joked.

We ate more and more bites of our food until our plates were practically wiped clean—a telltale sign that the meal was beyond delicious. But as I leaned back onto the couch, belly full and satisfied, I also remembered the other reason we'd met up tonight: Thomas had admitted to having a hard day at work, and I didn't want to let that just sit in the air without acknowledging it.

I moved in a little closer to him and put my hand on his thigh.

"All right, Mr. Wright," I began. "Did you want to talk about today and what was so stressful?"

"Mmm. Right. I almost forgot about that," he replied, turning toward me and leaning his head into the couch as well so that we were both facing each other, our foreheads almost touching.

"We don't have to if you don't want to," I offered as a consolation.

I knew I wasn't always the most talkative, either, when

things bothered me, so I wanted to let him know I wasn't
pressuring him to be so, either.

"I just thought it might be helpful to talk about it—"

"No, I appreciate that," he replied before sighing heavily. "Really, it was just a tale as old as time. Sometimes one
of the partners I work with will show up and just be on a
tear all day. So, despite the fact that I've even brought clients into the firm myself and how many cases I've helped
them win over the past seven years, he'll get on this kick
where he feels like nothing I do that day is right. Today
was one of those days."

"I'm sorry, Thomas. You definitely don't deserve that."

"Yeah, it's not the best feeling. But I also know how
much the other partners value me as a senior associate,
and I think that might be part of the issue with this guy,
honestly. I had one of the other partners approach me recently about taking that next step up, so it kinda feels like
it's not a coincidence that today of all days he came in trying to take me down a notch."

"Mmm, I know how that can go—jealous of your rise
but also has no clue all the work you put in to get where
you are."

"Exactly."

"I went through something similar at my last investment firm. There was this one woman who just couldn't
get past the fact that I was a young portfolio manager and
from Brixton and doing better than she was."

"What did you do about it?"

"I just kept beating her." I laughed. "Until a better opportunity came around and I left that investment group
for my current one."

"I guess that is always an option," he replied, a slight
dejection forming on his face.

Oh no, I realized. That was the last thing I wanted him

to feel, not when I believed he could move the moon if he wanted to.

"I'm not saying that's what you should do at all," I hurriedly added. "But I do think you will keep winning and you'll keep showing him that he can't stop you."

"Thanks, Liv," Thomas replied, his smile slowly starting to return to his face. "You're right, but sometimes it's nice to hear it from someone else."

"Well, I can be here to remind you of that every day if you want, with balloons and bells and some more of your dad's jambalaya, if that's what it takes."

"Ha ha, I'm not sure I need all that." He laughed, his head cocking to the side in the way that he did when he was sort of teasing me.

What he didn't know was that those were the same kinds of words men had used toward me in the past, right around the time they'd started to realize I was the girl who did "all that" type things for the people in my life. That was usually the signal that the end was near. So, while Thomas was enjoying himself, I silently started to panic, holding my breath and waiting to see if his laugh would turn sinister or if his dimple would fade away into an abyss as he began to chastise me for doing too much.

It never did. Instead, his smile grew wider as he leaned in closer to me, his cologne starting to come into focus and attempting to cloud my thoughts like the times before.

"But I kinda like the sound of it," he said. "Especially the part where you said you'd be here every day."

"That did sound nice, right?" I replied, finally allowing myself to breathe in and out again.

"Yeah."

"To me, too."

Now that my moment of panic had disappeared, I stared into Thomas's eyes, really seeing the man before me—the very same one who'd captured my attention since the moment we met and hadn't let it go. Who'd shown me over and over again that I could trust him with my heart. Who hadn't asked me to be different than who I was or choose him over my ambitions. *So really, what is it that has me scared?* I wondered.

Time passed in silence as neither of us wanted to break the spell we had over the other. But eventually, our hands slowly found their way to each other and our fingers intertwined in the still quiet of the room. I watched with my breath caught in between my lips as Thomas's eyes traced my face, then down my neck, over my cleavage and then returning to my eyes before he replaced the tiny space in between us with one small tug. Like it was always meant to be connected to his, my body naturally followed along as our faces and mouths collided and the two of us frantically sucked our way along the other's lips.

I moaned softly into his mouth, desperate for more and suddenly never wanting to know what it felt like to have his lips removed from mine. A small whimper escaped from me when he did eventually pull away, but thankfully he soon began to follow the path he'd first established with his eyes, tracing his tongue gently along the edges of my jawline, down my neck, onto my collarbone and finally right where the fabric of my bodysuit left just enough cleavage for him to graze the tops of my breasts—sending waves of chills down my spine the entire time.

"I think it might be time for dessert," I whispered as his kisses began making their way back up my neck with one hand grabbing my twists to give him better access.

"Dessert," he repeated, groaning into my ear like a man greedy for more but willing to wait until he heard exactly what he needed. "Ha! Tell me what you really want, Olivia."

Thomas stopped kissing me and looked me square in my eyes, daring me to be bold enough to tell him all the dirty things I'd thought of doing with him when I was alone late at night.

"I want you," I replied.

"How?"

His eyes never left mine as I squirmed under his gaze. I'd never had someone ask me to be this blunt before, and I was all at once thrilled and nervous at the same time. After all, I was the same woman constantly accused of being extra and doing too much, and here he was, imploring me to let go of everything that was stopping me before and do more, say more, tell him exactly what I wanted.

"I want you..." I said, hesitating slightly and then building my courage back up. "Inside of me, on top of me, enveloping me, pleasing me...until we're both spent and satisfied beyond measure."

"Mmm. I can definitely do that," he replied, returning his lips to my body and placing some bites along the side of my neck. "I want to do that. But also, I told you I'd wait until you were absolutely ready. And I didn't just mean about sex. So, do you still have doubts, Olivia?"

"No. Not about this. Not about you. And not about us."

Thomas smiled at me with one of those smiles that makes the other person smile back, and instantly I knew just how right I was. Everything about this man was what I'd always wanted but had been too afraid to even pray for. He was kind, he didn't want to change me, he had his own ambitions and could easily relate to my goals and doubts in my job...but more than that, he'd been presented with an unexpected encounter, just like I had. And he hadn't run away. He'd chosen me over everything he'd thought he wanted before. And that was sexy as hell.

I bit my bottom lip as I waited to find out what he would say or do next.

"Okay, then," he said, and picked me up off the couch, carrying me over his shoulder and to my bedroom.

Once inside, Thomas flicked the switch for the string lights, which I'd placed meticulously throughout my room, wrapping them around the mirror and other items so that it created an almost moonlit atmosphere. Gently, he placed me back on my feet, facing the mirror and, piece by piece, began slowly peeling off my clothes while we both admired our reflection. Standing behind me, he then unbuttoned and unzipped my trousers, following along my hips and thighs with his hands as they fell to the ground. Next, he peeled the bodysuit straps down my arms, grazing my skin as the fabric folded down my breasts and torso until I stood in front of him and the mirror with just my black thong on.

"You're so beautiful," he whispered, staring into my eyes through our reflection in the mirror before grabbing my hair and giving himself full access to the side of my neck down to my chest. He took his time for the next several minutes, building the tension in my body as he alternated between tracing his fingers down my spine and kneading my nipples, causing intermittent goose bumps along my skin and then crystal clear juices sliding down my inner thighs.

"Take your panties off," he finally commanded.

And without another word, I did just as he said, grabbing the fabric at my hips and watching it roll down my legs as Thomas undressed himself behind me and slid a condom onto the meaty penis that I now desperately wanted inside of me.

A few seconds later, I got exactly what I'd been craving as he gently lifted my butt cheeks and slipped inside my vagina, rocking my entire world with each thrust from behind.

Chapter Fourteen

The next morning, I woke up happy, relaxed and basking in the feeling of Thomas's arms wrapped around my bare skin.

It was honestly quite startling how normal it felt, like the spot next to me in my queen-size bed had been waiting for him to occupy it all this time. And finally, after pushing past my fears, he was here, where he belonged—with me. After a quick glance at my clock to check the time, I snuggled in closer to his body, breathing in deeply as he enveloped himself even tighter around my slender frame even as he remained asleep. With at least another hour and a half before I needed to leave for work, I intended to take advantage of every still, quiet minute in his embrace.

As I lay there, eyes now closed again, I contemplated all the times I'd got it wrong before him. How I'd allowed those relationships to make me question whether anyone could ever want me for me. Question if I'd ever know the kind of connection that so many of the people around me had found, even my own little brother, who'd managed to snag one of the women I trusted and admired the most. And yet something about Thomas was easy from the very start. Not that it had been easy allowing myself to fall for him, but that our connection, no matter how hard I'd tried to run from it, had been palpable from the moment we'd met and only continued growing as we'd gotten to know more about each other. That was something I'd never experienced before, and it felt damn good.

I squeezed myself even closer to his chest and breathed in deeply. How had I gotten so lucky, I wondered...and then just as suddenly, did I need to enjoy this time with him while I could? *Because it can't very well last, right?* That was the silent fear still lingering that I didn't want to admit.

"Mmm. Well, that's one way to wake up from a good night's sleep," Thomas said, awaking suddenly and moaning into my ear. "Good morning."

"Oy, I'm sorry. I didn't mean to disturb you," I replied, realizing I'd probably startled him by holding on so tightly.

Before he could do it for me, I loosened my grip around his torso ever so slightly and began the process of removing myself from his grasp.

"You didn't."

Thomas rubbed his sleepy eyes and then, before I could slip out any farther, pulled me back into the nook that had been my sanctuary just moments before. Once I was returned to my rightful place, he stretched his bare, sculpted arms wide and gently kissed me on my forehead—taking the time he needed to loosen his limbs from a full night of sleep before wrapping them all back around me. Even his long legs, like with our hands the night before, found mine under the covers and twisted around each one, so that within seconds, no part of my body was left unconnected to him.

"Did you sleep well?" he asked, that deep baritone voice of his eliciting flashbacks in my mind to the night before and all the ways that I'd never even known my body could experience pleasure.

Whether with simple instructive commands or affirmations of how good I felt, over and over, that same voice had been what kept me grounded throughout the night as he'd encouraged me to let my guard down and open myself up to him. It was also the same voice that had moaned my name softly through staggered breaths as I climbed on top of him and rode his penis until we both climaxed. And then, that voice (and the man behind it) had practically rocked me to sleep while whispering sweet nothings in my ear as I drifted off in his arms. Talk about a sensory overload in the best way.

"I did," I replied, grinning under the covers as I continued down memory lane in my mind. "Probably one of my best nights of sleep in a while."

"Oh yeah? Well, I'll take that as a compliment in more ways than one."

"You should," I said, giggling briefly and then allowing the beauty of silence to overwhelm me as we both stopped our banter to just be present and still in each other's arms.

For several minutes, we lay just like that, no words spoken, just inhaling and exhaling as one, until my internal clock told me that if I didn't get up, I'd never make it out of my flat in time for work.

"Do you want some coffee?" I asked as I once again began trying to peel myself out of his embrace. "I'm going to make some while I get dressed, so…"

"Yeah, that would be nice. I think I'm going to need it to get out of this bed this morning, for sure."

"Same. I kind of wish it were Saturday and we could just be here all day actually. But it's not, innit."

With one last regrettable heave, I fully rolled myself out of Thomas's arms, climbed out of my bed and finally stood up to begin my day. If we were going to be together (*a wild thing to even contemplate, I know*), I was going to have to get used to nights and mornings with him and still getting up and being to work by 7:30 a.m. That was the routine I'd established after all, and I wasn't about to change it now. So, today was as good a day as any to begin the practice.

"How do you like it?" I asked, grabbing my robe and wrapping it around my body before making my way toward the kitchen.

"More cream and sugar than coffee," he admitted with a chuckle.

"Ha ha, okay, noted."

Step by step, I slowly dragged myself away from Thomas and the bed I still desperately wanted to be in, momentarily paused by his large hand that jutted out and grabbed mine as I started walking by him in what felt like one last attempt to get me to come back. I pressed on, however, undeterred from my goal at hand, and made it to the kitchen, where I went about pouring just enough grounded beans and water into the machine for us to both have a large mug of coffee each.

As I waited for the magical brown liquid to begin filling my flat with its sweet aroma, Jhené Aiko's "New Balance" suddenly started playing in my head—another reminder of just how infatuated I'd seemingly become over the naked man currently lying in my bed. It hadn't happened overnight. But it had very obviously been building for quite some time, as evidenced by my friends' comments on our trip. And last night I'd finally stopped fighting it, leaning into the idea that maybe, just maybe, I did deserve someone who saw things in me that even I couldn't—and loved what he saw.

Realizing that I probably needed to multitask while I continued waiting for the coffee to brew, I scooped up my phone from the coffee table in the sitting room, where we'd left it behind the night before.

"By the way," I said out loud as I began scrolling to see if there were any urgent emails I needed to handle before work, "not sure if you remember, but I think I might have said I wanted to be with you—as in, like, us officially be together—last night."

"Oh, is that what you said?" Thomas responded from inside my bedroom. "I may vaguely recall something close to that, but it's the strangest thing, I don't remember those exact words being used."

Amazingly, even without seeing him, I knew he was smiling from under the covers in my bed. Still teasing me even after the way he'd handled my body like a pro last night. Now that was just rude.

"I didn't say those exact words, but I mean—"

"You're right, you didn't," he interjected, suddenly standing at the junction between my bedroom door and the sitting room. "And yet I did, right?"

The smirk I'd assumed he had on his face was now replaced with something different, something more earnest and sincere.

"You did."

"Mmm."

He stood in exactly the same spot, not moving any further toward me but not yet retreating as he waited for me to say more.

"Well, I do want us to be together, if that's still a question in your mind," I answered.

"Good," he replied, pausing his words as he stepped toward me in the dim light. "I wouldn't say it was still a question, but sometimes a man needs to hear it, too, you know."

"Yeah, okay."

With one last step, Thomas reached his destination (me) and once again pulled me toward him, his hands now sitting on the small of my back as I instinctually leaned into him, climbed onto my tippy toes and joined my lips with his. We moaned in unison as I bit his lower lip and used it as my leverage to thrust my tongue into his mouth, which he sucked at feverishly. It wasn't until I felt his penis jumping as it grazed my thigh that I realized we should stop before I lost all control of my senses and allowed him to carry me right back to bed or, better yet, bend me over the coffee table or couch right before us.

"You," I said breathlessly, laughing and stepping down onto the heels of my feet. "You and your best friend need to go back over there so I can get myself together."

I pointed toward my bedroom to emphasize my point.

"You sure?" he asked, those gray eyes once again staring daggers into my soul.

"Yes!" I exclaimed, trying to convince myself just as much as him.

"Okay, okay—but I don't have to be happy about it."

"Well, neither do I, but you still need to do it."

I giggled silently as I watched him dramatically turn around and walk back toward my bedroom door, his firm butt cheeks threatening to distract me once again. I quickly cleared my throat and pulled myself together, turning back to my phone just as a new message came through from Walter.

Olivia, I have great news, it read. I'm probably not supposed to tell you this, but I've been talking to some of the C-suite brass, and you are most definitely on their radar. In fact, apparently the head of the UK portfolio division is looking to step down as early as next year, and after what they've seen from you in just a few months here, plus what you were doing in London, I think they might be interested in offering you the top position. You get what this means, right? You're on the precipice of everything you've wanted, and even earlier than you expected.

I read Walter's note in shock probably six times in a row before anything he'd written was able to really sink in. Was he for real? I questioned. Was it all just right here all of a sudden? The dream I barely had enough courage to say aloud except for one late night when Walter and I were working at the office, and he'd randomly asked me what I wanted to get out of New York. I'd hesitated at first, but after some proper cajoling, he'd gotten me to admit it all—my whole kick-ass list down to the ultimate goal.

I smiled deeply as the joy finally replaced the shock and washed over my body. Sure, I still had some time before it was final—but it was here! I'd done it. The young Black girl from Brixton had grown into a woman who was on her way to being head of her management group's UK portfolio division. *My God!*

I messaged Walter back saying that he'd already made my whole month and the sun hadn't even come up yet, then swung myself around, throwing my head back, and fully took in the news. I only paused briefly from my swing fest so that I could read the note once more. *You're on the precipice of everything you've wanted,* he'd said.

I sure in the hell was.

Seconds later, I heard the coffee machine switch off, and suddenly dread washed over me. *Thomas.* Sweet, unaware Thomas was waiting in my bed for his cup of coffee while I received what was equally the best career news ever and the thing that spelled impending doom for us. Sure, he'd been understanding last night, I thought, but how understanding would he be when I told him that there was no way I'd be staying in America now. And even though he hadn't yet asked me to, that conversation of where we both lived was always going to eventually come up, right? Months down the line, the only thing that would change was that it would hurt more, but I was always going to have to say goodbye.

This was what I'd been avoiding. This was why I'd tried

to keep choosing Door Number Two over and over again, so I wouldn't get lulled into a false belief he might be the one man who didn't mind how important my career was to me. And yet I'd ultimately failed—falling for the man who looked at me with sincere eyes and who'd chosen me over his own comfort level—and now I was going to have to shatter both of our hearts. When I never should have given him mine in the first place. I knew better… I knew.

I walked over to the coffee machine and poured out two cups of coffee into the mugs beside it, prepared them individually according to our preferences and braced myself for heartbreak. I needed to tell Thomas now that I'd been wrong and we shouldn't be together, but I really, really didn't want to. With a heavy sigh, I picked up both mugs and walked to my bedroom, trying to figure out the words I'd use to let us both down gently.

"Just like you like it," I said once I'd walked back into the room, handing Thomas his mug as he finished sliding up and then buttoning his trousers.

"Thank you, love," he replied, gently grazing my fingers as he took the cup out of my hand and then kissing me on the cheek before indulging in a large, satisfying gulp.

I took my own sip of coffee to steady my hands and breathing before finally getting up the nerve to broach the topic I was sure would make me want to go cry in the shower after.

"So…" I started with hesitation. "I just got a note from Walter saying that he thinks C-suite wants to skip the senior portfolio manager promotion I wanted and that they're contemplating offering me the division head spot when I return."

I held my breath as I waited for Thomas's response, holding back the tears threatening to fall down my face from the inevitable disappointment.

"Liv, wait, are you serious?" he asked.

"Very."

"That's...that's amazing, babe! Damn, I'm so proud of you."

Thomas sat down his coffee and, in one swoop, scooped me into his arms and held me tightly to his chest. "I knew they would see what I see," he whispered in my ear.

"Yeah," I replied softly, holding on to him for dear life as my eyes began to water.

Once again, Thomas had surprised me, exuding only joy from my announcement. That was the kind of man he was, I realized. The same one who had been concerned about not wanting my time in New York to become about him because he knew only moments after we'd met how important this time was for me. He *wasn't* David. He wasn't anything like all the others who had disappointed me time and time again, really. And yet, as I clung to him, feeling every vein in his muscles on my skin, I knew I was still going to have to say goodbye.

Just not now, I thought. For now, I wanted to pretend that it mattered that he was perfect for me. Even though every bone in my body knew the awful truth.

Part 3

"So maybe it won't look like you thought it would in high school, but it's important to remember that love is possible. Anything is possible. This is New York."

—*Sex and the City*

Chapter Fifteen

A week later, I found myself uptown, in Jake's condo for Christmas dinner, dressed in a winter white sweater dress with knee-high chestnut-brown boots and surrounded by the group I'd dubbed Reagan's New York village—Keisha, Giselle, Jake and his two friends, Brandon and Lucas. For different reasons, we'd all found ourselves still in the city on Christmas Day, so when Jake had suggested a friends' dinner, we all jumped at the chance to spend the day and evening laughing, drinking and eating good food. I was particularly glad not to be spending the day alone, where my mind had time to wander about me and Thomas and the fact that I'd yet to tell him I needed to end things.

Jake's place was just the home away from home I needed and everything that I'd expected from a Harlem condo decorated by an alum of Howard University and the boyfriend of Reagan Doucet. From the moment I walked in, I was greeted with the sounds, smells and sights of American Blackness, beginning with the smell of the soul food he and Reagan had cooking in the kitchen all the way to the Jackson 5 Christmas album playing on his record player as background tunes. On every wall, except the one that had been turned into a floor-to-ceiling bookshelf, were collages of black-and-white photographs of Black luminaries, the likes of everyone from James Baldwin to Josephine Baker. And scattered throughout his place, matching seamlessly with his Williams Sonoma and Neiman Marcus furniture, were various hints of what he obviously found to be most important in his life, such as the coasters on his coffee table that featured *Life* magazine images from Howard University in the 1940s, the Mardi Gras mask that was presumably from Reagan and had been given prime positioning on his bookshelf, and the Alpha Phi Alpha notebook-and-pen set seated on the corner of one of his end tables.

"This food is so good," I said, leaning over toward Reagan from the midnight blue ottoman I was perched on while eating. "I can't believe you eat this every Christmas."

"Thanks, *cher*," she replied with a smile. "It's probably hard to believe, but this is the truncated version of my family's Christmas meal. I couldn't have pulled all that off with just me and Jake."

"Oh, if you guys needed help, I could have come over," I said quickly, suddenly feeling guilty for not just asking.

"No, I appreciate that. But today you're our guest, so don't let your head take that thought any further."

"Oy, okay," I replied, marveling at the fact that we knew each other well enough at this point for her to know I would have started ruminating about whether I was a good friend or not.

I was glad to have Rae in my life—that much I was certain of, if nothing else. And if the company and the prospect of not spending Christmas alone hadn't been enticing enough, the food she and Jake cooked would have lured me uptown all on its own. On their menu, and subsequently stuffed into my belly, were the following:

Seafood filé gumbo
Baked macaroni and cheese
Seafood-stuffed bell peppers
Southern-style green beans
Potato salad

Crawfish pies
Shrimp and rice–stuffed chicken
And each piece of food tasted better than the next.

To my right, Keish and Gigi were just as happy and full as I was but also in the process of jump-starting the next conversation for us to dig into as a framily. Already, we'd covered everything from the advent of "podcast bros" to all the white celebrities randomly admitting that they didn't shower. We'd even had a short-lived deep dive into all three Megan/Meghans—Fox, Thee Stallion and Markle, respectively—until Jake let us know that the lemon pie he and Reagan had made was finally ready to devour. Just as well, I realized, for I was pretty sure that my only commentary about the Markles was going to be that I was glad they'd found their way to America, a statement that in hindsight might have been pretty ironic to all the Americans sitting around me, who still faced tons of discrimination in their own country.

"Okay, so looking a year ahead from now," Keisha began, crossing her legs and putting down her now empty saucer as she garnered everyone's attention, "what are some of the things you want to say you've done by next Christmas?"

She looked around the room, waiting for the first person to jump in with their answer. It took a few minutes, but Jake was the first to take the plunge.

"I want us to be living together by then," he replied, turning his attention to Reagan and effectively breaking the silence in the room.

"Whoa, really?" Lucas asked as the rest of the room oooh-ed in a stunned Reagan's direction.

"Yeah, I mean, I love this woman," he said, pulling her toward him and wrapping his left arm around her waist.

"Why wouldn't I want us to start building what a lifetime looks like?"

"Does that mean you're proposing next year, too?" I overheard her ask him quietly as we all screamed and giggled in response to their love.

"Yeah, babe," he responded, and then kissed her reassuringly. "I figured that part was kind of a given."

"It wasn't, but good to hear it's on your radar."

"And in my budget."

"Even better." She laughed.

I watched from the sidelines as the two lovebirds continued their private conversation in the midst of our very public discussion, but then again, that was indicative of everything I'd learned about Reagan and Jake—they somehow found a way to insulate themselves when they needed to even if among a crowd. It was something I admired about their connection. Something I thought Thomas and I probably had, too, but... *Oh, crap. Thomas.*

I bristled at the thought of what I still had to do with him, how I was only delaying the inevitable break of both our hearts, and quickly tried to turn my mind back to the discussion at hand. The one thing that slightly comforted me was knowing he was home for Christmas, and so I at least had until he got back to the city before I needed to say the actual words—that we were over.

"Okay, okay, that's a great start," Keisha interjected, quieting down all our remaining whistles and hoots. "I don't know who's topping that, but someone else, please try."

"I expect to have all my student loans paid off by then," Giselle replied, jumping in as she curled her legs into the right corner of Jake's couch and wrapped herself in one of his plush throw blankets.

"Gigi, that's boss!" Brandon screamed out, leaning over

to high-five her before quickly tempering his response back into his seat when we all turned our attention his way. "Sorry, I'm just... I'm just saying that's a big deal. I'm happy for you, friend."

"Thank you," she said, blushing. "I appreciate the excitement. I'm excited, too!"

"That's great, Gigi," Keisha added. "As y'all know, I'm about to take on even more student-loan debt when I start business school this summer, so you just make sure you remember the little ones when you're Navient free, okay?"

"I got you," Giselle replied, laughing at Keisha's sarcasm.

"What about you, Liv?" Reagan asked as she walked into the sitting room from the kitchen after having sufficiently completed her private conversation with Jake. "Are you still going to be with us come next Christmas?"

She poked me playfully in my side as she sat back down across from me in the chaise lounge attached to the sofa, relaxing into what I could only guess was her normal spot when she and Jake were home alone.

"Actually... I hadn't had a chance to tell you yet, but according to Walter, I might be head of the UK portfolio division this time next year."

"Wait, what?" she screamed out, excitement fluttering on her face. "Oh, Liv, that's amazing! That's like everything you wanted when you took this year opportunity in the city!"

"Yeah," I replied with a strained smile on my face. "Even more than, honestly, because I never expected they would shoot me straight past senior portfolio manager to leading the entire division."

"Well, I did. You're badass, and clearly everyone there knows it."

As the rest of the room joined in with cheers and exclamations of my awesomeness, Rae paused to look me in my eyes, and I could instantly tell she knew there was a *but* to all my exuberance. Her read of me reminded me of the first time Thomas had been able to see through my banter in the airport, but this time, I wasn't sure I had it in me to hold back the tears that wanted to pour out. I could do that with a stranger at the time, but not Reagan. Not after the friendship we'd built over the last several months. Thankfully, the rest of the group turned back to discussing Keisha's plans for business school before they could catch my breakdown starting.

"What's wrong, Liv? Why don't you seem as happy as we are?" Reagan asked, drawing me into a conversation of just the two of us.

"I am happy," I replied, as one lone tear dripped down my left cheek. "I just… It's everything I've ever wanted—"

"Yeah, it is, *cher.*"

"But it also means, once again, I'm the girl who gets to accomplish her career goals but loses the guy."

There it is. I finally said the quiet part out loud.

"Wait, what?" Jake interjected, sliding next to Reagan.

It wasn't lost on me that they even used the same language to express their shock at something. If I didn't adore them both so much, it would be sickening.

"Take me from the start. How did you jump from this amazing, exciting, thrilling accomplishment to you losing my guy Thomas? Did he say something to make you believe you needed to choose between him and your career?"

"Wait, Jake, before you answer that," Reagan interrupted. "Have you even told him about this, Liv?"

Reagan's eyes trained in on mine, seemingly so that she could determine whether I was telling her the truth. But also, there seemed to be genuine care behind her gaze, like she honestly thought I wasn't giving us a fair shot. She was probably right.

"I did, yes. Right after I got Walter's note."

"And?" Jake asked, leaning toward me as if he was prepared to fight somebody no matter what my response.

"He was excited for me. But... I know how this goes, okay. I just do. And the reality is we've never talked about trying to have an international, long-distance relationship. I'm not even sure that's something I'd want, really. So it just feels...inevitable. This time next year, I'll be back in London, living out my dream, and he'll be here, without me, living out his."

"Oh, Liv, that's a lot to assume, babe," Reagan replied, reaching out her hand and placing it on my thigh. "Especially if you haven't actually talked to Thomas about it. Who knows what ideas he might have for y'all to make it work."

"You do want to make it work, right?" Jake asked, looking at me earnestly as if that was the simplest question in the world.

It wasn't, of course. Sure, I wanted to make it work. What woman wouldn't want her dream partner and her dream job at the same time? And yet I was intimately aware from every past relationship that that wasn't how life worked...at least not for me. I could understand why Jake and Reagan didn't see it that way, of course. She'd bet on herself, convinced her job to let her move to New York and gotten the man and the job at once. But everyone couldn't be so lucky. My position wasn't available in New York, and even if it was, I didn't want to stay here. I wanted to go back home, where I could see my parents in less than twenty minutes just by hopping on the Tube. Where my best girlfriends since primary school were waiting to welcome me back with open arms. Where I could go to

Nando's or Dirty Martini with Craig and Robin and Frank without having to plan an eight-hour trip to see them. It was just that I also wanted Thomas, the unexpected blessing that had come into my life and shaken everything up.

But Thomas, well, he had made a perfect life for himself in New York. A life he loved so much he resisted dating me at first because he hadn't wanted to risk changing it. A life he deserved, and I wanted him to have, after all the hard work he'd put in at his firm—one that was about to make him a partner, for God's sake.

None of those realities changed just because I *wanted* to make things work.

"It's not that easy," I replied.

"Nothing worth having ever is," he answered.

I looked away from them both, with their eager hearts trying to impress upon me a reality I knew simply wasn't true, desperate to hold my composure and not draw the rest of the group's attention our way. But in my attempt at distraction, I noticed—and therefore they also noticed— the FaceTime call from Thomas trying to come through right at the worst possible time. I quickly silenced the call before anyone else could see it and stared Reagan and Jake down to hopefully, telepathically, let them know I didn't want to discuss what had just transpired.

"Does he know yet?" Reagan asked, somewhat taking the hint, but not really.

"Does he know what?"

"That you're giving up?"

Wow, what a gut punch.

I'd sort of expected it since Reagan wasn't one for mincing her words, but hearing it, as blunt as she'd said it, still stung a whole lot.

"I haven't told him that we shouldn't continue seeing each other yet, if that's what you mean."

"And so, he's still calling."

"He is."

"And you're not answering?"

I sighed heavily.

"I'm not."

"On Christmas."

Crap. She had a point there.

"So you're just, what, ghosting him?" Jake asked, now seemingly fired up at me in the same way he'd been ready to go to war when he'd thought Thomas to be the potential bad guy in all of this.

"I'm not… No, that's not…" I fumbled with my words, unsure of exactly what to say. "I just don't know how to tell him yet. Or what to say. I almost thought about writing a letter and leaving it at his flat—"

"Oh God, definitely don't do that," Reagan interrupted. "He deserves better than that, Liv. What you all have built deserves better. You know that."

"Yeah," I replied. "I know."

I slumped my shoulders and wished I could rewind things back to when Reagan had first come into the sitting room, figured out a way to put on a braver face, and then maybe we wouldn't be having this conversation. It was a faulty plan, but it was all I had in the moment.

"Okay, you three," Keisha shouted out, turning to us with her eyebrow raised. "If you're done with your little side conversation now, we'd all like you to rejoin the discussion."

"Sorry," Reagan replied, once again sitting back into her corner of the chaise lounge. "You're right. We're being rude."

"It's all good," Keisha replied. "Plus, you're back just in time for something I know you'll have an opinion on… 'Confessions One' or 'Two'?"

"Oh, that's easy," Jake replied, perking back up after having chastised me for the past couple minutes. "It's 'Confessions Two,' and it's not even close."

"Are you kidding me?" Reagan asked, flummoxed and turning toward him with her arms folded. "The first 'Confessions' is iconic. All you have to do is play the first few notes, and everyone will start oooh-ooh-ing!"

"Yeah, babe, that might be true, but 'Two' has that bop with it. And I guarantee you most people know all the lyrics to that way more than they know the first one."

"I can't believe what you're saying right now." She laughed, playfully pushing him away from her as they continued on their debate, pulling in Gigi, Lucas and Brandon to defend their points.

I sat off to the side, pretending to laugh and be part of the discussion while silently taking in all that they'd just said to me. It had been very hard to hear, but they'd probably been at least right about the fact that Thomas deserved better than the way I was treating him. Not probably—I knew they were. That didn't make what I had to do any easier.

Turning to the side, I caught Keisha's eyes as she mouthed *You're welcome* to me and winked in my direction. I guess I had a Christmas angel on my side, someone who could tell I'd needed saving from Reagan and Jake's interrogation. I returned the favor and mouthed *Thank you* as I shook myself out of my thoughts and forced myself to be present again—to enjoy the beautiful people all around me, all clad in either warm earth tones or some combination of white or cream fabric. None of us with any stains after having devoured all that food...now that was what I called Black girl and boy magic!

"If it helps," I interjected, finally actively joining in the debate, "from a global perspective, I don't think the first one charted in the UK."

"Et tu, Olivia?" Reagan asked, dropping her mouth in shock.

"I'm just saying," I said with a shrug.

"Well, you can say all you want, but that doesn't mean it's not the better song."

She laughed, poking her lips out at me.

"Nah, let the woman cook. It's her only chance to be right today, so let her have it," Jake replied.

Oh brother. I can see now I won't be living this whole Thomas thing down anytime soon.

Chapter Sixteen

"Time check!" Reagan screamed out from the confines of her bathroom to anyone and no one, briefly startling me, Keisha and Gigi to attention before we each realized we were nowhere near a clock or phone to answer her.

"9:48 p.m.!" Jake called out from the sitting room, seated calmly on Rae's couch and sipping from his whiskey tumbler.

To his left was Brandon, also fully dressed and ready to go, the two of them decked out in their finest attire—Jake with his sky blue trousers, charcoal-gray oxfords and a black-and-silver striped button-down that he wore only half closed, and Brandon with his rust-colored tailored suit that he'd paired with a fitted white T-shirt and a pair of matching white Vans. Together, they sat and watched in awe as we ran around Reagan's apartment, trying to finalize the last bits of our outfits for New Year's Eve.

"Ugh," Reagan cried, finally fitting the last eyelash strip perfectly to her face, then waving her hand over it to make sure it was dry. "We are going to be sooo late."

I looked up from tying the final knot on my silver lace-up heels just in time to catch Gigi roll her eyes in exasperation. I could understand her frustration, as I'd been struggling to wrap the laces around my calves (and most importantly, have them stay there) for what had felt like hours, igniting my anxiety, too, which was only worsened by the feeling of being rushed. This heightened every extra minute it took me to get everything to work. But also, I'd finally got my thing done, so I also had the experience of jubilation that I was at once finally among the ready few. Gigi, beautiful as she was, was definitely not.

"See, this is why I don't like to go out for New Year's Eve...especially in New York City!" she said. "It's too much pressure."

Standing in front of Reagan's full-length mirror, Gigi slid her hands over her dress once more, smoothing down the cocoa-brown fabric to make sure the Spanx she wore underneath didn't show through. She turned to the right and left, inspecting all the angles where her shapewear secret could be exposed, finally spinning in a complete 180 to where her backside faced the mirror for one last check across her shoulders. Once satisfied with her look, Gigi glanced over at me, at first, I thought for my approval, but then her eyes lit up, beaming in a way that felt completely incongruent with her demeanor just a couple minutes before.

"Liv!" she exclaimed, swishing her way over to me. "You're done, right? Can you please zip me up? I could only get it to go so far up."

"Of course," I replied, motioning for her to spin around so I had access to her back. "It's like they make these things as torture devices to remind single women that they don't have an extra set of hands to help them."

"Seriously. But that's why we just end up all getting dressed together, I guess."

"Except Reagan only has one bathroom...and it's four of us." I bristled, reminding myself of why we were all feeling the angst and rush of the moment.

"Exactly. Yet another reason I don't like doing this."

I finished zipping Giselle's dress up and patted her on the back to signal my effort was complete, which she promptly thanked me for and went about trying to find the shoes she'd brought with her to wear for the evening. I knew they were somewhere among the litany of clothes and shoes tossed about Reagan's flat, but I wasn't entirely convinced she was going to find them in the little bit of time we had left.

"I knowwwww, you guys. I know," Reagan called out, seemingly overhearing our conversation while she delicately applied her red Fenty Beauty Stunna Lip Paint.

After she let it sit for a second to not get any on her teeth, she continued her thoughts.

"But you know this is Liv's one and only time to experience New Year's Eve in the city, so we had to do it right. We couldn't just be in Jake's condo, chilling and drinking champagne."

"I mean, but that sounds like a lot of fun to me," Jake interjected.

"Of course it does…to you!" she replied, finally emerging from the bathroom in a bright yellow-gold satin dress, the top shaped almost like a bustier with the straps meant to fall past her shoulders and midway down her upper arm.

The bottom of the dress was equally as fitted, showing off her small waist, with a high slit on the right that exposed almost her full size-ten thighs. Most importantly, she was now done and counted among the growing crew of people ready to leave.

"I want Liv to have a moment," she protested. "There are no New Year's Eve moments happening on One Hundred Thirty-Third in Harlem. That's why we're going to Magic Hour, and we're going to have a great time, damn it."

Jake chuckled and threw his hands up in defeat. If it was one thing he knew, it was when not to try to get Reagan off an idea she had in mind.

"Okay, guys," she said, again to no one and everyone all at the same time. "I'm calling the UberXL. It's almost ten o'clock now, and if we don't get out of here soon, we're going to be in line during the countdown…"

"And that will most definitely not be a moment," Gigi interrupted, joining our ever-growing group in the sitting room.

Pretending to wipe her forehead from exhaustion, she breathed in a huge sigh of relief. "All done," she said. "I cut it close, but you can never say Gigi Lewis is going to be late."

Reagan laughed and pressed Choose UberXL on her phone, knowing exactly who Gigi was referring to—the one person who'd yet to join us in the sitting room. Keisha had a lot of great qualities about her: loyalty, superb conversation skills, drive and ambition…but timeliness was just not one of them.

"We know, Gig. Thank you for that."

"Don't think I don't know that was a dig at me," Keisha called out as she finally came bouncing up to us, her velvet hot-pink dress and diagonal-patterned fishnet stockings stopping everyone in their tracks. "I'm ready, too, now, so there."

"I mean, if the shoe fits, babe." Reagan laughed, rolling her eyes. "But either way, I'm glad we're all ready now, with not a moment to spare."

She paused, checking her phone once again, and then said the dreaded words we'd all been worried would come too soon.

"Car's here."

Like we'd been waiting for the person at a racetrack who shoots the gun to let you know when you can finally start running, we all immediately sprang into action, quickly gathered our purses, phones, coats and other accessories, and began piling out of Reagan's flat. Brandon and Jake lagged a few steps behind us, still calm and unfazed. Clearly they'd got used to the chaos of the crew by now, refusing to let the women they called partner and friend rile them up on occasions such as this.

Must be nice, I thought. Chaos still very much left me flustered. And the night had only just begun.

It was nearly 11:00 p.m. when we finally walked into the winter wonderland rooftop party being hosted at Magic Hour NY in Midtown, just off Seventh Avenue. Once inside, we were immediately greeted by an après-themed pink-and-white explosion of decor, featuring everything from frosted Christmas trees to a sparkly dining carousel with over twenty-five thousand crystals and a pink-and-white winter lodge flanked incredibly by even more iced-out forestry. In the distance, I saw a group of women gathered on the makeshift dance floor, drinking and singing loudly to Pitbull and Ne-Yo's definitive dance song, the ever iconic "Give Me Everything," while others were seated in booths sipping spiked hot chocolate with their dates or posing for Instagram-worthy photos.

I guess Reagan was right, I thought to myself. *This, and not Jake's condo, is exactly what a New Year's Eve in New York City should look like—decadence, elegance and iced-out decor, all under the beautiful and lit-up gaze of the Empire State Building.*

The six of us took our time walking through the crowd, making our way to the bar while simultaneously people watching and scoping the scene for who Keisha, Gigi and Brandon might want to kiss as the clock struck midnight. As for me—the only other sort of single person in the crew—I planned to ring in the new year simply sipping on a glass of champagne under the moonlight and trying to forget all the ways I was likely actively hurting the one person who made my whole face smile just thinking about him.

If I could pull that off and spend one night not internally beating myself up for letting Thomas down over and over, well, that...would be a New Year's Eve miracle all on its own.

Since that fated morning after I received Walter's message, I'd managed to do the exact opposite almost every day. To be fair, our random conversations didn't change instantly, but any time Thomas broached the idea of us seeing each other again, I clammed up and made an excuse for why we couldn't. In my heart, I knew I was wrong. But I was paralyzed in a way I'd never been before—hating the idea of having to end things with him and simultaneously realizing I was doing it anyway, but with no real closure. It was the ultimate coward's way out, and eventually, he took the hint. Our calls and texts grew fewer and fewer until we'd barely talked to each other in days.

Tonight had to be different, I thought. If only just for the prospect of truly starting the year off as a new beginning.

After we finally reached the bar and gave our orders to Jake to place, I looked around and let my eyes land on a group of guys standing in a corner laughing. Their faces were filled with so much happiness and exuberance as they slapped each other on the shoulders and curled over in laughter. It was a beautiful sight to behold, men just expressing joy around each other, in their own element and not at all aware of anyone else paying them any attention.

I made a mental note to myself that a few of them seemed like they could be good prospects for Gigi or Keish.

The only thing was, as I stared in closer, it almost looked as if Thomas was standing in the midst of those friends. But that wasn't possible, right? In a city as big as New York, there was no way we'd somehow ended up at the same party. It was just my brain pranking me out of guilt.

I blinked my eyes feverishly to make sure I wasn't making up what I saw before me, but after several seconds of trying, I could no longer deny the truth. There he was. Standing off to the side with a fitted white shirt rolled halfway up his forearms and buttoned about three-fourths up his chest with a pair of gray-striped plaid pants that seemed as if they'd been tailor-made for him. And of course, his smile (that dimple!) was in full effect—bright enough to compete with the Empire State Building towering over us all.

Caught up in the moment, I couldn't stop myself from staring. First, I was stunned by his outfit choice, not because he didn't look great—of course he did; he always did—but because we had barely talked in the past week and somehow his outfit managed to perfectly complement my silver deep V-neck disco dress with its low scoop back and the silky white oversize blazer that I paired it with.

Wonderful, I thought. It was as if God and the universe were trying to troll me.

"Reagan," I said, grabbing her toward me. "Is this what you meant by a New Year's Eve moment? Please tell me you didn't plan this."

Her curious look told me she had no idea what I was talking about. So, in my best attempt to not draw attention to us, I positioned her head in direct eyesight of Thomas to clue her in on what I was rambling about. Reagan's eyes instantly bulged out as she turned toward me to protest the idea that she had anything to do with Thomas and me being in the same space tonight.

"Oh, no, Liv, this definitely isn't me. I know how hard

this week has been for you—I promise I wouldn't set you up like this."

I breathed a sigh of relief. She was right. I knew that this was beyond what she would go through to put us together. She might have pushed me to attend that first party because we'd known he would be there, but she wouldn't orchestrate an ambush—that wasn't her style.

"You're right. I'm sorry for even asking. I just… What do I do now? I mean, he's literally standing right there."

Reagan looked at me sympathetically and then turned to her left as Jake tapped her on her shoulder and passed her two shot glasses.

"The only thing you can do, *cher*. Take this shot and hope he doesn't see you."

She passed me one of the chilled shot glasses, and without another word, the two of us poured the smooth white tequila down our throats and then promptly chased it with the limes that had come stuck on the rim of the glasses.

"I may need a few more of those," I replied.

"Uhh, you might actually need a bucket, Liv."

I watched Reagan's face turn sideways as she saw, and then I saw, that any hope I'd had of Thomas missing me was long gone. In an instant, we locked eyes from across the room, his deep gray eyes staring daggers into my soul. Like all the times before, his intense gaze halted any movement or breaths from me, but this time it wasn't because of how turned on I was. It was because I was being forced to face him, after having told him I no longer had doubts and then immediately going back on that word the very next day, slowly and horribly ticking away at us with my inaction. The awful things he must have thought about me.

"Here, take another shot," Reagan said, briefly grabbing my attention as she passed me another chilled glass.

I dutifully took the smooth liquor out of her hands and

happily obliged, as if my actions were no longer under my control. Take a shot? Sure. Stand paralyzed while the man of your dreams glares at you from a corner? Why not. There was nothing I could do about it anyway. Nothing I could do except once again pour the white liquid down my throat, suck the lime, ask for another one and repeat.

By the time I downed my fourth one, my glazed-over eyes were finally able to somewhat protect me from Thomas's insistent stares. I still felt them, don't get me wrong, and all the disappointment hidden behind them, but at least I could no longer clearly see just how much I'd hurt him. And that was a win I'd readily take since there seemed to be no others in sight. That look, now blurry despite its persistence, held within it all the times he'd tried to call or text me and I'd made excuses for why I was busy or unavailable.

I continued watching him through my now distorted view, studying his every move as he interacted with his friends but never dropped his eyes from mine for more than a few seconds. Each time he did, I could barely count to the number five on my hand before once again, we were locked in, neither of us knowing what to say or do but somehow understanding the magnetic draw we still had with each other.

"I'll be right back," I said, leaning over to Reagan as the rest of our friends toasted to the pending new year behind us.

"Wait, where are you going?"

"You know where."

Filled with a ton of liquid confidence, I slammed my latest empty shot glass down onto the bar, ran my hands through my passion twists and stepped toward him, one uneasy foot at a time. My entire way there, through the thick of the growing New Year's Eve crowd, my eyes stayed on his, almost begging him to forgive me, still adore me, not hate me. And as I got closer, the pounding of my heartbeat steadily increased, regret beginning to overtake the liquid courage. But I pressed on, knowing that at this point, there was no turning back. That would have been even more humiliating.

"Hi, Liv," he said as I walked up to him, his eyes tracing the length of my body.

"Hi, there. Do you think we could talk?"

I bit my bottom lip nervously, praying that he wasn't going to immediately reject my request. I hadn't thought that part completely through when I'd started on my journey, when I'd decided I needed to speak to him immediately. The ugly truth I didn't want to face was that he had every right to react in whatever way made him comfortable. And I knew that, glazed-over eyes and all. So, I stood there awaiting his response and braced myself for the worst-case scenario.

"Sure," he replied, stepping off to the side and guiding me to do the same with his large hand lightly placed on my back.

"You look really handsome," I admitted with a sigh once we were on our own, just a few steps away from his watchful friends but secluded enough for there to be at least somewhat of a private conversation.

"Thank you. You look stunning, per usual."

His eyes lit up almost uncontrollably and the smirk I'd once been thrilled by slipped out from his face. It reminded me of the look he'd had on our first non-date, one of awe, where he seemed to be asking me *How did I get so lucky?* without a single word. I missed that look. It had at one time made me believe I could have it all. Now it just felt like it came with a lot of unsaid, really sad words and maybe even a heaping load of regret.

Thomas must have felt similarly as he quickly corrected himself and returned back to the stoic look that he'd been giving me since he saw I was there.

"It's been a while, Liv," he said, his deep voice matching the serious expression on his face.

"I know."

"Not cool."

"I know."

I adjusted my stance in my heels as I awkwardly readied myself to receive whatever verbal punishment he wanted to lay on me. I deserved it after all. And lowest of keys, some part of me kind of needed it to feel better about hurting the one person I'd never wanted to let down.

"I definitely wasn't expecting to see you here," I added.

"Yeah, same. But maybe it's for the best, since I think you've been avoiding me, right?"

And there it was. Not a verbal punishment at all, but a truthful acknowledgment. That was maybe worse.

"Honestly, Thomas, I just haven't known exactly what to say," I admitted, holding myself back from drawing in closer to him.

"Is it because of the job back home? Is that why you started pulling back from me?"

"Yeah," I said quietly.

Of course he'd figured it out, I realized. At the end of the day, it wasn't that hard to understand. With me now most certainly leaving, I'd *had* to cut my ties and run off before I got too deep with him, before I allowed myself to believe…

Thomas nodded silently with a full understanding washing over his face. Then, as if he needed the space to process his thoughts, he backed up a few steps from me before continuing. "Did you ever think you weren't the only one whose feelings needed protecting?"

"Yeah. Every day, really."

I locked eyes with him once more, tears threatening to fall from mine, but desperate to cry out to him and remind him how I wasn't an evil person. I'd just been scared. And was that so hard to understand?

"And yet you still..."

"And yet I still... I just—"

"Chose to shield yourself from me, of all people," he interjected.

I stood in silence, once again at a loss for words, watching the man before me admit how my actions had affected him. How in my haste to take care of me, like I'd *always* had to do before—you know, get in front of the pending rejection, focus on my career and my friends, not let it break me down too much—I'd failed to trust him. I'd failed.

Neither of us moved, even as it was clear that the conversation had ended, our legs or minds or both somehow paralyzed into this one position. What else more was there left to say, really? We'd been a thing, a beautiful thing, an unexpected thing for months—but ultimately something I couldn't rely on not to eventually hurt me. And so then, we weren't a thing...not anymore.

All around us, the energy of the rooftop grew exponentially as it suddenly dawned on me that we were nearing the time of the NYE countdown. To my left and right, I saw people frantically pouring champagne into their flutes, getting their noisemakers ready and signaling to their smooch partners they were indeed the one. Behind me, I knew my crew was doing about the same, going through the motions to prepare themselves for the moment Reagan had promised me...the whole reason we were here in the first place. I knew they were getting their toasts ready, each one with their favorite drink in their hand and maybe a glass of champagne, too. That they were likely watching us from afar, waiting to see if we'd break our gaze in time so I could rejoin them, dancing and shouting my way into the new year.

And yet I couldn't move. Thomas didn't, either. Our feet plastered just a few steps apart, our bodies barely within arms' length, but our eyes remained locked in—refusing, for some reason, to let go, even as we finally heard the crowd begin its countdown.

Ten, nine, eight, seven, six, five, four, three, two...one! Happy New Year!

As shouts of joy filled every speck of the rooftop except one, so did bursts of confetti and the sound of clinking drinks and noisemakers. We'd made it to a new year, spent it together, in fact, but not like either of us had expected.

Thomas stepped toward me, the closest he'd dared to get all night, and finally leaned over and kissed me on my cheek. It was achingly close to my lips and provided me with just enough time to smell his signature Le Labo scent, but it was over in two seconds.

"Good night, Olivia," he said. "I really do hope you get out of New York everything you came here for."

"Happy New Year, Thomas," I replied, my voice barely coming out as it got caught in my throat, a signal that even my body knew it was really, really over this time.

As he walked away, the tears I'd been successfully holding back instantly began pouring out. And my body, once poised and braced for the verbal punishment that of course never came—because that wasn't the kind of man he'd ever been—slumped over with exhaustion, trying desperately to prevent the heaving and wailing I felt coming on.

Thankfully, before I could fully melt down in front of what felt like the world, I felt a small hand on my shoulder and the reassuring voice that had been with me since I'd stepped out of the JFK International Airport months before.

"It's okay, Liv," Reagan said, bringing me into her embrace. "It's going to be okay. I promise."

I didn't have the heart or the ability to tell her how much it wasn't.

"Okay, let's go to the bathroom," she added.

With her arm still around me, Reagan started walking me out of the rooftop toward the hallway where the bathrooms were and holding me up so that if you didn't know the situation, you might have just thought she was helping a friend who'd had a bit too much to drink. We passed by tables and sections of the fanciest-clothed people, all dancing, all happy, all oblivious to the two women trying to get past them so that the one in the sequined minidress could cry her heart out in private. So I could finally release every fear I'd been holding in ever since I'd gotten Walter's message.

When we finally reached our destination and stepped inside, Reagan quickly locked the door behind us and turned to me with sympathetic eyes.

"It's okay, now, Liv," she repeated from earlier. "You can let it all out now."

And I did.

Under the cover of the loud music and the insulated bathroom, I let out the loudest wail and cried and cried and cried until I didn't think I had any tears left in me.

Chapter Seventeen

In the privacy of a Midtown bathroom, Reagan stood by, without judgment, and let me cry until my screams eventually turned to sniffles. Only then did she reach for some tissue to pass to me, somehow knowing that doing so before then would have been a futile effort on her part. Thankfully, after about fifteen to twenty minutes of uninterrupted tears, I calmed down enough to be able to take it from her hand and try—at least attempt—to pull myself together.

"I'm so sorry," I said to her once I felt I could finally get words successfully out of my mouth. "You shouldn't have to see me like this."

"For what? Please don't apologize for having feelings or needing a friend."

"I just don't do this, you know. I don't break down crying in front of people."

I wiped the tissue all around my face, effectively removing the majority of the makeup I'd painstakingly applied just hours before in her flat. But it didn't matter in that moment. I needed to try to start erasing the remnants of this embarrassing situation away, so if that meant my Fenty foundation went with it, then so be it.

"I'm used to being there for others," I admitted. "Not the other way around."

"We all need support sometimes, Liv," Reagan replied, passing me another tissue, but this one she'd wet slightly beforehand to keep me from having pieces of tissue stuck to my face. "Maybe the people who are always there for others even more so. And honestly, if you can't cry with your friends, who can you cry with?"

"Yeah," I answered softly. "I know."

It dawned on me that this was the same refrain I'd had in my conversation with Thomas, and the tears started pouring out again as I recalled the expression on his face as he'd watched me, unable to say anything back to him except a continuous acknowledgment that he was right. I was the bad guy, the villain in our story. *Where can the waterworks still be coming from?* I wondered. *Isn't there a limit to just how much any one person can cry?*

"Do you want to talk about what you're feeling right now?" she asked. "You don't have to, but if you want to, I'm here."

"I appreciate that, Rae. Genuinely."

Through more sniffles, I attempted once again to dry up my tears, breathing in and out deeply to calm down my nervous system.

"And I do want to talk about it," I admitted. "I just don't know if I have the words to fully express everything running in my head right now."

"I know, *cher*," Reagan said, drawing near to me and taking my hands in hers. "But try."

Those were the exact same words she'd said to me at the party in Brooklyn months before, indicative of the kind of unconditional support she offered her friends with just a smidge of challenging when needed. Indeed, with those five small words, she conveyed so much. That she understood the difficulty I was having, that she could relate to my fear and regrets, that she was there for me if I spoke about it or not—but importantly, in addition to all that, she wanted me to give it a shot. Try. Just try. Three little letters, yet they carried so much weight.

"Well, you know I'm not someone who gets swept off her feet," I started up, wiping at my eyelids again with the wet tissue. "I had a plan, Rae! And it was a good plan, a *perfect plan*, one that would set me up for the kind of future I could only dream of as a young girl living in Brixton."

I glanced over at her and saw how attentively she was listening and was all at once comforted and uneasy. Needing to distract myself with something while I spoke, I walked toward the bathroom mirror and began fluffing my hair, as if the curls in my passion twists really mattered at a time like this. Somehow it helped me continue, however; just the act of focusing on something mundane gave me the strength I needed to explain the devastation I was dealing with.

"But Thomas did the thing that never happens," I continued. "He literally came into my life and changed everything. He made me start to believe that I could have real love. That someone might want me for me and not suggest that I had to choose him over my career. That someone would actually desire me, all of me, with all my quirks and my extra-ness. For a brief moment, I thought I could have it all, but we know that's not true. I'm not living in a Disney movie here. And so before I could get hurt again, be disappointed once again…before I got caught up too much…"

I paused to try to gather my thoughts, realizing that I was fumbling over my words toward the end of my explanation as I continued struggling trying to describe the conflict in my head and heart to someone else. I hoped that Reagan could understand the gist of what I was saying…that she could hear me even through my failed words.

"Walter's message about the promotion, it just reminded

me what my priorities were supposed to be. The perfect plan. And nothing else," I added.

"So you ended things to prevent yourself from being hurt again?" she asked.

"Something like that. I guess."

Except I never actually said the words to him; I just slowly disappeared before he could eventually disappoint me and turn out like every other guy before him, I thought to myself.

"But aren't you hurt now, anyway, *cher*?"

Reagan's question, while genuine and meaningful, still stung. And it instantly made me pause the fluffing of my hair in the mirror. I turned back around to her and quietly mouthed, *Yes*.

Seeing the way my body slumped over, Rae sprang into action and immediately removed the space between us, grabbing me and pulling me into another one of her warm embraces. At first, I barely allowed my arms to hug her back, but as she stood unrelenting and unwilling to let me go, I slowly gave in and finally squeezed her back. All this did, of course, was incite more tears, but by then, I had no more fight left in me to try to swallow them down or prevent them from tumbling down my face. Instead, I just held on to her tightly and let the tears do as they wished, wetting up her bare left shoulder in the process.

"Listen, you know I know a thing or two about making perfect plans," she whispered, still gripping me tightly. "I mean, I created a list and a rewards plan to finally begin taking risks in my life for God's sake, and even then, it was really hard for me to stop relying on the crutch of perfectionism in the areas of my life where I was trying to mask my fear. So, I get it. I get why you've needed to make your plans and stick to them, because not doing so is really scary, right?"

"Yeah," I replied.

"But here's the thing, *cher*. I would never tell you not to make your plans. I just would ask you to consider how it can actually *be* a perfect plan if it doesn't allow room for you to fall in love with a man who literally makes your heart jump. How is a plan like that really serving you?"

I stood there in silence, still holding on to Reagan and thinking really hard about her last set of questions. The truth was I didn't have a ready response for her. I don't think she actually expected me to. But that, in only a way that a true friend could, her job was simply to toss the challenging thought into the universe and allow me to consider it, to question what it meant that I'd given up hope that my plans made room for love, and the moment I was presented with the opposite—I ran.

After a few more minutes, I finally started releasing my grip on her, allowing my arms and then hers to slowly fall back by our sides. I'd got the strength and the love and the challenge I needed to proceed forward, so now it was time to do so—and at least try to enjoy what was left of the party. After all, we'd come here presumably for me. I'd be letting myself and the others down if I just stayed in the bathroom all night.

I moved back to the mirror so I could reassess my look. From the neck down, at least, I still appeared as if I was a woman ready to party. Amazingly, the straps that were wrapped around my calves were even still intact. And because Reagan had had the foresight to take my white blazer off me as soon as we'd entered the bathroom, that had also been saved from any potential makeup and tearstains. But oh, my face was a wreck.

"Don't worry—I got you," Reagan said as she joined me in the mirror and began pulling makeup essentials out of her clutch, including her mascara, blotting papers, eyeliner, bronzer and red lipstick. "Now, obviously, I don't have your foundation, but your skin is gorgeous, so we won't worry too much about that and just focus on everything else. I do think the blotting papers might be able to help us smooth out some areas where there are tear streaks, so we can try that, too. That, with some mascara and eyeliner, and you'll be brand-new."

"Rae, who are you?" I laughed. "Why do you just have all this stuff in your purse? Not that I'm complaining, but...wow."

"Girl, you know I stay ready so I don't have to get ready. Plus, ever since Jake revealed that a proposal is coming soon, I keep some small essentials with me just in case. Because you know I will be a mess when it happens, and before we take any photos, I'm going to need someone to help me wipe my face down!"

I chuckled along with her, realizing suddenly that it was the first time I'd laughed in hours and just how much I'd needed it.

"Well, if it happens while I'm still here, I got you, too."

"Oh, I know," she said with a wink. "That's not even a question."

Once Reagan was done prepping her makeup area, stacking up the items in the order she planned to use them, she went about the business of repairing my once flawlessly applied makeup.

Gently, she used a combination of the blotting papers and some damply wet napkins to reduce the smearing that had occurred as a result of my tears, lightly dabbing each part of my face, from my forehead to the areas that creased around my full lips. Then she motioned for me to lift my eyes upward so that she could reapply my eyeliner unobstructed to my lower lash line and then smudge it a bit, allowing my eyes to still pop despite no longer having the sparkly mauve eye shadow I'd previously worn. After that, Reagan moved to the mascara, dipping the wand into its case multiple times before she finally pulled it out and added three full coats to each of my lashes. I legit looked as if I had on false lashes when she was done, which was no small feat since I'd always felt that mine were never as long or as full as I wanted them to be. Lastly, she took the fleshy part of her middle finger and swiped the bronzer onto it, and then circled that around the upper parts of my cheeks.

By the time she was done, you could barely tell that this wasn't my original look. The only slight giveaway was some of the puffiness that remained near my eyes from all the damn crying, but honestly, she'd basically performed a miracle.

"Wow," I said, staring into the mirror in awe. "You might have missed your calling as a makeup artist, babes."

"Oh, definitely not. This was one of those *desperate times call for desperate measures* kind of things. I would never want to do this for anyone else regularly. The pressure alone…no, I'll stick with writing."

"Fair, fair," I replied, laughing with a slight roll of my eyes.

It felt nice to smile again—cathartic, even.

"Okay, now there's one thing left to do," Reagan said as she meticulously began putting all her makeup back into her purse.

"Okayyy," I replied with only a small bit of hesitation.

"When we walk out of here, I want you to strut out of this bathroom like nothing just happened. Pretend you're a nineties supermodel on the runway, for all I care. But you walk out of here with your head held high, your shoulders arched back and your toes pointing forward. For all anyone should know, you came to the bathroom for the same reason we all do—to freshen up or to use it. That's it."

"So what you're telling me," I said with a smirk, already pre-giggling at the TikTok reference I was getting ready to use. "Nobody's gonna know."

"How would they know?" she replied with a wink, and unlocked the door back to reality.

In a flash, I quickly scooped up my blazer, put my arms back through it and walked out just as Reagan had directed—all the way back to the rest of the crew, who had by now migrated from the bar to an open area near the carousel. As we approached them, we were instantly greeted with smiles and cheers, and two glasses of champagne—one for me, and one for Reagan.

"Welcome back," Keisha said, dancing circles around us and cajoling us into joining her party groove as she swayed side to side while Usher's "Bad Girl" played in the background. "You may have missed the first toast, dear Liv, but guess what? The beauty of a New Year's Eve party is that there's always a chance for another one. So, we saved these for y'all because you can't very well start the new year without some bubbly. I won't allow you to jinx yourself like that. Not on my watch. No, ma'am."

"I'm very down for that," I replied.

"Tuh. Say less then, my girl!"

Keisha turned around briefly and grabbed her own glass of champagne, nudging Gigi, Jake and Brandon to join us while I playfully bumped Reagan on her side, silently thanking her again for everything. It took another couple minutes for everyone to have a full glass in their hands, but once the logistics were all handled, there we were, all in a circle, our smiles and glasses lifted high, giving me a new shot at a new beginning without ever needing to acknowledge all the sadness that preceded it.

"Cheers!" we all screamed out in unison, clanking our glasses together and then dutifully taking our individual sips of the sparkling wine meant for celebrations.

It was just the reset I needed after such a hard and draining experience, and I couldn't have been more grateful for this set of human beings if I tried.

I looked around briefly to see if Thomas was still around but never found him again. It was just as well, I thought. Reagan had given me a lot to consider in the bathroom, and I didn't need to see him again until I could firmly and assertively answer all the questions she'd posed once and for all.

Chapter Eighteen

At approximately 6:15 p.m., with the office quiet and no sign of Walter's stomping feet coming down the hallway, I closed my laptop, put my Slack notifications on Away and set about packing up all my stuff to head home.

This was the new me.

Still Team Extra, still utterly committed to my job, but finally starting to trust myself and the work I'd put in for our management group enough that I didn't feel obligated to stay until 9:00 p.m. every night to prove I belonged there. This meant that if the building wasn't metaphorically burning down, there was no good reason that I couldn't leave out before 6:30 p.m. like everyone else—even, critically, Walter, who'd made a New Year's resolution to spend more nights at home with his fiancée.

To be fair, it was winter in New York City, so I still wasn't beating the sunset home. But this was progress I was very proud of. Progress that hadn't come about as part of some easy revelation, but one that had come through countless nights of self-examination and finally, at the end, a sense of calm and self-assurance that washed over me. These nightly self-check-ins had started off as just excuses to agonize over Reagan's questions, but slowly they'd begun evolving so that by week three, the whole thing had turned into revelation after revelation about how I wanted to live my life going forward.

And so, in the three weeks since the infamous New

Year's Eve party meltdown, I'd come to understand a few important things about myself:

1. I'd never, not once, failed to give something in my career my all. This was the number one thing everyone at work knew about me: if Liv was on the case, she would move mountains before she let you down. And while that meant some long nights and sometimes not having the people in my life understand my dedication, it had also gotten me to where I was right now—on the precipice of everything I wanted. I'd take that exchange any day!

2. Despite this shining example of what happened when I didn't quit staring me in my face, I'd stopped myself over and over when it came to my love life, cutting things off before things got too hard or going numb before I was vulnerable enough with my partner that they could hurt me if they wanted to. That was what David had meant in our last conversation in London, I realized. He was an insensitive idiot for saying I'd chosen my ambition over us, but he'd been right that I'd checked out on him a long time before that talk and nothing he could have said would have stopped me.

It was in the nightly check-ins that I'd come to understand this was all part of my way to protect myself because I could never count on the men I dated. But what I could always count on was my career going exactly as I planned if I put in the work, and so I relied heavily on that. I was essentially like the woman who didn't consciously understand that the reason she loved shopping for shoes so much was because, unlike with her clothing, she could confidently say which shoes would look good on her and what size worked for her in different styles, etcetera. If you knew that a 40 always fit no matter what shoe store you shopped at, for example, why even deal with the messiness of trying to figure out which clothes fit and looked nice on you when that could vary so much in every store across the UK and America? *Because you still need clothes is eventually what that woman might realize, just like I eventually realized I wanted/needed love, too.*

3. I was a damn rock star! Clearly everyone at my job saw it, and so I needed to believe it, too, instead of constantly taking on more and more work to prove my worth. That was how I'd ended up in New York after all, right? With no sense of what I'd be doing but a belief that if I excelled at yet another thing they put before me, I'd prove once again that I deserved what I'd already proved I deserved.

4. I desperately missed Thomas, and even more than that, I loved him…and that—that realization—had been the most eye-opening. For I'd never really loved anyone like that before, not really. My parents, my brother, my friends, yes…but a man who could get up and leave at any moment? No. I'd never dared. And so the part of my brain that hadn't been ready for that had needed to run away as fast as humanly possible. But I'd been a fool to let my fears prevent me from just letting him love me back. *What a mess.*

On this day, however, at now 6:25 p.m., I, Olivia Robinson, was not a mess. In fact, more than anything, I was clear and prepared for whatever came next. With my workbag fully repacked, I grabbed my cherry-red coat, tied it around my waist and headed for the door. As I walked past Walter's office, I saw him engaged in a similar fashion, hurriedly closing down his work so he could get out of the building on time. I nodded toward him, and with a simple wink, he reaffirmed my decision.

"See you tomorrow, Olivia," he said, stuffing stacks of papers into his briefcase.

"Have a good night, Walter," I replied, continuing my

procession forward, past the cubicles, then to Wendy's desk, to the lifts on our floor and through the atrium once I made it downstairs.

As I walked through the now equally silent atrium—the only sounds being the echoes of my heels click-clacking on the floor—I reached into my workbag and scooped up my phone. I'd followed through on one commitment to myself—now it was time to make good on the second. I clicked on Thomas's name and waited for the phone to start dialing.

"Liv," he said, answering on the second or third ring.

His voice sounded gravelly—his deep baritone piercing through the raspy whisper he was attempting—but also incredibly familiar, like the way it felt to hear my mum's *Welcome home* after a long day of work.

"Is everything okay?"

In the background, I heard the also unmistakable sounds of New York bustling all around him, the way the idle chatter resounded in the walls of the train, the muffled announcement from the conductor probably alerting passengers that the doors were closing and then the whoosh that told me he was on the move again.

"Yes, everything's fine," I replied. "I... I..."

I breathed in deeply, trying to steady my nerves for what I was getting ready to say, and then with a burst of energy, I blurted it out as fast as I could before I stopped myself. "I'm really sorry about the way I handled things with us, but I was hoping we could talk sometime this week if you're free."

Seconds went by as I awaited his response with bated breath, wondering if he'd even heard me, if his phone had cut off on the train or if it had come through loud and clear and he was just trying to figure out how to nicely tell me no.

Finally, after what felt like an hour of torture, I heard his voice saying something into the phone, jolting me out of my thoughts in time to get back present into the conversation.

"Did you want to meet up?" he asked.

"Yeah, I think that would be nice."

"Okay."

He paused yet another set of painstakingly long seconds, and I couldn't help but wonder what was going through his mind. We hadn't spoken to each other in weeks, after all, and here I was, calling him out of the blue. If it were me, I'd be saying, *You barely had any words to say the last time we saw each other, and now you want to talk?* if I even answered the phone.

Thank God he's not like me.

"I can do tomorrow after work if you're free then," he said.

"That would be perfect. Thank you."

"Sure, it's no problem. Are you good to come to my place? Feels like somewhere quiet might be best for us."

"Absolutely," I replied, maybe a little too eagerly. "Does seven o'clock work for you?"

"Yeah, I'll be home by then. I'll text you my address."

"Okay, great. I'll see you then."

"Good night, Liv."

"Good night, Thomas."

And with that, we both ended the call, his voice still reverberating in my ears and making me miss him that much more. The silence at the end of the call was maybe even worse than the pauses as he'd gathered himself throughout, but that was okay...it was just my central nervous system realizing what I already knew, I told myself. Yes, what I was doing was terrifying, but I owed it to myself to do the scary thing in pursuit of love for once.

After a series of deep breaths in and out, I slipped my phone back into my workbag and continued on my walk out of the building, past the maze of wooden benches and perfectly manicured, plush green bushes and out into the cold, damp January air. It was just the bolt I needed to not start overthinking. In fact, January in New York felt a lot like London, with its gray skies, frigid weather and an energy that propelled me forward, toward my train station and then eventually home, where I had only one thing on my agenda for the night: pick out a killer outfit worthy of getting my man back.

Standing in front of Thomas's prewar walk-up building on West Seventy-Fifth Street in my camel-brown nude sweaterdress with its asymmetrical collar that dipped past my left shoulder, cinched at the waist and then fell to about mid-calf like a proper pencil skirt, I had an epiphany that I was planning to use as my saving grace no matter his reaction.

This might end in failure, I thought, *but I'm not going to let fear talk me out of trying yet again.*

With all the courage I could muster, I made my way up the redbrick steps winding toward the front door and dialed his apartment number into the call box. Within a few seconds, his voice boomed through the speaker, calling out my name as both a question and a response.

"Liv?" he asked.

"It's me, yeah," I replied, trying not to awkwardly fidget before I even saw him.

"Okay, come on up."

He sounded calm—chill, even—which stopped me in my tracks only briefly as I pondered if that meant good or bad things for my prospects. I also knew I had to catch the door before it locked again, so with another deep breath in and out, I quickly pulled the handle and walked into the building. *There's no turning back now.*

Thomas's flat sat on the second floor of the building, like mine, which gave me even more time to gather my thoughts. It was odd even being here, really. As much time as we'd spent together and even FaceTimed while he was home, it hit me sort of ironically that this would be my first time seeing it in person. It was like telling someone you loved them only after you'd broken up.

Oh, right. I'm planning to do that, too, I said to myself. Well, I guess this made more sense than I'd realized, then.

After carefully making my way up the stairs so that I didn't trip in the deep chocolate knee-high boots that fit perfectly under my dress, I turned to the left and saw a door swing open. And there he was, waiting for me. Still somewhat dressed in his clothes from work but far more relaxed, he wore a pair of black trousers that looked like they would have made any tailor proud. He'd also unbuttoned his shirt at least twice and taken it out of his pants, letting it casually fall across his torso.

If I wasn't careful, I could easily see myself getting swept up in all the ways he physically enticed me—that part was easy. But I wanted tonight to be about something deeper, a chance for us to be emotionally honest with each other and experience the type of intimacy I'd always wanted but never believed I could have.

"You made it," he said, holding the door open wide so that I could slide past him and into his entryway.

"I did, yeah," I replied, staring into his eyes as he closed the door behind him. "I said I would."

"Yeah, you did."

His voice dropped to a soft whisper, and it instantly broke my heart because I knew what that meant. I'd also told him I was ready to be with him and had gone back on that statement, so who was I to suddenly have my words believed? He didn't have to say that out loud. He probably never would. But I felt every bit of the sting in just those three words alone.

I cleared my throat and tried to start again.

"Is this a shoes-off place?" I asked him, still standing in his entryway, flanked by two closets that faced each other.

The way the space was set up, he couldn't exactly get by me unless he touched me, whether it was to brush my shoulder or maybe guide me to the side by placing his gentle hand on the small of my back. Part of me wanted to see if he'd try, if he was as desperate as I was for his touch—not necessarily sexually, but in that way that told a person you hadn't completely closed yourself off from them. He waited by the door, however, nodding yes as his reply and then watching me as I gingerly slipped the boots down my legs and off my feet.

"Do you need help?" he asked eventually, maybe suddenly remembering that we weren't strangers and he could, in fact, put his hands on me without it being a problem.

By then, however, I was practically done and slightly deflated that it had taken him so long to offer. "No, I'm good. Thank you."

Now able to proceed further into his place, I walked into the sitting room that somehow looked exactly as I pictured it and also sort of not. There were parts of it, like the double-paned windows, which took up almost the whole wall next to the kitchen, that looked much larger in person. Then there were other things, like his coffee-brown sofa and the matching entertainment center underneath his TV, that were a perfect match from what I'd seen over the phone. In a way it reminded me of us and how I could have been looking at us for so long and while I'd had some stuff very right, some parts I'd had so, so very wrong.

"Do you want something to drink?" he asked, following me into the sitting room and watching me marvel beside him.

"Water would be good, yes, thanks."

God, we sounded like two people who'd never met each other before, still trying to be incredibly polite and tiptoe around each other. *This is not at all what I want.*

Thomas dipped into the kitchen, which was visible from the sitting room via a built-in bar/counter, where he'd added two tan-and-brown bar stools since the last time we'd been on video.

"Are these new?" I asked, pointing toward them as he closed the fridge door and passed me a chilled bottle of water.

"Yeah, they are. I got them as a beginning-of-the-year gift for myself."

"Oh, okay," I replied, cringing inside at the reference to the new year. "Well, that's great, Thomas. They look great."

We both stared into the other's eyes, not really knowing what else to say or maybe having so much to say, we didn't know where to start. Either way, the tension was palpable as I opened up my bottle and gulped down as many droplets of the refreshing liquid as I could without choking. After I finished the water in one fell swoop, I turned back to him and finally pushed the words out of my mouth.

"So, I wanted to…" I began.

"So, you wanted to…" he chimed in, both of us starting at the same time and realizing at once that the other was about to say something, too.

"I'm sorry—you go first," I added…only it was once again at the same time as he tried to tell me the same.

"Wow, we really suck at this," he said, finally daring to smile at me due to the insanity of the moment.

"Yeah, very much so," I agreed, grinning as well.

If nothing else, the absurdity had broken the ice between us. It also reminded me how much I missed laughing with him.

"Why don't we sit down first?" Thomas offered, gesturing toward his couch. "Then at least we're comfortable and you can tell me what you wanted to talk about."

"Okay," I said, obliging and plopping down onto the brown wool cushions.

Once I got comfortable and steadied my breathing, I looked across the couch toward Thomas and began the speech I'd practiced in my bathroom mirror all night.

"Let me start by saying I know how much I hurt you, and I'm really sorry for that. It's no excuse, but I was scared and couldn't see my way past all my worries that I would inevitably fall in love with you—a man who needs to stay here—while I need to go back home, and by the summer, I'd be a wreck. The ironic part of it all is that I was already in love with you. I just didn't want to admit it because, honestly, everything about us is a disruption to the life I planned for myself. And that's…thrilling in a way that is hard to explain, but it also terrified me to the point where I'd lay in bed all night, chest tight, agonizing about how I got myself in this situation."

Thomas listened attentively as I continued talking, barely moving on his side of the couch, but by his facial expressions, I could tell he was trying to understand me even as I sometimes fumbled over my words while trying to explain my thought process. It wasn't like I was ever really going to be able to fully explain all the fears I'd been experiencing at the time because I barely understood them, but I knew I owed it to him—to us—to try.

"So, anyway," I continued with a sigh, "I don't want you to think it was an easy decision to back up from us—

because it wasn't. One part of me was sure that it was the best thing to do to avoid either of us getting even more hurt than we already were, and the other part was so angry at myself for running away from the first man outside of my family who ever supported me and didn't want to change me and just… You just wanted me for me. And I wanted you for you, but I didn't… I don't know, I guess I didn't know how to handle that when it was in front of me."

"Do you regret us meeting and getting to know each other?" he asked, finally interjecting, and thankfully stopping me before I spiraled down a word vomit rabbit hole.

"No, absolutely not."

"Okay."

His mouth might have said *okay*, but his body language seemed unbelieving still.

I leaned my chest slightly toward his to emphasize my point. "Honestly, I don't. I just wish I'd really been ready for it, for us, when I said I was."

"Hmm."

Thomas sat still on his side of the couch, not moving toward me at all but staring deeply into my eyes and effectively cutting off whatever was left of my speech. Really, I wasn't doing that great of a job anyway, so that was probably for the best. After a few moments in silence, he spoke again.

"Sooo, did you come here tonight to basically say what you couldn't say on New Year's Eve, or…"

"No," I answered, interrupting him this time. "I came by because I miss you, and I wanted to tell you that I loved you…love you…and even if you don't feel the same, I wanted you to know that you're one of the best things that has come from my trip to America. And you're a great guy. And I love you. I…"

My voice broke as I tried to get my words out, pausing

each time I admitted my love for him, as the tears started flowing down my cheeks and replacing any last remaining chance that I had at keeping my composure.

"Hey, hey, it's okay," he said, finally removing the space between us on the couch as he jumped toward me in a flash.

Once our thighs were nearly touching, Thomas wrapped his arms around my shoulders and pulled me into him, providing me with the comfort I probably didn't deserve since I was the one trying to apologize.

"I'm really sorry," I said, crying into his chest. "I was an idiot. I didn't fight for us... I was Dwayne Wayne!"

"Liv," he said, interrupting me again. "You weren't an idiot. And you're not Dwayne Wayne because you're here now."

Thomas chuckled softly and then lifted my chin so that I could see his face and look into his eyes as he spoke.

"You were scared. I knew that. I mean, I was, too, for that matter. It's why I didn't pursue anything with you for months, but listen... I've never met a woman like you before. I've never had someone capture my thoughts so wholly and intensely and as quickly as you did. That's the only reason I stopped fighting what we so clearly had with each other. I just got to the point where I was willing to do it scared.

"But I knew... Hear me out, babe. I knew that you still weren't ready even when you said you were. I just really wanted you to be. I wanted you to be willing to do it scared with me."

"I am now," I whispered, slowly starting to wipe the tearstains off my face. "I am now, Thomas."

With regained confidence, I repeated myself, louder this time so that he'd know this was different than the last.

"Are *you* still? Maybe?" I asked.

"I wouldn't have even answered the phone the other day if I wasn't, Liv."

I raised my head again, and Thomas leaned back slightly, tilting his head to the side. It was reminiscent of the first day we'd met, sparking up the smirk that had always forced me to catch my breath no matter our surroundings. That smirk had literally been my kryptonite from day one, but tonight, while still incredibly sexy, it was more than that; it was a glimmer of hope that I hadn't completely blown my best chance at love.

"Does that mean...?"

"It means that I love you, too. And yes, I was hurt, but I never stopped loving you. And I'm here. Now. In the only place I'd want to be, with the only woman I want to be with."

Thomas's last few words came out slowly and intentionally, like he wanted to make sure I heard every syllable, and it penetrated my memory in a way that it couldn't be erased. In response, I leaned back into him, dropping my head onto his chest and scooping my arms around his torso. I squeezed him tightly and, closing my eyes, breathed in a sigh of relief that I hadn't messed up so royally that things couldn't be fixed.

Because he loves me. And he's here, I reminded myself. *Thank God for that.*

In return, Thomas enveloped my entire body, wrapping his thick arms around me and making sure that almost every part of our bodies was connected. Then, with nothing else left to say, he sunk his head onto my shoulder, inhaling me in.

We stayed exactly like that as the next several minutes turned into thirty, holding each other closely in a beautiful silence that was equal parts calming and secure. Eventually, our heartbeats and our breath patterns fell into the same pace, and I realized, in that very moment, that this was what my friends had been trying to talk about during the bachelorette weekend. This kind of elemental connection was rare, and once I'd stopped fighting it, it no longer felt scary at all—it was just…safe.

"You know," Thomas said, his deep and endearing voice sounding like a frog was trying to come out, as neither of us had spoken a word in quite a while, "you never actually asked me if I was willing to move to London when you go back home."

"What?" I asked, lifting my head slightly, unsure if I was confused and had misheard him or if he'd said what I thought he said.

"I said you never asked me," he repeated.

"Well, of course I wouldn't," I replied. "How many times have we talked about you loving the life you've built here? I wouldn't ask you to give that up."

"Yeah, I don't mean it in that way, not as in asking me to choose. I mean you never asked me what *my* thoughts were on it. You just assumed I'd be conflicted, but I'm not, Liv."

"What are you saying?" I asked, daring to actually look him in the eyes for this conversation.

I wanted—no, needed—him to be very clear, and I had to make sure I wasn't just hearing what I wanted to.

"I'm saying that I already work with clients in the UK. You know this. That's why I was on that flight that day. So, yeah, I'm not going to lie—it would be a big change, but not an impossible one. I'd already started talking to one of the partners I work with, and he was excited about the chance to have me overseas to give more face time to our clients there. But then…"

"I freaked out and started breadcrumbing you."

"Something like that, yeah."

"Wow. I just didn't think you'd be willing to give up all of this...for me."

"I know, but it's you. And for you, for us, I'm more than willing to take that chance."

"Okay," I said softly, and forced myself to let his words once again sit in my spirit.

I didn't want to run away from this feeling. I wanted to just take it in and enjoy it.

"To us doing it scared, then," I added, and then dropped my head back onto his chest, tucking myself into his embrace once again.

Correction, Olivia, I said to myself. *This is what it feels like to be fully and wholly loved for who you are.*

There was no way I was letting it or him go again.

Epilogue

"Are you still in your office, Olivia?"

Thomas's baritone voice boomed through my phone, somehow equally chastising and teasing me at the same time. I could hear his smirk even as he spoke, which made me move that much faster at packing up my tan Chanel tote bag so that I would prove him wrong.

"Yes," I said, hesitantly. "But... I promise I'm leaving now. I won't be late for lunch this time."

"Mmm-hmm. This is what you said the last time."

"I know, I know. But give a girl some credit. You know I'm still getting used to actually leaving the office during the day. But I am because I want to see you."

"And yet you're still in the office," he replied, his laugh bellowing into my ear.

"Because you're still on my phone! Okay, I'm leaving it now. Love you. See you soon."

"Love you, too."

As soon as I ended the call, I slipped my phone into my bag, made sure to silence my Slack notifications and headed out, passed the scores of other staff preparing to leave for lunch, too. I smiled to myself, vividly remembering the days when I'd be holed up in my office, save a welcome interruption from Wendy or Julie, too scared to enjoy lunch like every other person who worked at our company. For months, I'd worked through breakfast, lunch and dinner—always trying to outdo myself, prove that I could excel at the next thing and the next thing...and yet here I was, still excelling *and* making time to meet up with Thomas for lunch. It was nice. I guess Walter was right about his work-life balance motto.

Wendy's desk was my last hurdle to making it on time for my third lunch date with Thomas in two months—which, despite his lighthearted complaints about my tardiness for them, I'd really come to love. Not that Wendy herself was an obstacle, but a) her desk was positioned right by the lifts in the lobby, so you had to walk past her before you left out, and b) if anyone would know that Walter was looking for me or needed me to stay for some kind of emergency, it was her.

I braced myself as I walked up to her, the smile on my face hopefully sending signals that read *Please don't stop me!*

"Hey, Wends," I said, slowing down my stride but purposely not stopping. "I'll be back in a bit. If Walter asks..."

"Please," she said, shushing me off. "Go enjoy your lunch with your very handsome and charming boyfriend. Walter and the work will be here when you get back."

"Thanks, Wendy," I said, my smile growing wider and wider as I picked my pace back up, hit the button for the down lift and waved goodbye as I disappeared into it.

Moments later, I found myself walking into the cool air that only an early May afternoon in New York City could bring, joining the bustling crowd of people headed to the train. Now that it was officially spring, I'd taken the liberty to brighten up my wardrobe and today had worn a hot-pink sleeveless turtleneck shirt tucked into my rust-orange high-waisted wide-leg trousers. So, between that and the way my skin was glowing under the sun's bright gaze, I knew I was making a statement among the blues, blacks and tans most people still gravitated toward in the

Financial District, and I kind of loved it. It was just another way I was enjoying this new version of me. Plus, I'd been taking Reagan up on her offer to see her hairstylist, so my brown-and-blond highlighted passion twists had been replaced by my natural dark brown tresses, which fell right below my shoulders and blew effortlessly in the cool breeze.

It would be another twenty-five minutes before I walked onto Pier 45, my yellow stiletto pumps guiding me along the way, just in time to meet Thomas. It was the perfect middle ground between the Financial District and his office space in Midtown, but it was also known for some of the most amazing views in the city. I looked around the pier, checking to see if I'd missed him or shown up to the wrong place, when he suddenly appeared, handsome as always, and dressed in a navy blue blazer and white button-down that I was going to have to desperately stop myself from ripping off when he came nearer.

"Hey," he said, smiling brightly at me as he walked up to me.

"Hi, there."

I licked my lips to stop myself from jumping on top of him.

"You made it on time," he replied, his gray eyes twinkling under the sun and making my cheeks hurt from how much I couldn't drop them, either.

"I said I would."

"That you did, love. That you did."

As he leaned in to give me a hug and a kiss, his Le Labo cologne threatening to make me weak in my knees as always, I finally noticed the black plastic bag he had in his hand and instantly had an idea for what he'd brought us for lunch.

"Is that what I think it is?" I asked.

His wink told me everything I needed to know. Before he could stop me, I dipped my hand into the bag and grabbed one of the two foil-wrapped sandwiches out of it, claiming it as my own.

"You went to Hajji's and got us chopped cheese sandwiches for lunch?" I asked rhetorically, clearly already having the evidence in my hands.

"Well, you know, we're officially on countdown mode to leave here in a few months, so I figured we should make sure to get in all the bad-good food New York has to offer before we do."

"You're a genius," I said, unwrapping the top part of my sandwich and taking the biggest, most satisfying bite. "And OMG. I'm definitely going to miss this."

Thomas watched in awe, still unable to stop smiling as I savored the gloriously delicious and greasy beef-and-cheese treat. I very clearly enjoyed the decision he'd made and the effort it must have taken for him to go there and come back and still get here at the time we'd said. No wonder he'd been pestering me about being on time. It all made sense now.

"Don't worry," he said with a wink. "I might know a thing or two about how to make them myself. So you won't have to miss them too much."

"What? How have you kept this from me all this time?"

"A man's gotta keep some secrets, Liv. You already know about Rihanna… I can't tell you everything all at once."

I laughed heartily in between bites and then with my free hand, grabbed his so we could finally find our way to a bench to sit down and eat properly.

"I guess you're right," I replied. "But how did I get so lucky to find a man who can cook and who loves me?"

Out the corner of our eyes, we both spotted a couple getting ready to get up from a bench just a few steps away, so before he could respond, we instinctually looked at each other and booked it in our best dress shoes, not wanting to lose the spot. It was like old times' sake anyway, the way we banded together and made magic happen. We'd done that from the very start, as he'd helped me wrestle down not one but two pieces of luggage on that fateful September day. Now we'd bested the busy New York crowd all trying to find an empty spot near the water. What a team!

As we plopped down onto the bench, Thomas finally took his own sandwich out of the bag and passed me one of the bottles of water to wash mine down.

"I guess sometimes the best things come unexpectedly," he said, answering my question from before in such a Thomas-like way, one filled with hope even when I didn't have enough for us both.

But he was right. Everything about us had been unexpected. And yet probably the best thing that had ever happened to me.

"How much time do you have for us today?" he asked, biting into his chopped cheese as he awaited my reply.

"How about a lifetime?" I replied with a devious smile, knowing that he would get that I was only partially kidding.

I checked my watch and rolled my eyes at the time. "But also, probably another forty-five minutes."

"Perfect," he replied. "I'll take these forty-five minutes and the lifetime as long as I get to spend it all with you."

"Deal," I said, and leaned my back into his chest, enjoying the sun on our bodies, the chopped cheese in my belly and the man—my teammate—who I wanted to spend forever and ever with.

If New York never gave me anything else, that was all I ever needed from her and more.

* * * * *

A Deal With Mr Wrong
Anna James

MILLS & BOON

Anna James writes contemporary romance novels with strong, confident heroes and heroines who conquer life's trials and find their happily-ever-afters.

Want to learn more about Anna and her books?

Sign up for her newsletter: authorannajames.com.

Follow her on Instagram: @author_anna_james.

Visit the Author Profile page
at millsandboon.com.au.

Dear Reader,

What happens when your mother won't stop fixing you up with every eligible bachelor in town? Out of desperation to stop the endless stream of potential husbands, you strike a deal with your sworn enemy to act as each other's significant other for the next five weeks.

The trouble is, said enemy is sinfully sexy, devilishly handsome, and his kisses are to die for.

Sparks will fly...

Thank you for picking up this copy of *A Deal with Mr. Wrong*—book two in my Sisterhood of Chocolate & Wine series! For those who don't know me, I'm Anna James. I write contemporary romance, and although I've been writing for years, this is my first series with Harlequin. I hope you enjoy *A Deal with Mr. Wrong* as much as I enjoyed writing it. I'd love to hear what you think of Cooper and Piper's story. Please share your thoughts with me on Facebook and Twitter (annajames.author, @authorannajames) or drop me a line through my website, authorannajames.com.

Happy reading,

Anna James

PS: If you haven't read book one yet, you can pick up a copy of *A Taste of Home*, Layla and Shane's story, at Harlequin.com.

DEDICATION

For my cousin, Sue. Thanks for all your love,
your support and your encouragement. I miss you.

Chapter One

Piper Kavanaugh pulled her Honda Fit into the parking lot of the old, colonial mansion and parked in an empty space. Grabbing her purse, she exited the car and walked over to the side entrance to the building that would take her to the second floor and the three thousand square feet of space that would become her gallery.

Her gallery. Something she'd imagined opening ever since she visited the Museum of Modern Art in New York City as a little kid.

She grinned. That dream was about to become a reality now.

She punched in the code on the keypad and opened the door, making sure to relock it behind her. The room was empty now, except for the dining tables scattered throughout the space.

One of the first orders of business would be to put up walls separating the private dining room that was part of the Sea Shack restaurant that Layla Williams, the current owner of the mansion, ran on the first floor, from the grand staircase that led to the entrance to her gallery on the second floor.

Piper climbed the stairs, stopping at the top to fish out the keys Layla had given her from her purse.

She'd replace this standard wood door with something more appropriate for her gallery entrance. Perhaps a double door with glass panes? Yes. That would work.

"Piper," a familiar voice called.

She glanced over the rail to the room below and waved. Her older sister stood at the bottom of the stairs with a big grin on her face. "Hey, Mia. Come on up. Wait. How'd you get in?"

Another thing she'd need to change when she was open for business, since patrons would access her gallery directly from the parking lot and not— "Did Layla let you in from the restaurant?"

Mia nodded. "I hope you don't mind. I wanted to surprise you."

"No. Not at all." She'd never mind a visit from her sister, but the two businesses needed to be independent of each other. That included access.

Mia took the stairs two at a time and threw her arms around her when she reached the landing. "You're finally here."

Piper grinned and eased out of her sister's embrace. "The New Suffolk building department finally approved my renovation plans yesterday." Months after she'd submitted the layouts.

Mia laughed. "You know how small towns are."

"Local governments are all the same. It's called bureaucracy."

"When did you get in?" Mia asked.

Piper glanced at her watch. "A few hours ago. I grabbed the red-eye out of LAX last night. Mom picked me up at the airport in Boston this morning. I picked up the car you helped me find at Mom's place. Drove over to my new apartment and dumped my bags, grabbed a quick shower and came straight here."

"You must be exhausted," Mia said.

"Nah." Piper waved off Mia's concern. "I'm too excited.

And I grabbed a quick catnap on the drive from the airport to Mom's. Now come on, let's go inside." Piper smiled a mile-wide grin.

How lucky was she to find the perfect place for her gallery on a trip home to see her family a few months ago? Especially since she'd been searching for a location for some time.

Really lucky—or maybe it was fate? Dad would have said the latter. A sad smile crossed her face. He'd always believed in that stuff. As for her...not so much. She believed you carved out your own path in life.

Piper waited for the gut-clenching grief to choke her, like it always had before when she thought about her father. It didn't happen. Her stomach wasn't tied up in knots.

A mix of surprise and relief flooded through her. Surprise because she'd carried her grief with her for so long it was like a physical weight on her shoulders, and relief because that burden was now gone. Unlocking the door, she stepped inside and Mia followed.

"So, what do you think?" Piper gestured around the massive space with its classic crown molding and oak plank flooring. Her chest filled to bursting point. It was just as she remembered. "It's pretty great—right?"

"I'm just glad you're home to stay." Mia slung an arm around Piper's shoulder.

"Me, too." She missed the closeness she and Mia had shared growing up together. They'd been each other's confidantes throughout childhood.

Mia locked her gaze on Piper. "Ten years away was too long."

Piper sighed. Leaving right after high school graduation had seemed like her only option at the time. Life in

New Suffolk had been suffocating. She could…breathe in Los Angeles.

"I've missed having my little sister around," Mia continued.

"That won't be a problem anymore." With the help of a great counselor, she'd worked through the loss of her father. Yes, the ache was still there, but the anger and grief that consumed her in the years after his death had finally faded. Coming home now seemed right.

She mock-punched her sister in the arm. "Pretty soon you're going to complain I'm around too much."

Mia grinned. "Not a chance. So, what are you going to do with all this space?"

Piper laughed. "You always did like a renovation project. Tell me again why you're teaching instead of going back to TK Construction?" Her sister had been happy working at the family-owned construction company started thirty-five years ago by her father and his best friend, Ron Turner.

Mia shook her head. "This is about you, not me. Now, come on. Out with it. What are your plans for this place?"

Piper wouldn't press her sister further. Now was not the time. Once she settled in, she'd invite Mia over to her place. They'd have a bottle of wine and maybe some pastries from the Coffee Palace and she'd get Mia to open up.

"I'm going to close this area off." Piper walked over to the kitchen Layla's grandfather had installed when he'd made this upstairs an open-concept apartment for himself and his wife. Lucky for her he'd retired and moved to Florida a couple of years ago, when Layla bought the mansion. "Although I'll keep the island and turn it into a small bar." Fingers crossed the state would issue her permit to serve alcohol on the premises before her grand opening in a few weeks. She couldn't imagine hosting a show without serving something sophisticated to drink.

"This big space—" she wandered back into the living room, where they'd come in "—needs to be divided into smaller sections so I can display different art collections at the same time.

"I need to reconfigure the master bedroom to allow access to the bathroom from the main hall. That way I'll have two for public use. I'll use the remaining part of that room for my personal studio."

She couldn't wait to get back to painting and sculpting again—managing Blue Space gallery, in Los Angeles, over the past few years had made it difficult to pursue her own creativity.

"I assumed TK Construction will do the work?" Mia asked.

"Yes. I'd do the modifications myself if I had more time." Her father had made sure all three of his kids could swing a hammer. "But since I'm in a rush, I hired the best in town."

Mia glanced at her watch. "Hey, I've got to get to the Coffee Palace. My shift starts in fifteen minutes."

That was another thing she and her sister would talk about. Mia working part-time at the Coffee Palace made no sense. At least not to Piper. "No worries." Piper picked up the cylinder containing the final floor plans for the gallery renovation. "I need to get going, too. I'm supposed to meet Mom at the diner. I'm going to give her these—" she tapped the cylinder "—and we're going to have lunch."

"That's right. She mentioned meeting up with you for lunch today when we spoke earlier." Mia looked her in the eye. "She's really happy you decided to come home. She's missed you."

"I know. And I'm glad I'm home, too." It felt good. Piper

glanced around the space. It felt…right to come back now. "To new beginnings." She lifted her to-go coffee cup in the air.

Mia nodded and touched her cup to Piper's. "Cheers. I've really gotta go." She gave Piper a quick hug and started toward the exit. "Oh, one more thing." Mia stopped and turned to face her. "Big Brother is playing tonight at Donahue's."

Her eyes widened. "Nick Turner's band?"

Mia laughed. "Yes. They've gotten really good in the last few years."

"They must have if they're playing venues. What time does the band go on?"

"Eight."

"Sounds great. I'll see you there."

Mia gave her a thumbs-up. "Bye." She gave a little wave before she left.

Piper slung her purse and the cylinder containing the gallery floor plans over her shoulder. Stepping into the small hall, she locked the door and headed out.

Outside, the January cold surrounded her and she shivered. She was going to miss the warmer climate in LA, for sure, but at least the sun was shining. It took the edge off the frigid temperatures.

Piper walked along Main Street and passed the town entrance to the beach. The scent of salt and sea filled the air. In the summer months, umbrellas would dot the sand as far as the eye could see. Hordes of tourists and locals would bronze themselves beneath the sun and frolic in the salty ocean. Not a soul could be seen on the shore today. She passed by several tourist shops with signs in the windows indicating they were closed for the season. Crossing the street when she reached the New Suffolk Bank, she stepped inside the nearby diner.

Mom waved from a booth in the rear.

She strode over and dropped a kiss on her mother's cheek. Removing her winter parka, she slid into the booth opposite her.

"Don't you look lovely." Mom smiled.

Piper glanced at herself. The black trousers and teal long-sleeved, fitted, button-down cotton blouse with matching belt and low black pumps were more casual than the work attire she would normally wear, but this was small-town Massachusetts, not Los Angeles. "Thanks. I've made arrangements to meet with an artist later this afternoon whose work I want to feature in the gallery, so I wanted to change out of my comfy travel clothes."

"I already ordered our meals," Mom said.

"Oh, great." She grabbed the tube containing her floor plans. "I'm surprised you wanted to go over these here instead of the TK offices."

"I don't anticipate any significant changes since the last time we reviewed them. This way we get to have lunch together."

Piper smiled. Yes, it was good to be home. She handed the cylinder to Mom. "And these are perfect as is."

"Great. I'll take a look at the schedule and let you know who's available to start the renovations."

"No need." Piper waved off the notion. "I already spoke to Levi. He can start the day after tomorrow."

She and Levi Turner had kept in constant communication over the past few months so he could hit the ground running as soon as the building permits were approved.

"Okay." Mom nodded her head. "I'll give him the plans. He'll let you know if he has any questions."

A waitress approached with three dishes in her hand. "A Greek salad with chicken for you." She placed one of the plates in front of Piper. "And the same for you." She set an identical dish in front of Mom.

"I see you're planning to have leftovers." Piper pointed to the to-go container the server handed mom.

"Yes." Mom chuckled.

"Where would you like this?" The waitress gestured to the third plate.

"You can set that right here." Mom pointed to the empty space beside her.

"Who's that for?" Piper asked when the waitress left. "Is someone else joining us?"

Instead of answering, Mom stood and waved her hand in the air, as if trying to get someone's attention.

A tall man, in his late thirties if she had to guess, appeared in front of the table. He wore a gray suit with a white dress shirt and a gray-and-red striped tie. Formal attire for the diner, if you asked her.

"Hello, Jane." The man smiled.

"Blake." Mom slid out of her seat. "Please, join us. I hope you're in the mood for a turkey club."

"Oh." Blake gave a hesitant nod. "Sure. Sounds great."

Piper crooked a brow and sent an inquiring glance at her mother as Blake slid into the booth. She mouthed silently, "What's going on?"

Mom flashed an I-have-no-idea-what-you're-talking-about smile.

"You must be Piper," Blake said.

"I am." She offered him her hand and he shook it.

"Blake is the new bank president," Mom said.

Why was the new bank president joining them for lunch?

"I'll let you two talk." Mom dumped the contents of her plate into the plastic container the server had handed her earlier. She grabbed her purse, the salad and the tube containing the gallery floor plans. "See you later."

"Wait." Piper's eyes bugged out. "Where are you going?"

"I need to get back to the office." Mom flashed a quick smile and bolted before Piper could object further.

What the hell? She turned her attention back to Blake. "I'm sorry about that."

"It's no trouble. I'm sure she wanted to give us some privacy to discuss matters."

Discuss what matters? What was going on? She drew in a deep breath and blew it out.

Blake removed the turkey from the sandwich and set it aside. "I'm a vegetarian," he explained. "But I didn't want to be rude to your mother."

Great. Just great. You missed that little nugget, Mom. Your investigative skills are failing you. "I can order something else for you, if you'd like."

"No, thanks. This is fine." He lifted the sandwich, pausing before he bit into it. "So, what questions did you have?"

"I'm sorry. You have me at a disadvantage. I don't know what you're talking about."

His brows furrowed. "I'm here to talk to you about what types of business accounts we offer so you can find the type that best suits your needs."

"I opened my business accounts at your bank a few months ago." She'd worked with one of his employees last summer when she'd come home to meet with the town's planning and zoning department. Piper dug into her purse and withdrew the business card the man had given her and handed it to Blake.

"Ah." Blake nodded and handed the card back to her. "Your mother must not have known. We talked when she came in yesterday and she was under the impression you could use some advice."

Piper's gaze widened. Her mother knew damned well she'd already opened her business accounts. She'd gone with her to do some banking that very day.

"She suggested we meet for dinner—"

A red haze filled her vision. She didn't hear the rest of what Blake was saying.

Piper couldn't believe it. She'd been back in New Suffolk for less than twenty-four hours and her mother was up to her old tricks. Again.

How dare she try to set her up? With the bank president, no less.

Mom had made it her mission to find Piper a husband, even though that was the last thing she wanted. Why couldn't her mother understand that?

Blake shot her a quizzical glance.

Piper sighed. "I'm sorry this misunderstanding has inconvenienced you, Blake." She would read her mother the riot act for sure. For all the good it would do.

"It's no trouble." Blake grinned. "After all, I got a free lunch." He pointed to his plate. "I should get back to the bank."

Piper flashed a nervous smile. "Of course. Thanks again for coming this afternoon. And again, I apologize for the misunderstanding."

Blake smiled. He rose from the table and headed out.

Piper grabbed her cell and called her sister. "Did you know about this?" she demanded when Mia answered.

"Know about what?"

Piper dragged a hand through her hair. "That this lunch with Mom was really a setup?"

"What are you talking about? A setup for what?" Mia asked.

Piper explained.

"Oh, no. She's at it again," Mia said.

"Yes. How am I going to stop her?" Piper wasn't interested in dating Blake, or any of the others her mother had
tried to set her up with over the years.

Mia sighed. "She just wants you to be happy."

"I *am*." Which was more than she could say for her
mother. Piper couldn't imagine loving someone as much as
her mother had loved her father. Fifteen years after Dad's
death, she was still devastated by the loss.

"I don't need a man to make me happy." No way would
she end up like her mother.

Cooper Turner concentrated on the files in front of him.
Once again, his gaze strayed to the upper right corner of
his desk, like a grisly image you couldn't turn away from.
The large white envelope embossed with a lace pattern
taunted him.

He refocused on the task at hand. His response for the
wedding wasn't due for another week. Not that he could
decline the invitation. He'd agreed to be Everett Burke's
best man months ago, but things had changed since then.
Now he couldn't bring himself to drop the response card
in the mail.

Cooper closed his eyes and allowed his shoulders and
back to melt into the soft, cushioned leather of his chair.
He drew in a deep breath and exhaled, enjoying the moment of peace and quiet after another chaotic day at work.

"You're still here." Levi's voice echoed in the now-
empty Turner Kavanaugh Construction headquarters.

Maybe his brother would go away if he didn't acknowledge him? Cooper kept his eyes closed and remained still.

"I know you can hear me and I'm not going away,"
Levi continued.

He let out a muffled curse and opened his eyes. "It's
seven thirty. Shouldn't you be home with your son?"

"Noah is with his mother tonight. I don't have to be anywhere right now." Levi arched a brow. "What are you doing here this late?"

"I'm working." Coop gestured to his desk.

"We both know you're caught up on all of your projects."

He wouldn't deny it. There was nothing that couldn't wait until morning.

"Come out with me tonight. We can go to Donahue's."

He shook his head. "I'm not in the mood."

"I get it." His brother shuffled into the office and dropped down in the chair in front of his desk. "You've been in a funk since Rachel broke things off with you. That's normal. I went through the same thing when Wendy and I split, but you have to get on with your life."

He dragged his fingers through his hair. None of it made any sense. They'd spent two fantastic years together. Why had she ended things between them?

"You can't keep hiding out here," Levi said.

What his brother didn't know—what no one knew— was he'd planned to ask Rachel to marry him. The receipt for the diamond solitaire set high on a thin platinum band still sat in his wallet as a sad reminder.

What a fool he'd made of himself. There he'd sat at a table for two at the little hole-in-the-wall Italian restaurant they'd found on their first date. Rachel had fallen in love with the romantic ambience. He'd loved the food. Of course he'd booked a table at her favorite place to pop the question.

He'd started the evening with such optimism. The waiter would bring Rachel's favorite starter. The lightly breaded fried calamari with capers in a tasty lemon sauce was his favorite, too. They'd enjoy their favorite meals: vegetable lasagna for her, chicken piccata for him. Rachel would ask him for a bite of his chicken and end up eating his meal because it tasted much better than hers, and he'd eat her lasagna, but he wouldn't care. He'd get down on one knee after they'd eaten their cannoli and the restaurant owner would bring a chilled bottle of his best champagne to celebrate their engagement.

He should have left after thirty minutes of waiting but he'd stayed. An hour later, he'd convinced himself she'd left the office late and was stuck in traffic, even though all his calls to her went straight to voice mail. The waiter approached at some point with a large vase of water—for the two dozen red roses he'd brought, so they wouldn't wilt any more than they already had.

He'd never forget the look of pity on the owner's face when he came over to inform him they were closing soon.

Cooper shook his head. He'd trashed the flowers and tipped the waiter two hundred bucks for the bread and bottle of wine he'd consumed. It was the least he could do for taking up a table for four hours on a Saturday night.

Rachel's text came as he sat in the cab on his way back to the upscale hotel in Boston on the water—so much for the romantic evening he'd planned for the two of them. He hated sentences that started with *we need to talk*, especially when they came from a woman.

It's me, not you, she'd told him.

Yes, he was a fool all right.

"Big Brother is playing tonight. You know how Mom likes us all to go when Nick's playing," Levi said.

Coop snorted. "You're as bad as Mom with the guilt."

"Whatever works, bro."

Coop heaved out a resigned sigh. "Fine. Donahue's it is. Maybe we can get a quick game in before Nick starts playing."

"Sounds good. Let's get out of here." Levi jerked his

head toward the exit. "I'll even buy the first round, cuz I'm such a nice guy."

"Yeah, right." Coop rolled his eyes skyward. He rose, flicked off the light on his desk and followed his brother out.

"Wanna ride?" Levi asked as they strode to the parking lot.

"Nah. I'll take my own car." Coop waved off the offer. That way he could leave whenever he wanted to.

"Okay. See you there." Levi slid behind the wheel of his SUV and started the engine.

He did the same and pulled out of the TK Construction parking lot.

Coop pulled his car into the parking lot at Donahue's a few minutes later. He hated driving his Camaro in the winter weather and couldn't wait for the repair shop to finish fixing his truck. It was just his luck that someone slammed into his F-150 when it was parked at the mall a few weeks ago. Whoever hit him hadn't bothered to leave a note. Worse, the repair shop was having trouble locating the parts they needed to fix his vehicle.

This time he'd take every precaution to protect his car. He pulled into a spot far away from all the others.

He hopped out and headed toward the back entrance.

"Wait up, Cooper," a voice called from behind him.

Every muscle in his body stiffened. He knew that voice all too well. He turned. "Rachel." His heart slammed against his chest hard enough to break a rib. Damn it. He should have known she'd show up tonight. Thanks to him, Big Brother was one of her favorite bands, too.

"No Tom tonight?" He couldn't hide the sarcasm in his voice. It still stung, even after all these months, that she dumped him for his best friend. Talk about a kick in the teeth.

"He's working late. I'm meeting a friend of mine from work. Um, about Tom—"

She raised her left hand. That was when he saw it. "What the hell?" He stared at the massive rock on her third finger. "You're engaged to Tom?"

She jerked at the anger—or shock?—in his tone. "Yes. He asked me a few days ago."

Coop didn't know what to say. The woman he'd wanted to marry planned to marry someone else. His heart iced over and it would stay that way.

No way would he ever let another woman get close enough to melt it.

Piper heard the din of the crowd as she approached the front entrance to Donahue's Irish Pub. She stared through the glass door. The place was packed. Grabbing the handle, she pulled the door open and stepped inside. She peered around. The long, glossy wood bar sat to her right with a couple of dozen high wood chairs. Four square, high-top tables stood in a not-so-straight line in the center of the room. Booths with green leather benches lined the outside perimeter of the room and three round tables in the back. Three pool tables stood in the space to her left.

The place looked exactly the same as it had the last time she came here. Right down to the sports paraphernalia that covered every inch of the walls, except for the spots where beer signs hung. However, the owner had finally upgraded the old televisions to flat screens.

It seemed surreal to be back in New Suffolk again. Time seemed to have stood still here while the rest of the world marched on, or maybe it was just that Los Angeles had been the complete opposite of life in this sleepy seaside town.

Still, she liked the fact that things stayed the same

around here. Took comfort in the fact that people here built businesses that lasted, like Donahue's Irish Pub, and the Coffee Palace. She would, too.

"Hey, Piper." Nick Turner came up and gave her a big bear hug. "Welcome home. Glad you made it tonight."

She grinned. "Thanks. I'm looking forward to hearing you guys play."

Nick released her and draped his arm around the petite blonde who stood by his side. "You remember my fiancée, Isabelle, don't you?"

Piper nodded. "We met last spring." When she'd come back for her sister's thirtieth birthday party. "It's nice to see you again."

"You, too." Isabelle seemed…uncomfortable. Yes, that word best described the vibe she gave off.

"Hey, I've got to get back to the band. We're starting in a few minutes. Oh, Abby said you were going to join them. She's with Elle, Layla and your sister at one of the tables in front of the stage," Nick said.

"Great. Thanks." She had been wondering how she was going to find them with all the people here.

"Catch you later." Nick grasped Isabelle's hand and strode toward the back of the room.

Piper followed suit. As she walked through the crowd, she spotted a group of guys she remembered from high school. As she got closer to their table, she heard one of the guys chanting, "Chug, chug, chug." The others joined in, except for one guy who lifted his growler and slugged the entire sixty-four ounces of beer in one shot.

Piper rolled her gaze skyward. Of all the foolish, juvenile… This wasn't high school anymore. They were adults. "At least some of us are," she murmured to herself.

She caught a glimpse of Elle Patterson waving at her out of the corner of her eye and headed over to where she sat.

"Good. You found us," Mia said when Piper sat in the only empty chair at the table.

"How are you settling in to your new place?" Layla asked.

"Great. I'm going to love living in your old apartment above the Coffee Palace," Piper answered.

"And I love having a new neighbor now that Layla has moved in with her hot EMT." Elle sipped from her glass of white wine.

"Eww." Mia made a face. "That's our brother you're talking about."

"Yeah." Piper plucked up a tortilla chip covered with gooey cheese from the plate of nachos in the center of the table. "It's hard to think of Shane as 'hot.'" It was also a little weird that her brother's girlfriend was *her* friend, as well. Not to mention her business landlord. Funny how that had never happened before, given New Suffolk was such a small town, and their closeness in age—the three of them were only a little more than a year apart—but it hadn't.

She glanced around. "Which server is ours? I'd like to order a glass of wine."

"Yes. I need a refill." Layla lifted her empty glass.

"Oh, there she is."

The light glinted off Elle's necklace as she waved to their server.

The woman nodded as she passed by with a full tray.

"I love your choker," Piper said to Elle.

"Oh, thanks. I got it at the jewelers in town. You know, the one next door to the diner. Now that the son has taken over, they're finally selling some modern pieces."

Piper nodded. "I'll check it out."

"In the meantime..." Abby propped her elbows on the table and laced her fingers together. Attention trained on Piper, she said, "I want to hear about the gallery you're opening."

Elle nodded. "Me, too."

"What do you want to know?" Piper asked.

"What made you decide on opening a place here?" Abby tucked a lock of titian hair behind her ear. "I mean, you can't compare New Suffolk to Los Angeles, or New York."

"True," Piper agreed. "But our quaint little town has a lot to offer. Sandy beaches in the summer, the harvest celebration in the fall and Christmas festivities throughout December. All of these events bring tons of people here each year, and I plan on taking advantage of that."

"And don't forget the annual ice art festival in the middle of February," Elle added.

"Exactly." Piper grinned. "That event is gaining in popularity. Groups from all over the East Coast come to New Suffolk during that time."

"Your plans sound awesome," Elle said. "I'm so excited for you."

"We're all happy for you," Abby agreed. "We need more female-owned businesses in this town."

"Like you," Mia said. "And Layla, of course."

"That's right." Abby grinned. "Everyone loves coffee. And the amazing French fusion food Layla cooks."

"I know I do." Piper lifted both arms in the air and lowered her palms to the table. "All hail the Coffee Palace and The Sea Shack."

Everyone laughed.

How lucky was she to have found such a great group of friends since she'd decided to return home? They'd included her in their circle and offered their friendship and support the moment she'd met them.

"So, when is the grand opening?" Elle asked.

"The first day of the ice art festival," she answered.

"That's only five weeks away," Abby gasped. "How are you going to do it? You're going to have to renovate the space to make it work for what you want to do and all of the local construction companies are booked for months," Abby continued. "I tried getting someone in to make a few minor changes to the Coffee Palace last month and no one was available until this summer."

"You should have told me." Mia turned her attention to Abby. "Our family co-owns TK Construction. I know they're busy, but I'm sure someone can help you before then."

"You own TK Construction?" Abby asked.

"Technically my mother and Ron Turner own the company," Piper said. "Ron and my father started the business almost thirty-five years ago."

"I never knew TK stood for Turner Kavanaugh," Elle said.

Piper picked up another tortilla chip from the plate. "Most people don't, since it's just initials."

"Any chance you can ask someone from TK to come out and give me an estimate?" Abby asked.

"Sure." Mia smiled. "It's too bad we didn't know earlier. Piper could have asked our mother to set something up for you when she had lunch with her today."

Piper cringed as she remembered the fiasco with the bank president. "I could have, if I'd actually had lunch with Mom."

"Oh, right." Mia sighed.

"Did something happen?" Layla asked. "Is Jane okay?"

"She's fine." Piper rolled her gaze skyward and related the story.

Abby, Layla and Elle chuckled.

"Do you have any idea how embarrassed I was?" Piper asked.

"I can only imagine," Elle agreed. "Do you think he realized what was going on?"

"He didn't let on if he did." She shook her head.

"Unfortunately, this isn't the first time Mom has tried this," Mia said.

"Oh, do tell." Layla grinned.

Piper rested her elbows on the table and steepled her fingers. "The most recent time was last year. She tried to set me up with one of my coworkers when she came out to LA to visit me. And yes, *he* definitely understood what she was up to."

Abby doubled over laughing. "Oh, God. I would have been mortified."

Heat flooded her face just remembering George's reaction. "What's even worse is that he was interested." He'd confessed to having a crush on her for a long time.

"But you weren't," Elle stated.

"Actually, I was. He was pretty damn hot." Piper grinned. "But I got the feeling he was looking for something long-term, and that was the last thing I wanted." She shrugged. "I'm not looking for anything serious right now." *Not ever.* "I just wish my mother could understand."

"Maybe you should find a fake boyfriend," Elle suggested. "That would get your mother off your back."

Her eyes went wide. "That's not a bad idea."

Mia shook her head. "It won't work. Mom would double down on her efforts the minute Piper ended the relationship."

Mia was right. Piper's shoulders slumped. Mom was relentless.

The server breezed by their table again without stopping.

Piper stood. "I'm going to go to the bar. Anyone else want anything?"

Elle and Layla rattled off their requests.

"Coming right up." Piper made her way through the crowd to the bar and placed her order.

A man stepped up beside her while she waited for the bartender to return with her drinks. Her pulse soared. With those bulging biceps on display and that thick, wavy golden brown, hair...he looked like a Greek god. Not to mention that hard-core five o'clock shadow. *Oh, yeah. Sexy as all get-out.* She wasn't looking for Mr. Forever, but he could be Mr. Right Now.

"Hey, Cooper. What'll you have?" the bartender asked.

Cooper? No. It couldn't be. She jerked her gaze back to the man and stared.

"I'll take a Macallan on the rocks," the man said.

Shit. She'd know that voice anywhere. "Cooper Turner," Piper blurted.

He didn't respond.

Maybe she was wrong? This wasn't the tall, gangly geek with shaggy hair she remembered. Not with those broad shoulders and lean, narrow hips. Lord have mercy!

The man shot a side-glance her way. "Piper Kavanaugh." He couldn't hide the disdain in his voice. "Heard you were back in town." He looked none too pleased about it.

"Yes." She'd known they wouldn't be able to avoid each other the way they had during her few and brief visits home over the years, but she'd hoped to evade him for at least a little while. She should have realized he'd come to see his brother play, but she hadn't given it any thought when Mia had mentioned Nick's band was playing tonight.

Cooper grabbed his glass, slugged down the contents, and walked away without another word.

The old anger and resentment roiled around inside her as potent as ever.

What had she expected? That he'd welcome her with open arms—like his brothers had? *Hah!* Cooper Turner didn't care about anyone but himself.

This was the guy who'd played countless pranks over the years and left her to take the blame when things went wrong.

Her father had loved him like another son. And Cooper…couldn't even pay his respects when Dad passed.

He thought no one had noticed him leave—moments after he and his family had arrived—and go skateboarding in the funeral parlor parking lot during Dad's wake.

Her lips tightened into a thin line. *She* had.

Piper shook her head. How could he have done such a thing?

Cooper stopped walking when one of the guys she'd recognized from high school grabbed his arm and shoved a chair at him. He placed his empty glass on the table and picked up the beer one of the other guys slid toward him.

"Chug, chug, chug," the guys started chanting.

Cooper grinned and lifted his growler.

She ripped her gaze away. He might be gorgeous and sexy, but it was clear to her he was still the same jerk she remembered.

Chapter Two

Piper walked into the TK Construction offices the next morning at eight o'clock sharp. She couldn't be late for her meeting.

"Hi, Piper." Laura Hawkins smiled at her as she approached the reception desk. "Welcome back. It's so nice to see you again."

"It's nice to see you, too. Your hair looks fantastic."

Laura grinned and touched her fingers to her short bob with blond highlights. "This is my post-divorce hairdo. My friends say it takes twenty years off me. I guess that means I can pass for a woman in her mid-thirties." Laura winked.

"Maybe even younger." Piper nodded. "Is my mother in her office?" She'd called this morning and asked if they could meet at the Coffee Palace for breakfast to discuss a couple of things regarding her layouts. Piper assumed Levi must have had questions when he'd reviewed her final plans. Given what happened at the diner yesterday, Piper wasn't taking any chances. She'd insisted they meet at the TK offices. Once bitten, twice shy.

"Let me check." Laura picked up the phone on her desk.

Piper peered around the lobby as she waited. They needed to redecorate. It hadn't changed since she was last here years ago, except... She walked over to where two large photos sat mounted on the wall that stood to the left side of the double glass doors separating the lobby from the offices. Each sleek metal frame held an image of an ice sculpture. The first was a massive dragon with its wings spread wide and the second an enormous, graceful swan.

"Your mom will be out in a minute." Laura came to stand beside her. "Aren't they fantastic?"

"Yes," Piper agreed.

"This one won first place at the festival last year." Laura pointed to the dragon.

Piper could see why. The details on the piece were incredible. The scales on the beast looked almost lifelike. "Who is the artist?" A TK employee maybe, or it could be an artist TK had sponsored. She wondered if it were too late to find her own artist to sponsor?

Laura opened her mouth to speak just as her mother burst through the double doors.

"Sweetheart." Mom hugged Piper and gave her a quick peck on the cheek. "You're right on time. Come on back." She yanked open one of the glass doors and gestured for Piper to precede her.

Piper stepped into the hall and Mom followed.

"Head into the conference room. We're set up for you in there."

"You don't need to do that. Your office is fine. It's just going to be you, me and Levi, and the table in your office is big enough to review the drawings." Piper stopped short and turned to face her mother. "Oh, and by the way. I won't be having dinner with the bank president."

Her mother shot a perplexed expression in Piper's direction. "Excuse me?"

"Are you going to deny you tried to set me up with Blake?"

"I don't know what you're talking about, darling." Jane darted into the conference room.

Piper gritted her teeth and followed her in. "You need to stop—" She froze when she spotted Cooper sitting at the conference table. Dressed in a pair of tan trousers and a navy button-down shirt, he looked even yummier than last night.

No, no, no. Jerk. *Remember? Get a grip.*

Piper sucked in a deep, steadying breath. "Where is Levi? I thought we were meeting with him this morning."

"We can finish up later, Jane." Cooper stood and headed for the door.

"Stop," Mom commanded.

Piper gawked at her mother. What was going on?

Jane pointed to the table. "Please have a seat, Cooper. You, too, Piper."

Her gaze narrowed. What was her mother up to now? She wasn't going to stay here and find out. "I only have thirty minutes before my next meeting." Piper glanced at her watch. Okay, that was a little white lie. She wasn't supposed to meet with a sculptor, whose work she wanted to feature when she opened her gallery, for another couple of hours, but… She headed toward the exit. "I'll find Levi and—"

"Levi isn't here," Mom cut in.

Piper executed a 180-degree turn. "What do you mean? I thought we were supposed to go over the floor plans for my gallery?"

"That's what I'm trying to do. Now—" Mom huffed out a breath "—if you would both sit down, we can get started."

"What are you talking about, Jane?" Cooper began.

"Mom, Levi should be here for this," Piper reiterated.

This *couldn't* be what she thought it was. Why would Mom even suggest such a thing? Okay, Mom didn't know about what Cooper had done at her father's wake, no one in her family did, but she did know about all the jerky pranks he'd played on her over the years.

Why would her mother believe Piper would agree with her suggestion?

"You." Mom pointed to Cooper and spoke in a calm, rational manner. "Are the only TK employee who has availability in your schedule to accommodate Piper's tight timeline."

Piper shook her head. "But Levi said…"

Her mother propped her elbows on the table and steepled her fingers. She looked Piper in the eye. "He is already slated for another project. Which he would have realized if he'd double-checked the schedule before making a commitment to you."

"What about—" Cooper began.

Mom held up a hand. "All the crews are out on other jobs right now. I wish I had an alternative, but I don't. Unless—" she peered at Piper "—you're willing to hold off on your renovations until someone else becomes available."

Piper dragged a hand through her hair and blew out a breath. "You know I can't do that." She'd already lost months due to permit delays. Not to mention all the money she'd paid out in rent for a business that wasn't generating any income. Thank goodness her boss had allowed her to stay on at her job in LA until things got straightened out here; otherwise she would have gone under before she'd ever opened her doors. "The gallery needs to open at the start of the ice art festival." She couldn't afford to wait any longer.

Cooper leaned back in his chair and folded his arms in front of his chest. "Then I guess you're stuck with me." His tone challenged her to deny it.

She couldn't, even though she wanted to.

They'd have to spend almost every day of the next five weeks together. Piper groaned. She opened her mouth to object, but her mother cut her off before she could say anything.

"This is the *only* solution I can offer you. We hadn't anticipated taking on this extra work right now. I know it's not your fault the town took so long to approve your permits, but the timing sucks for TK."

Piper gritted her teeth. What choice did she have if she wanted to make her new business venture a success? *None, that's what.* "Okay."

Cooper nodded. "I'll order the materials today." He extended his hand to her.

Piper hesitated for a brief moment, then pressed her palm to his. A bolt of electricity shot through her. Cooper felt it, too, if his surprised expression was anything to go by. She jerked her hand away.

Lord help her. She'd just made a deal with the devil.

Thirty minutes later, Piper exited the TK Construction offices. She glanced at her watch. She had plenty of time to grab a coffee before her meeting with the sculptor.

Piper drove the short distance to the Coffee Palace and parked in an empty space on Main Street. She walked inside.

"Hey, Piper." Elle smiled. "What can I get for you today?"

"I'll take a large toasted almond coffee." She glanced at all of the pastry trays. "And one of those chocolate cupcakes." She'd need to run five miles to work off the calories for the copious amounts of creamy frosting alone, but it would be so worth it.

Mia walked into the front of the shop from the kitchen. "Hey, sis. How did your meeting with Levi go? Oo-oh, not so good, if the look on your face is anything to go by."

"Levi has been assigned to another project. Cooper will be completing the renovations for the gallery."

"Oh, boy," Mia said.

"Why is that a problem?" Elle asked.

Mia snorted. "Piper and Cooper don't get along."

Elle propped her hands on the counter and sent an inquiring glance Piper's way. "Oh, do tell, because last night, I was pretty sure you felt differently."

"What?" Mia's jaw nearly hit the floor.

Elle smirked. "I saw Piper checking him out when she was standing at the bar."

"Ah…" Mia still wore a stunned expression. "I think you need to explain."

Piper sucked in a deep breath and exhaled slowly. "There's nothing to explain. Cooper and I don't get along. Never have. Never will."

Mia chuckled. "You guys have rubbed each other the wrong way since you were in diapers." She turned to Elle and grinned. "Apparently Cooper stole one of Piper's toys and she's never forgiven him."

Piper straightened her shoulders. "That was the first of many indiscretions over the years."

"This is true. Let's see. Whoopee cushions left on the teachers' chairs and fake tarantula spiders let loose in the cafeteria come to mind." Mia turned thoughtful. "Some of the more memorable offences included setting alarm clocks to go off at various hours in the early morning during the eighth-grade class trip to Camp Jewel, and, oh, the toothpaste cookies—I can't remember when that happened."

Piper's lips tightened. "Home Economics, freshman year. We thought he was being nice when he offered them to our team."

Elle grinned. "Cooper sounds like quite the prankster."

"Oh, yes." Mia snapped her fingers. "The water balloons he and his friends dropped on you guys at what's-her-name's sweet sixteen. And of course, there was the skunk incident."

"Skunk incident? What happened?" Elle's gaze widened and she rubbed her hands together. "Details, please."

Piper shot Mia an I-am-going-to kill-you look.

Mia smirked. "Have you ever been over to the Turner house?" she asked.

Elle shook her head.

"They have a lot of acreage and in the back, near the property line, there's an open field. We used to ride dirt bikes—"

"You and Shane used to ride with Nick, Levi and Cooper," Piper corrected.

Elle studied her from head to toes, taking in her persimmon-colored stretch sheath dress and her cream leather boots. "Definitely not a mini bike kind of girl."

Piper straightened her shoulders. "Absolutely not."

"Anyway," Mia continued. "We used to have bonfires on the weekends in the cooler months as well. A bunch of kids from school would come and we'd all hang out. It was tons of fun."

"It was," Piper agreed. "Until Valentine's Day my senior year of high school."

"So, what happened?" Elle looked from Piper to Mia and back to Piper again.

Piper heaved out a sigh. "As usual, we were all hanging out at the bonfire all afternoon. It was about four o'clock and a bunch of us girls were getting ready to head home and get ready for the Seniors' Sweetheart Dance."

"Some of the guys, including Cooper, had been riding around on the dirt bikes earlier," Mia added. "Apparently, one of the guys dared Cooper to jump over the fire on his bike."

Elle shook her head. "Please tell me he wasn't foolish enough to agree."

"No can do, girlfriend," Piper scoffed. "The fool backed up the bike and turned the throttle full force. He headed straight for the flames."

"But he chickened out at the last minute," Mia said. "He swerved around the fire."

"Driving at top speed. A bunch of us were in his path. He came straight at us."

Elle's eyes widened. "Oh my God. Did he run into you?"

"No." Piper shook her head. "Everyone ran for it and luckily no one got hurt." Although they would have if Cooper hadn't ditched the bike to avoid crashing into them. Not that Cooper would have cared. He'd hadn't given a damn about anyone else. He'd bolted instead of sticking around to make sure everyone was okay.

Not true.

Cooper had left to go to the hospital. She and her friends may not have been injured, but he'd suffered a concussion and a broken arm.

Which she hadn't learned until the next day, so yeah, that evening, she'd thought him heartless.

Looking back on it now, *she* was the one who hadn't cared. Worse, she'd been a complete jerk to him, too.

Piper clenched her hands into tight fists. She was just so damned angry with him. All the pranks he'd played on her over the years. Not paying his respects at her father's wake. It had all melded together that evening and, well, she'd lost it with him. Big-time.

Not one of my finer moments. Piper sighed.

Elle's brows furrowed. "So, where does the skunk come in?"

"Remember how Piper said everyone ran for it?" Mia

asked. Not waiting for Elle's answer, she added, "Piper ran into the shed at top speed.

"Fun fact." Mia's eyes danced with delight. "One of the common places skunks make their winter dens are in sheds."

Elle gasped. "You got sprayed." She doubled over in a fit of laughter.

Piper rolled her eyes. "I stunk to high heaven, even after I washed with peroxide and tomato juice."

"That tomato juice thing is just a myth." Mia grinned. "It doesn't take away the smell."

"My date dumped me. No one would get near me." Piper gritted her teeth. Was it any wonder she and Cooper didn't get along? "Worst Valentine's Day ever."

"I don't know, I still think you have the hots for Cooper." Elle flashed a smug smile.

An image of him formed in her head. His sexy smile sent shivers down her spine. "Not in this lifetime."

"Thanks a lot, Levi." Cooper marched into his brother's office in the TK Construction building. Bright sunlight filtered in the small space through the shuttered blinds, casting a glow on the potted plants set on a bookshelf near the window. The faint sound of rock music played from the computer set atop his brother's gleaming metal-and-glass desk. "I thought you were going to handle Piper's gallery renovations."

Levi held up his hands as if surrendering. "I thought I was free, but Jane already had me scheduled to handle a new client. I'm sorry."

Cooper dropped down into the seat opposite his brother. "Let me take the new customer." *Please.*

"I can't. It's the Xaviers. I did their kitchen reno about

five years ago. They're remodeling their master bed and bath and asked for me by name."

"Come on." Coop scrubbed his hands over his face. He looked up at his brother. "Is there really no one else who can do this?"

"You're it. Everyone else is tied up on another job."

"I *so* don't need this right now." Coop shook his head.

"What's up?" Levi propped his elbows up on his desk.

Coop closed his eyes for a moment and sucked in a deep breath. "I saw Rachel at Donahue's last night."

His brother nodded. "Yeah. I saw her, too. I was hoping that with all those people there you might have missed her."

He shook his head. "No such luck. I ran into her in the parking lot on my way in. She and Tom got engaged a few days ago."

Levi's gaze widened before he pinned a neutral expression in place. "Good riddance."

He let loose a derisive laugh. "Leave it to you to give it to me straight."

Levi shook his head. "The woman cheated on you for more than two months before she finally ended things."

"I know. I know." He dragged a hand through his hair. His head understood that it was over between them, but his heart… Wasn't involved anymore. He'd been upset when Rachel shared her news last night, but truth be told, he'd forgotten about her the minute he spotted Piper. God, she'd always been beautiful, but the woman she'd turned into… Long blond hair kissed by the sun, sky blue eyes, curves in all the right places…

What was wrong with him? He was *not* interested in Piper Kavanaugh. The woman was wound tighter than the Timex watch his father wore.

"I agree," Levi smirked. "Rachel is pretty uptight."

He jerked his gaze to his brother. "What are you talking about?"

Levi stared at him as if he were delusional. "You just muttered something about her being wound tight."

He hadn't realized he'd said that aloud. "I was talking about Piper."

Levi's brows furrowed. "How did we go from Rachel to Piper?"

He'd been thinking of her. How the smile she'd flashed at him when he first stepped up to the bar…could light up the darkest skies.

No, no, no. Once she'd recognized him the brilliance had faded to distain. Suddenly everything was his fault again.

His mind drifted back to that night she'd been sprayed by the skunk.

Cooper blinked and opened his eyes. Multiple faces filled his view. What was he doing lying on the ground?

Everyone was shouting at the same time. "Are you all right? Are you hurt?"

The bike. He'd dumped it to avoid hitting the group of girls. What an idiot he'd been to allow those guys to goad him into jumping the fire.

Levi appeared. He pushed all the others out of the way. "Can you sit up?" he asked.

He pushed up to a sitting position. Stars exploded in front of his eyes. His left arm throbbed.

Levi must have realized what happened. He removed Coop's helmet for him, muttering to himself about how Mom and Dad were going to kill him for letting his little brother pull such a crazy stunt.

"Help me up." Cooper extended his right hand to his brother and cradled his left arm against his chest.

Levi pulled him to his feet.

Everyone started clapping and he grinned.

Everyone started talking again. His head started to pound. He felt like he was going to get sick.

Levi looked at him and said something about getting him to a doctor. They started toward the house.

Piper appeared in front of him, blocking the path. She looked like...her whole world had come crashing down on her.

She started screaming at him, and if looks could kill, he'd be a goner for sure.

Cooper couldn't make out most of what she was saying but juvenile, it's your fault, *and* ruined everything *came through loud and clear.*

He started walking again. Levi's arm was around him propelling him forward.

Levi said something to Piper. It made her even angrier.

"I hate you, Cooper Turner," she said.

She looked as if she meant every word.

"Hello, Earth to Cooper." Levi waved his hand in front of Coop's face. "You still with me?"

Cooper blinked. "Yeah. Sorry."

"Where'd you go?" Levi stared at him as if he were trying to determine if he was okay.

You don't want to know. Cooper waved off the question. He focused his attention on his brother. "How the hell am I supposed to work with her?" She hadn't given a damn that he'd broken his arm in two places and received a mild concussion when he'd hit the ground all those years ago.

Levi shrugged. "You're a smart man. I'm sure you'll think of something."

He straightened his shoulders and gave his brother a pleading smile. "Can you at least talk to Jane for me? Have her reassign me?"

Levi arched a brow. "What makes you think she'll listen to me any more than you?"

"I'm desperate here."

"For crying out loud." Levi rolled his gaze skyward. "Piper is not that bad."

"Are you kidding me?" Coop jumped up from his seat and started pacing back and forth. The girl had all the compassion of a snake about to eat its prey.

"Okay, okay." Levi spoke as if he was trying to placate a child. "I'll admit Piper can be a little...standoffish sometimes."

Cooper stopped midstride and turned to face his brother. He crossed his arms in front of his chest. "Well, that's a polite way of putting it." He'd have said she was arrogant, unfriendly and, yes, downright rude *all* of the time.

"I'm sure you'll figure out something."

Cooper shook his head. Convincing his brother to help him get out of this *was* his plan.

"It's only five weeks. What's the big deal?"

Thirty-five days of her hostility, the condescending attitude, that's what. "She has no sense of humor."

"Fine." Levi heaved out a sigh. "So she doesn't like to laugh."

"She needs to lighten up," Coop continued. "Have a little fun."

Levi threw his hands up in the air. "What does it matter? We're asking you to renovate her place, not date her."

Date Piper? A shiver of excitement ran through him.

He stiffened. *No way. Never gonna happen.* Not in this lifetime or any other.

Chapter Three

Piper grabbed her backpack and purse and headed out of her apartment. The overhead light lit the staircase as she walked down to the parking lot behind the Coffee Palace. Darkness still filled the early-morning sky. She wouldn't see the sun for at least another two hours this time of year.

She hurried to her car and drove the short distance to the mansion that housed her gallery.

Parking by the side entrance, she hopped out of the car and headed to the door.

Twin beams of light pierced the darkness. A moment later Cooper slid from the driver's seat of his car. She couldn't help admiring the sleek lines of his vintage Chevy Camaro. And the turquoise color with the two white stripes across the hood... Yeah, that was pretty hot.

"Hey." He wouldn't look at her. His body language indicated he'd rather be anywhere else but here with her.

"Morning." She practically choked out the word.

Piper blew out a breath. This wasn't going to work if this was how it was going to be between them. She tried again. "Thanks for agreeing to five a.m. starts."

"Not like I had any choice in the matter."

She gritted her teeth. The gallery was located above The Sea Shack, Layla's restaurant. Of course Layla would want the construction noise to stop when her customers were dining. They needed to start early in the day in order to finish up by noon.

"So…" Cooper arched a brow. "Are we going to stand here all morning chitchatting, or are you going to unlock the door so we can get started?"

Piper threw her hands up in the air. The man made it his mission in life to drive her crazy. "You are impossible."

He rolled his eyes. "Can we get to work now?"

Piper wanted to scream. She stabbed the combination of numbers on the keypad that unlocked the door and shoved it open. "Please." She gestured for him to precede her. "Don't let me hold you up." *Immature and juvenile. That's what you are.* She huffed out a breath.

He marched up the stairs, turning to face her when they reached the top. "I am neither immature nor juvenile," he shot at her.

"What?" How could he know what she was thinking?

He glared at her. "Are you going to deny that's what you just called me?"

Crap! She'd said that out loud? Not the smartest thing to do. Piper's shoulder slumped. Why was she letting him get to her? She folded her arms across her chest. "Nope. That's what I said. I call it like I see it."

"What are you talking about?" He mimicked her stance.

Besides the eye rolling of a few minutes ago? "You downed a whiskey the other night at Donahue's and followed it with a sixty-four-ounce beer chaser. Are you going to deny that?" She arched a brow.

His hands clenched into tight fists. "There you go judging me again. Did you ever stop to ask yourself why I would do such a thing?" He didn't wait for her to answer. "No, of course not. Once again, the Ice Queen convicts without knowing any of the facts." He walked away from her.

Ice Queen? Was that how he saw her? Her stomach twisted. No. He was just trying to make her mad. It was what he did. Piper glared at his back. "Fine. By all means, explain." She couldn't hide the sarcasm in her voice.

He turned back to face her. A muscle in his neck jerked. "I don't need to."

Of course not.

"I don't need your help today. I can handle the framing myself."

Her mouth fell open. He didn't want her around? No problem, because being here with him was the last thing she wanted. "Great. Have at it." Piper gestured to the pile of two-by-four planks stacked in the middle of the room.

She stormed down the stairs and exited the building. The slamming door punctuated her mood.

Piper drove the short distance back to her apartment. She glanced at the dashboard clock before hopping out of her car—5:30 a.m. The Coffee Palace would be open now. She walked around to the front of the building and entered the coffee shop.

"Hey, Piper." Elle waved from behind the counter. "What can I get you this morning?"

"A toasted almond coffee with cream and two stevia." She eyed the pastry trays. "And a chocolate cream–filled doughnut. Make it two." It was that kind of day.

"Two?" Elle eyed her curiously. "Are you okay?"

Piper blew out a breath. She was letting Cooper get to her again. She needed to clear her head. Only one way to do that. A jog on the beach. "On second thought, cancel the doughnuts."

Elle nodded. "A toasted almond coffee coming right up."

Five minutes later, Piper exited the Coffee Palace and made her way up to her apartment. She changed out of her jeans and sweatshirt and into a pair of fleece-lined yoga pants. Layering a moisture-wicking long-sleeved shirt under a zip-up jacket, she shoved her feet into her running shoes. She shrugged into a safety vest—it was still dark out—grabbed a water bottle, and headed out.

Piper set a brisk pace as she walked along Main Street. She didn't mind the cool temperature this morning. She might have goose bumps now, but she'd be sweating in a few minutes. She passed the New Suffolk Bank, the police station and the row of boutiques, turning when she reached the entrance to the town beach.

She peered around. Stars still twinkled in the clear dark sky, and the seagulls squawked in time with the waves crashing on shore.

She'd love to run like the wind with the sand beneath her feet. Having the entire beach to herself was what she needed right now.

But she'd settle for pounding the pavement on the main road until the sun came up. Piper retraced her steps and broke into a light jog when she reached the road. She'd forgotten just how beautiful New Suffolk could be at this time of year with the holiday lights still displayed on storefronts and streetlights.

She lengthened her stride, but even with all of the beauty surrounding her she couldn't find the serenity she desperately craved. Thoughts of Cooper kept intruding.

She wasn't an Ice Queen. She cared about others. She'd even given him the benefit of the doubt and he refused to explain.

Not true, a little voice inside her head persisted.

Piper sighed and slowed her pace. Okay, so maybe she had convicted him without due process.

No maybe about it. She'd assessed the situation at face value. Acting as judge and jury, she'd found him guilty as charged. He was right about that.

Crap.

What was she going to do now?

* * *

Cooper hummed along to the music as he tapped the nails into the studs. Nailing them in at a forty-five-degree angle would provide the flexibility he needed to slide the frame into place. He'd shore it up after he confirmed the position was correct.

All of a sudden, the music stopped.

Why had the Bluetooth disconnected? He stuck the hammer in the looped holder attached to his belt and walked over to where he'd left his cell phone on the kitchen island.

Piper came into view.

Son of a gun. He so didn't need this right now. He'd had enough of her condemnation over the years.

Okay. Maybe, just maybe, he'd deserved some of it. As an adult, he could see how some of his childhood antics could've rubbed her the wrong way.

Still, she never stopped to consider what other people were going through.

His stomach plummeted as he remembered the service for her father.

Coop tugged at his tie as he walked into the building. It felt like a boa constrictor around his neck. And the suit jacket... He was going to sweat to death if he couldn't take it off soon.

"Stop fidgeting." Nick elbowed him in the ribs.

"Give him a break." Levi shoved Nick's arm away. "He's already green, if you haven't noticed."

Nick shook his head. "For Pete's sake, we're not kids anymore."

Maybe not, but at thirteen, Coop wasn't an adult either. He glanced back at the car. Maybe he could wait in there while Mom, Dad, Nick and Levi went in? No one would even notice he wasn't there, would they?

Nick grabbed the collar of his coat and Cooper jerked to a stop. "Don't even think about it."

"Lay off, Nick," Levi said.

"You think I want to go in there?" Nick pointed to the two-story brick Georgian manor that loomed in front of them. "Well, I don't, but we have to."

Coop's stomach churned. How could he face the Kavanaughs—especially Piper—when he was responsible for Victor's death?

He hadn't caused the heart attack, but if he'd called 911 faster, instead of freaking out when Victor fell to the ground, he might be alive today.

Dad turned to face them. "That's enough, boys." He looked madder than he had when Nick and Levi got caught skipping school last year so they could go to the beach.

Hands on her hips, Mom added, "Stop your arguing. You should know better."

They walked the rest of the way in silence.

The smell struck him when they stepped inside. Like they hadn't opened any windows since the turn of the century. All the dark wood made him feel like the walls were closing in on him. His insides lurched. He hated antique furniture, at least he did now.

Piper looked at him as he came into the room. *Your fault.* That's what the look on her face said. Sweat poured off him. He couldn't breathe.

Coop raised his hand to his tie again, but stopped when Levi glared at him.

They waited for what seemed like hours to go through the receiving line. Hushed whispers were the only sounds he heard.

It was their turn to kneel on the pew in front of the casket.

Nick and Levi dropped down.

Dad motioned for him to join them.

Coop swallowed hard.

It was one thing to be prepped for what he'd experience—Mom and Dad had done their best to explain what was going to happen since neither he or his brothers had ever been to a wake before—and something a hell of a lot different to go through it.

His stomach heaved. Cooper covered his mouth and bolted outside.

Dad found him puking in the bushes on the other side of the parking lot a few minutes later.

He helped him clean up and told him he didn't have to go back inside.

But Dad did.

How was Dad supposed to say goodbye to his best friend? How were any of them?

Coop wasn't sure how long he'd been sitting in Mom's Pathfinder, but the parking lot was almost empty now, so he figured it had been a while. When were his parents and brothers going to come back?

He stared at the massive brick building. All he wanted was to get away from this place. Now.

Coop needed to do something. Sitting here... His mind kept drifting back to that day. If he'd gone with Dad and Nick to grab lunch, he wouldn't have been there, but he'd stayed behind to help Victor tack up the Sheetrock on the wall they'd just framed.

When Victor fell to the ground... Tears flooded his eyes. No, no, no.

He jumped out of the SUV and dug around in the back for his skateboard.

The only thing he thought about was holding his balance as he glided back and forth across the parking lot.

Coop sucked in a lungful of much needed air. Finally, he could breathe.

He spotted Piper descending the stairs to the parking lot. The look on her face... His stomach plummeted.

Yep, she definitely blamed him for what had happened to her father.

"Cooper." Piper waved a hand in front of his face.

He blinked and looked around the space. *The art gallery.* Piper's place. He blew out a breath. He couldn't stop her from being here, but he wasn't going to allow her to start in on him again. He'd had enough of that over the years.

"You turned off my music." He wasn't accusing, just stating a fact.

She shrugged off her zip-up jacket and laid it on the counter next to his phone. "I called out to you a couple of times but you didn't answer."

He couldn't help noticing how the yoga pants and long-sleeved top she wore displayed her curves to perfection. Coop blew out a breath. *No, damn it.* What was wrong with him today? "What do you want?" He dragged a hand through his hair.

"To apologize."

Cooper stared at her and he was pretty sure his mouth was hanging open. No. He must have misunderstood what she'd just said. "Excuse me?"

Hands on hips, she shot him an annoyed glance. "I'm not going to say it again."

"For what?" He wasn't trying to be sarcastic. He just couldn't believe what he was hearing.

Piper looked him in the eyes. "You were right. I shouldn't have said what I did earlier."

"Um...thanks." He couldn't think of anything else to

say. The truth was, he might have jumped to the same conclusion if he'd witnessed what she had. He'd downed the whiskey, after all.

"I didn't drink the beer." Coop wasn't sure why he told her that. He didn't owe her an explanation.

Piper's brows furrowed. "But I saw you—"

"I set it down without drinking any." It would have been foolish, and yes, juvenile. She was right about that.

Piper blew out a breath. "I was wrong to assume. I'm sorry."

His jaw nearly hit the ground. He couldn't help it. "I appreciate you saying that."

She opened her mouth. Closed it without saying anything, then opened it again. "I think we should call a truce." Her words came out in a rush.

His mouth gaped open. He couldn't have heard her right.

"We're both adults now. We shouldn't be sniping at each other."

She was right about that.

"I'm not proposing we become best friends. That's never going to happen."

She was right about that, too.

"But I do think we can be civil to each other while we're working together."

Could they? Neither of them had managed it thus far. Then again, neither of them had tried.

"What do you say?" She shot him a hopeful glance.

If she was willing to try, he could, too. "Count me in."

Chapter Four

The next morning, Piper stepped out onto the patio at the gallery that overlooked the ocean.

The stars had disappeared and hints of light touched the early-morning sky. She closed her eyes and breathed in the cold, salty air.

She couldn't remember the last time she'd experienced this sense of serenity.

"So this is where you disappeared to."

She opened her eyes and Cooper came into view.

"Yes." Piper crossed the deck and leaned her elbows on the railing.

"What are you doing out here?" he asked. "It's cold." Cooper ran his hands up and down his coatless arms.

"I haven't seen an East Coast sunrise in quite some time." She might have been up in time to see it yesterday morning, but with all the arguing they'd done, she'd missed it.

Piper returned her attention to the view. The stars had disappeared now and streaks of blue and yellow had appeared.

Seagulls squawked in the light breeze while the waves crashed on the shore below.

"It's beautiful." She'd never appreciated that before. What teenager did? But now... She loved the peace and tranquility. The quiet beauty. Yes, she was glad to be home.

"Morning is always my favorite part of the day." Cooper moved beside her and mimicked her stance. "It's a new beginning. A time of possibilities."

She turned to face him. "I never thought of it that way before, but you're right." Piper lifted her mug to her lips, but no coffee came out when she tipped it. She peered inside. "Ugh. Empty." *Damn.* That was the last of the thermos she'd filled this morning before leaving her apartment.

"There's more inside if you want some." Cooper pointed his thumb behind him.

She eyed him curiously. "Are you offering to share your coffee with me, Cooper Turner?"

He let loose a chuckle. "I believe I am."

"Thank you." A rush of warmth flooded through her. "That's nice of you." She wouldn't have expected that from him, given their history. They might have called a truce yesterday, but there was a big difference between being civil to each other and being nice.

"You're welcome." His genuine smile sent another wave of heat rushing through her.

"Um…" She jerked her gaze away from him. "I'm going to grab another cup." She brandished her empty mug for effect.

"It's just regular, not the flavored stuff you seem to prefer."

She stopped midstride and turned to face him. "How do you know I like flavored coffee?" It wasn't something she'd told him.

He pointed to her cup. "I could smell it when you were drinking earlier."

"Oh." That made sense. Piper started walking again.

"There's cream in the fridge and some sugar packets on the counter, too," Cooper called.

"Great. Thanks." Piper slid the door open and stepped inside.

She stepped up to the kitchen island and poured the hot liquid into her cup. Cooper was being nice to her. She didn't know what to make of this new development. Not that she was complaining. It was just...foreign. They'd sniped at each other for so long now, she hadn't been sure they'd be capable of anything else. He'd proved her wrong.

"Ready to get back to work?" she asked as she heard Cooper enter behind her.

His long legs crossed the room quickly. "Yes. Did you want to frame another wall or put up the Sheetrock on the ones I built yesterday?"

Piper pursed her lips as she considered. "Let's do the Sheetrock. That way I can tape the seams this afternoon." The work would be quiet enough so as not to disturb Layla's customers dining on the first floor.

He nodded. "That'll work. Let's get started." He walked over and grabbed a four-foot-by-eight-foot sheet off the stack.

Piper joined him and lifted one end while he boosted the other. They carried it across the room and into the hall they'd formed to create access to the second bathroom.

As much as she'd wanted to put up the walls to separate Layla's private dining room from what would become the entryway for her gallery, they didn't have enough time to construct and finish them before Layla opened for business at eleven thirty. They'd have to wait until Sunday, when the restaurant was closed for the day, before that could happen.

They'd nailed in four sheets, enough to cover one side of the wood frame, when Cooper's phone rang.

He pulled it from his holder. Stabbing the screen, he lifted it to his ear.

Piper walked into the main room to give him some privacy.

Cooper appeared a few minutes later, walked toward the grand staircase that led downstairs to the private entrance they used to access the gallery, and disappeared.

Piper stared, dumfounded, at the spot where Cooper had been standing a moment ago. "What the hell?" He'd left in the middle of what they'd been doing without so much as a word, let alone an explanation. Of all the irresponsible, negligent...

There you go judging him again.

Crap. The little voice in her head was right. She'd jumped to conclusions without bothering to ask if there was a reason he'd do such a thing.

She'd done a lot of that over the years. Not once had she stopped to consider if there was a reason why he'd acted the way he did.

She was starting to think that she'd earned the Ice Queen title fair and square.

Piper didn't want that name anymore.

So what was she going to do to change it?

Coop hit the redial button on his cell as soon as he reached the parking lot.

"Hey, man," Everett answered.

"What's up? It's like seven thirty in the morning." A light breeze blew, sending a chill through him. Damn. *Should have grabbed my coat.* He started walking to stay warm.

"It's after eight," Everett retorted.

Coop frowned. They must have been working longer than he'd thought.

"Don't tell me I'm interrupting your beauty sleep."

Coop let out a soft chuckle. "If I recall from our college days, you're the one who needed beauty sleep, not me. I've been at work since five."

Everett let out a groan. "That's cruel and unusual punishment."

"That's why you're a desk jockey and I'm boots on the ground. So, what's going on?"

The long silent pause made his gut tighten.

"So…" Everett dragged out the word.

His insides churned. "Spit it out, Ev. What gives?" Coop knew instinctively that this call had something to do with his ex. It was why he'd bolted before taking the call.

"We received Rachel's response card last night. She's bringing Tom."

His hand clenched around the phone. "Yeah. I know." That's why he didn't want to go to this shindig.

"There's more," Everett continued.

He gritted his teeth. "I already know she and Tom got engaged."

"That's good." Everett's relief was palpable. "Not for you. I meant that you already know."

His blood boiled just thinking about how the two of them had deceived him.

"You know that if it were up to me, I'd disinvite her to the wedding," Everett said.

That wasn't going to happen. Rachel was Everett's fiancée's cousin—and the maid of honor.

How the hell was he supposed to get through the day with her by his side? How was he supposed to act like everything was fine between them, when it wasn't? Just thinking about how she'd cheated on him with his best friend made Coop's stomach churn.

"I'm sorry, man." Everett's voice was full of compassion.

Great. Just great. The last thing he needed was people feeling sorry for him.

"It's fine." He clipped out the words.

"You're sure? You're...ah... Not gonna bail on me, are you?"

If only that were an option. Coop sighed. "Not unless you want me to."

"No way, dude. You and I go way back. We pledged together. Got through rush week together. Not to mention all the antics we pulled over our four years of college."

Coop smiled, remembering all the fun they'd had together over the years.

"I want you to be my best man," Everett insisted. "That's why I asked you."

Coop dragged his hand through his hair and nodded. "I won't let you down." Rachel and Tom be damned. He could handle this. He had to.

"Good," Everett said. "You had me worried. We haven't received your response yet."

"I'll be there," he said.

"Are you bringing a plus-one?" Everett's voice was filled with hope.

"Yes." Who that would be, Coop couldn't say, but no way would he show up alone. It was bad enough Everett felt sorry for him. He didn't want the rest of the grooms-men or his frat brothers to feel that way, too.

"You're seeing someone." Everett whooped. The sound of a hand slapping a tabletop echoed down the line. "I knew it. The Cooper Turner I know wouldn't let a breakup get him down for long. Way to go, bro. So, what's her name? What does she look like?"

Crap. What was he supposed to say now? He had no prospects on the horizon. He hadn't even thought about finding a date. "I gotta go now. Talk later."

"Wait a minute. I want to know about the woman you're bringing. Who is she?"

He sure as heck didn't know the answer. "You'll meet her at the wedding." He blew out a breath. "I really need to get back to work. I walked out in the middle of something." Piper was going to rip him a new one for walking out in the middle of what they'd been doing.

She might be justified in this case. He should have said something, even if all he'd said was he needed to take the call.

You never explained about anything you were going through. Not once.

How could he blame Piper for jumping to conclusions over the years? He couldn't.

"Fine. But don't think you're off the hook regarding this mystery woman, especially once Annalise finds out. She's gonna want to meet her. She's still feeling bad about how things turned out with you and Rachel."

"It's not her fault." Annalise might have set him and Rachel up, but she wasn't responsible for Rachel's actions. "I was the one who introduced Rachel to Tom." Coop's hands clenched into tight fists. More than twenty-five years of friendship and comradery ended in the blink of an eye.

I fell in love. Tom had made a point of telling him that. Like that fact justified the two of them sneaking around behind his back.

"Let's do dinner together soon. I'll check with Annalise and get back to you." Everett's words pulled him from his thoughts.

He needed to find a date for this wedding. Fast. "Talk soon." He ended the call before Everett could say anything more.

Coop shoved the phone back in its holder. It was time to face Piper's wrath. He looked around. Hell, he'd walked all the way to the center of town while he and Everett were talking. Which meant he'd be further delayed getting back. *Crap.*

He started back toward the gallery, passing the post office and the library. The aroma of freshly ground coffee hit him as he approached the Coffee Palace. Maybe Piper would be in a better mood if he brought a peace offering? Regardless, he could use another cup of caffeine.

Coop walked inside. He peered around. Most of the tables were full, but no one stood in line to order. He approached the counter.

"Hi, Cooper." Mia smiled at him.

"Hey." His brows furrowed. "What are you doing here?"

She let out a soft chuckle. "Ah, I work here."

"Still?" he asked. "I thought you were teaching at the private elementary school in the next town over."

"I am. I'm only here when school is on break." A delicate flush stained her cheeks. "We're off for the Christmas holiday until next week. We go back later than the public schools."

Coop frowned. Was she struggling financially now that she and her husband had split? Working at TK Construction would pay more than her teaching position and whatever she was making here combined. So why was she killing herself with two jobs?

"Right." He eyed her curiously. "You know we'd love to have you back at TK Construction." His father had been disappointed when she stopped working after her second daughter, Brooke, was born, although he'd respected her decision to stay home and raise her children.

"Thanks. I appreciate that. Mom and your dad told me the same thing."

"Perfect. You can start today." He grinned. "As a matter of fact, I've got a job for you right now. You can help Piper renovate her gallery. You could always swing a hammer with the best of them."

"Hey, no stealing my employees, Turner." Abby walked in from the kitchen and flashed a grin.

"You don't have to worry," Mia said to Abby. To him, she added, "Even if I was interested in going back to TK, which I'm not, I couldn't work on the gallery renovation. You start way too early for me. I have to get the kids off to school most mornings."

He sighed. "You are always welcome back at TK if you change your mind."

"I know, and I appreciate that. So, what can I get for you?" Mia asked.

He ordered his usual. "Large regular coffee with half-and-half and two sugars." He may as well grab something to eat as long as he was here. "And a bacon, egg and cheese breakfast sandwich, too."

"Is that all?" Mia asked.

Coop shook his head. "I thought I'd pick up something for your sister, too. What type of coffee does she like?"

Mia gawked at him. "A large toasted almond—light." She arched a brow. "She'd also appreciate a ham, egg and cheese croissant to go with it."

Cooper laughed. "Okay, sure. Why not." This was a peace offering, after all.

Mia shot him a curious glance. "It's awfully nice of you to bring something for Piper."

"Contrary to some opinions, I'm a nice guy." Coop grinned and waggled his brows.

Mia chuckled. "Yes, you are." She handed him his drinks and indicated he'd need to wait a few minutes for the rest of his order.

Fifteen minutes later, Coop entered the old mansion and took the elevator to the second floor. He found Piper kneeling on the floor over a couple of wood studs with a tape measure in her hand.

She looked up when he called her name.

"You're back. Good. I got to work on the next wall while you were gone. If it's all right with you, we can finish this one, and then go back to Sheetrocking."

"Yeah, sure. No problem." He stared at her, waiting for the lecture to come, but she just got back to measuring the boards. "Um, sorry I ran out on you."

"No problem. I figured you needed to deal with whoever called you."

He nodded. "It was Everett. He's getting married in a few weeks. I'm his best man." Why was he telling her this? He sounded like a bumbling fool. "Here." He thrust the foam cup at her and the bag containing her food.

"What's this?" Her brows drew together in a deep V.

"It's a toasted almond coffee with extra cream and a ham, egg and cheese croissant. Mia said that's what you like."

"Yeah." She stared at him as if he were an alien who'd just landed on the planet. "It is. Thank you."

Heat crept up his neck and flooded his face. Why he was so pleased with her response, he couldn't say. He just was. "You're welcome." Coop grinned.

Maybe there was hope for them yet.

No, damn it. There was no *them*.

He didn't want there to be.

Chapter Five

"Why are you ignoring me?" Coop's brother Nick walked into his office at TK Construction on Wednesday evening.

Coop's brow furrowed. "What are you talking about?"

"I texted you an hour ago and called twice in the last fifteen minutes. Why haven't you answered?" Nick flashed an exasperated look at him.

"I haven't received any texts or calls all afternoon." He glanced to his right, ready to pick up his cell and prove his point, but it wasn't there. He scanned the entire desktop. It wasn't anywhere. Coop patted the holder attached to his belt. No luck. He flashed back to earlier today. *Crap.* "Sorry. I must have left my phone at the gallery." He stood. Closing his computer, he disengaged it from the docking station. "I need to go and grab it." He shoved his laptop into his backpack and started toward the door. "What did you want?" he asked his brother.

"Are you still planning to go to Levi's to watch the game tonight?" Nick asked.

"Yeah. I'll see you at eight."

Coop stepped outside. Clouds covered the early evening sky, leaving a blanket of inky darkness behind. He shivered as he hurried to his vehicle. Hopping inside, Coop drove the short distance to the old, colonial mansion that housed Piper's gallery. The parking lot was packed, which meant Layla's restaurant must be busy. He pulled his Camaro into an empty spot near the side entrance and hopped out.

Punching the code in on the keypad, he pulled open the door and hurried up the stairs two at a time. He spotted his phone where he'd left it—next to the circular saw in the far corner of the room.

Coop grabbed it and thrust it in his belt holder.

He heard muffled music coming from the opposite side of the space. Was that the soundtrack from that Disney movie his nephew, Noah, liked to watch?

He listened again. Magic carpets and genies. Yes, definitely children's songs. Who was here and why were they playing kids' music? Cooper headed in the direction the sounds came from to investigate.

A squeal of laughter came from the room Piper had designated as her studio. The music came from there, too.

Coop arched a brow. What was she doing? More laughter filtered into the hall. Muffled voices, too.

"Piper?" He knocked on the closed door.

No response.

"Hello?" He thrust the door open and walked in.

Piper whirled around and stared at him, a startled expression on her face.

"Uncle Coop!" A paint-covered Noah smiled. "What are you doing here?"

"I have the same question." Piper shot him a curious glance. She grabbed her mobile from the table that stood in the far corner of the room. The music stopped.

"I forgot my phone." He tapped the holder on his belt. "Came back to get it. What's going on in here?" He stared at walls covered with various streaks and stripes and four equally colorful children.

"We're helping Auntie Piper decorate her studio," Aurora, Piper's eldest niece, said.

"It's really fun," Kiera, the youngest of the three girls, added.

"Yeah," Brooke, the middle sister, agreed. "Do you want to help?"

"I…ah…" He didn't know what to say. He doubted Piper would appreciate anything he contributed.

"You can grab a brush and some paint from the table if you want," Piper said.

He trained his gaze on her. Something flickered in her expression. Curiosity, maybe? He wasn't sure, but at least it wasn't the condemnation he usually saw when she looked at him. He supposed that was a good thing.

"Look what I did." Noah dragged him over to where he'd drawn a few squiggly lines in various colors. "Piper said I could write my name so everyone knows who painted it."

Cooper studied the oversize letters. "You did a great job, buddy."

"Yes, they all did." Piper pointed to the rest of the pictures. "I'm so proud of all of you."

His nephew and her three nieces beamed.

Coop frowned. Why were the kids even here?

"Hey, Coop." Levi appeared by his side.

"Daddy!" Noah raced toward his father. "We had so much fun today with Piper."

"Whoa." Levi held him at arm's length. "You've got wet paint all over you. I don't want it on me."

"Hey, Levi." Piper waved. To Noah she said, "Go and change into the clothes you were wearing earlier."

"But I don't want to go home yet," Noah protested. "Aurora, Brooke and Kiera get to stay."

"No, they don't." Mia walked into the room. "Go and get changed, girls. You've got swim lessons in twenty minutes."

A round of grumbling ensued.

Piper laughed as she herded them toward the door.

"Thanks again for volunteering to watch the girls this afternoon." Mia started cleaning up.

"And thanks for including Noah," Levi said.

Coop frowned. He wouldn't have expected the uptight woman he knew to go out of her way to do such a thing. Let alone allow the kids to splatter paint all over her walls.

"You're a lifesaver." His brother helped Mia put things away. "I can't believe I forgot to hire a sitter. My mother told me last week that she couldn't watch Noah, but with the holidays, I forgot to call someone."

"You're welcome. It was no trouble. I had a lot of fun with them. Check out the artwork they created." Piper walked to the front of the room where three easels sat.

There was more than just the walls? Coop followed Levi and Mia to where Piper stood.

"We went over how to draw some basic shapes and this is what they came up with." Piper pointed to the first canvas. "Noah created these fish out of ovals and triangles."

Coop's gaze widened. "Hey, that's pretty good for a five-year-old."

Piper nodded. "Yes. It is."

"This must be Kiera's drawing." Mia pointed to the second easel. "She loves flowers. And Brooke loves butterflies." She examined the last canvas. "Where's Aurora's drawing?"

"She opted for a different media for her project." Piper grinned and pulled out her cell. She stepped close to her sister. "Look at these." She swiped her finger across the screen.

"Oh my gosh, that's a great picture of Brooke and

Kiera," Mia said. "This one's great, too." Mia scrolled through what he assumed were more photos.

Cooper studied her. Piper hadn't just watched the kids today, she'd taken the time to do things with them and teach them something, too.

"She's a natural," Piper said. "You should have seen the smile on her face as she was taking the pictures. You would have thought I'd given her a million dollars when I gave her my phone and told her to have at it."

"I had no idea," Mia said. "Can you teach her?"

"Absolutely. I'd be happy to." Piper let out a little chuckle. "Although don't be surprised if we surpass what I know sooner, rather than later. She's a quick study."

Mia hugged her sister. "You're the best. I'm so glad you're home."

The kids rushed into the room, each trying to talk above the other.

"Okay, okay, girls." Mia held up her hand. "First, I need you to help Auntie Piper finish tidying up." She glanced at her watch. "We need to leave in five minutes if we're going to make it to the YMCA in time for your swim lessons."

"You, too, sport." Levi pointed to Noah.

"Come on, guys." Piper sang a song about everyone helping to put things away and the kids joined in.

Coop marveled at how good she was with children. Even more surprising, she seemed to enjoy being with them. The persona didn't fit the woman he had believed her to be.

"Thanks for your help, guys." Piper capped the last paint jar.

Noah ran over to her and threw his arms around Piper. "I had so much fun today."

"I'm so glad." Her smile lit up the room.

"Me, too," Noah said.

"I'll see you guys later." Piper hugged Noah tight, and then her nieces.

"Let's go, girls. Chop, chop." Mia clapped her hands together.

"We're going to head out now, too." Levi motioned for Noah to join him. "Thanks again, Piper." He waved and headed out the door.

"Bye, Auntie Piper," the three girls called together.

Piper waved as they exited.

When they were alone, Piper turned to him, hands on hips. "Why are you staring at me?"

Coop hadn't realized he was. "Sorry." He'd been trying to reconcile the Piper he remembered with the woman who stood before him, and couldn't.

"That doesn't answer my question. You've obviously got something to say, so you might as well say it."

All right, then. "I can understand why you'd watch your nieces for the afternoon, but why Noah? You barely know him."

She gawked at him. "What did you expect me to do, leave him in the dungeon all alone?"

She was talking about the converted conference room at the TK Construction offices. He and his brothers and the three Kavanaughs would go there on days off from elementary school, and early closings, if no one was available to watch them. The six of them had nicknamed the place the dungeon because they hated their time spent there. He smiled to himself. Looking back, it wasn't as bad as he'd once thought. They'd had a television, an air hockey table and lots of video games to play.

Piper crossed her arms and glared at him. "Of course you did. After all, I'm the Ice Queen. I'm not capable of caring or compassion."

He might have believed that once upon a time, but what

he'd witnessed here today proved otherwise. "No. I was clearly wrong about that."

Dead wrong.

Chapter Six

"Thanks again for meeting with me today. I appreciate you taking time out of your Saturday afternoon to accommodate my schedule. It was a pleasure meeting you," Talia said.

"You, too." Piper smiled at the woman standing a few feet away. "And you're welcome." This appointment had been well worth the time. She was looking forward to featuring Talia's work in her gallery. Piper glanced around the studio. The woman was quite a talented sculptor. "I'll be in touch with the details as we get closer to our grand opening." She gave a little wave and exited Talia's studio.

A cold midday breeze struck her the moment she walked outside and she shivered. Would she ever get reacclimated to the cold January weather in New England? She zipped up her parka and tied the pashmina scarf Mom had given her for Christmas around her neck.

Hurrying to her car, she climbed inside and started the engine. Cool air blasted her. She shut the vent until the car warmed up.

Piper pulled out of the parking lot that housed the building where Talia's studio was located. Humming along with the radio, she headed toward town.

Her cell rang. She pushed the phone button on her steering wheel and connected the call. "Hi, sis. What's up?"

"Have you eaten lunch yet?" Mia asked.

"No." She glanced at the clock on the dashboard. It was already one thirty. No wonder she was hungry.

"Me either. I just got off my shift at the Coffee Palace, and for once, Kyle is around."

Piper cringed. She'd never liked her brother-in-law. Kyle had always been pleasant to her—to everyone in her family—but there was something about him that had rubbed her the wrong way from the start. Personally, she was glad her sister was no longer married to him.

"He has the girls, so I'm free as a bird. Want to meet me for a bite to eat?"

Piper turned left onto Rainbow Road. "Sounds good. Where do you want to go?"

"How about Layla's place? Maybe after we eat you can show me the progress you've made on the gallery. I can't wait to see what you've done."

She chuckled. "I knew it. You can't help yourself. You love the construction world."

"What I like is transforming a space, or in the case of a new build, creating a vision," Mia corrected.

Piper shook her head. "If you like it so much, why don't you go back to TK? I'm sure Mom and Ron would love to have you back."

"That was a long time ago." Was that a hint of regret in Mia's voice? "I have other priorities these days and their names are Aurora, Brooke and Keira. Teaching fits the girls' schedule. Besides, I spent all that time and money getting my teaching certificate. It would be a waste if I didn't use it."

"Maybe, but there's something to be said for being happy."

Mia sighed. "I'll live vicariously through you for now. So, Layla's place?"

She and Mia needed some alone time. Something wasn't

right with her sister and she needed to figure out what it was. "You bet. I'll see you in about ten minutes. I'm coming from a meeting with an artist on the other side of town."

"Perfect. I should arrive around the same time. Grab a table if you get there first."

"See you there. Bye." She ended the call.

Piper continued driving toward town. The four new houses that sat side by side under various stages of construction caught her eye. She tried to remember what was there before. The Walker property, if she remembered correctly. At least it used to be. Three old barns in major disrepair had once stood where the new houses did. Yes. That was it.

Those structures had always reminded her of the old outbuildings at Ron and Debby Turner's place. She'd always loved the century-old dwellings. Could remember playing hide-and-seek in the Turner barns when they were little kids and they'd go over for big family barbecues during the hot summer months.

Maybe that was why some of the kids had started hanging out at the Walker property after Ron and Debby had stopped the bonfires at their place.

After Cooper had gotten hurt their senior year.

Piper sighed. She'd been so…furious and upset that evening. All her plans had turned to dust.

The truth was, she'd been looking forward to that evening with Tom Anderson. It was the first time, in a very long time, that she'd let someone in. Let herself feel something for someone else.

Losing her dad… Piper shuddered and stopped that thought in its tracks. It hurt too much to feel.

She'd really gone off on Cooper that night. No wonder he thought of her as an ice queen. He'd suffered a broken arm and a concussion and she hadn't given a damn about anyone or anything but herself.

Piper gasped when the Homes for Humanity sign came into view. Wait. The four houses were Humanity homes?

She turned around and drove back to where the sign stood.

Piper grinned. Yes. Homes for Humanity was building homes in New Suffolk. Dad would have been thrilled. He, too, had believed everyone should have a decent place to live, and he'd helped the nonprofit build homes throughout the state for as long as she could remember. Piper was sure he would have continued to volunteer if he was still alive today.

She pulled into the parking area to turn around. The turquoise-colored car parked separately from the others in the parking area caught her attention as she backed up and turned toward the road. Was that Cooper's car? She looked in the rearview mirror to see if the car had twin white stripes across the hood, but she couldn't tell from this vantage point. It couldn't be Cooper's, could it? Piper dismissed the thought. She couldn't imagine Cooper volunteering his time for such a cause.

Not the old Cooper, anyway. But the current version…

She couldn't say. Piper didn't know him well enough. Why that thought made her heart pang, she wasn't sure, but it did.

She arrived at The Sea Shack a few minutes later. Parking in a free spot in the parking lot, Piper hopped out of her car. The Coffee Palace bag and the commercial coffeemakers she'd purchased earlier today sat in the back seat. She decided to bring the bag containing the coffee and one of the makers up to the gallery now, so she wouldn't have to juggle all three of them tomorrow morning. Opening the rear passenger door, Piper grabbed the packages and nudged it shut with her hip.

"What have you got there?" a familiar voice asked.

Piper turned and spotted Mia parked one spot away from her. "Some things for the gallery. I thought I'd run them up before we had lunch."

"Looks like you have your hands full. Let me help." Mia rolled up her car window. Sliding from the driver's seat, she pressed her key fob and locked her vehicle. She slung her purse over her shoulder and reached for the box Piper held. "This is going to make a *lot* of coffee."

"A lot of people come to shows." Wine and beer weren't the only beverages she'd serve her customers. Piper unlocked her car and grabbed the other coffeemaker from her back seat. "I need to make sure we don't run out."

They entered through the side entrance and into the room that Layla used as a private dining space.

"Let's take the elevator." Piper gestured to the door that looked like a closet to the right of the grand staircase.

Mia opened the door with her free hand. "You're lucky Layla's grandfather had this installed when he and his wife used the second floor of the mansion as a residence."

Piper nodded. "I wouldn't have rented the space if it wasn't here. I wouldn't have the proper accessibility required by the state."

The elevator door opened a minute later. They exited into the hall that led to the main space if you turned left, and her studio if you turned right.

They headed toward the main space.

Piper set her box and the bag of coffee on the island and Mia did the same.

Mia glanced toward the main space. "You haven't gotten much done in here yet."

Piper chuckled. "First off, it's only been a few days.

Second, we've been focusing on creating access from the hall to what was the primary bedroom en suite. Modifying that bathroom so that it's only a sink and commode is taking a lot more work that I thought."

Mia slanted a sidelong gaze at her. "Are you sure it's not taking longer because you and Cooper can't get along?"

"Actually, Cooper and I called a truce. We're both adults now and we're managing to work together just fine." Piper burst out laughing at the shocked expression on her sister's face. "You might want to pick your jaw up off the ground."

"I can't help it. You couldn't have surprised me more."

"We're not bosom buddies, if that's what you're thinking." She still didn't *like* him. Images of his handsome face and sexy smile flooded her brain. Her pulse kicked up a notch.

No, no, no. Piper turned away to hide the color she knew had stained her cheeks.

"Still…" Mia flashed a smug smirk. "Levi and I thought you two would have killed each other by now."

"Gee, thanks." Piper rolled her eyes skyward. She walked back to the island that would soon be converted to her bar. Grabbing the bag from the granite surface, she placed the four bags of grounds into the cupboard.

"Why is the stove pulled away from the wall?" Mia asked.

She spared a quick glance into what was currently the kitchen. "I can't keep it. As a business, I don't have a permit to cook up here. My insurance company wants it gone."

"What do you plan to do with it?" Mia asked.

"Layla suggested I donate it." She shot her sister a quizzical look. "Unless you want it. I'm sure she wouldn't have a problem with that."

"No." Mia shook her head. "I was going to propose the same. There's a donation center over in Carver. The money earned from the donations people make goes to support the Homes for Humanity houses."

She nodded. "Perfect. And it's so close by, too." Piper sucked in a breath and released it. "Speaking of Homes for Humanity. I noticed they were building a few homes on the outskirts of town."

Mia grinned. "Yes. They started those projects a couple of months ago."

"Is Cooper one of the volunteers?" Her insides jumped and jittered. Why was she so nervous about asking such a simple question?

"I assume so. He's been helping build Humanity homes for a long time now."

He has? Her brows furrowed. "How long?"

"Ever since he was old enough to volunteer."

Piper shook her head. "No way." You had to be sixteen to help build Humanity homes. That would have meant he started while they were in high school. "I would have known."

Mia's expression turned contemplative. "Not necessarily."

"Oh, come on. I lived here back then." She definitely would have known unless… "He didn't want me to know? Why?"

Mia pulled a face. "Do you really have to ask?"

Her shoulders fell. No. She didn't. They'd hated each other back then.

"It was his way of honoring Dad," Mia said. "You know how close they were."

Yes. Dad was Cooper's godfather. They'd shared a special bond. That was why it had been so hard when she'd caught him skateboarding at Dad's wake. Dad had loved Cooper like another son, and Piper thought Cooper couldn't have cared less about Dad.

"I wish I'd known." Piper dragged her hand through her hair.

"Would it have made a difference back then?" Mia's soft voice thundered in the silent room.

Yes. No. The truth was, Piper wasn't sure. She'd been caught up in her own grief back then. And Mom's depression… It hit all of them hard. Mia, Shane and especially her. At least it felt that way. It was as if she'd lost both her parents.

Was it any wonder why she wanted no part of a serious relationship after watching what her mother went through?

"Piper?" Mia waved a hand in front of her face. She repeated the question.

She sucked in a deep breath and released it. "I don't know."

Ice Queen. Oh, yes. Cooper had been more than right about that. Lord, no wonder he'd hated her back then.

Hates. Present tense. As in, still does.

They might have called a truce, but she wasn't under any illusions his feelings about her had changed.

Her stomach plummeted.

Chapter Seven

The aroma of fresh coffee brewing hit Cooper the minute he walked through the main entrance of the gallery on Sunday morning. That was the good news. The bad news was it smelled like the toasted almond flavor Piper preferred.

Tapping his backpack, he sighed. At least he had a thirty-ounce YETI full of the regular brew he enjoyed. He'd made it fresh this morning before he'd left the house. It would have to do.

"Hey, Cooper." Piper walked into the main space from the hall that led to her studio. She flashed a smile in his direction.

What was it about her smile that sent a flood of warmth rushing through him every time he saw it? Coop gave himself a mental shake. So what if she had a nice smile? *A great smile.* He shouldn't be wasting time thinking about it now. He shouldn't be thinking of Piper in any way, shape or form, other than as a client, because that was what she was, for all intents and purposes. A TK Construction customer. No more. No less.

Focus on the job and nothing more. "You're here early." It was barely five in the morning.

Piper nodded. "I got here about an hour ago. I needed to finish sanding the walls so I can paint later. I ran out of time yesterday."

A part of him felt bad for leaving her to work alone,

but no way would he cancel on the Humanity crew. They counted on his help.

"I had meetings with a couple of artists I'm interested in featuring once the gallery opens."

"How'd that go?" he asked. Part of him still couldn't believe he was standing here talking to her like she was an old friend.

A client, he mentally corrected. He was making small talk with a client. That was all. He would do that from time to time with other TK customers. It was appropriate to do this with Piper, especially since they were also working together.

It helped that they'd been getting along great these past few days. Who would have guessed that getting along with her was much easier than he'd expected? Not him. That was for sure. But here they were.

Piper smiled and his heartbeat kicked up a notch. That was another thing that had surprised him these past few days. How much she smiled. He couldn't remember ever seeing the old Piper smile—not at him, anyway.

The woman before him smiled a lot, and the happiness that radiated from her when she flashed those pearly whites… It stole the breath from him.

You're not supposed to be thinking about her smile. But he couldn't help it. He liked seeing it. It brightened his day.

"Great, thanks. I'm going to showcase both of them during the festival." She snapped her fingers. "That reminds me. I've got another artist I need to interview. I tried to set up the appointment for after we finished up here, but her schedule is full for the next few days, so I've got to speak with her this morning. I'm leaving at ten thirty. I should be gone about an hour and a half at the most."

He nodded. "No problem. I can handle things here while

you're gone." *Look at us, communicating like normal people.* He chuckled to himself.

Cooper set his backpack on the workstation and yanked out the thermos.

"There's a fresh pot of coffee for you on the kitchen island." Piper pointed a thumb over her shoulder.

He glanced over. Two coffeemakers stood side by side on the counter top.

"Where'd these come from?" Coop pointed to the coffeemakers as he walked to the island and inhaled the aromatic brew.

"I bought them at the store yesterday afternoon, after my meetings. I'll need them for when we start having shows. The coffee is from the Coffee Palace. Toasted almond for me and a pound of Abby's special blend for you. It's a medium dark roast. She thought you'd like it."

Of course he liked it. He ordered a large every time he visited Abby's place.

"I figured it would be easier than having to bring it in each day," Piper finished.

"Thank you. That was really nice of you." More than nice. She'd gone out of her way. For him. He wouldn't have expected her to consider his preferences.

Now who's judging who?

This was the same woman who'd included his nephew in the fun and games she'd played with her nieces the other day so he wouldn't be left out.

The old Piper might have been an ice queen, but the woman who stood before him now was anything but.

"You're welcome." Piper wiggled her brows. "Let's face it. We both go through a lot of java each day."

He laughed. "Yes, we do." A love of caffeine was another thing he'd realized they had in common.

Coop spotted the stove in the middle of the kitchen. "What are you doing with this?"

"Shane is going to stop by later with his truck and he's going to take it to the Homes for Humanity donation center for me. There's one close by."

He shot her a quizzical glance. "How did you know that?" The store she referred to had only opened a short time ago.

Piper cocked her head to the side. "Mia told me about it." She waited a beat and added, "She also told me that you've been a Humanity volunteer for years."

"Yes." It might have started as a way to honor Victor in the beginning, but somewhere along the line things had changed. Coop loved the work and the charity's mission. He continued volunteering because it was something he wanted to do.

A soft smile filled her face. "That's really great." She walked over to where he stood and captured his hands with hers. Giving them a gentle squeeze, she said, "Thank you."

Her sincerity sent a flood of warmth rushing through him and filled his chest to bursting point.

Focus on the job. No more, no less. Coop walked over to the island. He spotted two large mugs resting beside the coffeepots. "I see you grabbed these, too." One cup had a picture of a harried cartoon with the caption I Drink Coffee for Your Protection, and the other had a bunch of flowers on it with the inscription A Cup of Happy. He grabbed the cartoon character mug and held it up in the air. Nodding, he said, "This is rather appropriate."

Piper laughed. The sweet sound surrounded him like a soft cloud of silk.

Coop did his best to ignore the fluttering in his stomach and filled the mug. "Thanks again for doing this."

"You're welcome. Shall we get started on the wall to

separate Layla's private dining room from the gallery entrance?" She gestured to the stack of wood studs lying on the floor.

He gave her a thumbs-up and walked to the pile. Grabbing a board, he started measuring.

A few minutes later, he caught Piper staring at him, an odd expression on her face.

"What?" he asked.

She looked like a kid who got caught stealing a cookie from the cookie jar. "You were whistling."

Coop shook his head. "I don't think so." He never whistled—unless he was happy.

"You were whistling. No doubt about it." Piper grinned. *Holy crap.* He gawked at her, nonplussed.

"Cooper. You're here." Jane Kavanaugh walked into the gallery from the main entrance on Monday afternoon.

His brows furrowed. "Yes. Why are you so surprised?"

"Don't you usually wrap things up by this time so you don't disturb Layla's customers dining downstairs?"

He nodded. "I'm just finishing up now."

Jane peered around the space. A look of concern crossed her face, but she said nothing.

She was probably thinking they hadn't made any progress over the last few days, but she couldn't see the walls he and Piper had created to allow access to the bathroom from the main hall, or the new entrance they'd created to Piper's art studio.

"Is there something that I can do for you?" His gaze shot to the man who stood next to Jane. Tall and lanky, he was dressed in a pair of dark tapered pants with a matching button-down shirt, his long, dark brown hair tied back in a ponytail. He didn't look familiar.

Why was he here with Jane?

None of my business.

"Is Piper around? I wanted to speak with her," Jane asked.

Coop shook his head. "Not right now. She said she had an appointment this morning and would be back around noon."

"Yes. She mentioned that when we spoke earlier." Tapping her watch, she added, "It's almost ten after."

Coop arched a brow. "I'm sure she'll be back any minute."

Jane walked over to where he stood by the workstation. "You can go ahead and call it a day. I'm sure Piper won't mind. We'll just wait here until she returns. It won't be a problem."

Coop frowned. Was she trying to get rid of him? "Okay. If that's what you want."

Relief flooded through Jane's features. "I know you have better things to do with your time than sitting around and waiting for Piper to return."

"Rii-ight." He dragged out the word. Why was Jane acting so...not normal? "Let me just finish up what I'm doing and I'll head out. Help yourself to some coffee if you want." He pointed to the kitchen island that was partially visible from where he stood.

"Sounds good." Jane flashed a tight smile and walked away.

Coop frowned. *Definitely not normal.* He needed to finish up and get out of here. He grabbed another stud from the pile on the floor and laid it across the workstation. Grabbing the tape measure, he began measuring.

"Hey, Mom," Piper greeted. "What are you doing here?"

His gaze strayed to where Piper stood a short distance away. He swallowed hard. Gone were the jeans she'd worn when she'd walked out of here earlier. She'd replaced them with a slim-fitting black pencil skirt. A wide fabric belt was cinched around her narrow waist. The sweatshirt she'd worn had disappeared as well. In its place was a white, figure-hugging blouse. And those heels... How she managed to stand upright, let alone walk in them, was beyond him, but they made her legs look great.

His heart beat a rapid tattoo.

No, damn it. He needed to concentrate on building the frame for the next wall, not gawk at Piper.

"Hello, I'm Piper Kavanaugh." She extended her hand to the guy.

She didn't know the man standing next to her mother either? Why had Jane brought him here?

"This is Donny," Jane said. "He's my friend Miriam's son."

Dead silence followed Jane's introduction.

What was going on? He shot a covert look in Piper's direction. She stood stiff as a board.

Coop gave up all pretense of working. Whatever was happening here was much more interesting.

Piper jerked her gaze to Donny. She was none too happy, if the tight smile on her face was anything to go by. "It's nice to meet you."

"You, too." Donny shook Piper's hand.

"Donny is an artist," Jane said.

Comprehension dawned. Jane's friend had probably asked her to introduce her son to Piper in the hopes that Piper would look at his work. Best-case scenario, Piper would display his art—whatever that might be—in her gallery.

He almost felt sorry for her. Almost.

"I'm a computer programmer," Donny said.

Coop frowned. Why would Jane say he was an artist if it wasn't true? It didn't make any sense.

Jane patted Donny's arm. "But you like to paint." It was a statement, not a question.

"Um, yeah." Donny flashed a nervous smile.

Something weird was happening. Piper seemed to know what it was, if the expression on her face was anything to go by, but she seemed helpless to stop whatever it was.

"You have a great smile." Jane turned her attention to Piper. "Don't you think?"

Coop's jaw dropped. Why on earth would Piper care if Donny had a great smile or not? Why would Jane even say such a thing?

"And you're a snappy dresser, too," Jane added.

Donny brightened. "Thank you, Mrs. Kavanaugh."

"Mom—" Piper began. She looked like she was about to explode.

"Donny, tell Piper about the paintings you showed me." Jane's words came out in a rush.

Donny turned his attention to Piper. "It would be better if I could show you."

"What a great idea," Jane enthused. "As a matter of fact, you could grab a bite to eat on the way. Why don't you go and do that now? You know, I have a table booked downstairs at Layla's restaurant for twelve thirty. You two can take it. I'm sure she won't mind if you're a few minutes early."

Coop's jaw dropped. He couldn't help it. Now he understood why Donny was here. Jane wanted to set him up with Piper.

A loud clang filled the now-silent space. He glanced down. Damn. He'd dropped the tape measure he'd been holding. Coop bent to pick it up. When he stood up again, Piper was staring at him. Her face flushed fire-engine red. She probably hadn't realized he was still there.

Piper marched over to him and dragged him down the hall and into her studio. "Stay here."

"Not a chance." He wasn't some minion she could order around. Coop headed toward the door.

"Please." Her shaky voice stopped him dead in his tracks.

He turned around and faced her. The breath caught in his throat. She looked like she wanted to crawl under a rock and die. He knew that feeling all too well. The embarrassment and mortification he'd experienced when he'd learned of Rachel and Tom's affair... Coop blew out a breath. He wasn't about to kick her when she was down. He wasn't a teenager who played pranks anymore. "Okay." He nodded. "I'll stay."

Relief flooded her features. "Thank you."

His hand brushed hers as she passed by him on her way to the door.

Sparks of electricity zipped down his spine from the accidental touch.

She stopped and stared at him.

Something hot and needy pulsed between them. His heart slammed against his chest.

Her lips parted and a soft little gasp came out of her mouth.

White-hot heat pooled low in his belly.

Piper jerked her gaze from him. Holding her head high, she strode from the room.

Coop stared at the closed door. What the hell had just happened?

Piper sucked in a deep, steadying breath as she walked along the hall toward the main part of the gallery. She was losing her mind. Yes. That had to be it. It was the only reason she could come up with that would explain why she'd almost grabbed Cooper Turner and started devouring his mouth like a starving person feasting at an all-you-can-eat buffet.

One minute she thought she might burst into tears—she'd never been this angry and frustrated in all her life—the next minute Cooper's hand brushed against hers. It was the lightest of touches, but the intense, fiery need it ignited inside her...holy hell. She'd never experienced anything like it before.

"Hey." Donny flashed a nervous smile and gave a little wave as she walked down the short hall to where he stood.

"Hi. Sorry for disappearing on you like that." Piper peered around the empty space. "Where's my mother?"

"She got a phone call and had to leave."

"I see." Her hands clenched into fists. She'd bet the commission from her first sale after the gallery opened that mom had bolted to avoid a confrontation. Well, that wouldn't save her. Not this time. She was going to march down to the TK offices right now and lay down the law once and for all. Piper had had enough of her interfering to last a lifetime.

Donny eyed her curiously. "I...ah...guess you didn't know we were coming."

She shook her head and gave him an apologetic smile. "No, I didn't. I'm so sorry."

"That explains why your mom was acting so weird. Did you still want to have lunch together?" Donny's voice sounded hopeful.

What was she supposed to say now? She didn't want to hurt him. He was as much of a victim of her mother's manipulations as she, but she didn't want to lead him on either.

"Sorry, dude." Cooper strode into the room like he owned the place. "She already has lunch plans. With me."

Now it was her turn for her jaw to drop.

Donny jerked his attention to her. "Is that true?"

It was now. She'd buy Cooper whatever he wanted to eat this afternoon for throwing her this life preserver. "Yes. As you said, I wasn't expecting you."

"Well." Donny looked from her to Cooper and back to her again. "Maybe another time?"

"I don't think so, pal." Cooper walked over to where she stood. He flashed a brilliant smile and draped an arm around her shoulder.

It took every ounce of inner strength she could muster not to gasp at him.

Donny stared at them for a moment. "I guess I misunderstood."

Piper shook her head. "This is my mother's fault, not yours. I'm so sorry."

Donny nodded and left without another word.

Piper let out the breath she was holding and added some much-needed space between her and Cooper. She peered over at him. She still couldn't quite believe what he'd done for her. "Thank you."

"You're welcome." His expression turned quizzical.

Piper could only imagine what he must be thinking. Lord, how was she going to put a stop to Mom's matchmaking ways once and for all? Talking to her wasn't going to help. She'd already tried that.

"Does she do that often? Your mom, I mean." He shook his head. "If I hadn't witnessed it for myself, I wouldn't have believed she would do such a thing. It's so unlike the Jane Kavanaugh I know."

Piper nodded. "She does this a lot. Twice since I came back to town and I've been back less than a week."

Cooper's eyes rounded. "I don't understand. I've never seen her do this before. Shane never mentioned her doing anything like this and neither has Mia."

"That's because she's never done it to them."

Cooper shook his head. "So, why you and not them? It doesn't make any sense."

She might as well tell him. She probably owed him that much for bailing her out with Donny. "Shane and Mia both got married."

Piper couldn't help but laugh at the expression on his face.

"Let me get this straight. She wanted you to marry Donny?"

"He was potential husband material, in her mind," she corrected.

Cooper nodded. "But you're not interested in getting married."

"Exactly. But she thinks if she keeps presenting good prospects—or what she believes are good prospects—I'll somehow change my mind."

His brows drew together in a deep V. "So, why don't you just tell her you're not interested?"

Piper snorted. "You don't think I've tried that? Repeatedly? When I confront her, she tells me she has no idea what I'm talking about. I bet you a hundred bucks she'll do the same thing when I try and talk to her about what she did this afternoon." She started pacing back and forth across the room. "I'm beginning to think Elle was right."

"About what?" he asked.

"About finding a fake boyfriend to get my mother off my back."

His disapproving glance made her hands clench into tight fists.

Piper glared at him. How dare he condemn her? "Obviously, you disagree."

"Actually—" His cell started to buzz. Cooper grabbed

it from the holder and glanced at the screen. He uttered a muffled curse.

"Don't let me stop you from getting that." She was going to find her mother and head back. It was well past noon now. They couldn't do any more construction today. She headed down the hall.

"Wait a minute," Cooper called.

"Hey, Piper. Are you here?" her brother called.

"Yes." She pivoted and returned to the main space. Shane came into view a moment later.

"Hi." Shane came over and kissed her cheek. He turned his attention to Cooper. "What's up?"

"Finishing up for today." Cooper gestured around the space.

"Thanks for coming," she said to her brother. "The stove is in there." Piper pointed toward the kitchen.

"Okay, but first I've got a surprise." Shane waggled his brows. He turned toward the entrance. "You can come in now."

Her brows drew together in a deep V. "Who are you talking to?"

The door to the main gallery entrance opened and her brother's best friend, Jax Rawlins, walked in.

Piper grinned and walked over to meet Jax as he stepped through the door. "What are you doing here?"

"Just taking care of a few things here in town. Bumped in to Shane at Donahue's and he told me what you're up to. Figured I'd stop by and see how you're doing." He threw his arms around her and gave her a big bear hug.

"I'm great. How about you?"

"Doing well." He eased her back, but left his arms loose around her waist. "Look at you." He winked. "Lookin' good, baby."

She grinned. He wasn't too shabby himself. As a matter of fact, with that sexy smile he was aiming at her, he was pretty hot.

Shane cleared his throat. He tapped Jax on the shoulder. "You know that's my baby sister, right?"

Piper glared at Shane. "Knock it off already. I'm not a kid anymore. I'm a grown woman."

Shane straightened his shoulders and smirked. "You're still my baby sister."

Jax let go of her and held up his hands as if surrendering. "I know. Best friend code."

"What does that mean?" Piper asked.

"You can't go after your best friend's sister," Shane answered.

Jax nodded. "He's one hundred percent right."

Piper shook her head. "That's the most absurd thing I've ever heard."

"It's true." Cooper walked over to where she, Jax and Shane stood. He extended his hand to Jax. "It's good to see you."

Jax grasped his hand and clapped him on the shoulder. "You, too, Turner."

Shane's phone rang. He pulled out his cell and glanced at the screen. "I've got to take this. I'll be right back." He exited the gallery.

"So…" Jax winked at her. Draping his arm around her shoulder, he said, "Talk to me, beautiful."

She laughed. "I see you're still a terrible flirt."

Jax pounded a fist to his heart. "You wound me, woman."

"Oh please. I know you." He'd been her brother's best friend for more than twenty-five years. "You've left a trail of broken hearts all over town. Heck, all over the country, now that you're a famous photographer."

An idea hit her. He'd make a *great* fake boyfriend. He

was sinfully handsome, sexy as all get-out, and the best part…like her, he'd never been interested in a serious relationship. She arched a brow and shot him a curious glance. "How long are you in town for?"

"A couple of days, then I've got a bunch of shows back-to-back, so I'm traveling for the next month. I'm back in New Suffolk for a few days in the middle of February. Why?"

Oh, yes. He was perfect all right. No one would be surprised when he dumped her for someone else and left her brokenhearted. She grinned like a Cheshire cat and placed her arm around his waist. "I've got a proposition for you."

"Oh yeah?" He sent her an inquiring glance. "What is it?"

She winked and gave him her best sexy smile. "Come with me and I'll tell you about it."

Chapter Eight

"Wait a minute," Cooper called as Piper dragged Jax down the hall toward her studio.

Piper looked over her shoulder at him, but kept going. "I'll be back in a minute."

No. That wouldn't work. She was going to ask Jax to be her fake boyfriend. He was sure of it. That was the last thing Coop wanted—because he wanted her to be *his* fake girlfriend.

His phone rang again. He didn't have to look at the caller ID to know who it was. It was Everett's ring tone. He knew Ev was calling to set up a time when he and Annalise could get together with him and his new girlfriend. Coop hadn't made any progress in finding anyone.

When Piper had told him about Elle's idea of a fake boyfriend, he thought they could help each other. Was about to suggest as much when Shane and Jax had showed up.

"This can't wait. It's important," he insisted.

Piper looked annoyed, but she gave him a reluctant nod. Turning to Jax, she said, "Can you give me a minute? I promise this won't take long."

Jax nodded. "Sure. No problem."

Piper grasped Jax's hands and squeezed them. "Please don't leave before we have a chance to talk."

Jax gave her a speculative glance and nodded. "I'll be in the other room." He jerked his head in the direction of the main space.

Piper thrust open the door to her studio and gestured for Coop to proceed her in.

He stepped inside.

She followed and closed the door. "Okay. What's so important that it couldn't wait a few minutes?"

Coop opened his mouth, but no words came out. Was he really considering Piper Kavanaugh, of all people, to be his fake girlfriend for a few weeks?

Coop started pacing from one end of the room to the other. They'd been at each other's throats less than a week ago. How could they possibly pull this off?

He peered around the room. The art projects Noah and her nieces had painted a couple of nights ago were still on prominent display.

He'd been wrong about her. The old Piper may have been an ice queen—*no maybe about it*—but the grown woman who stood before him was anything but.

"I don't have time for games." Piper threw her hands up in the air and headed toward the door.

Crap. "You need a fake boyfriend, right?"

She turned back to face him. "That's none of your business." She folded her arms across her chest.

Coop blew out a breath. "Just hear me out, please."

"Okay. Fine. Yes. I need a fake boyfriend. What of it?"

"How about me?" His words came out in a rush.

She stared at him as if he were delusional. "Ha ha. So funny." Piper shook her head. "Look. I appreciate you bailing me out with Donny, but come on… I need a real solution to my problem."

"I'm serious. We could be the perfect solution for each other."

He almost laughed at the confused look on her face, but he figured she wouldn't appreciate it. "A situation has developed and I find myself in need of a temporary girlfriend. For the next few weeks, to be exact. It wouldn't require much commitment on your part. One, maybe two outings with some friends of mine, and a date for a wedding I'm in the first week of February."

A thoughtful expression appeared on her face. "So, you're talking two or three dates?"

She was considering his proposal. He wanted to pump his fists in the air.

She cast a curious glance in his direction. "Would you be willing to include a lunch or something with my mother—you know, to make it look real?"

Hell, yes. He'd do whatever she needed. "I can do that. Do we have a deal?" He flashed what he hoped was a winsome smile.

Her face fell. "Oh my God. What am I thinking?" Piper dragged a hand through her hair.

Coop wouldn't give up now. He needed this to work. He was running out of options. "Piper." He moved closer.

The air between them thickened, sparking and crackling with energy.

Piper stared at him. Her eyes turned a smoky shade of gray.

His heart rate kicked up a notch.

"Who would believe you and I are an item?" Her voice was a soft caress against his skin.

A shudder ran down his spine.

Coop swallowed hard and fought the overwhelming urge to close the infinitesimal distance between them. "Donny found it plausible."

"He doesn't know our history." A lock of hair fell forward as she shook her head.

He reached out and tucked the strands behind her ear. Coop closed his eyes for a moment and enjoyed the feel of the soft, silky tresses against his calloused fingertips.

She drew in a swift breath. "We don't even like each other."

"You're right." He gave a sage nod.

"We can barely tolerate being in the same room together." Her lips parted and the way she was looking at him, like maybe he could make her wildest fantasies come true...

All sense of reason vanished. Coop snaked an arm around her waist and hauled her up against him.

"Cooper!" Her cry sounded desperate. She wrapped every inch of her supple form around his body and held on tight.

A jolt of electricity sizzled through him, sending a thousand watts of need racing through his system. He crushed his lips to hers.

"Oh God." Her mouth ravaged his while her hands explored every inch of him.

The heady sent of roses and jasmine filled his senses. His blood roared through his veins, pounding out a deafening beat.

"What the hell is going on?" Shane's voice thundered through the room.

Oh, shit. Coop jerked away from her. "I...ah..."

Jax chuckled. "You two need to get a room."

"Like hell they do." Shane grabbed two fistfuls of Coop's T-shirt and dragged him close.

His eyes widened. He'd never seen Shane so mad.

"Stop it." Piper pushed her way between them and shoved her brother hard. Caught off-balance, he fell backward and hit the floor. "You're acting like a caveman, for goodness' sake."

"It's not her fault," he blurted. He didn't want Shane to be mad at Piper. He'd started this and he'd take full responsibility.

Piper looked him in the eye. "While I appreciate you

trying to help, I don't need you to defend me or take the blame on my behalf. Neither of us has done anything wrong."

"Like hell he hasn't." Shane stood and pointed at him.

Piper turned to her brother, who was walking toward them again. "This is none of your damned business."

She was right, but that fact wouldn't stop Shane from butting in. He wanted to safeguard his sister. Coop couldn't blame him. Family meant everything to Shane. He'd do anything for them.

He admired Shane's protective nature.

Shane advanced on him, growling like a grizzly bear protecting its cub.

Coop didn't flinch, but it was a near thing. "Calm down, Shane."

Shane invaded his space and glowered at him.

Coop stood his ground.

"How dare you walk in here unannounced and uninvited and start yelling like you're some lord and master?" Hands on hips, head held high, Piper looked magnificent.

Shane blinked and turned to face her. "You're my little sister," he announced, as if that explained everything.

"I'm not a kid anymore. I'm a grown woman. I can, and will, kiss whoever I want, whenever and wherever I deem fit. You have no say in the matter. Do I make myself clear?"

Shane stared at her, a stunned expression on his face. "Are you telling me that you two…" He didn't complete the rest of his sentence.

"Are together." Piper looped her arms around his waist.

He liked the feel of her hands on him. The rightness of it.

Wait. What? Coop frowned. Where had that thought come from? The only thing between them was a little lust. Pure and simple.

"Come again?" Shane's eyes bugged out.

Coop released the breath he was holding. "We haven't told anyone yet."

"You two... Are you really..." Shane shook his head, a perplexed expression on his face. "No way. I don't believe it."

Piper looked at Coop and grinned. "I guess my brother here needs more convincing." She rose up on her tiptoes and yanked his head down to hers.

"Okay, okay." Shane held up a hand. "I believe you."

Jax smirked. "All that anger you directed to each other over the years was really just pent-up sexual frustration."

"You're not helping." Shane clapped his hands over his ears.

"I'm not trying to help." Jax grinned. He turned to Piper. "I've got to get going, but I'm on board."

"What are you talking about?" Shane asked.

"Piper said she had a proposition for me," Jax said.

"Um, about that..." Heat crept up Piper's neck and flooded her cheeks. "You don't have to worry about it anymore."

Jax's brows furrowed. "Are you sure? I don't mind doing a show here at your gallery. That is what you wanted, right? Why you asked me when I was going to be back in town?"

Piper walked over to where Jax was standing and linked her arm through his. "Of course. What else could I want?"

She turned an even brighter shade of red. Coop chuckled.

"Great. I'll give you a call and we can settle the details before I leave." He gave her a quick kiss on the cheek.

"Jax." Coop practically growled the name.

Piper gave him a what-the-heck glance.

He was only playing the part of her besotted boyfriend. He wasn't *really* jealous.

Liar.

"Sorry. Old habits die hard." Jax grinned and released Piper's arm. "I'll talk to you later." He waved and exited the room.

Shane looked at Coop and then at Piper. He shook his head, a dumbfounded expression on his face. "I should get going, too."

"I'll see you out." Piper ushered her astounded brother through the door. She glanced back at Coop and mouthed a silent "Stay here."

Coop stayed put and waited for her to return. He heard their muffled voices and the noise when they moved the stove onto the dolly. The sound of the elevator car a moment later signaled Shane's departure.

Coop paced back and forth across the space. What if she said no?

What if she said yes?

Anticipation hummed and buzzed inside him.

Shit.

Chapter Nine

Piper's mind raced as she walked alongside her brother. She'd just kissed Cooper Turner—and liked it. More than just liked, if she was being honest. How was that possible?

One minute she was explaining why his crazy idea of having a fake relationship with each other wouldn't work and the next...

Driving need thrummed through her body and all she wanted was for him to ravage her like there was no tomorrow. She would have begged him to do as much if Shane and Jax hadn't walked in when they did.

Thank goodness for small favors. Her brother had saved her from making a complete fool of herself. Piper shuddered.

They stopped when they reached the kitchen.

"So..." Shane grabbed the dolly and moved it behind the stove. He looked Piper in the eyes. "You want to tell me what that was all about in there?"

Piper locked her gaze with his and folded her arms across her chest. "No." How could she when she wasn't sure herself?

"Come on. I walk in there and Cooper, of all people, looks like he's about to—" Shane didn't finish the sentence.

A shiver raced down her spine as she filled in the blank. *No, no, no.* "I'm a grown woman, Shane."

He moved the stove onto the dolly and secured it with

straps. "You're my baby sister. I don't want to see you get hurt."

She grinned. "That's not going to happen." It's not like she was going to fall for Cooper.

"You don't know that. I like Cooper. He's like a brother to me, but he's also a guy. I saw the way he looked at you." Shane shook his head. "I don't like it."

Despite her objections, she was happy Shane had her back.

Another reason it was great to be home. She'd missed her family. Missed the closeness she'd shared with Mia and Shane. But she wasn't about to allow any of them—not her brother, not her sister, and especially not her mother—to interfere with her love life.

Her mother, of all people, had no right. Talk about the pot calling the kettle black. She wanted Piper to fall in love, when she had never moved on and done the same. *Fifteen years* since she'd lost her husband. And Mom hadn't so much as glanced at another man. No, Piper could and would decide relationship matters, or lack thereof, for herself.

"You have nothing to worry about." She kissed her brother's cheek.

Cooper Turner wasn't a love interest. He wasn't even a *like* interest. They couldn't stand to be around one another.

Okay, that wasn't true anymore. The truth was, he wasn't as hard to be around as she'd once imagined. This past week had proved that. They'd worked well together and the days had flown by.

"You two really like each other?" Shane asked.

"Yes." She could admit that Cooper, the man, wasn't at all like Cooper, the boy, who'd been the bane of her existence ten years ago.

And she wasn't anything like the young woman who thought cutting herself off from everyone and everything she'd once held dear was her only option. She was ten years older. Ten years wiser. She'd learned to deal with the loss of her father and was starting to see the past from a new perspective.

"This thing with Cooper... It's what you want?" Shane pressed.

Piper nodded. "It is." With any luck, Mom would stop the husband search once and for all.

"Okay." He sighed. "I guess I can get used to you guys together."

Piper laughed because Shane's expression conveyed anything but confidence.

"Thank you." She threw her arms around him.

"For what?" Shane asked.

"For being my big brother. I couldn't ask for a better one."

"You got it. I'm always here for you."

"You always have been."

Shane arched a brow and slung an arm around her shoulder. "You know I'm going to kick Cooper's ass if he hurts you."

She grinned. "I know."

Shane released her and grabbed the dolly handles. "I'll see you later. Oh, and tell the rest of the family so they don't find out about you and Cooper the way I did." He shook his head. "Sooner rather than later."

"I will." Piper walked beside him as he strode to the elevator. "Thanks again for taking the stove."

The door opened and Shane moved inside. "You're welcome."

The car door closed.

Piper glanced down the hall at her studio. "Here goes nothing."

Cooper paced back and forth across the room as she entered. He stopped short when he saw her.

He trained his gaze on her. "Well?"

"We have a deal."

Cooper flashed a smile that made her go weak in the knees.

He strode toward her. Would he kiss her again? A frisson of pleasure washed over her. Who knew the man could kiss like…like all her schoolgirl fantasies come true.

Just thinking about it now… Piper fanned herself. She touched her palms to her cheeks. Lord, they were hot as Hades and probably fire-engine red.

Heaven help her, she wanted his lips on hers again. Wanted to drown in the sweet pleasure rushing through her veins. The—

No, no, no. Not happening. Not again.

Something flickered in his gaze. He felt it, too. The heady beat of desire that pulsed between them. Her heart beat a rapid tattoo.

"So… What should we do now?" Cooper dragged a hand through his already disheveled hair.

She'd done that. Messed up those short soft tresses with her hands. She licked her suddenly dry lips.

Get a grip.

"We should tell our families about us, and not let them find out like Shane did." Piper shuddered. How were they supposed to do that? Her mother and Mia would be as shocked as Shane. She could only assume all the Turners would react to the news in the same fashion.

Cooper nodded. "Yeah. That makes sense."

"Any ideas on how we should break the news?" she asked.

"I know that Shane finding us…" He twirled his finger in the air.

A shiver ran down her spine at the thought of what they'd been doing.

"That wasn't ideal, but in the long run, I think it was a good thing. He witnessed..." Cooper blew out a breath. "You know what your brother saw. What I'm trying to say is..."

Piper sucked in some much-needed air and blew it out slowly. "We made our claim credible."

He stopped and looked her in the eye. "Yes. Let's go to the TK offices. We can kill two birds with one stone."

"You want to tell our parents first?" Piper swallowed hard. Never in her wildest imaginings would she have ever come up with a scenario where she'd tell her mother she was dating Cooper Turner. She shook her head. What was she supposed to say?

"I was thinking more like we could get them in the same room and tell them together. That way we make sure we get our story straight. The last thing we need is for you to say one thing and me to say another."

She nodded. He had a point. They needed to be on the same page with this.

"Ready?" Cooper held out his hand to her.

She grasped his palm in hers and ignored the tingles racing up and down her arm. She looked at him. "As I'll ever be."

Cooper nodded. "Let's do this."

They exited the gallery space and walked down the grand staircase to the first floor.

Piper slanted her gaze to their joined hands. His large hand engulfed her much smaller one. His grip was strong but gentle at the same time. She liked it.

Good grief. She'd fallen down the rabbit hole, headfirst, and knocked herself silly. Yes, that must be why she was thinking such ridiculous thoughts.

He dropped her hand when they exited the building.

She missed the sensation of his calloused palm against her softer skin.

Earth to Piper. Come in, Piper. This whole thing is a farce—remember? A part they'd each agreed to play. A means to an end.

"My car or yours?" she asked. "We should drive together. Like you said, we need to get our story straight."

"I'll drive." He jerked his head toward his Camaro.

"Heck, yes." She'd admired it the moment he'd pulled it into the parking lot on the first day they'd started construction. "Who wouldn't love to ride in this baby? She's gorgeous. What year is she?"

He looked at her, nonplussed. "You like my car?"

Piper laughed. "Heck, yeah. It's cool-looking." And just a little bit sexy, or maybe that was the guy driving it. She shook her head. *Down the rabbit hole, all right.* "It's a classic—right?"

He nodded. "1968."

"It's in perfect condition."

Cooper chuckled. "You should have seen her when I first got her a couple of years ago. I rebuilt the whole thing."

"That's impressive."

He flashed a cocky grin. "I'm a man of many talents."

The sensation of his lips sliding over hers while his hands touched every inch of her flooded her brain. Piper sucked in a deep, steadying breath. *Oh my, yes, you are.*

Cooper unlocked the car and held the door open for her.

A gentleman. She approved. "Thank you." Piper slid onto the cool leather seat.

Cooper slid in beside her a moment later.

"I know it's cold out, but can you put the top down? We could crank up the heat to keep us warm." Piper sent him a winsome smile.

"A girl after my own heart, but we're not going to be able to talk if I do that."

Damn. He was right, and they needed to talk.

"Another time?" he asked.

"Sounds good."

He started the car and pulled out onto the main road.

"So, how are we going to explain—" She couldn't bring herself to say the words so she just pointed to him and back to herself again.

"I've been thinking about that." His sexy grin sent her heart thudding and her stomach flip-flopped.

"Jax's explanation is out of the question."

He laughed, a deep, rumbly sound that vibrated through her in the most delicious way. "Don't worry. I wasn't about to suggest we tell our mothers that."

Thank God for small mercies. Piper shook her head. "Good. So, what are we going to tell them?"

"Keep it simple and believable. After spending so much time together over the last week, we realized we have a lot in common."

That made sense and it was true, too.

Cooper continued. "The more we talked, the more we liked each other."

Piper sucked in a deep breath. That was true, too. The more she got to know Cooper Turner, the more she did like him.

Chapter Ten

Cooper pulled his car into a parking space at the TK Construction offices a few minutes later. He removed the key from the ignition and looked at her. "Ready?"

Yes. No. Lord, she didn't know if she could go through with this. Piper sucked in a deep breath to steady her jangling nerves.

Nerves. Yes. That was all this jumping and jittering inside her was.

Cooper looked her in the eyes. "Think about Donny if you need to stiffen your resolve."

No way did she want to go through another setup again. It wasn't fair to her or to any potential guy Mom chose to match her up with.

"We've got this. Together." Cooper reached for her hand and gave it a firm squeeze.

He was right. They could do this.

Piper nodded. "Let's get this over with." She jumped out of the passenger seat and shut the door.

They reached the front entrance and walked inside.

"Where's Laura?" she asked. The receptionist desk was vacant.

"She takes a late lunch." Cooper glanced at his watch. "She should be back in a few minutes. Don't worry. We can still get into the office."

Cooper held his badge to the scanner by the double glass

doors. Pulling the door on the right open, he gestured for her to go through.

Piper walked past the conference room and down the quiet corridor that led to the executive offices. She stopped at her mother's, but found the room empty.

"She's not here." Piper wasn't sure if she was mad or relieved.

The faint sound of female voices drifted into the corridor.

"That sounds like your mom." Cooper gestured to an office farther down. "She's in my mother's office. Come on." He grabbed her hand and practically dragged her along.

"How mad was Piper?" Debby asked.

Piper stopped short at the mention of her name.

Cooper turned because she'd jerked his arm, hard, with her sudden halt.

"Hold on," she whispered in his ear. Piper wanted to hear what they were saying. They were talking about her, after all.

"Pretty mad, if the look on her face was anything to go by," Mom said. "She figured out what I was up to pretty fast. I really thought she'd have a lot in common with Donny."

It was bad enough that Mom tried to play matchmaker at Piper's expense, but to brag about her exploits to Debby... Piper's hands clenched into tight fists.

"I told you—you were too hasty. You didn't even give her and Cooper a chance," Debby said. "I still think they belong together. We just need to give them a little more time together to realize it for themselves."

Debby Turner thought they *belonged* together? Her jaw dropped. Lord, the woman must be a card short of a full deck if she thought that.

Cooper's hand clenched around hers. She turned and

saw the same stunned expression on his face that must be on hers.

"Maybe you're right," Mom agreed. "I just hope they don't realize what we've done. It was pretty risky making them work together."

"Desperate times call for desperate measures," Debby quipped.

Cooper blew out a harsh breath.

Piper turned to him. "*Be quiet*," she mouthed. She couldn't believe what she'd just heard. How dare they conspire against her and Cooper! What right did they have?

"That's it," Cooper whispered in her ear. "I'm going to give them a piece of my mind." He started toward the open office door.

"No. Wait." She tugged him back to her. "I've got a better idea. Come with me." Piper walked back the way they came.

"But!" Cooper protested.

"No buts. We need to get out of here before anyone spots us. I'll explain everything when we get back to your car."

"This way." He marched them to the side exit. "We don't want to risk running into Laura."

Once outside, they hurried to Cooper's car and jumped inside.

"Quick. Get us out of here. This car is way too conspicuous." Piper started laughing. She couldn't help it. The whole situation reminded her of a television sitcom.

"What's so funny?" Cooper looked at her as if she'd grown two heads. "I'm furious with the two of them. I would think you would be, too."

"Oh, I'm pissed off. Believe me. They have some nerve messing with our lives, but confronting them doesn't solve our problem. I've tried that before with my mother and she acts as if she has no idea what I'm talking about. What we need is to make sure they never try this again. With either of us."

Cooper pulled out into traffic. "How are we going to do that?"

She grinned and patted his knee. "You, my friend, are going to break my heart."

Coop jerked his attention from the road for a brief minute to look at Piper. "I'm going to what?"

Her soft chuckle sent shivers zinging up and down his spine.

"You heard me right."

He shook his head. "I don't get it."

Piper covered her heart with her hands. "When you break things off with me, I'm going to be so devastated that both our moms will feel guilty for throwing us together. If they see how upset I am, they won't try it again. With either of us."

He was all for that. No way did he want his mother, or anyone else, for that matter, playing matchmaker for him. But… "I'm going to need a good reason to dump you."

"I know. You can say you fell for someone else. An old girlfriend, maybe? You know someone who you had a relationship with in the past. You called it quits, but with some time and distance you've both realized how right you were together."

An image of Rachel floated into his mind. The idea of reconnecting with her now made him nauseous. "No." His forceful decline had her eyes going wide.

"Okay." She nodded. "No problem. We've got a little time to figure it out. We just need to make sure we're on the same page about it."

Coop blew out a breath and tried to calm the churning

in his stomach. "So, what are we going to do about tell-ing our families?"

"I haven't figured that out yet." Piper's stomach rum-bled audibly.

Coop slated a quick glance in her direction and smiled at the pink staining her cheeks. "Hungry?"

"Yes. With everything going on today I missed lunch."

"I never ate either. Have you had one of Layla's burg-ers since you've been back?"

"I have not. Are they good?" Piper asked.

"They're the best in the state. Today is your lucky day, because I'm treating."

"Then maybe I'll have two."

He caught her smirk out of the corner of his eye and laughed.

Coop pulled into a parking spot at the restaurant a few minutes later.

Exiting the car, they walked toward the entrance.

Coop couldn't be sure how they ended up holding hands. Maybe his hand had been by his side and Piper reached for it, or it was the other way around. Either way, he liked the feel of her slender fingers entwined with his.

He pulled open the door and they walked in. Approach-ing the hostess, he asked for a table for two.

"It's a forty-five-minute wait," the woman said. "Would you like to wait in the bar?"

Piper looked at him and gave a brief shake of her head. She pulled him aside. "Let's go somewhere else."

They were on the same page. "How about the diner in town?"

"Perfect." Piper smiled. "I'll drive. I'm going to come back here anyway to finish up some of what we were work-ing on in the gallery earlier, so I can drop you off."

"Or we could walk. It will probably be faster than driving between here and there. The stoplights on Main Street will delay us for sure. Not to mention finding a parking spot. Even at—" he glanced at his watch "—one thirty on a Monday." He gave her his best winsome smile.

She looked at him as if he'd lost his mind. "It's cold out there."

"By Southern California standards, maybe, but forty-five degrees Fahrenheit is downright balmy for New England in January. Come on." He held out his hand. "It won't take long."

She let out a resigned sigh. "I see you're still a big fan of walking places."

"I am," he nodded. "I problem-solve when I walk."

"Fine." Piper zipped up her coat and threw the hood up over her head. "Problem-solve how we're going to convince people we're a real couple, especially our families."

"Yes, ma'am." He gave a jaunty salute.

They exited Layla's restaurant and headed toward town.

If he was going to come up with a solution to their problem, he needed to know the facts. "What did you say to Shane about us?"

Piper looked at him. "Not much, really. He was still reeling from finding us…" She gave a little twirl of her finger. "Well, you know what he saw."

Coop's pulse quickened just thinking about their interlude. *So not the time.* "Did you mention anything about the length of time we've been seeing each other?"

"I've only been back in New Suffolk for a few days." She shook her head. "Lord, how are we going to convince anyone we're for real?"

He'd thought about that. "What if we told everyone that we reconnected last April when you were here for Mia's thirtieth birthday party, and we found we had more in common than we realized."

She stared at him. "But I never saw you."

"You never saw me at the party." He'd stayed away on purpose to avoid her. It was what they both did on those few occasions when she came to town over the years. Sometimes he begged off if the families got together and sometimes Piper would. "But you were in town for a couple of weeks, weren't you? We can say we ran into each other and got to talking."

She shrugged. "I guess that could work, but we're going to need a little more than that."

"Agreed. You came back last July, right?"

Her eyes widened. "How did you know that? I was only in town for four days to see if I could expedite getting the building permits for the gallery."

"My mother told me." He snorted. She always told him when Piper came to town. He used to think it was because she wanted to give him a heads-up so that he could avoid running into her while she was here, but after her comment to Jane earlier, he wasn't so sure. Lord, why would she believe he and Piper belonged together? That made no sense. They'd been at odds with each other for as long as he could remember. What could she possibly know that he didn't?

Coop gave himself a mental shake. Why was he wasting time even thinking about it? Mom was wrong. End of story.

"Did you stay with your mom during that time?" he asked.

"I stayed at her house, but she wasn't there the last couple of days. That reminds me, have you met her friend Chris? Mom said they met at book club last spring."

"No." Coop shook his head. "What does this Chris have to do with what we're talking about?"

"She's the reason Mom wasn't home. She and Chris went to Cape Cod for a few days. Neither Mia or Shane have met her either, so I was wondering if you have."

"I haven't," he confirmed. "But I know your mom is really into her book club. Maybe Chris is a new member." Coop shrugged. "If you're concerned, ask her to introduce you."

Piper grinned. "I can definitely do that now that I'm back in New Suffolk."

He steered the conversation back to the problem at hand. "Is it plausible that we ran into each other again the times you were here?"

"I didn't socialize much, but yes, I suppose it would have been possible. Maybe we ran into each other at town hall? I spent a lot of time waiting to see the planning and zoning commissioner."

He grinned. "We had a cup of that sludge that passes for coffee."

"That's good." She nodded. "But when did we start dating?"

"When I came out to LA."

"You were in LA last summer?" Her eyes rounded.

"No, but my fraternity brother, Jack, lives out there. I could say I went out to see him the second week of August."

She shot him a curious glance. "Why the second week of August? That's rather specific."

"Because I took off for a couple of weeks during that time period, and I didn't mention where I was going." He'd been down in the dumps about his breakup with Rachel and had needed to get away.

Coop continued, "So I decided to look you up while I was there."

"Now, why would you do that?" She looked him in the eye.

He shrugged. "Things seemed to be better between us

after we talked in July so I thought I'd say hi while I was in town."

Piper nodded. "Okay, so we got together while you were in LA and we talked some more and…" She shot a sideways glance at him.

"We went out a few times. Got to know each other better and decided to keep seeing each other since you were moving back to New Suffolk. We didn't say anything because we wanted the opportunity to see where the relationship was going without interference from our families."

"Amen to that." Piper grinned and pumped her fist in the air.

He chuckled. "I thought you might like that reason."

"Oh, yes. And what you just said could work, but what about what happened between us that day at TK when my mother told us we had to work together?"

"It wasn't that bad," he said.

"Really, 'cause I'm pretty sure I tried to walk out." The tone of her voice dared him to deny it.

"All right. I still need to think about how to finesse that," he admitted.

"You'd better think fast because we've already reached the center of town. The diner is only a block away." She pointed up the street.

Coop grinned. "We can keep walking."

"You can keep walking. I'm starving. I'm going to the diner." Piper stopped short. "But first." She gazed at the jewelry store window display. "I forgot this place was so close to the diner. Elle told me they feature some pieces made by a local artist."

"Did you want to go inside?" he asked.

"Not now. I'll come back later when I have more time. That's her stuff next to that gorgeous engagement ring on display." She pointed to an eclectic diamond solitaire with a thin strip of gold that was shaped like a curlicue, with the stone mounted between the bottom and top points.

"You like that ring, huh?" Cooper chuckled.

She smiled. "I do. I mean it's gorgeous. Classy. Understated." She flexed her left hand out in front of her and glanced at her third finger, as if she were imagining what it would look like there.

He chuckled. "I thought you didn't want to get married."

Color invaded her cheeks. "I don't. Definitely not."

"Then why are you admiring engagement rings?" *Damn.* The words slipped out of his mouth before his brain could engage. He shouldn't have tried joking with her. She used to hate when he did that. He held his breath, waiting for her condescending reply.

Piper let out something between a laugh and snort. "Touché."

He grinned. He couldn't help it. He liked this friendly rapport they were developing. "It's definitely not a traditional diamond solitaire."

Piper laughed out loud. "If you haven't noticed, I'm not traditional either."

"That's okay. I like unique."

She flashed that gorgeous smile again and everything seemed right with his world.

"Piper Kavanaugh, is that you?" A short, rotund woman approached them.

"Do you know her?" Coop didn't recognize her.

"Hellen Francis. She's Mom's next-door neighbor. White colonial house on the right."

He nodded. "The nosy neighbor with the cardboard-tasting sugar cookies." He hadn't seen her for years.

"Yup," Piper whispered to him. "I can't believe you remember her cookies. She used to use them as an excuse to come over and find out what was going on."

"They were pretty bad."

Piper wiggled her brows. "No kidding."

Hellen stopped in front of them. "Yes, it's you, Piper."

Piper smiled. "Hi, Mrs. Francis."

"I think you're old enough to call me Hellen." She pulled Piper against her chest and wrapped her arms around her. "It's so good to see you again. Your mother told me you were moving home, but she didn't tell me you were already back."

"It's only been a few days." Eyes wide, Piper looked at him and mouthed, "Help."

Coop grinned. "Hello, Mrs. Francis." He extended his arm toward the woman in the hopes that she'd release her death grip on Piper to shake his outstretched hand. "I'm Cooper Turner. Do you remember me?"

"Ron and Debby's youngest. Of course." Hellen released Piper and grasped his palm with hers. "I didn't recognize you. It's been a while since I've seen you."

"Yes," he agreed. "It has been."

"What are you two doing here?" Hellen eyed them curiously.

"Just a little window shopping." Piper pointed behind her.

Hellen looked at the display. *"Oh!"* Her eyes widened and she shot Piper a coy smile. "I see." She winked and said, "Well, I won't keep you anymore. You have a good day." She gave a little wave and continued down the street.

"Bye," he and Piper called in unison.

"That was interesting," he said as they watched her retreating form.

"Come on, let's get going." Piper started toward the diner.

"So…back to the problem at hand." Coop heaved out a sigh.

"You've come up with a solution?" She chuckled. "Boy this walking thing really works for you."

"If you are referring to that day at TK, we can say we had a fight. And we were still annoyed at each other when your mom dropped her bomb about us having to work together."

"Okay. That works for me." Piper crossed her fingers. "Let's hope everyone buys it."

Coop pulled open the door to the diner. The place was still packed, even this late in the afternoon. He peered around. "There's an empty booth in the back, on the right."

"I see it." Piper walked in the direction of the vacant table.

She slid into the bench seat on the right and he sat next to her.

Piper grabbed two of the laminated menus and passed one to him. "How's the burger here?" she asked.

"Pretty good, but not as good as Layla's, if you ask me."

Their server appeared a moment later and set two glasses of water on the table. "What'll you have?"

"A cheeseburger, medium rare, with fries, and a Diet Coke." Piper slotted her menu back in the holder behind the salt and pepper.

Coop nodded. "Make it two." When their server departed, he asked Piper, "When do you want to tell the rest of the family about us?"

Piper's cell rang. "Let me see who this is. I'm expecting a call from another artist I interviewed."

"Sure. No problem."

Her gaze widened. "It's my mother. I wouldn't have expected her to call me so soon after that act she pulled today with Donny. She usually avoids me like the plague after one of her matchmaking stunts."

"Maybe Shane told her about finding us together this morning?"

She shook her head. "I don't think so. As far as I know, he was heading to work after he dropped off the stove at the donation center." Piper connected the call. "Hi, Mom. What's up?"

Coop could hear Jane's excited voice emanating out of Piper's phone, but he couldn't make out what she was saying.

Piper gawked at him and whispered, "Oh my God." To her mother, she said, "As a matter of fact, yes."

"What's going on?" he whispered.

She shook her head and he heard Jane start talking again.

She let out a lighthearted laugh. "Yes, Mom." Piper looked at him and grinned like a Cheshire cat.

He heard more of Jane's indistinct chatter.

Piper glanced at him and rolled her eyes. "Unbelievable," she murmured to him. To Jane, she said, "It's not like you gave me the opportunity when I saw you this morning. You were too busy trying to set me up with Donny."

Did Jane know he'd made Donny believe he was Piper's boyfriend? *Crap.* Had Donny said something to her?

"Wait. *What?*" Piper shook her head. "You're joking, right?" She smacked her hand to her head. "No. Absolutely not. That's the craziest thing I've ever heard." Her gaze widened. "No, she was… Mom? Are you still there?" She lowered the phone and stared at it.

The color drained from Piper's face.

Holy shit. He wrapped an arm around her. "What's wrong?"

"She hung up on me." Piper stared at him, a dazed expression on her face. "I forgot how the rumor mill works in this town."

His brows furrowed and he eased away from her. She seemed more confused now than upset. "What are you talking about?"

"Hellen Francis." Piper shook her head. "We can add notorious gossip to her nosy neighbor description. She couldn't wait to call my mother and tell her how she saw the two of us together."

"You're kidding." He let loose a hearty chuckle.

"Nope." Piper blew out a breath. "She watched us walk into the diner together."

"Man, you had me worried for a minute. From the look on your face, I thought something was seriously wrong."

"We were holding hands."

Why did she still look as if they were in a heap of trouble? "So what?" He waved off her concern. "Don't worry about blabbermouth Hellen. Actually, we should thank her. She did us a huge favor. She's solved our problem for us."

"I don't think so." She shook her head.

"Jane knows we're a couple now. She's probably on the phone with my mom right now." He'd get a call any minute from her asking if what Jane had told her about him and Piper was true. Problem solved as far as he could see.

Piper looked him in the eye. "You'd better hope not. Because you don't want her to tell Debby what she said to me."

"Why not?" This was the perfect solution as far as he was concerned. "What did she say?"

"She thinks we're about to become engaged."

He gawked at her. "Come again?"

"Betrothed. Affianced. Promised to each other." She cradled her face in her palms and shook her head.

Coop couldn't believe it. "How the hell did Hellen come up with that?"

"Remember when I said we were window shopping?"

Coop nodded. "Yes. What of it?"

"Apparently Hellen thought we were shopping for an engagement ring."

His jaw just about hit the floor. What the hell were they going to do now?

Chapter Eleven

How the hell had this happened? One minute Mom was asking if it was true that she was having lunch with Cooper and the next...

Piper replayed her conversation with Hellen in her mind again. Not once had she indicated anything about being engaged to Cooper. Heck, she hadn't even referred to him as her boyfriend.

Okay, yes. There were some diamond rings in the window display. A lot of them, in fact, but there'd been other pieces on display, too. How the woman had come up with her and Cooper shopping for rings was beyond her. She only knew she needed to nip this in the bud now before Mom went off on a rampage and told everyone in town. Assuming Hellen hadn't already done that.

Oh, dear Lord. Please no.

"Here you go." The server appeared holding two burger platters.

She'd get sick if she ate anything now.

"Change in plan," Cooper said. "We need these to go. And the check, too, please."

"No problem. I'll be right back." The server picked up the dishes and disappeared a moment later.

Coop clasped her hands in his. "It's going to be all right. We'll go and talk to your mother and straighten everything out."

"I tried doing that when I spoke to her just now. She

wouldn't listen. She just gets something in her head and she just runs with it. She even denied trying to set me up with Donny this morning." Piper gritted her teeth. "'I have no idea what you're talking about, dear,'" Piper mimicked. "Good grief. She wants to go friggin' *wedding dress* shopping tomorrow. Not that I agreed to that. I gave Mom a hard no. Do you think she listened?" Piper didn't wait for Cooper to respond before she continued. "No sirree. She just kept chattering away as if I hadn't spoken a word." She shook her head. "I don't even have a diamond on my hand and she's planning the wedding already." Her stomach jumped and jittered.

"Piper." Coop lifted her chin and waited for her gaze to settle on his. "Is it possible that this is just your mom trying to set you up again?"

Piper threw her hands in the air. "That makes no sense."

He grasped her hands in his again. The gentle squeeze gave her comfort and she relaxed.

"I'm sorry. I didn't mean to snap at you. This whole thing has me rattled."

"It's all right." He offered a reassuring smile.

The server approached. She set a bag with the to-go boxes on the table and handed Cooper the check. He placed several bills in the holder. Handing it to the server, he said, "It's all set." To Piper, he said, "Come on, let's get out of here."

Grabbing the bag with one hand, he guided her to the exit.

She thought about what he'd said right before she'd lost it. "What did you mean about Mom setting me up again?"

"Think about it. As far as everyone knows, you just returned to New Suffolk a few days ago. I know we came up with a story to make our relationship plausible, but no one else knows that. There's no way anyone would even think we were engaged after just a few days."

Piper stopped walking midstride. "You're right."

"So why would your mother?" he asked. "What, exactly, did she say to you?"

Piper pursed her lips as she tried to remember the conversation. "First, she told me that she'd just gotten off a call with Hellen Francis and that she'd seen us together."

"Blabbermouth," Coop quipped.

Piper chuckled. "Yes, indeed. Then, Mom wanted to know if the two of us were having a late lunch together. After that she mentioned something about Hellen seeing us holding hands and did that mean what she thought it meant and why hadn't we told her."

"To be fair, you wouldn't have had anything to tell her about you and me. That all happened post Donny setup."

Piper scowled up at him. "Whose side are you on?"

"Ours." He grinned. "Now, how did she go from lunch and us being a couple to planning the wedding?"

"She said, and I quote, 'What Hellen told me is true then?'"

"And you answered yes."

"Of course." Piper agreed. "I thought Hellen had told her we were a couple, but apparently, she told her we were shopping for engagement rings. Unless...do you think my mom made that part up?"

"I think Hellen embellished her story and now Jane is trying to make sure it sticks. I mean, we did just hear both our moms confess to trying to set us up."

"Oh. My. God." Piper's eyes widened as comprehension dawned. "She's up to her old tricks again."

"So what do you want to do?" he asked.

She wanted to stop this once and for all. A plan hatched in her brain. She looked at him and grinned.

Grasping his hand in hers, she said, "Cooper Turner, will you fake marry me?"

"Have you lost your mind?" he asked.

Her smile lit up the sky that had turned dark with storm clouds. "No. I'm just trying to use the current situation to our advantage."

He shook his head. "You're going to have to explain, because I have no idea what's going on in that pretty head of yours."

"You think I'm pretty?" Her surprised expression made him chuckle.

He'd have thought that much was obvious from the way he'd been kissing her earlier today. "Don't play coy with me."

"I wasn't—" She shook her head.

Was that hurt in her gaze? Could she really not know how attractive he found her?

She straightened her shoulders. "What I was talking about was using what Hellen said about us window shopping for an engagement ring to our advantage."

They began walking again.

"Let's go to my place and we can warm up those burgers we ordered. They're probably cold by now, and I'm feeling hungry again." Piper turned and headed back the way they came.

He shook his head and followed. "Where are you going?"

"To my place. I live above the Coffee Palace. It's only a few blocks away and it's toasty warm inside." She rubbed her hands over her arms. "Now that the sun has disappeared behind the clouds, it's cold for this California girl."

"You're a New Suffolk native." He grinned. "Don't worry, you'll get used to the New England winters again soon."

"I hope so. Now let me explain what I'm thinking." She grabbed his hand. "You know, you're right about this walking thing. It helps me to think better, too."

"I daresay it's another thing we have in common." He winked at her.

She grinned. "I do believe you're correct in your assumption, my dear."

Her dear. He liked the sound of that. "All right. Let's hear it."

Piper told him her plan.

"Let me get this straight. You're going to pretend to be crazy about me over the next five weeks and not so subtly drop hints that you're expecting an engagement ring for Valentine's Day."

"You've got it." Piper nodded. "It fits in well with what you said earlier, that we've been dating since last summer when you came to LA. We might have to spend a little more time together than we initially planned." She shot him a speculative glance. "I can manage that, if you can."

Spending time with Piper was turning out to be much more pleasant than he'd ever imagined. "Sure. No problem."

"You'll end things right after the gallery opens, and tell everyone you're not ready for that kind of commitment. It's too soon."

He and Rachel had dated almost two years before he was ready to pop the question. He couldn't imagine proposing in such a short time frame. "That's the only part of all this that's true."

Her expression turned curious, but he wasn't going to elaborate.

"This plan gives both of us what we want and no one is the bad guy." She patted him on the arm. "Don't worry. I'll realize you dumping me was all for the best. Everything will be back to normal for the two of us in a couple of months."

"You don't think Jane will try her matchmaking again?" he asked.

"I don't think so. I'm banking on her not wanting to see me hurt again anytime soon. What about you? Will Debby interfere in your love life after this?" she asked.

"I don't see how she could. We'll prove to her once and for all that we don't belong together. Lord only knows why she thinks we do."

"I know." Piper's brows furrowed. "I was wondering the same thing when I heard her say that. She's obviously mistaken."

No doubt about it.

"Hey, Cooper." Fiona Carter, a fellow Humanity volunteer, came toward them.

"Hi, Fee." He smiled.

"It's great to see you. We missed you yesterday." Fiona gave him a quick hug.

Coop's brows furrowed. He never volunteered at Humanity on Sundays. Fiona knew that.

"Honey…are you going to introduce me to your friend?" Piper asked.

He couldn't help noticing how she emphasized the word *honey*, like she was trying to prove a point.

Fiona jerked away from him.

"I was just about to do that. Piper, this is Fiona Carter."

Piper extended her hand to Fiona. "Hi. I'm Cooper's girlfriend."

Fiona flicked a quick glance to him and back to Piper.

"I didn't realize Cooper was seeing anyone. It's...ah... nice to meet you." She shook Piper's outstretched hand.

"You, too." Piper grabbed his hand with her free one and squeezed tight enough to cause some pain.

He flinched. What was with her?

Piper flashed an overbright smile. "So, how do you know Cooper?" she asked.

"We volunteer at Homes for Humanity," he said.

"Oh, how nice." Piper sounded none too pleased about that. "It was nice meeting you." She tugged on his hand. "We should get going." She pointed to the bag he carried containing their meals. "Our lunch is probably getting cold."

"Take care," he called as Piper practically dragged him away.

"See you on Saturday," Fiona called.

He waited a couple of minutes, until they were out of earshot of any passersby, and said, "You know, there's no need to be jealous of Fiona. There's nothing going on between us."

She looked up at him. Color invaded her face.

Coop grinned. He couldn't help it.

Piper looked him in the eye. "I'm not jealous."

He laughed and the heat on her face kicked up a notch. Could this situation get any more embarrassing?

"You could have fooled me," Coop said. "You made it damned clear that Fiona needed to keep her hands off me."

He was right, but she'd never admit that to him. "I reacted the same way any female would when a gorgeous woman she doesn't know comes up to her man on the street and plasters herself against him."

"I'm your man?" Cooper flashed a smug smirk.

Piper pulled a face. "You are for now, if this plan is going to work."

"She gave me a friendly hug," he protested. "That's all."

Piper grinned. "The way Jax hugged me this morning?" She'd almost forgotten about that. Jax's flirting was harmless. She didn't believe he was actually interested in her. He mostly flirted with her and Mia to annoy Shane. "I guess that makes you jealous, too."

It was Cooper's turn to blush profusely. "That was different. Jax was all over you. I had to make it believable. He and Shane would have known the truth if I hadn't said anything."

Piper nodded. "Exactly. Which is why I did the same thing."

"Fiona and I are just friends," Cooper grumbled.

"So are Jax and me. And you're kidding yourself if you don't think that girl is interested in you. Either that or you're blind as a bat. Did you not notice her reaction when I called you *honey*? She un-plastered herself pronto." Which was why she'd done it.

"Okay, fine. We're both just playing our parts," he said.

"Exactly," she agreed. Cooper was just as jealous as her. The thought made her grin.

Chapter Twelve

"I've got to get going. Mia is waiting for me. We're going to Donahue's to watch Monday Night Football." Piper rose from the club chair in her mother's living room.

"I'm so happy for you and Cooper. I have to say, you two really know how to keep a secret." Jane kissed her cheek.

Piper straightened her shoulders. "Given how close the families are, we wanted to see how things went before we said anything." It was sort of the truth. Her stomach plummeted. Good grief. There wasn't an ounce of truth in any of those words. Lying to her mother was proving to be much more difficult than she'd expected.

Think of Donny and Blake, she told herself. Piper sucked in a slow, deep breath and relaxed. Mom wouldn't stop her matchmaking. She'd made that perfectly clear. Piper was doing what she had to do.

"And things are good between you?" Mom asked.

Piper grinned. "They're the best they've ever been." That was the God's honest truth.

"I couldn't be happier for you." Mom looked as if a heavy weight had been lifted from her shoulders.

"Thanks." She couldn't help smiling. "I'm happy, too." Because Mom would finally stop interfering in her love life. Yes. That was why she was happy. It had nothing to do with Cooper. And the excitement swirling around her stomach at the thought of seeing him later tonight at Donahue's... She was playing the part of besotted girlfriend. *That's all.*

"You know, I'm free this weekend. It wouldn't hurt to look at wedding dresses. Just to see what's out there." Jane walked her to the front door.

Piper pulled a face. "Mom! I told you. Cooper and I are not engaged."

"But you're hoping that will change in the near future," Mom insisted. "You were looking at rings."

Piper chuckled. Hellen Francis was such a busybody. "Well, I did see something I liked in the window display and I did mention to Cooper that I liked it." Now, that was 100 percent the truth.

"I guess we'll have to wait and see." Mom crossed her fingers.

Piper laughed. She couldn't help it. "I'll see you later."

Mom flicked on the front porch light and opened the door. Gesturing for Piper to step through the opening, she said, "Love you, darling."

"I love you, too."

She hurried down the front steps and strode to where she'd parked her car in Mom's driveway.

Her phone pinged as she started the engine. She glanced at the text from her sister.

Front door open. Come in when you get here. I'm hopping in the shower now.

Piper sent a quick note back. Will do. On my way.

A few minutes later, she pulled her car into the driveway of the colonial blue, Cape Cod–style house where Mia and her daughters lived.

Exiting her car, she walked along the gray paver stone

walkway to the front door and stepped inside. "Hey, Mia. I'm here."

"I'm upstairs," Mia shouted. "Come on up."

Piper climbed the stairs two at a time. She reached the small landing at the same time her sister raced out of the hall bathroom with towels wrapped around her body and hair.

"Come in." Mia jerked her head toward the master bedroom. "Have a seat on the bed."

Piper sat. She peered around the space. "This looks different than the last time I saw it."

"It is. I started remodeling about a month ago." Mia grabbed clothes from her dresser. "This is my current project." She pointed toward the master bath. "I pulled out the tub, which is why I was showering in the girls' bathroom. Not ideal sharing a bathroom with the kids." She shrugged. "Should have waited because I don't have much time to work on it until my February break. Be right back." She walked into the bathroom.

Piper spotted a stack of photo albums sitting on Mia's dresser. "Hey, are these mom's pictures?"

"Yeah. She dropped them off yesterday. Aurora's class is doing an ancestry project. We're going to go through the old pictures and put a collage together so she can tell everyone about her family."

"Sounds like a lot of work for a third grader," Piper said.

"She's just doing immediate family and grandparents," Mia responded.

The sound of a hair dryer made it impossible to continue their conversation.

Piper wandered over to the dresser and opened the first book. Images from their family vacation to Disney World right before her thirteenth birthday filled several pages and Piper grinned as she looked through the photos.

Pictures of Christmas of that same year came next. The one of Dad dressed as Santa brought a somewhat sad smile to her face. Who would have guessed that would be his last holiday with them? Not his three kids, who'd made gentle fun of him for dressing up like he'd done every year since Mia was born. He always insisted he was the real deal and told them only kids that believed would get presents.

Piper flipped the page. She found an image of her standing with her friend Ilana. They were both dressed in party dresses. She laughed. Ilana's bat mitzvah had been the first major party she'd been allowed to attend without her parents. Of course they didn't need to be there. The Kepelmanns had invited the entire Turner family since they were friends and Ron and Debby made sure she didn't get into any trouble. Not that it had even been an issue.

Several more images from Ilana's party followed. The last one had her doing a double take. Was that her *slow dancing* with Cooper?

No. It couldn't be. Piper removed the image from the protective cover and walked with it into the hall, which had brighter light. She scrutinized the image and...yes, that was her with her arms around thirteen-year-old Cooper's neck.

Piper gawked at the image. She couldn't remember dancing with him. Okay, yes, it was fifteen years ago, but you'd think she'd remember that.

Why would she be dancing with him? They didn't like each other.

She peered at the photo again. They were both grinning ear to ear. Good grief, not only were they wrapped in each other's arms, they seemed happy about it.

"Oh, here you are." Mia walked into the hall. "I was wondering where you'd gone. So, what do you think?" She did a little twirl.

Piper shoved the picture in the back pocket of her jeans and focused on her sister. "You straightened your hair. It's so much longer this way. Oh, and I love the highlights. When did you do this?" Piper picked up a lock of Mia's brown, highlighted hair. "It wasn't this way when I saw you the other day."

"This afternoon," Mia answered.

Piper's brows furrowed. "Didn't you have school?"

"I had to take some personal time. We met with the judge this morning. As of eleven a.m., I'm officially a single woman again." Mia smiled an overbright smile.

Piper hugged her sister. "Are you all right?" She couldn't imagine what Mia had gone through this last year.

Mia gave a nervous smile and eased away. "To be honest, I'm not sure how I feel. We spent eight years together. Well, ten, if you count the two years we dated in college before we got married. That's almost a third of my life."

Mia straightened her shoulders and looked Piper in the eyes. "But, yes. I'm all right. I'm looking forward to the next chapter of my life. Whatever that might bring. Now, do these clothes say thirty and flirty or frumpy mom? I'm outta practice."

Piper grinned. "You look great. You're gonna knock 'em dead, sis."

Mia didn't look convinced.

"You're a knockout. Trust me," Piper said. "Let's get going. Layla, Abby and Elle are probably already there."

Mia glanced at her watch. "You're right. We need to get there soon if we want a table. The place is usually packed for Monday Night Football. Let's do this."

Piper crooked her elbow and linked her arm with her sister's. "I'll drive. You have fun."

Mia snorted. "I can't drink that much. I still have to face a classroom full of first graders tomorrow."

They arrived at Donahue's pub fifteen minutes later. As they walked into the bar, Mia said, "Hey, you said you wanted to tell me something when we hopped in the car, but I never gave you a chance to say what it was. I've pretty much monopolized the conversation since you arrived."

"Yeah, there is something." She opened the door to the bar and gestured for Mia to proceed her.

Mia walked inside. "What is it?" she asked.

"It's about Cooper and me," she started.

Mia rolled her gaze skyward. "Don't tell me you guys got into another fight again."

"No-oo." She dragged out the word. "I wouldn't say that."

Hand on hip, Mia turned to face her. "Then what would you say? Hey, is that Jax Rawlins coming toward us?"

"Yes. He's in town for a couple of days. He and Shane stopped by the gallery earlier." That reminded her. She needed to nail down the details for Jax's show. She couldn't believe he'd volunteered to allow her to feature his pictures. People came from all over the world to view his work. This one show could skyrocket her gallery to elite status in no time flat. Talk about a stroke of good luck.

"Hello, ladies." Jax gave her a quick hug and released her. He turned his attention to Mia. "It's great to see you again."

Mia flashed a nervous smile. "Yeah, you, too."

"How long has it been?" Jax asked Mia. He couldn't take his gaze off her.

"Almost ten years," Mia admitted.

"Too long." Jax's tone held a hint of longing.

Piper's brows furrowed. Was there something between her sister and Jax? They both looked…wistful.

"Hey, Mia." Cooper came over and gave her sister a hug.

"It's good to see you." He turned his attention to Piper. His gaze smoldered with heat.

Piper's pulse kicked up a notch.

"Piper, honey." Cooper pulled her into his arms and planted his lips on hers.

His hungry mouth devoured hers. Tasting, teasing, until every inch of her was on fire.

"What the heck!" Mia sputtered.

He released her and she swayed. Good Lord, the man could kiss.

"You can't seem to keep your hands off each other." Jax smirked. "You really need to get a room."

"*What* is going on?" Mia gasped.

Cooper threw his arm around her waist and steadied her. "You didn't tell your sister about us?"

"I was, ah, just about to." She sucked in a breath. Lord, she couldn't think straight when he was this close.

"Well…" Mia pointed back and forth a couple of times between her and Cooper. "This is an interesting development."

"I'll say," Jax snorted.

Cooper looked at her, his gaze filled with heat.

Her pulse soared into overdrive. Oh, this was quite an interesting development all right.

How the hell had this happened?

Chapter Thirteen

On Wednesday evening, Piper pulled her car into Mia's driveway. Elle and Abby waved as they exited the car next to hers.

She grabbed from the front passenger seat the big bowl of salad she'd prepared for their dinner.

"Hey, Piper. How's Cooper doing?" Elle flashed a smug smirk.

She wasn't sure. She hadn't seen much of him since he'd planted that smoldering kiss on her at Donahue's.

A shiver raced down her spine. The skill and talent that man possessed.

"Piper?" Elle nudged her.

"Cooper is fine." At least she assumed he was. She'd done her best to avoid him by scheduling artist interviews over most of the last two days.

What was she supposed to say to him?

Hey, Cooper, that was one hell of a performance the other night. You certainly convinced everyone we're a couple with that kiss.

Feel free to indulge anytime you like.

No, no, no. What was she thinking? This thing they'd started was complicated enough. They didn't need to add sex into the mix.

Anticipation hummed and buzzed inside her.

She needed to change the subject. Fast. "So, what are we celebrating?" Mia had told her Elle had big news to share.

"I've been accepted to Boston University. I'm going to finish my business administration degree." Elle brandished the bottle of champagne in her hand.

"We're so proud of you." Abby slung an arm around her cousin's shoulder.

Elle's cheeks flushed crimson. "It's not that big a deal."

"It is, given everything you've gone through over the last few years." Layla walked up behind them carrying two platters of food. "And that's why we're celebrating tonight."

Elle gazed from Abby to Piper and to Mia's house. "I can't think of anyone else I'd love to celebrate with more."

Piper marveled at the bond these women shared. She'd never experienced anything resembling this closeness, this loving support, with her friends in LA, nor here in New Suffolk, when she was younger.

Or maybe you've never been open to the concept before. Maybe you pushed people away. Kept them at arm's distance so you couldn't get hurt the way Mom was hurt when Dad died.

She shook off the uncomfortable, unwelcome thoughts. "Let's break open that bubbly."

Piper knocked on her sister's front door. It opened and three giggling girls appeared. "Hello, ladies."

"Hi, Auntie Piper," Aurora greeted.

Brooke waved.

"Are you gonna come in?" Kiera asked.

Piper chuckled. "You guys have to move out of the way first. You're blocking the doorway."

"Come on in." Mia's voice came from somewhere inside the house.

Aurora, Brooke and Kiera ran into the living room and the adults stepped inside.

"Why don't you set the food on the island." Mia walked in from the kitchen that was open to the living room and dining area. A renovation Mia had done right after she and her ex had bought the place.

Mia and her brother, Shane, had inherited their father's creativity when it came to home makeovers and construction. Piper had inherited Dad's love of painting and sculpting, although Dad had liked to work with metals and she preferred clay.

"Hey, I love your necklace." Elle walked over and touched the antique silver, chunky, Bohemian bib choker fastened around Piper's neck. "Is it from the shop in town?"

Piper nodded. "I saw it in the window display the other day." She'd gone back to buy it yesterday afternoon.

"That's not all you were looking at." Mia winked. "I do believe you spotted a ring you might like." She held up her left hand and waggled her third finger.

"Wait. What?" Layla gasped.

Mia smirked and started humming Mendelssohn's *Wedding March.*

Heat crept up Piper's neck and flooded her cheeks. "Gossipmonger."

"Did Cooper give you a ring?" Abby grabbed Piper's left hand and held it up for inspection.

"Daddy gave Oriana a ring but she didn't like it." Kiera pointed to Piper's bare fingers.

Piper gasped. Oriana was the woman Kyle had left Mia for.

The room went silent and everyone stared at her sister.

"Okay, girls." Mia straightened her shoulders. "Time for you to go into the den and watch your movie."

"We want to stay out here with you guys." Brooke pointed to Piper and the others.

"That's not an option." Mia gestured toward the den, which sat to the right of where she was standing. "It's either a movie or bed."

The girls scurried away.

Mia followed and returned to the others a moment later.

"Your ex got engaged?" Layla asked.

"Are you okay?" Piper moved to Mia's side.

"I'm fine, and no, Kyle and Oriana are not engaged. He asked her on Monday. Right after he signed our divorce papers."

Elle pulled a face. "Oh, that's just poor form."

Piper agreed. "You knew he was going to ask her?"

Mia nodded. "He told me at the courthouse."

Piper slung her arm around Mia's shoulder and gave her a firm squeeze. No wonder her sister had gone out and gotten a makeover.

Abby snorted. "What a jerk."

"Yep," Elle agreed.

"Yes." Mia nodded. "That was a crappy thing to do, but I'm glad he told me so that I could reassure the girls that everything was okay."

"You're a really good mom." Piper pressed a kiss to Mia's cheek.

"So, what happened?" Elle asked.

"She turned him down." Mia held up a hand. She disappeared into the hall for a moment and returned. "I just wanted to make sure the door was still closed." In a hushed voice she added, "Apparently Oriana isn't ready to take on the responsibility of three kids, even part-time."

"Did Kyle tell you that?" Abby asked.

Mia nodded. "Yesterday morning." A hint of pink touched her cheeks. "He came over after he dropped the kids off at school."

Mia's cheeks went from pink to scarlet.

"What happened?" Piper asked. "Something must have, because you're bright red."

"Did you and your ex…" Abby made a funny motion with her hand.

Mia's brows furrowed. "Did we what?"

"She's asking if you and Kyle did the horizontal tango?" Elle smirked.

Piper smacked her hand to her head. "Please tell me you didn't sleep with him."

"Oh God no," Mia denied.

"Then why are your cheeks on fire?" Layla laughed.

"Oh my God!" Elle covered her mouth with her palm. "You were with Jax Rawlins. Ms. I-have-to-get-up-early-for-work-tomorrow-so-I-need-to-leave-now."

Mia's eyes went wide. "How did you know?"

"I'm not blind. You two couldn't keep your eyes off each other." Elle looked at Piper. "It was the same with you and Cooper. And I was right." Elle flashed a smug smile. "Even though you denied it."

"About you and Cooper," Mia began.

Piper shook her head. "Oh no. This time you don't get to change the subject. So, you and Jax?" Elle wasn't the only one who'd seen the sparks the other night, but she'd dismissed them because it was Jax. As Shane's best friend since childhood, he'd been around for as long as Piper could remember.

Mia held up a hand. "There is no me and Jax. It was one night only."

"But," Piper protested.

"No buts." Mia smiled. "I don't want a relationship. I just ended my marriage. The last thing I want is something serious. And I would appreciate it if we could keep this between the five of us." She turned her attention to Layla. "Please don't say anything to Shane. He can be a little overprotective at times."

"Yes, he can," Piper agreed. She remembered all too

well his reaction when he'd found her and Cooper. Heat pooled low in her belly just remembering the feel of Cooper's hands as they stroked along her spine and over her shoulders. And his scent. Fresh and clean with something more. Something she couldn't identify, but it drove her wild.

Stop it, stop it, stop it right now. She gave herself a mental shake.

"I know he means well, and I love my brother dearly, but this isn't any of his business," Mia said.

Layla lifted a finger to her lips. "Mum's the word."

Elle rubbed her hands together. "Now, I want to hear all the deets about you and Cooper."

"Um…" Piper's breathing quickened.

Abby chuckled. "Oh yeah. Check out that expression. She's got it bad for the hot construction guy."

Piper opened her mouth to deny the claim, but stopped before the words came out. This was what she'd hoped for. They believed she and Cooper were a couple.

Mia crossed her arms in front of her chest and smirked. "You, little sis, have a lot of explaining to do. Come on. Confession time. Is it true what Mom said? Are you hoping for a ring by Valentine's Day?"

"Yes." A little thrill raced through her. Because everything was going according to plan. *Not* because the thought of her and Cooper together sent shivers racing down her spine.

Nope. Nope. Nope.

The next morning, Coop zipped into a parking space at the mansion and booked it upstairs to Piper's gallery. He found her sitting at the kitchen island reviewing a large portfolio.

"Hey, Piper. Sorry I'm late. I slept through my alarm."

She peered up at him. "You must have been pretty tired."

Not exactly. Coop had tossed and turned until almost two thirty, and it was all Piper's fault. His imagination had gone into hyperdrive the last couple of days, conjuring pictures of their naked bodies entwined together, her long blond hair fanned over his pillow. He swallowed hard.

The cold shower he'd taken hadn't done anything to cool his libido. Even when he'd slept, he'd dreamed of her.

"It's no wonder you're tired. That client of yours has got you working six days a week with no time off for good behavior. She must be a real taskmaster."

Images of her dressed in tight black leather, holding a whip, flooded his brain.

Son of a... Coop yanked off his coat and casually held it in front of him to hide the sudden bulge in his pants.

What the hell was wrong with him? He wasn't even into BDSM. Although, with her... He shook his head.

"She's not that bad," he said.

"Seriously, you've been working hard since we started this renovation and I really appreciate it, but I don't want you to burn out. Between the work you're doing here and the time you volunteer at Homes for Humanity, you're working seven days a week. We've gotten a lot done. You deserve a day of rest. Take tomorrow off."

He shook his head. "No need. I'm fine."

"Cooper." Piper walked over to where he stood near the entrance to the gallery and squeezed his arm. "You deserve some time off."

He couldn't miss the care in her gaze.

"Okay. I'll take tomorrow off, but only if you do, too. You've been working just as hard as I have." He gestured about the space with his free hand. "You stay long after noon most days to tackle the painting. That's why we're ahead of schedule."

"It's my place," she reasoned.

"Take the deal, Piper. We can do something fun together." The words came out of his mouth before his brain could stop them.

Piper blinked. "Are you asking me out on a date?"

Oh crap. Yes. No. Coop dragged a hand through his hair. He studied Piper. She looked…okay, maybe horrified was too harsh a description, but she didn't seem thrilled either.

Awkward. What was he supposed to say now?

"You mean we'll go on one of the 'dates' we talked about having? So that people believe we're a real couple?" she clarified.

"Right." If he nodded any faster, she might think he was a bobblehead. "Of course I did." Coop stopped nodding and released the breath he'd been holding. "What else would I mean?"

"Nothing." Relief flooded her features. "Good thinking. We need to keep up appearances."

Thank you, Universe, for small favors.

"Coffee's ready if you want some. The one on the left is yours." She pointed to the two pots resting side by side on one end of the island. "There's a breakfast sandwich from the Coffee Palace in the bag for you, too. It should still be hot. I just picked it up a few minutes ago."

He smiled. "Hey, thank you. I didn't get a chance to eat anything and I am starving."

"You're welcome." Piper grinned.

Cooper strode toward the island. "Hey, these are new." He gestured to the two bar-height chairs lined up in front of the counter.

"Layla is letting me borrow them until the ones I ordered arrive."

She'd been sitting in one when he first arrived, but his brain hadn't registered the fact. He was definitely sleep-deprived today.

Coop pulled out the chair Piper hadn't been sitting in. Something went flying off the seat and thudded on the ground. He glanced down. The contents of Piper's purse lay scattered on the floor.

"I'm so sorry," he said.

Piper rushed over. "No. It's my fault. I shouldn't have left my purse on the chair."

He started picking up the items and handed them to her. "Hey, what's this?"

"A picture of you and me when we were kids. I've been meaning to ask you about it." She handed the photo back to him. "Do you remember where it was taken?"

He studied the image and smiled. "At Ilana Kepelmann's bat mitzvah."

"That's what I thought." She looked him in the eye. "I don't remember dancing with you at that party."

He couldn't possibly forget. Some of the other boys at the party had dared him to ask her to dance, but the truth was, he'd wanted to.

Sometime between the end of seventh grade and the beginning of eighth, Piper went from annoying as all get-out to intriguing. His stomach would flip-flop every time she came near him.

Not that he would have admitted as much to anyone. His brothers would have teased the crap out of him if they'd known. His friends would have, too.

Still, he'd done his best to get her to notice him in the only way he knew how. Too bad his thirteen-year-old self didn't know pranks and dares were not the way to go. All he'd succeeded in doing was to make her even more aggravated with him than ever.

Until that night. When she smiled at him on the dance floor...

"Hey, Piper." Cooper stopped in front of Piper and Ilana on the edge of the dance floor in the ballroom of the New Suffolk Bay Beach Club, New Suffolk's version of a country club.

Piper's nostrils flared as she stared at him.

His stomach turned a loop the loop. Lord, why was he so nervous? All he had to do was ask her. It shouldn't be hard. So why did he feel like he might puke up the food they'd just eaten?

"Hi, Cooper," Ilana said, smirking at him.

"Hey," he said. "Nice party." His parents would be pissed if he wasn't polite. "Thanks for inviting me."

"You're welcome," Ilana said.

He returned his attention to Piper. She looked so pretty in the long coral dress she wore.

Ilana waved a hand in front of his face. "Did you want something, or are you just going to stand there staring?"

Coop swallowed hard. His stomach jumped and jittered. "You wanna dance, Piper?" His words came out in a rush.

She stared at him as if he'd grown another head, but said nothing.

Coop held his breath as what seemed like hours passed with no response from her.

"Piper." Ilana nudged her with her elbow.

She opened her mouth but no words came out.

"She'd love to." Ilana shoved her forward.

That was good enough for him. He rubbed his sweaty palm against his trousers and grasped her hand.

Coop led her to the dance floor, stopping when he found an empty space. He started moving, praying he wasn't making a complete fool of himself.

The hint of a smile crossed her face as she did the same.

That had to be a good sign. Maybe he wasn't as bad at this as Nick and Levi claimed he was. Coop breathed a sigh of relief.

The rock song ended and another started, a slow song.

His pulse soared. He'd never slow danced before. What the heck was he supposed to do?

Piper stood stock-still. She stared at him. Panic etched her bright blue gaze.

He peered around the room and stared at Dad and Mom. Dad had one hand on Mom's hip. His other held her hand. Coop grabbed Piper's hand with what was clearly too much force, because she bounced against his chest.

He didn't fall, thank God, but he did stumble back a couple of steps.

"Sorry," she mumbled.

"It's okay." He placed his hand on Piper's hip. Glancing at Dad, he noticed he swayed from side to side. Cooper tried to do the same but his movements weren't as smooth as Dad's.

Piper slanted a couple of worried looks in his direction as they moved.

Was he doing it all wrong? Cooper started to sweat. He jerked his gaze toward the other couples on the dance floor. No. He'd copied them the best he could.

The song ended too soon as far as he was concerned. He would have liked to keep dancing with her like this.

Piper looked up at him. A brilliant smile crossed her face. "Thanks. That was fun."

She'd liked dancing with him.

He grinned.

* * *

"Cooper?" Piper nudged him.

He blinked. "What?"

She repeated her statement. "I don't remember dancing with you."

He nodded. "It was a long time ago."

"Fifteen years. It looks like we were having a good time together." It was more of a question than a statement.

He peered at the image again. *A great time.* Dancing with her had been the best part of that party.

Who would have guessed that three days later her world would come crumbling down and that nothing would ever be the same between them again?

Not the boy who blamed himself for not saving her father, and not the girl who would never forgive him.

Coop gave himself a mental shake. He needed to stop thinking about the past. He couldn't change it.

"I'm sorry I don't remember." Piper rested her hand on his arm.

It was time to lighten the mood. His lips curved into a smile. "I wasn't a great dancer back then. You probably blocked it out because I stepped on your feet all night."

Her sweet chuckle sent a flood of warmth rushing through him.

"I'm serious. I didn't have the mad skills I do today." He mimicked a few waltz steps in the area where they stood.

She laughed harder. "Sorry, I'm just not seeing it."

"Is that a challenge, Ms. Kavanaugh?"

"I believe it is, Mr. Turner."

He grinned. "Oh, it's on." Coop grabbed his phone. He opened his music app and typed in "slow dance music." He set the phone on the countertop when the melody started.

Extending his hand to her, he said, "May I have this dance?"

Surprise flickered across her face as she extended her hand to his.

Coop set his right hand on Piper's hip and grasped her right hand with his left. "What do you think of this?" He spun her out and back in again.

She smiled up at him. "Not too shabby."

He moved them about the space for a few minutes, adding more twirls and spins as they made their way across the room. When the song ended, he dipped her.

"Oh my." Her startled gaze landed on his. "That was pretty good."

The next song started to play.

Like all those years ago, he wasn't ready to end this yet. He liked holding her in his arms. Coop wrapped his arms around her waist, and enjoyed the press of her body against his. "How am I doing so far?" he murmured.

"Shh." Piper twined her arms around his neck and laid her head on his shoulder.

They moved together to the slow, sensual beat.

"Cooper. Piper." His mother appeared in the entry.

He froze at the sudden intrusion. So did Piper. They jerked away from each other as if they'd been caught doing something wrong.

"Mom." Coop ran a hand through his hair. "What are you doing here?"

Chapter Fourteen

"Debby." *Crap, crap, crap.* Heat scorched Piper's cheeks and flooded her face. She peered around the room, looking everywhere but at Cooper.

"I hope I'm not interrupting anything." Debby cast a knowing look in her direction.

Piper was pretty sure her cheeks flamed even brighter. Could she be any more embarrassed? She shoved her hands in her pockets and rocked back and forth on her heels. Lord, she felt like a teenager who just got caught making out with her boyfriend, which was totally ridiculous.

Get a grip. Piper sucked in a steadying breath and blew it out slowly. *You're a grown woman.* It wasn't as if she and Cooper had done anything wrong. They were just dancing, for goodness' sake. A frisson of pleasure trickled down her spine.

She shuddered. *So not the time to be thinking about that.*

"Of course not." Piper waved off Debby's concern. "This is a pleasant surprise." She needed to start locking the door on the lower level so people couldn't walk in unannounced.

"I'm so glad." Debby grinned.

"What are you doing here?" Cooper asked again.

"I wanted to see if you two were free for dinner on Saturday evening." She turned her attention to Piper. "Ron and I would love it if you could join us."

"You could have just called," Cooper grumbled. "You

didn't have to drop by." He turned and strode to the island. Grabbing a mug, he filled it with coffee. He moved to the side opposite the coffeemaker, hiding the lower half of his body from view. Setting his cup down, he propped his elbows on the granite surface.

Unfortunately, the island wouldn't hide her arousal. She grabbed her cardigan off the chair back and tugged it on.

"So, what do you say?" Debby flashed a hopeful smile.

Piper understood why Debby had stopped by in person to issue the invitation. It was a lot harder to say no to her face.

Cooper shot a sidelong glance at her and she nodded.

"I can't, Mom. I've already got plans."

"Me, too," Piper said.

"How about sometime next week?" Cooper suggested.

"What about next Friday?" Debby asked.

Cooper's birthday.

"That works for me." Cooper sent her an enquiring glance. "How about you?"

"Yes," she agreed. "I'm available, too."

"Six o'clock?" Debby asked.

"Sounds good," Piper said.

Cooper nodded. "That will give me time to shower and change after I get home from working on the Humanity houses."

An image of the stunningly gorgeous Fiona flashed into her mind. Piper gritted her teeth. Oh, she was jealous all right. Which made absolutely no sense. She and Cooper... There *was* no Piper and Cooper. Their relationship was a farce. A means to an end.

Okay, so she was attracted to him. Piper sucked in a deep, steadying breath. She could deny it all she wanted, but that didn't make it untrue.

How had this happened? A week ago, they couldn't

stand to be in the same room with each other. Now... She glanced at him. He still stood on the other side of the island. Piper shivered. He wanted her as much as she wanted him. He'd proven that a few minutes ago when he'd held her close.

What did she want? The truth was she wasn't sure. She liked Cooper. She couldn't deny *that* any longer either.

Lord, just admitting that fact sent her head spinning.

"I'll make a reservation at the Italian place in Plymouth." Debby turned to Piper. "Ron and I love it there. The food is excellent."

"Great." She pasted a bright smile in place, grateful for the diversion from her musings. "I can't wait."

Debby hugged her. "I'm just so happy you two finally got together."

Piper swallowed hard. A pang of guilt swept through her for the deception they were playing.

"Mom," Cooper warned. He sent her an annoyed glance. "We talked about this."

"I'm just saying." Debby let go of Piper and crossed to her son. "See you later." She kissed him on the cheek.

Waving at Piper, she walked to the doors and exited the room.

"I'm sorry about that." Cooper came over to where she stood.

Piper laughed. "Which part? The dinner invitation we couldn't say no to, or your mom walking in on us?" At least she hadn't caught them in a compromising position the way her brother had.

"Both, but mainly the walking in on us." He flashed a heart-stopping smile. "Her timing is lousy."

Everything inside her went soft and mushy.

Heaven help her. She was in big trouble now.

* * *

Piper hummed along to the song blasting from the speaker as she painted. She frowned when the music stopped. Walking into the main part of the gallery, she jumped when she saw Cooper. "Oh my god, you scared me! I didn't hear you come in."

"I'm sorry! Didn't mean to startle you. I saw the windows open and wondered what you were doing here," he said. "I thought we agreed to take today off. We're supposed to go on a date. You're not standing me up, are you?"

Not a snowball's chance in hell. Oh, good grief. Get a hold of yourself. "No. Of course not." Piper tapped her watch. "It's only eleven o'clock. I figured we wouldn't head out until later. In the meantime, I thought I'd get a little painting done."

Cooper shook his head. "The date starts now."

She blinked. "Oh, okay. Where are we going?" Piper stared at her old jeans, sweatshirt and work boots. "I need to go home and change."

"You're fine as is." Heat flickered in his gaze as he eyed her from head to toe.

She laughed as she shook her head. "I'm not going out dressed like this."

"Okay. You'll need to wear something warm. And winter boots, too." Cooper grinned.

"We're going someplace outdoors?" She sent him a wary glance.

"The artist in you is going to love it." He grinned.

Okay. He'd piqued her interest. "All right. Let me finish up what I was doing and we can go."

Cooper nodded. "I'll meet you at your place."

Fifteen minutes later, she pulled her vehicle into her designated spot in the parking lot behind the Coffee Palace.

Exiting her car, she walked to the back door of the building. Cooper jumped out of a silver F-150 and joined her.

"You have a truck, too?" she asked.

He nodded. "I don't usually drive the Camaro in the winter, especially when there's snow on the ground. I had to recently because my truck was in the shop."

She nodded. "Makes sense."

Piper opened the external door and stepped into the back hall. She climbed the stairs and unlocked the door to her apartment when they reached the landing on the second floor.

Walking inside, she turned to Cooper, and said, "I'll be right back. Make yourself at home."

She hurried into her bedroom and changed into a pair of skinny jeans and her light blue V-neck cashmere sweater. Releasing her ponytail, she ran a brush through her hair and added lip gloss.

Glancing at her reflection in the mirror, she nodded and exited her bedroom.

Cooper stood when she walked into the living room. "This is a cute place."

Piper peered around. "It's good for now, but eventually I'd like to find a house."

"Oh yeah? What are you looking for? A place on the beach?"

She nodded. "Probably. I had a place near the ocean when I lived in Los Angeles. I loved living by the water. You can't beat a fresh sea breeze and your toes in the sand. What about you?"

"The beach is okay, but I prefer a little more solitude. A place where my next-door neighbor isn't on top of me."

Piper chuckled. "What, no Hellen Francis types stopping by with cookies?"

Cooper grinned. "Exactly."

"There is something to be said for privacy." Piper walked to the closet. She grabbed her winter boots.

"Bring shoes for later. We won't stay outside for too long."

She grinned. "Now you're talking." Piper slid her feet inside the plush fake fur lining.

"Let me get your coat for you. You'll need something to keep warm, seeing as you're used to much milder temperatures." He winked.

"That's an understatement. The average temperature in LA at this time of year is in the high sixties. We'll be lucky if it gets above freezing here today."

"You're an outdoor girl at heart. You'll be fine."

He remembered that about her? A rush of warmth flooded through her.

Grabbing her long, down parka from the hanger, Cooper held it open for her.

Sure, she could put the coat on all by herself, but his kind gesture made her feel...special. Her heart gave a little kick. "Thank you, kind sir."

"You're welcome. Ready to go?" he asked.

"I am." She grasped a pair of high-heeled suede booties and her purse, slinging the strap over her shoulder as she made her way to the door.

They exited the building and strode to Cooper's truck. Once inside, she asked, "Are you going to give me a hint as to where we're going? Other than some place outside followed by a place inside where I'll need shoes."

He pursed his lips as he started the engine. "We're going to stay in New Suffolk."

Piper let loose a chuckle. "So we're not going skiing or tubing at one of the nearby mountains?"

"Nope. Definitely staying more local." Cooper pulled

out of the parking lot and turned onto Main Street. "Oh, and we'll have lunch, too."

She couldn't imagine where he was taking her. What local attraction had outdoor activities and a restaurant? "You've got me stumped."

Cooper flashed a mile-wide grin. "Don't worry. You won't have to wait long to see where we're going. But first, I need to make a quick stop. It's on the way." He turned on the road that led to the outskirts of town. "We'll be there in less than ten minutes."

The downtown hustle and bustle faded to a more rural landscape as they drove.

Piper stared out the passenger window. She marveled at how the sunlight dappled through the pine trees and evergreens, glinting on the fresh coating of snow that covered the ground. "This part of town is really beautiful. I don't think I ever appreciated that as a kid."

"It's peaceful," Cooper said.

"Yes." The landscape filled her with a sense of calmness and tranquility. "I can see why your parents love living out this way."

"Actually, they sold their place last May and moved closer to town."

She jerked her gaze to his. "Really? I would never have guessed your dad would want to do such a thing."

"Dad and Mom want to start traveling more. The upkeep on the house and all that land was a huge time suck. They didn't want that anymore."

Piper nodded. "I can understand that."

"While not immediate, retirement is sooner rather than someday in the distant future for them."

It made sense. Her mother was in the same boat. She'd started talking about wanting more time to pursue interests outside of TK Construction. Piper looked at it as a good sign. For so long now, her mother's life seemed to have revolved around work and home, with no social life to speak of. *Those first few years after Dad's death...* She'd trudged, zombie-like, through her days.

Piper gave herself a mental shake. Mom had her book club friends now. Maybe she'd finally start moving on with her life.

"We had some fun times there when we were kids," she said. Flag football games at Thanksgiving, barbecues and pool parties on hot summer days, and ice-skating on the rink Ron had built when the weather turned cold.

"You've got a huge smile on your face," Cooper said, grinning. "What are you remembering?"

She trained her focus on him. "I just had this flash-back to when we were like six years old. We were all out in your parents' backyard and had a snowman building contest. Mia and Levi teamed up, and Shane and Nick, which left you and me.

"My dad decided the others had an unfair advantage, so he helped us and, of course, we won."

"You and me on the same team?" He snorted.

She laughed a deep belly laugh. "I know, right?"

"I don't remember that specific event, but you're still smiling, so it must be a good memory."

There went that crazy heart of hers again, beating a rapid tattoo. "Yes. It is." It was nice to finally be able to remember times spent with her father without being over-whelmed by sadness and despair. For too long, she'd sup-pressed all her memories in order to stop the bad ones. No emotions had been preferrable to grief.

"I'm glad," he said. His grin warmed her better than any fire could.

Piper sighed. "It must have been sad to see the place

go. You spent your childhood there. It must hold a lot of memories for you, too."

"I have to admit that I was upset when they first told me, Nick and Levi they were selling the place." Cooper brought the truck to a stop. "That's why I bought it." He gestured out the window.

Piper's mouth fell open. The house looked totally different than what she remembered. "I see you've made some changes." The vintage one-story farmhouse now boasted new, larger windows with slate blue shutters, and a covered, wraparound porch. Stone siding covered the two bumped-out areas on either side of the front door, and white, vertical boards covered the rest of the exterior. Dormers with windows added dimension and style to the old facade.

"I love it."

It felt like…home.

Chapter Fifteen

She liked what he'd done. Warmth radiated throughout his entire body. "Thanks." Cooper beamed. He couldn't wait to show her the rest. "Come on. I'll show you the inside."

"I can't wait to see everything." Piper opened her door and hopped out.

Cooper walked over to where she stood. "This way." He grasped her hand in his and they walked over the pavers to the front entrance. He probably looked like a big goofball with this stupid grin plastered on his face, but he didn't care.

"I love the double doors. And those tall glass panels are fabulous," she said.

"It was really dark when you first came in before, but now…" Cooper unlocked the door on the right and opened it. "Look how much sunlight shines in." He stepped aside to allow her entry.

Piper stepped inside. "Look at these floors. The wood actually gleams."

They'd better. He'd spent hours sanding and applying several coats of urethane to make them shine. "It's the original flooring. I just refinished them."

"They're gorgeous. You did a phenomenal job."

He grinned and, yes, his chest puffed out…just a little.

Piper looked to her left. "This used to be Nick's room, right?"

"Yes. I ripped out the carpet and painted. I'm using it as a study right now."

"I love the cool gray paint," Piper said. "It's very modern, but you need some artwork on the walls."

Coop chuckled. "I haven't gotten that far yet. You're the art expert. Do you have any suggestions?"

"I'll think about it and let you know."

"Sounds good." He pointed to his right. "I haven't tackled the other bedrooms and the bathrooms yet, but the kitchen, dining and family rooms are completed. We can head there now." He gestured for her to precede him down the short hall and into the main space.

"Oh. My. Goodness!" Piper rushed into the family room. "Look at this fireplace!"

Coop grinned. "You like it?" He'd covered the standard red brick with limestone that went from floor to ceiling.

"It's amazing." She looked up at the vaulted ceilings. "You added wood beams." Piper bounced up and down on the balls of her feet. "It looks so cool."

He loved her enthusiasm. "I'm glad you like it."

Piper glanced to her left. "Dear God." Her mouth fell open. "Look at this kitchen. You removed the wall and opened it to the family room." She rushed over and stroked her hand over the white marble covering the blue island. "Be honest. Did you hire someone to design this space?" She touched one of the white Shaker cabinets that lined the walls, and the stainless steel six-burner stove.

He shook his head. "I did it myself." He'd renovated enough kitchens in his career to know what he liked and what he didn't.

"You have excellent taste. This is exactly what I'd do if I were to design my dream kitchen." She jerked her gaze from one end of the room to the other. "It seems bigger, too."

"It is." He nodded. "I used part of the formal dining

room." He'd traded the space required to house his mother's china and buffet cabinets for more kitchen storage.

Piper nodded. "You removed the wall that used to separate the two rooms, too. I didn't realize that when I first walked in.

"I love how the kitchen, dining room and family room are open to each other. It's great for entertaining."

"I haven't done any of that yet. I've spent the last six months renovating, but I'm hoping to have a party to show everyone soon."

"You haven't shown this to anyone? Not even your family?" Piper turned an astonished glance in his direction.

"You're the first."

"Thank you. That means a lot." She brushed her lips against his cheek.

Coop closed his eyes for a moment. The fleeting touch sent shivers down his spine. He reveled in the sensation. "You're welcome." Was that gruff voice his? He cleared his throat. "Do you want to see more?"

She placed some much-needed space between them. "Yes, please."

He swallowed hard and tried to get his raging hormones under control. "It means going outside."

Piper flashed the sweetest grin, and his heart beat a rapid tattoo. "I think we can do that."

Two eight-foot sliders flanked the fireplace on either side. Cooper strode to the right side and opened the door. He stepped onto the patio and Piper followed.

"This is the same." He gestured to the hot tub and covered pool. "I added a putting green." He pointed to his left. "And the outdoor kitchen." He gestured to the built-in grill and mini fridge on his right.

"The gazebo looks new." Piper opened the gate to

the fence that surrounded the pool and moved toward the structure.

He followed her. "Newer," he corrected. "The old one rotted out and Dad replaced it a couple of years ago with this bigger one."

Piper broke into a run. "Look at the icicles on the roof. With all the fresh snow, it looks like an ice castle." She scooped up two armfuls of snow and threw it up in the air. "It's so pretty. Come on." Piper spread her arms wide and fell backward. She let out a loud "woo-hoo" as she hit the ground.

"What are you doing?" he called as he traversed the short distance.

"Making a snow angel." She motioned for him to join her.

"You know that won't last, right? The weather report said it's going to snow six to twelve inches later today."

Piper clasped her hands over her heart. "I'll always have the memory in here." She stood and admired her handy-work. "Perfect," she announced. "I forgot how much fun playing in the snow can be."

The smile on her face warmed him inside and out. "I'm glad you're enjoying yourself." This wasn't what he had planned—a quick trip to see the frozen waterfalls at Long Pond, to appeal to her artistic nature, and a trip to Layla's restaurant for one of the famous burgers he'd promised her the other day had topped his to-do list—but he'd go with it.

"Let's make a snowman." Excitement shone in her bright blue eyes. "I'll start on the base. Can you start roll-ing the ball for the middle section?" she asked.

She looked so happy. Coop's heart beat a rapid tattoo. "Yeah, sure. No problem." He'd do just about anything to keep that smile on her face.

They worked in silence for several minutes. She, kneeling on the ground and continuing to add to her base, as he accumulated a second sizable sphere. When he thought the ball was big enough, he called over to her. "Are you ready for me to add this on top of yours?" Coop pointed to the chunk of snow sitting at his feet.

"You betcha." She motioned with her arm. "Bring it on over."

He rolled the ball over to where she sat.

Piper stood. "Okay, we'll lift it together on three."

He bent over and she followed suit.

"One… Two… Three!" Her hands went up. The ball fell apart in the air. Piper went flying backward and landed on her back.

He chuckled. He couldn't help it. "Are you okay?" he asked.

"I'm fine." She was laughing so hard, tears leaked from her eyes. Piper reached out an arm. "Can you help me up, please?"

He grasped her hand and pulled. She pulled, too. He lost his footing and fell forward, almost landing on her.

"You did that on purpose." He scowled, but he wasn't angry.

Piper laughed even harder. "I didn't. Swear to God. It was an accident. I'm sorry," she said between gasps of breath and more rounds of laughter. "Now this…"

A handful of snow landed on his face.

"That was on purpose." Piper tried to roll away.

"Not so fast." He snaked out an arm and grabbed her. Rising to his knees, he scooped a handful of snow and held it over her face. "Hmm… What to do, what to do? Should I do the same to you as you did to me?"

She grinned up at him. "No. I don't think so."

Coop cocked his head to the side. "Why not?"

"Well…" She glanced at his hand poised above her head and then looked him in the eye. "This is our first date."

"That didn't stop you from taking the first shot," he reasoned.

Piper batted her eyelashes. "I'm having such a great time with you. You wouldn't want to ruin it, would you?"

He lowered his handful of snow. "Your arguments are not swaying me."

"I…" She shrugged. "Don't have a defense. I deserve payback." Piper closed her eyes and scrunched up her face. "Go ahead."

He chuckled and tossed the snow to the side. "I've decided to let you off the hook this one time. But this is a one-time deal. The next time I won't be this lenient." Rising, he brought both of them to a standing position.

"Thank you, kind sir, for your mercy." Piper flashed a saucy grin. "I am sorry for my…lapse in judgment."

"Huh." Coop let out a belly laugh. "You don't look sorry. Don't sound sorry either."

"Oh, but I am. I really am." She grabbed his hand and started walking toward the rear of the property. "So, what other changes have you made out here?" She pointed to a spot a short distance away. "No ice-skating rink this year?"

He shook his head. "We haven't had one in years. No one to use it anymore."

"I guess not. We're all adults now," she said.

They walked along in silence for a few minutes until they reached a clearing near the edge of the property.

"It's been a long time since I've been back here." The happy-go-lucky woman of a few minutes ago disappeared. Tension radiated off Piper in waves.

Shit. She was probably remembering that last bonfire their senior year of high school. It was the last time she came here.

"Not much has changed in the last ten years." She pointed to the outbuilding to her right. "Do the skunks still insist on making their homes there in the winter?"

Oh, yes. She was remembering that night, all right. *I hate you, Cooper Turner.* Her words echoed in his head.

He should never have brought her here. They'd been having a great time together. Why had he walked in this direction? "We should head back to the house."

"Wait a minute. Please." She lifted her gaze to his. "I'm sorry for the way that I treated you all those years ago. I was so awful to you, especially that night."

Coop blinked. He hadn't expected those words to come out of her mouth. Ever. "You were pretty mad."

"I know," she said. "Everything went wrong that night. I blamed you and I shouldn't have. It wasn't your fault." Piper flashed a rueful smile. "Well, not *all* of it. Some of it was Tom Anderson's fault."

Coop cringed. It had irked him beyond measure when he'd learned Tom had asked Piper to the Sweetheart dance. He'd viewed it as a betrayal of the worst kind. Still did, if he were honest.

"I'd wanted to go with him that night." She turned away and started pacing back and forth in a small area. "He was always so nice to me. Waiting for me so he could walk me to class. Offering to carry my books."

His hands clenched into tight fists. Tom had told him it was the other way around. That Piper had ordered him to do those things.

It wasn't outside the realm of possibility. They were both pretty geeky back then. Always struggling to fit in. An endless challenge for him, especially with two older brothers who'd always run with the popular crowd. And Piper...was the Ice Queen.

So, yeah, he'd believed Tom.

Idiot, idiot, idiot.

"When he backed out of our date after the skunk..." She waved a hand in the air again. "I was devastated."

Devastated? He blew out a breath. She'd really liked Tom back then. He would never have guessed Piper harbored such feelings. His heart gave a painful thud.

"The way Tom acted..."

He couldn't miss the hurt in her gaze. *Ah, hell.* "I'm sorry." His foolish behavior had made her miss out.

She stopped in front of him and grasped his hands in hers.

Lord, he could stare into her beautiful eyes forever.

He gave himself a mental shake. Where had that thought come from?

"It's not your fault. You didn't make me run into the shed. I chose to do that. Everyone else ran in the opposite direction." She let out a derisive laugh. "You weren't even that close to us. And Tom is the one who acted like I had the plague, not you." She shook her head. "But I blamed you nonetheless. I shouldn't have."

Coop blew out a breath. "Thank you for saying that."

"About damned time, right?" She gave him a tentative smile.

He laughed. He couldn't help it.

A gust of wind blew and Piper shivered.

"We should definitely head back to the house now," he said. Snow was starting to fall and the temperature was dropping.

"Agreed. Now would be a great time for the indoor portion of this date." Piper wrapped her arms around herself and rubbed her gloved hands up and down the sleeves of her parka. "I'm cold and wet from playing in the snow."

"Don't worry." He slung an arm around her shoulder

and tugged her close. "We can throw your jeans in the dryer. I'll loan you a pair of my sweats while they dry."

"Sounds like a plan." She draped her arm around his waist.

Coop marveled at the feel of her pressed close to him. He liked it. A lot.

Maybe more than he should.

They reached the house a few minutes later.

He opened the back slider and gestured for Piper to precede him in.

"It's nice and warm." Piper unzipped her parka and slid her arms from the sleeves.

"I'll take that for you." Coop grabbed her coat. Removing his boots, he walked into the front hall and hung their coats in the closet. He strode back to where Piper stood in the great room. "Now, let's get you warmed up. What do you need?"

"Pants and socks," she answered between chattering teeth.

He walked down the short hall to the main suite. Once inside, Coop searched through his drawers for a pair of sweats that might fit her. Everything he owned would fall from her petite frame. He found a pair made of navy fleece with a drawstring waist and elastic at the ankles. It was the best he could do. He laid out the pants and added the socks she'd requested. Returning to the great room, he said, "I left a change of clothes on the bed. You can change in there."

"Thanks." Piper disappeared.

Hot cocoa and a fire would warm her fast. He got busy making both. The fire was easy. He pushed a button on the remote and the flames burst to life. Hurrying into the kitchen, he prepared the hot cocoa. Not that it was difficult, although he used almond-coconut milk instead of water.

Piper reappeared as he poured the hot chocolate into two mugs. "What do you think?" She performed a pirouette. "Am I runway-ready or what?"

His pants billowed around her waist and ankles and the excess material of the socks flapped as she moved her feet. She looked utterly adorable. "Perfect," he said.

She chuckled and moved to the island. "Is one of these for me?" Piper pointed to the mugs.

He nodded. "I'm going to change." His jeans were damp as well. "Be right back." Cooper hurried back to his bedroom. Grabbing another pair of sweats, he changed and went back to the great room.

He found Piper sitting on the couch with one of his picture frames held in her hands.

Coop made his way over to her, noticing her hunched shoulders and downcast face as he approached. And were those tears in her eyes? He sucked in a breath.

Why was she crying?

Chapter Sixteen

"What's wrong?" Cooper rushed over and dropped down on the couch beside her.

"Nothing. I'm fine." She scrubbed the backs of her hands over her face. "Really." She gave him a watery smile.

"Why are you crying?" He tilted her chin up and waited for her gaze to settle on him.

Damn. Piper cringed. "This collage of pictures." She tilted the frame so he could see the images. "They caught me off guard."

Cooper stared at the images, a look of confusion on his face. "Yeah, they were taken when your dad took me to the arcade on the pier for my thirteenth birthday."

"I'd never seen them before." Piper shook her head. He probably thought she was one card short of a full deck. "It's like finding a treasure chest full of gold coins." She rubbed her thumb over a picture of her smiling father, remembering how soft the skin on his cheeks was and how he always smelled of Brut aftershave. "It doesn't bring him back, but for a second…" She kissed his cheek. "These brought him to life for me."

Cooper smiled. "I'm glad they made you happy. He was such a great guy. I was so fortunate that he was my godfather. He always made me feel special."

Piper glanced at the photos again. "You loved him a lot." She couldn't deny it. The images didn't lie.

"I did. Do. I miss having him in my life," Cooper said.

"Oh, Cooper." She buried her face in her hands. "I'm so sorry. So, so sorry. I was awful to you." She more than deserved his Ice Queen title. She deserved his condemnation, too. "All those years..." She'd gotten it all wrong. The truth had been staring her in the face for years. She'd chosen not to see it. How could she have been so blind? Cooper was never the villain she'd made him out to be. She'd needed someone to blame for all the anger and misery she was feeling, and she'd made Cooper the fall guy.

Piper lifted her head and gazed into his eyes. "Can you ever forgive me?"

"Piper." The look of devastation in his glittering gaze tore at her heart.

"Please, let me explain." Not that any explanation would justify her behavior toward him, but still, she had to try. She couldn't bear it if their story ended here. Piper grasped his hands in hers. She needed the contact.

"After my father died..." she began.

"You don't have to do this. I know how much losing him hurt you."

His concern for her—even after the horrible way she'd treated him all these years—showed him for the caring, compassionate person he always was. Shame on her for believing otherwise.

"I need to say this to you. It's important." Piper drew in a deep breath and blew it out slowly. "I missed him so much. I was angry—"

"At me. I know. You had every right to be. I let you down." Cooper dragged a hand through his hair.

She frowned. "What are you talking about?"

"I tried, Piper. I really did." He looked away from her. "But nothing I did helped."

She shook her head. "I don't understand. You're not making any sense." Piper grasped his shaking hands in hers and squeezed them tight. "It's okay, Cooper. You didn't do anything wrong." Why would he believe otherwise?

"I couldn't save him. I wanted to, but I couldn't." His breaths came out in short gasps.

Piper froze. Cooper blamed himself for her father's death? "No, you're wrong. You're not responsible. It's not your fault." How could he believe such a thing when it wasn't true by any stretch of the imagination?

He shook his head.

Piper jumped up and sat down on the other side of him. Grasping his face in her palms, she looked him in the eye. "Never once have any of us blamed you for Dad's death. Not me, not Mom, not Mia and not Shane.

"Cooper, I want you to listen to me very carefully. My dad had a massive heart attack that day. He died instantly. *No one* could have saved him. Not you. Not the paramedics. Not anyone. You've got to believe me, and you've got to stop blaming yourself. It was never your fault."

He looked at her and for the first time since they'd started this conversation, there was hope in his gaze.

"I thought that's why you hated me so much," he said.

"No. No." She kissed his cheek. "I was furious with my father for leaving us. I understand that now, but at thirteen, all I wanted to do was lash out." Piper stood and started pacing back and forth. "All of the rage and grief I was feeling bubbled up inside and erupted. Unfortunately, it landed on you." She stopped and looked at him. "When I saw you skateboarding in the parking lot of the funeral parlor, I thought..." Piper drew in a deep breath and released it. "There you were gliding over the pavement like it was just another normal day." She swallowed hard. "Like nothing was wrong while my whole world had crumbled to pieces. I thought you didn't care. About Dad, who I know loved you so much, or any of us, but most of all about me."

Cooper flinched and the hurt expression on his face broke her heart.

"That probably doesn't even make sense to you, because we were never particularly close growing up." Although… looking back on it now, something had changed between them the summer between seventh and eighth grade. She'd started…noticing him. He made her laugh, and having him around wasn't so bad anymore.

Then everything went wrong.

Piper clasped a hand over her mouth and swallowed her groan. She'd screwed everything up, big-time. "I know now that none of what I believed back then is true." Piper wrung her hands together. "But at thirteen…"

Cooper stood and walked out of the room.

She was all alone.

Again.

Ho-ly hell. Cooper couldn't believe what he'd just heard. All this time, he'd told himself that Piper couldn't forgive him for not saving her father, but he'd been wrong. About so many things.

He couldn't blame her for the conclusions she'd come to. Looking back on it, he may have believed the same if he were in her shoes. At least his younger self would have.

Coop dragged a hand through his hair. She wasn't the only one who'd messed things up back then. He'd done a good job of that himself.

His younger self couldn't understand why someone as vibrant and full of life as Victor would suddenly leave this earth. Someone should have been able to save him.

The idea that he hadn't done enough had lodged itself in his subconscious and had remained there ever since.

He'd failed, and the guilt he'd suffered as a result had driven every interaction with Piper since.

She'd never blamed him. He was the one who couldn't forgive himself.

Idiot, idiot, idiot.

Coop strode back into the great room.

Piper looked at him, devastation etched in her beautiful, delicate features.

A heavy weight settled in his chest. Yes, he'd messed up all right.

"I should go," she said, her voice void of all emotion.

"No. Please don't." Nausea roiled in his belly. "I don't want you to leave." He pulled her into his arms and held her tight. "I need you to stay."

She peered up at him, a wary expression on her face. "I assumed…"

Coop grasped her hands with his. He needed the contact. "We've both done a lot of that over the years." He shook his head. "I got it wrong, too. All of it. Let me explain."

Piper locked her gaze with his and nodded.

He told her everything. Pouring out his heart until there was nothing left unsaid between them.

When he finished it was like a heavy weight had been lifted from him.

She gazed at him, eyes glossy with unshed tears. "We're quite a pair, aren't we?"

He kissed their joined hands and smiled. "That we are."

"So…" Piper worried her bottom lip. "Where do we go from here?"

Before he could answer, his stomach gave a loud rumble.

Piper burst out laughing and all the tension he'd experienced earlier drained away.

"I'm thinking somewhere to eat." She rubbed her belly. "I'm a little hungry after this afternoon."

"I'm afraid you're going to have to settle for Chez Turner." Coop pointed toward the glass slider that led to the backyard. "The snow is really coming down now."

Piper walked toward the kitchen. "Works for me. My clothes are still wet and I'm not about to go out dressed like this. No offense." She gave a little smirk.

"None taken." His gaze traveled over her from head to toes. "But I think you look great." Although he'd never be able to wear those sweats again without thinking about how the material had caressed her soft skin. At least, he assumed it was soft.

His pulse soared. Oh yeah, he wanted to know for sure.

A happy grin crossed her face. "Good to know, Turner. Good to know. Now, what can we make?" She opened the fridge and stuck her head inside.

Coop liked the sound of *we*. He walked into the kitchen to join her.

Piper pulled out a Ziploc bag full of cooked chicken breasts he'd marinated in Italian dressing before grilling and veggies for a salad.

"These still good?" Piper held up the Ziploc bag.

He nodded. "Yep. Cooked them last night."

"Perfect. We can have a chicken salad." She handed him the head of lettuce and a cucumber. "You prep those and I'll take care of these."

"Bossy, aren't we?" He grinned.

"I'm a take-charge kind of girl. Got a problem with that?" She shot him a deadpan glance that lasted all of five seconds before she burst out laughing.

They peeled and chopped vegetables for a few minutes in companionable silence, then Piper turned a concerned expression in his direction.

"Are we okay?" she asked.

"We're more than okay. We're great." He brushed his lips against hers because he wanted to. Because he needed to. Because it had been too damned long since he last tasted the sweetness of her kiss.

Her supple lips met his in the most achingly tender kiss he'd ever experienced.

Coop slid one hand around her head and the other around her back and drew her closer. He reveled in the feel of her warm body pressed against his.

Piper twined her arms around his neck and clung to him. "Cooper." She moaned his name and deepened the kiss. "So damn good."

"You don't know the half of it." The taste of her lips, honeyed with the thrill of anticipation, sent a flood of heat rushing through him.

He lifted her into his arms, and a startled "Oh!" escaped from her mouth.

"Where are we going?" Her eyes danced with delight and she gave a soft chuckle.

"In here." Coop nodded to the sofa in the great room as he walked. "Where it's more comfortable."

Piper grinned. "Sounds like a plan."

Coop dropped down on the sofa and set Piper on his lap. A big mistake because she wriggled her sexy little bottom against him. He groaned. "You're going to kill me if you keep that up."

"We can't have that." Her lips brushed against his as she spoke. "I'm enjoying this too much."

Coop gazed into her bright blue eyes. "Me, too, sweetheart. Me, too." He brushed featherlight kisses along her jawline to the hollow beneath her ear.

He licked and nipped at the thrumming pulse and she shivered. "You like that." It was a statement, not a question.

"God, yes. I want to touch you."

At this moment, he wanted that more than he'd ever wanted anything in his life.

Her fingers grabbed at his shirt, fumbling with the buttons. She let out a cry of frustration. "Take off your shirt," she demanded.

"You *are* bossy." He grinned. With one swift movement, he set her on the cushion beside him and pulled his shirt over his head.

Piper grabbed the shirt from him and tossed it on the floor. "Like I said earlier, I'm a take-charge kind of girl."

Oh yes, she was, and he liked it.

Piper straddled him and laid her palms against his bare chest. She closed her eyes and slid her hands over his pecs and shoulders. "Your skin is as smooth as I imagined."

"Fantasizing about me, are you?" He sent her his best sexy grin.

Her lids opened and she looked him in the eye. "Since I saw you at Donahue's the evening Nick's band played."

All those weeks ago? Before they'd struck their deal? He couldn't believe it. Coop scrutinized her face. The stark vulnerability in her gaze touched him, soul-deep. Their relationship might be a farce, but this desire, no, this fierce attraction they held for one another was real. It was more tangible, more genuine than anything he'd experienced in a long time. "I haven't been able to get you off my mind either."

Piper tugged her sweater over her head. Her eyes glittered a deep sapphire blue as she gazed at him. "Touch me, Cooper. I need you to touch me."

She wouldn't have to ask him twice. Lord, she was beautiful. He skimmed his hands over the lacy cups of her bra and she moaned.

The sound sent all of his blood heading south. He unclasped her bra and slid the straps from her shoulders. He tossed the lacy garment toward the spot on the floor where his shirt lay in a heap. "Exquisite," he murmured. Perfect in every way.

Her smile sent a rush of heat coursing through his body. Cupping her breasts in his palms, he stroked his thumbs over the distended tips.

"Oh." Her head fell back and a long moan escaped her parted lips.

Coop savored her delightful cries of pleasure. He wanted, no, *needed* to hear more of them. He twisted the buds between his thumb and finger.

She cried out again and a sense of deep satisfaction rumbled through him.

She dragged his head to her and kissed him again. Slow and languid as she stroked her fingers over his chest and back.

Coop thought he might die from the sweet pleasure of her hands on him.

"I think we should take this into your room." She grinned against his lips. "There's a big bed and it will be much more comfortable than the couch."

"Your wish is my command." He gripped her bottom in his hands and stood in one swift motion.

Holding her tightly, he kissed her hard, and together they laughed as he stumbled towards the bedroom.

For the first time since he could remember, Coop never wanted to let her go.

Chapter Seventeen

Striding into the bedroom, Cooper stopped by the bed. He gazed at her as if she were the most precious, most important thing in the world to him.

No other lover—not that there'd been many over the years—had looked at her with such adoration, such passion.

What did that say about the choices she'd made thus far in her life? When it came to men, she'd opted for casual, easy, commitment-free. She'd never wanted anything more.

But now...

How could one look from Cooper turn her inside out and send her spinning out of control? Because that was how she felt right now.

He kissed her with such sweet tenderness. Everything went all soft and mushy inside her. How could she have lived without this warmth and genuine affection for so long?

He broke the kiss all too quickly, as far as she was concerned. She could stay here all night long just kissing him.

Coop flashed her the most heart-stopping grin and her heart melted.

"What?" she asked when he just kept smiling.

"I was such an idiot. You are kind, and gorgeous, and..." He glanced down at his sweatpants, which she was still wearing.

"And the best-dressed girlfriend you've ever had?" she quipped.

He chuckled. "Why did we waste so many years at odds with each other when we could have had this?"

One thing was certain, she never would have been ready for whatever this thing was between them, and she couldn't deny there was definitely something between them, if she hadn't worked through her grief. It was a long hard road, nearly ten years in the making, but she was glad she'd persevered.

"Maybe we needed to go through everything else to have this now?"

"Maybe so." He tumbled them onto his bed. "I'm glad we're here now."

Her heart slammed in her chest, beating so hard she thought it might break her ribs. "Me, too." It was the truth.

Piper gazed into his gorgeous green eyes. God, she could get lost in those fathomless pools. "Kiss me." She needed to feel connected with him.

"Bossy." His sexy grin devastated her.

"Desperate," she corrected.

His gaze turned smoky and a longing, both physical and something more, flooded through her. "I need you." More truth. "So much I ache inside." Piper didn't want to think about what any of that meant right now. She only wanted to feel. "I can't wait any longer." She removed the remainder of her clothes with one quick tug and tossed them over the edge of the bed.

"Slow down. We have all day."

"I can't." Not with all of this frantic need coursing through her body. "Next time, I promise we'll take it slow, but now…" Piper pulled him close and stripped off the rest of his garments.

"I have to admit, this is much better." He explored the soft lines of her back, her waist, her hips.

Piper let out a blissful sigh. This was heaven on earth. "Do you have any idea how much I like it when you touch me?"

Cooper flashed a wolfish grin. "As much as I love doing the touching? Your skin is so soft. So smooth." His fingers skated over her breast and across her silken belly.

She cried out when his skilled fingers found the sensitive spot between her thighs.

Cooper lowered his lips to hers. His tongue tasted, teased, demanded, and she thought she might go insane from the sheer pleasure of it.

"Now. *Please*, Cooper." He'd reduced her to a mass of jangling nerves.

"Hold on a second." He reached inside the nightstand drawer and grabbed a foil packet. Tearing it open with his teeth, he removed the condom and sheathed himself.

Cooper slid into her in one swift move, filling her completely.

He moved slowly at first, then faster and harder, driving the ache inside her to a fever pitch.

"So damned good." Her breaths came in sharp pants.

With a shout, they tumbled over the edge and drifted down to earth together.

Piper wasn't sure how much time had passed when Cooper stirred.

"I'll be right back." He slid out of bed.

She propped herself up on her elbows and watched as his naked form strode toward the bathroom. The statue of David couldn't hold a candle to Cooper Turner. The man was sexy as all get-out. And he was all hers...*for now*. She planned to take full advantage of him.

Piper grinned. She couldn't remember the last time she felt this alive, this exhilarated. This…ecstatic, exultant, joyful. *Happy.*

Yes, being with Cooper made her happy.

It wasn't just the sex—a frisson of pleasure trickled down her spine when she thought about what his hands and mouth could do to her body. Yes, the sex was phenomenal, unparalleled, best she'd ever had, if she was honest.

But she liked spending time with him, too. Cooper was kind and sweet and caring. He made her laugh and she felt content when they were together.

Which meant what?

Piper shook her head. She didn't want to think about it. She wanted to enjoy the here and now.

"Come back to bed, Cooper."

"Bossy!" he growled from the bathroom.

She cracked a smile even though he wasn't there to witness it.

"Just a second," he called.

Piper gazed around the space while she waited. She hadn't really looked at the room earlier when she'd come in here to change. She'd been too focused on removing her wet clothes to notice the blue-gray feature wall with a wooden diamond pattern behind the bed, the art deco nightstands, and the… "Whoa. Is that…?"

Piper jumped out of bed and hurried to the wall where two photos hung.

The ginormous dragon and delicate swan stared back at her.

"What are you doing?" Cooper slid his arms around her waist.

Her bottom came into contact with his hard shaft and she groaned.

"I saw the same photos in the TK Construction lobby a few weeks ago."

"Oh," he said.

Piper turned so they stood face-to-face. "Is that all you have to say?"

He shrugged. "Those are from the ice art festival."

"Why do you have—" Her gaze widened. "Did you carve those?"

"Yes." He nuzzled the sensitive spot where her neck joined her shoulders.

She laughed. "Stop trying to distract me. Seriously, you made them?"

"I did."

"Cooper, they're amazing. The scales… Those alone must have taken hours to etch."

He nodded. "The dragon took me a week."

"It's incredible." She turned and studied the image. "You're very talented." Turning back to face him, she asked, "Why didn't I know this about you?" She shook her head. "Don't answer that." She already knew the answer. All those years when they could have been…

Not hating each other. What a complete waste of time.

"The past is the past. There's nothing we can do about it now." Cooper dropped a tender kiss on her lips. "It's where we go from here that counts."

He was right. Piper planned to learn everything she could about this handsome, sexy, sweet, funny, wonderful man. She smiled. "Did you enter again this year?"

"Uh-huh." Cooper pressed a soft kiss to the hollow beneath her ear.

She giggled because it tickled. "What are you going to make?"

"I thought you wanted me to come back to bed?"

"I did. *Do*," she corrected. She grinned. "But first, I

want to hear what you're planning to sculpt. And—" she rubbed her belly "   I want you to feed me." She kissed his cheek.

"Honestly, I don't know what I'm going to make. The theme this year is love, since they're judging the sculptures on Valentine's Day. Got any ideas?"

"Not off the top of my head, but I'll think about it." She glanced around the room looking for her clothes. Damn. They'd never gotten around to tossing their wet items in the dryer. She walked over and picked up the pair of sweats Cooper had loaned her earlier.

"Hold on a second. I've got something more comfortable for you." Coop disappeared into the bathroom and returned a moment later with a huge white terrycloth robe. He tossed it to her.

"Thank you." She slid her arms into the soft, fluffy material. Overlapping the edges, she tugged the belt tight around her waist and tied it in a knot. She laughed when she caught a glimpse of her reflection in the mirror. The garment was three times her size.

Piper followed Cooper into the kitchen. They finished preparing the salad and filled two bowls.

"Let's eat in the family room. We can watch TV." Cooper, now dressed in the sweatpants he'd worn earlier, strode to the couch. He patted the spot next to him and Piper sat.

He draped an arm around her shoulder and pulled her close. "Are you warm enough?"

Piper breathed a contented sigh. She could get used to this. "I'm perfect."

Cooper powered on the television. "How about a movie?"

"As long as it's something funny." She pursed her lips. "Or they blow stuff up."

Cooper let out a deep belly laugh. "What, no chick flicks?"

"I'm not into the whole happy-ever-after theme."

"Is that why Jane has made it her mission in life to find you a husband?"

"You got it." Piper smirked and gave his cheek a gentle pinch. "She thinks that if she finds me the perfect man, I'll change my mind."

"But you won't?" He shot her a curious glance.

"Nope." She shook her head. "No way. No how."

Cooper grasped her jaw and gently lifted her head to meet his gaze. "Can I ask why?"

The care and compassion in his gaze touched her to the core. Piper swallowed hard. "I'm scared. What if…" She closed her eyes and drew in a deep breath. "Love doesn't last. People fall out of love every day, or they leave you. Look at Mia and Shane. They both thought they were in love and they ended up divorced. And my mother…" She shook her head.

Cooper nodded. "It's hard to put yourself out there again after you've been hurt, regardless of who or what may have caused that wound."

Finally, someone understood her. "Exactly. You get it."

"Unfortunately, yes." He couldn't hide the pain and bitterness he'd experienced.

The sadness in his gaze tore at her heart. "Someone hurt you, didn't they?"

For a moment he said nothing. He stared straight ahead as if he were lost in his own thoughts, but then he nodded. "Her name was Rachel. I thought she was as in love with me as I was with her." Cooper let loose a derisive laugh. "I even bought her a ring."

Piper's gaze widened. "You were engaged?"

"No." He shook his head. "I planned to propose, but she broke it off before I could."

She pressed her lips to his cheek. "I'm so sorry."

"Me, too, but at least no one knew what I'd planned to do. I didn't make a huge fool of myself."

"You didn't tell anyone? Not even your family?" Her mouth dropped open. "You guys are so close."

"Honestly, I don't know why I didn't tell them." Cooper shrugged. "Maybe I knew subconsciously that it wouldn't work out and I didn't want them feeling sorry for me." He locked his gaze on her.

"I can understand that," she said. If she were in his shoes, she wouldn't want people to pity her either.

"I know you do." Cooper grasped her hand in his. "It used to drive you crazy when people pitied you after your father died."

Piper nodded. She'd appreciated the care and compassion people had offered, but the pity… She'd *hated* it.

Piper released his hand. Lifting his arm, she draped it over her shoulder and snuggled in close to him. "She's a fool, if you ask me."

"Huh?" Cooper's brows furrowed into a deep V.

"Raquel, or whatever her name is."

Cooper chuckled. "It's Rachel, and why do you think she's a fool?"

"Because you're a great guy, Cooper Turner. How could she possibly do better?"

He laughed.

The joyful, deep sound rumbled through her and she smiled. "I'm serious."

"You're pretty great yourself." He kissed her soundly, and took her breath away. "Now, finish your salad, and let's watch that movie." Cooper wiggled his brows.

He wanted to change the subject, and that was fine by her. "Yes, sir." She gave him a jaunty salute.

He selected a James Bond movie and they settled in. After she finished her meal, Cooper collected the plates and brought them to the kitchen. When he returned, he pulled her into the crook of his arm and she snuggled in close.

"This is nice." Cooper dropped a quick kiss on the top of her head.

"It is," she agreed. She'd never experienced the simple intimacy of being held like this before. Sure, she'd had other relationships, but they'd lacked any real closeness.

This thing with Cooper...*isn't real*. She needed to remember that. They'd struck a deal out of mutual need. She needed to get her mother off her back once and for all and he needed a date to a wedding.

They were both playing a part. End of story.

Still...her heart ached at the idea of this thing between them ending.

Stop psychoanalyzing everything when you promised you'd just enjoy this time together. Live in the moment.

Cooper traced lazy circles over her shoulder and upper arm.

Frissons of pleasure trickled down her spine.

"Are you cold?" Cooper asked. "Do you want me to crank up the heat?"

Enjoy this time together.

"No-oo." She drew out the word. "Not in the least." Piper trailed a finger down Cooper's bare chest. "I'm plenty warm." She dipped her finger into the waistband of his sweatpants and withdrew it immediately. "In fact, one could say I'm hot." Piper licked her lips. "On fire, even."

"Maybe you should take some of your clothes off?" he suggested. The heat in his gaze contradicted the casual tone of his voice.

"You think it might cool me off?" Lord, she adored their banter, this playfulness. Another new experience with this sexy, kind man, and one she could definitely get used to.

"It's worth a try."

Piper nodded and stood. Releasing the belt, she shimmied out of the robe and let it pool on the floor around her feet.

"Better?" He arched a brow.

Piper sat on his lap, her legs straddling him. She grinned. "Oh, yes."

"Are you sure?" He nuzzled the crook of her neck.

A languid heat filled her. "Yes." This was what she wanted. What she needed... What was *real*. She couldn't deny it. This desire, or longing, or whatever name you called it, was tangible. And mutual.

When it came to pleasuring each other, neither of them was acting. She was damned sure of that.

It was the only thing she was sure of.

Her phone started to ring.

Oh, for crying out loud. "Ignore it," she commanded.

"Bossy," he growled but his lips continued skating over her skin.

The ringing stopped, thank God. Piper grasped his hands and placed them on her breasts. "Touch me. Please. I need your hands on me."

Her phone started ringing again.

Her head dropped forward. *You've got to be kidding.*

The ringing stopped but Mia's annoyed voice started yelling, "Your sister is calling, your sister is calling. What are you waiting for? Pick up the phone already."

Cooper chuckled. "That's an interesting ringtone."

She sighed as her phone repeated its demand. "Mia recorded it and downloaded the file to my phone so I wouldn't ignore her calls."

"You should probably get that."

"Right." Mia would keep calling until she answered.

She wiggled off his lap. He groaned and she flashed him a very satisfied grin.

Yes, this thing between them was real, all right.

Standing, she reached for the robe lying in a pile on the floor. She yanked her phone from the pocket. "Hey, Mia, what's up?"

"The power is out in town. I'm checking in on my little sister to make sure she's doing okay in this storm," Mia said.

"I'm fine."

Cooper stood and shed his pants.

She sucked in a breath. He was all hard planes and corded muscles. Piper reveled in his glorious arousal and the knowledge that she'd done this to him.

In one swift motion, she found herself planted on the couch with her back pressed firmly against the plush material.

"Just fine?" Cooper whispered in her other ear. "I'll have to see if I can do better."

Mia started speaking again. "Abby and Elle said to tell you they're riding out the storm at Elle's place, if you want to join them."

"I'm not home," Piper squeaked as Cooper closed his mouth over the tip of her breast. "I'm with Cooper." She didn't catch the rest of whatever her sister was saying because Cooper was doing delightful things with his hands as he skimmed them over her body.

"Ohhh," she moaned when he stroked his finger between her thighs. Her breaths came in short, sharp gasps.

"Enough talking," he growled. Grasping her phone with his free hand, he tossed it.

Piper heard Mia's startled gasp and her, "Are you and Cooper...? Oh, my God, you *are*!" as the phone hit the floor.

Cooper scooped her into his arms and strode toward his bedroom. "I can't get enough of you."

Piper looked into his eyes. Desire blazed from his emerald-gold gaze. And something more...

Something she couldn't—no, *wouldn't*—name.

Chapter Eighteen

The sun shone bright in the Saturday morning sky as
Cooper pulled his truck into the parking lot behind the
Coffee Palace.

Piper wanted to groan when she spotted the thick blanket of snow covering her car. She'd need to give herself an
extra fifteen or twenty minutes to clean it off and warm
the engine before she headed over to the gallery.

At least the parking lot is plowed already.

She turned to Cooper and dropped a kiss on his lips.
"I'll see you tomorrow." They both had plans this evening.
Poker night with the girls for her and watching the game
at her brother's place with the guys for him.

Piper hopped out of the truck and headed toward the
back door that led to her apartment. She touched the back
pocket of her jeans, making sure her phone hadn't fallen
out when she jumped out of Cooper's truck.

She couldn't forget to print out the pictures she'd
snapped of the exterior of Cooper's house while he was
clearing the snow earlier. She'd need to get started painting a portrait of the farmhouse today, if possible. Cooper's birthday was six days away and she wanted to have
it done by then.

Opening the door to her place, she stepped inside. A
shiver ran down her spine. Damn. No power all night
meant no heat either. How long would it take for the apartment to come up to temperature? Probably long enough

that she didn't want to sit here in the cold. She'd hop in the shower, and head to the Coffee Palace after.

Twenty minutes later, she exited the door that led out to the back parking lot.

"Ho-ly cow." Piper stopped dead in her tracks. She grinned at the sight of her car sans the snow last night's storm had deposited on it.

Cooper must be responsible. Who else would have cleaned away the snow for her?

She walked over to her vehicle. He'd even shoveled the two feet in front of her car that the plow hadn't removed.

Grabbing her phone, she found his number in her contacts and connected the call. "You sweet, sweet man," she said when he answered.

He gave a sexy little chuckle that turned her insides to mush. "Why, thank you. I see you found my little surprise."

"Yes, I did. You didn't have to clean my car off." She could have taken care of it. Was more than capable of removing a bit of snow. It came with the territory when you lived in New England in the winter. "But I really appreciate you doing it for me." She cleared her throat and murmured in her best sexy voice, "I'll have to give you a special thank-you the next time I see you."

"Sounds promising. What did you have in mind?" he asked.

"You'll have to wait and see." Piper heard a groan as she cut the connection. She flashed a smug smile to no one in particular as she walked around the front of the building and entered the Coffee Palace. A blast of heat hit her and she smiled.

"Hey, Piper." Elle gave a little wave from behind the counter.

"Good morning. It's nice and warm in here."

"Thank goodness for the generator," Elle said. "It was

freezing in my apartment when I got up. Needless to say, I was psyched when I got down here."

"It's still cold upstairs." Piper unzipped her parka. "That's why I'm here."

"Hey, Piper." Abby walked in from the back room. "We missed you last night."

"Yeah," Elle said. "We had a mini poker night."

She nodded. "Mia called to let me know."

"I would have called you myself, but I don't have your number," Abby said.

"Me either," Elle added.

"Let me give it to you now." Piper rattled off the digits and both Abby and Elle added her to their list of contacts. She did the same.

"How's Cooper?" Elle smirked. "Did you two have *fun* last night?"

Had Mia spilled the beans about what she and Cooper were doing when she'd called? Her cheeks burned. "He's, um…good." She needed to change the subject. "What's the coffee of the day?"

"There's a few." Elle laughed and pointed to the sign on the counter.

Piper eliminated the decaf flavors. She needed the caffeine. "I'll have a large chocolate raspberry with cream and two stevia."

"Anything else?" Elle asked.

Piper eyed the confections, looking for something yummy. She spotted a cupcake with loads of chocolate frosting and candy hearts on top.

Before she could order, a deep rumbly voice said, "She'll have one of those." And a finger pointed to her intended selection.

She whirled around and found Cooper standing behind her. A flood of warmth rushed through her, and she was pretty sure a goofy grin was plastered across her face. "Hey, stranger. Long time no see." Almost thirty whole minutes. She chuckled to herself.

The urge to launch herself into his arms was strong, but she resisted. Barely. Lord, what was it about seeing this man that made everything inside her go soft and gooey?

Cooper yanked her against him and crushed his mouth to hers. He kissed her as if she were all he could ever want. All he would ever need. Her heart filled to bursting point.

He released her a few moments later.

Breathless, she asked, "What are you doing here? I thought you needed to get over to the Humanity houses."

"I do, but I saw you walk in and wanted to see you again."

Piper flashed a mile-wide smile. "It's nice to see you again, too."

Elle cleared her throat.

Piper winced. "Oh, um… Sorry."

"Don't apologize." Elle flashed a wicked grin. To Cooper, she asked. "Anything for you?"

He pulled out his wallet and handed Elle his credit card. "Piper's order, two boxes of coffee and a couple dozen doughnuts. Gotta take care of the Humanity crew, too."

"Thank you." She kissed his cheek. He really was a sweet, sweet man.

Elle handed Piper her order. Turning her attention to Cooper, she said, "It'll be ten to fifteen minutes for the boxes. I need to brew the coffee."

Cooper nodded. "No trouble. I'll wait."

"Have a seat. Someone will bring you your order when it's ready," Abby said.

"Perfect." Cooper escorted Piper to the closest open table and pulled out her chair.

Piper sat. "So, how'd you know what I was going to

order?" She gestured to the sugary sweetness sitting atop her plate.

Cooper moved the other chair to sit by her side instead of across from her. "For as long as I can remember, you've always had a sweet tooth."

"You remember that?" A little thrill raced down her spine.

"I do. You used to hoard your Halloween candy and have a piece every day, and you never shared it with anyone else."

Piper laughed. "It's true."

"As far as chocolate is concerned…" He dipped his finger into the frosting and scooped up a smidge. "That's a love we both share."

He licked the frosting from his finger. Piper sucked in a deep breath as a languid heat filled her belly. *So not the time or the place. So not the time or the place.* She repeated the mantra hoping it would cool her fevered body.

More in control now, Piper cut the cupcake and handed half to Cooper. "Today is your lucky day. I'm feeling generous." She winked.

He shook his head. "I got that for you."

Piper kissed his cheek. "And I want to share it with you." She began plucking the chalky candies from atop the frosting on her half and set them on her plate.

"You don't like conversation hearts?" Cooper snagged one from his half.

"Is that what they're called?" she asked. "I never knew the proper name before. I've always called them the Valentine's candy with the sayings on them."

"That works, too." He popped a heart in his mouth. "I can't remember the last time I ate one of these."

"I haven't had them since I was a kid." She stuck a

candy on her tongue and savored the sugary sweetness. "I'd forgotten how tasty they are."

Cooper handed her a heart that had XOXO on the face. She grinned. "Aww, hugs and kisses. How sweet."

Cooper winked. "I'm a sweet guy. You said so yourself."

"Yes, I did, and I'd say it again." She plucked off more of the hearts and added them to the pile on the side of her plate.

"I thought you liked them." Cooper's brows furrowed.

"I do, but I'm a purist when it comes to chocolate." Grabbing another candy, she read the words etched on the surface. "Be Mine." The idea sent little thrills of excitement skating down her spine. "What do you say?" The words came out before she could stop them.

"Oh, man. Can I?" Batting his eyelashes in an exaggerated fashion, Cooper clasped his hand over his heart and sighed.

Piper shook her head, but she was smiling. "Ha, ha, ha."

"I know. You think I'm immature."

Not anymore. She understood now that he was just trying to fit in the best way he knew how. "Lighthearted," she corrected. "It's not a bad quality to have."

He let out a low, rumbly chuckle that sent her pulse skittering. Grasping the Be Mine candy from her hand, he set it aside. "I think we'll keep that one. Let's see what else we have here." Cooper picked up another candy from her plate. "Always and Forever." He scoffed. "I know that's not true."

"Agreed," she said.

"No use saving this one." He dropped the heart in his mouth and crunched it.

Piper laughed. She broke off a piece of her cupcake and lifted it to her mouth. "I'm totally with you on that score." *Always* and *forever* weren't words in her vocabulary when it came to relationships with the opposite sex.

He quirked his lips and grabbed another of her discarded candies. "Bossy." Cooper winked and gave her a sexy grin. "Now, *that* I'll agree with."

Piper arched a brow. "It does not say that."

"Yes, it does," Cooper insisted.

"I don't believe you." She gestured for him to hand over the heart. "Let me see."

"I don't think so." He popped it into his mouth.

"No fair." Piper shook her head.

He shrugged. "I guess you'll just have to take my word for it."

"Nope." She licked the chocolate frosting off the piece of cupcake she held in her hand.

"You did not just do that." He shot her a you-have-got-to-be-kidding look.

Piper chuckled. "I sure did." She flashed him an impish smile. "The frosting is the best part."

He laughed. A deep sound that rumbled through her.

God, she loved hearing that sound. It made her feel all warm and fuzzy inside. She grinned.

He grabbed another heart and read, "Marry Me." Snorting, he said, "For God's sake. Why would you include a statement like this in kids' candies?"

"I agree. We need to get rid of it." Grasping it from him, Piper dropped it on the floor and crushed it with her boot.

"I love it." Cooper smirked. "You're as jaded as me."

"Absolutely." She winked at him.

Elle walked over and set Cooper's order on the table. "Two dozen doughnuts and two boxes of coffee to go."

"Thanks," Cooper said.

Elle disappeared and they were alone at the table again.

He gave a reluctant sigh. "I've gotta get going." He ate the last of his cupcake and stood.

"I should get going, too. I'll walk out with you."

Cooper dropped a tip on the table and grasped a box of coffee in each hand.

"I'll take these for you." She grabbed the box of doughnuts and followed him to the door.

A tall man with short, black hair came toward them from the opposite direction as they walked to Cooper's truck. He stopped in front of them.

"Is that you, Piper?" the man asked.

At first glance, she couldn't recognize him, then comprehension dawned. "Tom Anderson." Cooper's best friend.

Piper pinned a congenial smile in place. "It's nice to see you."

"It's great to see you, too, Piper," Tom said.

Son of a bitch. Coop's hands clenched around each box handle he was carrying. Of all the people he could run into, it was just his bad luck he'd bump into Tom.

"What's it been? Ten years?" Tom wrapped his arms around her and gave her a hug.

Coop was going to lose his shit if Tom didn't step away from Piper. He didn't want him touching her in any way, shape or form.

He and Piper were...

The truth was, he wasn't sure what he and Piper were anymore. Last night had changed things. At least it had for him. Yeah, they'd had sex. Great sex. Fantastic for sure, but that wasn't what had changed things. He and Piper had shared...something potent, and compelling and powerful.

Something he'd never experienced with any other woman before. Not even Rachel.

Which meant what?

Hell if he knew. How was he supposed to approach

Piper and find out what was going on in her brain with all of this uncertainty roiling around inside his?

He couldn't.

The only thing he knew for sure was that he didn't want Tom anywhere near Piper. But he was going to look like a class A jerk if he went all caveman on her and threw her over his shoulder and walked away.

Even though that was exactly what he wanted to do.

"Yes. Can you believe it?" The smile Piper aimed at Tom sliced through his heart like a sharp knife. Which was crazy. She was just being polite.

He couldn't blame her. He hadn't told her about Tom and Rachel, because yeah, he still felt like a complete moron for not having figured out what was going on in front of his face.

Looking back on the situation, he should have figured it out sooner, but he'd been so caught up in the fantasy of what he believed was the perfect relationship, that he couldn't see the truth.

Or maybe he hadn't wanted to comprehend what was going on. The signs were there, but he chose to believe Rachel when she told him she was working late. And when he'd found Tom leaving her place one evening…

His gut plummeted. *Idiot, idiot, idiot.* Yeah, he'd wanted to believe Tom's story about helping Rachel plan a surprise birthday party for him.

He hadn't wanted to believe either of them were capable of such betrayal.

"Last I heard, you were living in Los Angeles and running a successful art gallery," Tom said.

It required every ounce of self-control Coop possessed not to reach over and slug Tom.

"I was, but I decided to come home and open my own place. The Kavanaugh gallery is opening in less than a month." Piper eased away from Tom and some of the tension inside him subsided.

Tom's grin broadened. "That's fantastic. We should get together soon and catch up."

Coop stiffened, every bone in his body going rigid. *No friggin' way.*

"Maybe in a few weeks," Piper said.

Wait. What? Coop jerked his attention to Piper. She wanted to get together with him? Did she still have a thing for him after all these years?

She moved to his side. "We're busy getting the space ready at the moment."

Coop pulled her close, so her shoulder and hip touched his. "We won't have any free time until after the gallery is up and running."

"You two are together?" Tom arched a brow.

"Yes." It gave him immense satisfaction to give Tom that news.

Chapter Nineteen

Piper pulled into Mia's driveway at seven o'clock sharp on Saturday night.

Her phone pinged. She pulled her cell from her pocket and glanced at the screen. Smiling, she read the text from Cooper.

How was your day?

A rush of heat radiated through her chest. Such a sweet guy to check in on her and see how she was doing.

She texted back. Been crazy busy since I left you this morning.

She still couldn't believe they'd run into Tom Anderson after leaving the Coffee Palace this morning. Although why she was surprised, she couldn't say. It was bound to happen, sooner or later. You couldn't hide in a small town.

Piper continued texting. Got a lot done at the gallery. She'd been able to do a good deal of work on the portrait she was painting of his house, too, but she couldn't tell him that. Wait until you see the progress I made with my art studio. It's really coming along. How was your day?

She snorted as she remembered the pole-axed expression on Tom's face when Cooper told him they were a couple. Like he couldn't believe it was possible. She wasn't sure whether he believed she was too good for Cooper, or the other way around. It was insulting either way.

Cooper's text came through. We worked on the interiors of the two houses that were enclosed. Just got home a few minutes ago. Grabbing a shower now and heading to Shane's to watch the game.

Have fun, she texted.

You, too. Save some chocolate for me.

Will do. Piper grinned as she shoved her phone back into her jeans pocket.

She hopped out of her car and noticed two others parked in the driveway. Elle and Layla must have arrived early.

The door opened before she reached the front stoop.

"Come on in," Layla said. "Mia is putting a movie on for the girls. She asked me to let you in."

Piper walked inside. "Am I the last to arrive?"

Layla closed the door. "Yes. Abby and Elle are already sitting at the table. They came together."

Piper laughed. "Here I was congratulating myself for being on time, and you all arrived early."

"Only by five minutes." Layla walked beside Piper as they moved toward the kitchen.

A woman Piper didn't recognize also sat with Elle and Abby at the table. "Hello." She walked over and held out her hand. "I'm Piper Kavanaugh."

"This is my sister, Zara," Layla said. "She's visiting from Manhattan. Piper is Shane's youngest sister," Layla said to Zara.

Zara grasped her hand. "It's nice to meet you."

Piper smiled. "You, too. How long are you in town for?"

Zara released Piper's hand. "A few days. I'll probably head home on Wednesday since I didn't end up arriving until today."

Layla sat in one of the empty chairs at the table. "She

was supposed to arrive yesterday, but got delayed because of last night's storm."

"We did get hit with a lot of snow." She'd awoken to the sound of a snowblower and found Cooper outside clearing the eighteen inches they'd received. She'd put on a pot of coffee and made eggs and toast when he finished the driveway. Piper smiled to herself. It was all very domestic. The thing was, she'd enjoyed starting her day with him.

She walked around the table and grabbed another of the empty chairs.

"Hey, Piper." Abby waved.

"Hey, Abby." She gave a little wave. "Elle, I meant to ask you this morning when I saw you at the Coffee Palace, have you started classes yet?"

Elle shook her head. "The semester starts on Monday. I can't wait to get back into the swing of things. I've heard really good things about my Marketing professor. One of my friends took his class last year and loved it. She told me we're going to get some real-life experience."

"That's great," Piper said. "What's going on with you, Abby?"

"Yeah, Abby." Elle nudged her in the ribs with her elbow. "What's going on with you?"

Abby rolled her eyes and shook her head. "There's nothing going on."

Elle arched a brow. "You looked pretty cozy with Nick Turner this afternoon."

"He asked me if I could cater an event. We were going over the menu. That's all," Abby said.

"I don't know. You two looked pretty chummy," Elle insisted.

Layla poured herself a glass of red wine from the bottle that was on the table. "Nick's engaged."

"*Exactly*," Abby confirmed.

Elle picked up her glass of white wine and sipped. "I heard there's trouble in paradise."

Piper remembered their meeting a few weeks ago when she'd run into Isabelle and Nick at Donahue's pub. Isabelle had seemed ill at ease. Maybe there was some truth to what Elle had heard.

"Oh, come on, Abby. I know you have a thing for him," Elle said. "You have his order ready and waiting for him every morning so he doesn't have to wait."

"To be fair, she does the same for me," Layla said.

Abby nodded. "That's because you come in every day, and so does Nick." Abby shook her head. "Nick and I have been friends since kindergarten. Honestly, I can't imagine being anything more than that with him." She looked at Piper. "How are your renovations going?"

Elle grinned. "Way to dodge, Abs."

Piper laughed. She'd been thinking the same thing. "The place is really coming together. With any luck we'll wrap up everything in a couple of weeks."

"That's great." Mia strode into the room with a stemmed glass in each hand. She set one in front of Piper and another in front of the last empty chair. With a smug smirk on her face, she added, "It's nice to know you and Cooper are getting some actual work done."

Elle and Abby started laughing.

Heat crept up her neck and flooded her cheeks. Yep, Mia had definitely told them what Piper and Cooper were doing while she and her sister were on the phone last night. She leaned back in her chair and crossed her arms over her chest. "Ha ha. You're funny."

"Okay. What happened?" Layla asked. She looked from Mia to Piper. "It must have been good, because your face is beet red."

"Oh, it was *good* all right." Mia doubled over laughing.

"Come on. Spill," Layla demanded. "Elle and Abby obviously know. I'm feeling very left out of the loop on this." She pouted her lips.

"It's not that big a deal." Piper grabbed the bottle of red wine and poured a healthy glass. Turning to her sister, she said, "By the way, I'm staying here tonight."

"No problem," Mia said.

"If it's not that big a deal, then how come you're not sharing?" Zara asked.

Piper glared at her sister, and Mia laughed even harder. "Fine, I'll spill." She told the group what happened.

"That's hysterical," Zara said. Turning to Layla, she said. "Do us both a favor and don't answer my call if you and Shane are in the middle of getting busy."

"We weren't… I wouldn't have…" Piper's cheeks burned hotter.

Everyone laughed even harder.

Piper let out a resigned sigh. She was never going to live this down.

"You two were so cute at the Coffee Palace this morning," Abby said.

"Yeah," Elle agreed. "You were acting all lovey-dovey."

"What are you talking about?" Mia asked.

"Piper—" Abby pointed to her "—and Cooper were kissing and touching and whispering sweet nothings in each other's ears. At least that's what it looked like from where I was standing behind the counter."

"You were?" Mia stared at Piper, a look of confusion on her face. "I've never known you to be all touchy-feely with a guy before. You're usually more…cool and reserved."

That much was true. Piper usually preferred a less sentimental, less sappy approach to her relationships, but Cooper was different.

She liked him. More than she believed possible. Piper

swallowed hard. Yeah, she couldn't deny it any longer. Somehow, he'd wormed his way past all her defenses and she'd fallen for him.

Holy. Friggin'. Crap.

Coop pulled his F-150 into the driveway of Shane's beachfront home. He could hear the soothing ebb and flow of the waves as they crashed on shore. A blanket of snow currently covered what would bloom into lush landscape come spring.

Was this the kind of house that Piper wanted to live in? He could see the appeal. Heck, the beach was Shane's backyard.

Still… She'd enjoyed frolicking in his large backyard yesterday.

Coop shook his head. Why was he even thinking about where Piper would want to live? Okay, yes, he liked her, but they weren't at the point of moving in together.

Although… No. *Absolutely not.* He'd dated Rachel for two years before he'd even thought about moving in with her. Now he was thinking about living with Piper after spending less than a month with her?

They weren't even a real couple at this point.

Yeah, he was losing his mind, all right.

Opening his door, he jumped out of his truck and walked along the pathway that led to the front porch.

Shane opened the door, but blocked the entrance, his arms crossed over his chest.

Crap. They hadn't talked since he'd found him and Piper… Groping each other. Yes, that was pretty much what they'd been doing to each other that day. If Shane knew about last night… Coop pulled at the collar of his shirt. "You gonna let me in?"

Shane shook his head. "Not until you tell me what your intentions are toward my sister."

Seriously? He scraped a hand through his hair. Okay, yes. Shane was overprotective when it came to his family. Coop should have seen this coming, especially after the way he'd reacted when he'd learned they were together. "I, ah, want to date your sister." That was the truth. What would Piper say if he told her as much? "Do I have your permission?"

Levi appeared in the open door frame beside Shane. The two of them doubled over with laughter.

Shane stepped aside and gestured for Coop to enter. "I'm just giving you shit."

Levi smirked. "You should have seen the look on your face."

"Priceless." Shane high-fived Levi.

Coop shook his head and stepped inside. "You guys are a barrelful of laughs tonight."

"Yep," Levi agreed.

Coop followed his brother and Shane across the hall.

"You remember Duncan, don't you?" Shane asked. He pointed to his fellow Emergency Medical Services responder.

Coop nodded and extended a hand. "It's been a while."

"Months," Duncan confirmed.

Shane slapped Duncan on the back. "Lover boy was seeing someone and she wouldn't allow Cruz here to come out and play, but now he's a single guy again."

Duncan rolled his eyes. "Yeah, yeah, yeah. Laugh it up, Wall Street. Not all of us are as lucky as you when it comes to finding the right match."

"I told you, I'm an EMT now, Cruz, just like you. My Wall Street days are over, but you're right about the lucky part. Layla is a treasure."

Levi made the sound of a whip cracking and they all laughed.

Coop scanned the room. "Where's Nick?"

Levi pointed in the general direction of Shane's kitchen. "Mr. Doom and Gloom is on the phone with Isabelle."

Coop's brows furrowed. "Is something wrong?"

Shane shrugged. "Not sure. He was pretty quiet when he arrived, then he got a call from Isabelle and he's been on the phone with her for thirty minutes now."

Nick walked into the room looking as if someone had smacked him upside the head.

"Hey, man. You okay?" Coop asked.

Nick sank onto the couch and dropped his head in his hands. "Isabelle wants to postpone the wedding."

"What?" Levi looked at Coop, a stunned expression on his face. "How come?"

Nick lifted his gaze. "She got an offer for a new job. In Tokyo."

"Japan?" Shane asked.

Coop sucked in a deep breath. That was a long way away from New Suffolk.

Nick nodded. "Her company offered her the job today. It's a one-year assignment. Apparently, it's a pretty big deal that they've selected her." His face fell. "We're supposed to get married next month and my fiancée and I won't even be on the same continent."

"Can you move the wedding up?" he asked.

Nick looked as if Coop had grown two heads. "First off, the wedding venue is booked solid for the next year and a half, and even if that weren't the case, we couldn't pull everything together before she has to leave."

Levi eyed Nick curiously. "When is that?"

"In a few days." Nick threw his hands in the air. "Talk about little to no notice." He jumped up from the couch and started pacing back and forth. "How is someone supposed to uproot their lives in a week? It's not enough time, damn it." Nick continued ranting as if no one else was there.

Coop couldn't understand most of what Nick was saying, but his last words came through loud and clear.

You think you know someone.

An image of Rachel flashed in his brain. Nausea roiled around in his gut and burned a path up his throat.

He'd thought he'd known Rachel. Look how that turned out.

And Piper... He'd known her since birth, but this thing with her was pretend. A deal they'd made.

He liked the Piper he'd gotten to know over the last few weeks, but how could he say for sure what she was really like?

Chapter Twenty

Piper headed back to the gallery at eleven o'clock on Wednesday morning. Flakes of snow drifted down from the gray sky.

Her phone rang as she reached the outskirts of town. She pressed the button on her steering wheel that connected the call.

"Hello."

"Hey, Piper. It's me." Cooper's voice boomed over her car speakers. "Were you able to get the things you needed at the hardware store for the bathrooms?"

She smiled. "Yes, although I had to drive to Plymouth because our local store was out of the fixtures I wanted. I'm on my way back now. I should be there in a few minutes."

"Actually, I won't be here when you arrive. I have to take off a little early today. I'm heading out now."

Her brows furrowed. He hadn't mentioned needing to leave early this morning. Usually, he gave her a heads-up when they started the day. "Everything all right?"

"Everything's fine," he answered. "I'll see you later, right?" he asked.

"Yes. I was planning to come to your place around dinnertime, if that's okay." She needed to spend the afternoon working on the portrait she was painting of his house. Cooper's birthday was only two days away.

"That works. I'll see you soon."

"Bye," she said and disconnected the call.

Her phone dinged a few minutes later, indicating she'd received a text. Piper wouldn't check it while she was driving. She'd wait until she arrived at the gallery. She'd be there soon.

Five minutes later, she pulled into a spot by the side entrance of the mansion and hopped out. Grabbing the bag with the boxes of fixtures from the passenger seat, she strode to the building. Piper entered the mansion and hurried up the stairs.

"Mom, Debby. What are you doing here?"

Her mother walked over and kissed her cheek. "We were wondering if we could convince you to have lunch with us today."

"How did you get in?" she asked. "The side door was locked." She'd needed to punch in the code in order to gain access. "Did Layla let you in?"

"No." Debby came over and gave her a big hug. "Cooper was walking out when we arrived." She chuckled. "He was very mysterious as to where he was going. All he said was he had something important to do."

"Yes." Mom flashed a mile-wide grin. "Very, very important."

"Maybe, just maybe…" Debby trailed off, but she raised her ring finger and waved it. "Valentine's Day *is* less than three weeks away."

Piper grinned. She couldn't help it. Everything was going according to plan. Time to play the part. "Do you really think it's true?"

Cooper always tells me where he's going, but this time he didn't.

What if… A lick of excitement swept through her.

No, no, no, no, no. He wasn't… They weren't…

Piper gave herself a mental shake. She was one card short of a full deck for even considering the idea.

Debby nodded. "I've always thought that you two belong together."

Why did Debby keep insisting that was true?

"I guess we'll just have to wait and see." Mom grinned.

"In the meantime, how about lunch?" Debby asked.

Piper blew out a breath, thankful for the subject change.

"Yes, I haven't seen you in forever," Mom said.

Piper rolled her gaze skyward. "Nothing like guilting me into it, Mom."

Mom just smiled. "I'll take that as a yes."

"A short lunch. I've got things to do here," she said.

"The place is really coming along." Debby circled her hand in a gesture that was meant to include the entire space. "I can't wait to see what it will look like with all the art in it."

Me either. A little thrill ran through her. "You'll have to come to my grand opening."

Debby gave her another hug. "Ron and I wouldn't miss it for the world. We're so proud of you."

"Me, too." Mom swiped at the corner of her eye.

"Aww, Mom. Don't cry." Piper wrapped her arms around her.

"I'm not." Mom held her tight. "I just wish your father could be here to see what you've done. He would love this."

He really would. Piper sucked in a deep breath and released it. *I wish he was here, too.*

She eased away from her mom. "Did you have some place in mind for lunch?" She walked to the bar and set the bag containing the bathroom fixtures on top.

"How about Layla's place? It's quick and convenient."

"Sounds good to me." She still wanted to taste the burger Cooper had told her about.

"Perfect," Debby agreed.

She pinned a smile in place. "Let's go."

They rode the elevator to the first floor and exited the building.

Walking into the restaurant, they requested a table in the main dining room. A hostess showed them to a table by the windows that overlooked the ocean.

There was no gentle ebb and flow of the water today. The icy water churned and the waves sounded like an explosion as they crashed on shore.

Piper gazed out the window, mesmerized. "It's beautiful, even at this time of year."

"It is," Debby agreed. "I can't think of a venue that has more spectacular views."

"Speaking of venues, did you know that Layla is doing weddings here now?" Mom's casual tone didn't fool Piper.

Debby shook her head. "I didn't know that. Did you, Piper?"

She leaned back in her chair and crossed her arms over her chest. "Did you two rehearse that?"

"I don't know what you're talking about, darling," her mother said.

Piper made a tsking sound. "You never do, Mom. You never do."

"Hello, Jane," their server greeted as she approached the table. "Layla is working on your tasting menu now and the first course should be out in a few minutes."

Jane nodded. "Thank you, Susan."

Piper gawked at her mother. "Don't know what I'm talking about, my ass," she mumbled under her breath. *So much for getting to taste the burger I've heard so much about.*

"What was that?" Mom shot her an annoyed look.

She flashed a bright grin. "I asked what we'd be eating today."

"The chef has prepared selections of beef, chicken and fish for the three of you this afternoon," their server said. "Along with a medley of starters. Would you care for anything to drink?"

A glass or three of wine would make sitting through Mom's pitch about having her nonexistent wedding here much more palatable, but alcohol in the afternoon made her sleepy. And let's face it. She needed to keep her wits about her. *More caffeine it is.* "I'll have a Diet Coke, please."

Mom and Debby each ordered a glass of chardonnay.

When their server left, Debby made a show of looking around the restaurant. "I just love all of the fairy lights woven through the potted plants."

"Yes," Mom agreed. "They were such a big hit for the EMT fundraiser Layla held last spring that she decided to keep them."

Debby nodded. "I remember that. All of the gold glitz and glamour. It's too bad you weren't here to see it, Piper. It really was quite lovely."

She wasn't into glitz and glamour. Piper preferred understated and classy to in-your-face.

Susan returned and set the drinks down in front of each of them. They thanked her, and she moved to another table.

Mom smiled. "All of the women wore elegant gowns. Just like they would for a wedding."

"Can't you just see it?" Debby asked.

And here we go...

Debby continued, "A ceremony on the beach, when the weather turns warmer, of course. At sunset, so the sky is streaked with vibrant shades of orange and purple."

"With only family and close friends," her mother added.

Actually, that sounded nice. Right up her alley, if she were to get married. Which she wasn't.

Their server placed small dishes of canapés, olives and cheeses on the table.

Piper served herself a canapé. Lifting the mini sandwich to her mouth, she bit into the savory goodness. "This is delicious."

Mom looked at Debby and winked. Piper tried but failed to hide a smile.

"Can you imagine eating hors d'oeuvres on the patio?" Debby pointed out the window to the massive space below, covered with sand-colored pavers and a bronze two-tier Greco Roman–style fountain in the center.

Piper nodded. She may as well make it worth their while. They were going to a lot of trouble to make her see the light. "Fresh urns of flowers mixed with the warm sea breeze. Wrought iron tables and chairs with linen tablecloths. Servers decked out in black pants and white shirts with bow ties mingling discreetly among the guests, serving trays of appetizers and champagne."

"Yes, yes." Mom's voice shook with excitement.

"When the bride and groom finished their photos, everyone would move back into the restaurant to dine on Layla's delicious food. While we gaze out at the stars twinkling in the evening sky." Piper slanted a glance at Mom and Debby. They hung on every word she said.

"Instead of a wedding cake, Abby would provide an assortment of cupcakes from the Coffee Palace." Because Abby's cupcakes had more frosting than cake, which was what she preferred. "The dessert would be served with her special blend coffee." For Cooper, of course.

"We could have a live band set up at the bar," Mom proposed.

"A DJ would be more fun," Piper insisted. After all this was supposed to be all about her and her groom.

Debby glowed with happiness. "It all sounds perfect."

Piper exhaled a wistful sigh. It really did. *What if...*

She looked at her mother. Images of her from right after Dad's death flooded her mind. She couldn't get out of bed most days. And the zombie-like person who greeted her when she did... She wasn't going to end up like her. *Nope. Never going to happen.*

She laid her palms on the white tablecloth and leaned forward. Locking her gaze on the two women sitting across from her, she said, "Too bad we don't have a bride and groom."

"Well, maybe not at this precise moment," Debby agreed. "But I'm sure we will soon."

Piper burst out laughing. They were persistent, if nothing else. "I surrender." She raised her hands in the air. It wasn't as if they could force her and Cooper to do something neither of them was interested in.

Except... If she were to get married... Piper gazed around the room. Layla's restaurant was a beautiful venue and she could picture this room filled with the people she loved most...

What was wrong with her today? *Love doesn't last. It devastates and destroys the one left behind.* How could she have forgotten that? All she had to do was look at her mother for the constant reminder.

Piper glanced across the table, and really looked at her, for once. The all-consuming sadness permanently etched on Mom's features was gone. And the heavy burden Mom used to carry seemed to have disappeared.

Before her sat a vibrant, vivacious, loving woman. The complete opposite of the mother Piper remembered from her childhood.

Why had she never noticed that before? When had this change happened?

"Here we are." Their server's voice pulled her from her musings.

Piper blinked and focused on the here and now.

"Everything looks so good, Susan," Mom said.

She set a large serving tray with three small platters sitting atop on a stand beside their table. "Beef tenderloin." She placed the first dish on the table in the center. "Pan seared salmon, and chicken in a red wine sauce." She positioned the two dishes next to the first.

"I can't wait to taste everything," Debby said.

"Is there anything else I can get you?" their server asked.

"Not right now, thanks," the three of them said at the same time.

"Okay. Enjoy your meals." Susan picked up her tray and headed back to the kitchen.

"Dig in," Mom said.

Thirty minutes later, Piper hugged her mother and Debby and waved goodbye as they strode out of the restaurant. She grabbed her purse and was heading to the main exit when Tom waved her over.

"Hi, Piper." Tom stood. Wrapping his arms around her, he gave her a big bear hug. "It's so good to see you again." He loosened his grip, but didn't let her go. "How are you?"

"I'm good." She stepped away from him and put some much-needed space between them. "Are you having lunch with someone?" Piper gestured to the empty plate opposite Tom, with a knife and fork laid across it.

"Yes." He nodded. "They had to leave. I was just finishing up. Care to join me?" Tom offered a winsome smile and reached for her hand. "I hate eating alone."

"Sorry, she can't." Cooper appeared by her side, a thunderous expression on his face. He wrapped a possessive arm around her and pulled her against him.

Piper gawked at Cooper. What had gotten into him?

"Hi, baby." Cooper planted a hard, demanding kiss on her mouth. "Sorry I left you alone."

What the hell? Piper felt like she'd just fallen down the rabbit hole.

"We need to get back to the gallery." Without letting go of her, Cooper marched them toward the exit.

"Bye, Piper. It was great seeing you again," Tom said. "Let's get together soon."

She tried to wave, but Cooper kept going.

Once outside, she stopped and stared at him. "What was that all about? Why did you frog-march me out of there?"

Something was up with Cooper, and she needed to know what.

Shit. What was he supposed to tell her? The truth was, he wasn't sure why he'd acted the way he had. He'd spotted her the minute he'd walked into the restaurant. He was on his way over to her when Tom stopped her.

His brain started screaming *danger, danger, danger.* His body took over, and the next thing he realized they were standing here in the parking lot.

"What are you talking about?" The words popped out of his mouth before he could stop them.

Piper slammed her hands on her hips and glared at him. "Now you sound like my mother."

Great. He wasn't sure which was worse, being lumped in with her mother or telling her the truth about Tom and Rachel.

What kind of moron doesn't realize his girlfriend and best friend are screwing around right under his nose?

Coop winced. Yeah, he'd take being lumped in with her mother.

"What is going on with you? You went all caveman on me in there."

A hint of a smile formed on his face. "I didn't throw you over my shoulder and drag you out of there." Even though he'd wanted to.

She rolled her eyes. "No. Thank goodness. I might have clobbered you if you had."

"Noted." He dragged a hand through his hair. "I'm sorry." What else could he say? Seeing Tom with Piper… Bile swirled in his gut and burned a path up his throat.

He didn't want Piper anywhere near Tom, or any other guy for that matter.

He didn't want to think about what that meant.

Chapter Twenty-One

Coop pulled his F-150 into the parking lot of the old co-lonial mansion at 5:00 a.m. sharp on Friday morning. An-other two weeks and these early starts would end.

That was a good thing—because he hated waking up at dark o'clock. He wasn't an early-morning kind of guy—so why was his stomach churning at the idea of them ending?

Who was he kidding? He knew why. When this project ended, he wouldn't see Piper every day.

He treasured this comradery, this rapport they'd devel-oped, since he started her gallery renovations. He liked having her around. Liked working with her all day and sharing a glass of wine in front of his roaring fireplace in the evenings. He enjoyed cooking a meal together. He adored sharing it while they watched a movie and tum-bling into bed after.

And yeah, he liked the lovemaking. *Loved*, he mentally corrected. Coop grinned. That part of their relationship was spectacular.

He would miss it. All of it.

He'd miss *her*. More than he would have ever guessed possible. A few weeks ago, he couldn't imagine how he was going to get through five weeks with her. It had felt like a long prison sentence with no time off for good be-havior. Now… He couldn't imagine not seeing her smil-ing face every day.

The million-dollar question was, what was he going to do about it?

Coop rubbed the back of his neck. Could he convince her to turn their fake relationship into something real? Sweat beaded on his brows and his hands turned clammy.

He rubbed his hands on his jeans-covered thighs. Sucking in a deep, slow breath, he blew it out slowly.

It wasn't like he was proposing marriage. *No friggin' way.* The idea of putting his heart out there again, of opening himself to that kind of pain… *Not gonna happen.* But… he'd be interested in extending this thing between them for longer than the time frame they'd originally agreed on.

Piper's grand opening was in fifteen days. He wanted more time with her.

Now he just needed to convince her she wanted the same.

Coop slugged down a gulp of coffee and hopped out of the truck. He strode across the empty parking lot to the gallery entrance and punched in the numbers on the keypad lock.

He rode the elevator to the second floor and stepped into the hall when the doors opened.

The lights were on. "Piper? Are you here?" She'd said something about needing to pick up a few things at her place before she headed to the gallery when she left his place this morning.

No answer came.

"Hello?" he called.

The scent of fresh-brewed coffee filled the room. Piper must be here. She was the only other person besides him with the entrance codes for both the external door and the one they'd erected on the first floor to separate her space from Layla's restaurant.

He walked into the main room, setting his phone next to the speaker on the island as he walked by.

The snap and pop of something sizzling filled his ears. Oh my gosh, was that bacon he smelled? He inhaled again. Yes indeed, it was. Coop grinned. "Come out, come out, wherever you are."

"I'm in the kitchenette," she called. "Come on back."

Coop ducked around the wall that now separated the kitchenette from the island that would be turned into a bar area as soon as he finished the construction. That was on today's agenda, along with a few other small projects, like adding baseboards to the newly installed walls that separated the main room into three smaller sections, and removing the carpet and the odd pieces of furniture stored in what was originally the third bedroom when Layla's grandparents had used this space as an apartment.

Piper was standing at the counter in front of an electric griddle. With her hair piled on her head in a haphazard bun and a large apron that read *Kiss the Cook* draped over the front of her, she looked adorable.

He snaked his arms around her waist and pulled her against him so they stood chest to chest. He crushed his lips to hers.

"What was that for?" she asked, breathless, a few minutes later.

"Just doing what you asked." He grinned and pointed to her apron.

"Ah." She chuckled. "I see."

"What's all this?" he asked.

Piper beamed at him. She removed her apron and set it on the counter. Opening the microwave that sat adjacent to the griddle, she pulled out a serving plate laden with food. "Chocolate chip pancakes with real maple syrup and bacon."

His favorite breakfast of all time. "Wow. What's the occasion?"

"Why, your birthday, of course." She kissed him again.

His eyes widened. "You remembered?" She hadn't said a word before leaving the house this morning. In fact, she hadn't said anything during all the time they'd spent together over the last five days.

"Of course, I did. I made all your favorites." She piled utensils on top of two empty plates that she grabbed with the other hand. "Would you mind getting the orange juice from the fridge?"

His favorite morning beverage—okay, his second favorite after coffee. He couldn't believe she'd gone to all this trouble for him.

It was, hands down, the nicest birthday gift he'd ever received from a woman, and the most thoughtful by far.

"No problem. Do you need me to bring anything else?" he asked.

"The glasses." She jerked her head toward the counter. "I already set out the coffee mugs on the island. We'll eat out there."

Coop got the juice and glasses and followed her out.

Piper set everything atop the marble surface. "Well, what are you waiting for? Dig in."

He frowned. "What about you? Aren't you joining me?"

"I will. I just need to grab one more thing. I'll be right back." She hurried down the hall toward her art studio and disappeared a moment later.

Coop stabbed his fork into the stack of pancakes and placed three on his plate. He added several slices of bacon. Setting his dish down in front of him, he reached for the jug of syrup, made on a farm just over the state line in Vermont.

"Close your eyes," Piper called. "I have a surprise for you."

"What is it?" he asked.

"If I told you, it wouldn't be a surprise, now would it?" She had a point.

"Are your eyes closed?" she asked.

He laid down his utensils and lowered his eyelids. "Yes." He grinned, feeling like a little kid again. "They are. You can come out now."

Her shoes echoed down the hall as she approached.

"Keep them closed while I get this set up," she said.

"Bossy." He chuckled.

"Damned straight." Piper snorted. "And no peeking."

"I'm not." Coop crossed his heart. "My eyes are closed. I swear."

"Make sure you keep them that way. I need to go back to my studio and grab one more thing. Be right back."

Coop's brows knit together. He couldn't imagine what she was doing. "Come on, you've got me really curious. Can't you give me just a little hint?"

"No. You'll find out soon enough." Her footsteps retreated. A moment later she returned. "Okay, I'm back. I need one more minute."

Something thudded against the wood floor and she let out a muffled curse.

Coop chuckled. "Everything okay?"

"I dropped something on my foot, but I'm fine." Piper mumbled something else he couldn't make out. "All right. I'm ready. You can open your eyes now."

He raised his eyelids. A large, framed picture sat propped against a black, shoulder-height easel.

Not a picture. A painting. Of his house. His jaw dropped. "Did you paint this?"

"Yes. You can put it in your study, or in a different room, if you want. I wouldn't want to tell you what to do with it." She flashed a cheeky grin.

Coop jumped off his chair and came closer to get a better view. He scrutinized the image. "The detail is amazing. It looks just like the front of my house. Landscape and all." He stared at her. "This is incredible. Thank you so much. I love it."

"Happy birthday." Her smile sent a flood of warmth rushing through him.

Coop just stared at her, awed that she'd given him such an extraordinary gift. She'd created something personal. No woman had ever done such a thing for him.

Such a loving, giving woman. And he thought he didn't know her. How ironic was that? "Thank you." He grasped her jaw and brushed his lips over hers. "I'll treasure it always."

Piper twined her arms around his neck. "I'm so glad you like it."

"Love it. I absolutely *love* it." He kissed her again.

Piper grinned and eased away from him. "We should probably eat before breakfast gets too cold."

"You're right." He clutched her hand and they walked back to the bar together. Sitting on the bar stool, he cut into the pancakes and he brought a bite to his mouth. Coop savored the buttery, sweet goodness. "Oh, man. These are delicious."

His phone buzzed.

Piper reached out and slid the phone over to where he sat.

He would have ignored it, but his father's number flashed across the screen. Coop connected the call. "Hey, Dad."

"Good morning, son. Happy birthday."

"Thanks."

"So, I know we stopped exchanging birthday gifts with each other years ago, but I've got a little something for you today."

Coop laughed. His parents said that every year, and every year they gave him something. "Thanks, Dad. You can give me my present tonight."

"I won't see you tonight," Dad said.

His brows furrowed. "We're having dinner together. Mom set it up with me and Piper a couple of weeks ago."

Piper chuckled and winked at him.

"We're not getting together tonight," Dad insisted. "That's my gift to you. We can get together another time."

"But Mom—" he started.

"I'll talk to her. Go have fun with Piper."

Coop grinned. "I will. Thanks, Dad."

Dad laughed. "You're welcome. I'll have your mom touch base with you next week."

"You're giving me the entire weekend, not just today? That's a hell of a present. I love it," he said and smirked, even though his father couldn't see his face.

Piper chuckled.

"Wiseass," Dad grumbled. "Have a good day. Love you, Cooper."

"Love you, too, Dad."

"Bye, son. See you soon." Dad ended the call.

He turned to Piper. "We're off the hook for tonight."

"Are you sure? Debby won't be happy. And I don't want to piss her off."

"Don't worry. Dad said he'd smooth things over with her." He stabbed his fork into another chunk of pancake. "So, tell me. How did you know all of my favorites?" he asked.

Piper plucked up a piece of bacon from the serving dish and munched on it. "We may not have been the best of friends growing up, but we did spend a lot of time together. Your dad used to make thin, almost crepe-like pancakes with chocolate chips for breakfast every Sunday." Piper gestured to his plate. "And you loved them." She served herself a pancake. "You used to hog the bacon, too." She winked and added three more slices to her plate.

He laughed. "What about the OJ? I never drank that as a kid."

"No," she agreed. "But I noticed you've consumed a glass every morning over the last five days while you waited for your first cup of coffee to finish brewing." Piper grinned and pointed her index finger to her head. "I used my mad deductive skills and figured you'd grown to like it."

"Brilliant, my dear. Simply brilliant." He gave her a quick peck on the lips. "But seriously. Thank you." He kissed her again because he wanted to. "You didn't have to do this."

Piper leaned close and wrapped her arms around his neck. She looked him in the eyes. "I know, but I wanted to."

Her smile filled his heart to bursting point.

"Now would you like to hear what else I have planned for your birthday celebration?" she asked.

His gaze widened. "There's more?"

"Yes sirree. We do have to work this morning, but I thought we could head to Boston this afternoon. Since you love to walk, I thought we could check out one of the Freedom Trails. Now that we have the evening free, how about a nice dinner in the city when we're done?"

"Sounds perfect." He leaned close, intending to kiss her once again, because yeah, kissing her was one of life's great pleasures, but his phone started to ring. Coop blew out a breath. Now who was calling him?

"You should probably get that," she said with a reluctant sigh. "It's probably someone calling to wish you a happy birthday."

He grabbed his phone and glanced at the caller ID. His brows furrowed. "Hey, Everett. It's pretty early for you to be calling. What's up?"

"Happy birthday, my friend."

He chuckled. "Thanks, man. I'm impressed you're up and cognizant at—" Coop glanced at his watch "—six a.m. to make this call."

"You should be. I don't have to head to the office for another three hours, but I know you start your day early, so I made the effort."

"Ha ha. Heading to the gym?"

Everett laughed. "Can't fool you, can I? Yeah. I'm on my way now. Figured I'd kill two birds with one stone."

"Huh?" Coop's brows drew together in a deep V. "What do you mean?"

"I haven't heard from you in a few weeks, and Annalise and I are still waiting to meet your new woman."

Damn. Coop pinched the bridge of his nose. He'd hoped Ev would have forgotten about that by now.

"Everything okay?" Piper asked.

"Is she with you right now?" Everett asked.

Piper must have heard Ev's question, because she answered. "Yes. I'm here with Cooper."

"Put the call on speakerphone," Everett demanded. "I want to talk to her."

He shook his head. "Not a chance."

In a surprise move, Piper grabbed his phone and pressed the speaker button. She danced away from him when he reached for the phone. "Hello, this is Piper. Who am I speaking with?" She grinned at him.

"I'm Everett, Coop's fraternity brother. I'm the one getting married next week. I take it you're Coop's new girlfriend and the person he's bringing to the wedding?"

"I am," she confirmed. "It's nice to meet you, Everett. So, what's up? Why do you want to talk to me?"

Coop let out a loud snort.

"I've been asking Coop to introduce you to us for a while now, but he refused," Everett said.

Coop shook his head. "Hey, that's not true. Piper and I have been busy. That's all."

"That is true," Piper said. "He's been working hard these past few weeks. I hear his client is very demanding."

"Bossy," Coop muttered.

Piper's smile lit up the whole room. God, he loved her smile.

"Sounds like he needs a break. How about dinner tonight? You can help us taste-test the food for the rehearsal dinner next Friday."

How could he have forgotten Everett's wedding was a week from tomorrow?

"That sounds fun," Piper said. "I'll let you two work out the details." She turned off the speaker and handed his phone back to him.

"Are you sure?" he asked Piper.

She nodded and kissed his cheek. "It's no problem."

"Okay, Ev. What time?" he asked.

Piper smirked and leaned in close. She whispered in his other ear, "Payback's a bitch."

He flashed a what-are-you-talking-about-woman look at her.

She tilted her head and nibbled his earlobe.

Coop swallowed hard. "What was that, Everett?"

Piper trailed her fingers over his chest.

He shuddered. Now he understood. She was getting even with him for doing the same thing to her when she was on the phone with her sister the other night.

Everett started speaking, but Coop couldn't make out what he was saying because Piper was doing delightful things to the pulse slamming at the base of his throat with her tongue.

Piper grabbed the phone from him again. "Text him the information." She disconnected the call and shoved his phone in his back pocket. "You were doing too much talking."

He sent her a wolfish grin. Lifting her, he placed her on top of the island.

"Touch me." She grabbed his hands and placed them on her breasts.

"Bossy." He skimmed his fingers under her sweater and pulled it over her head.

"You love it."

Yeah, he did. He loved everything about this beguiling, bewitching woman.

He *loved* her.

His heart thundered loud enough to wake the dead.

Chapter Twenty-Two

The smell of tasty treats filled the air as Piper walked hand in hand with Cooper around the food colonnade at Faneuil Hall in downtown Boston on Friday afternoon.

"How about some ice cream?" Cooper asked over the background noise of chatting passersby as they continued on their way.

It had been years since she'd last visited and she'd forgotten how massive the historical structure was and how many retailers occupied the enormous space.

"You do know that it's the middle of winter, right? We came in here to get out of the cold." She pointed to the mass of humanity surrounding them. "Do you see anyone else eating a frozen dessert on this cold, blustery day?"

He laughed. "No. That doesn't mean I can't have any. It's never the wrong season for ice cream, as far as I'm concerned."

"We just had a chocolate chip cookie. Are you planning on eating your way from one end of this place to the other?" she asked.

He linked her arm with his. "Now, that would be quite a feat. How many kiosks do you think there are?"

"Twenty-nine, according to this." Piper waved her folded marketplace map.

Coop nodded. "Impressive, but I'm not interested in trying something from all of them, just the sweets. So, is that a yes to the ice cream?"

She shook her head. "No, thanks. I'm going to pass on any more sugar before dinner."

"You're such a spoilsport. A little more sugar won't hurt you. We walked for hours on the Freedom Trail. Certainly that entitles us to a cupcake?" he asked as they passed the North End Bakery.

She chuckled. "Good try, Turner, but the Freedom Trail is only two and a half miles long. We spent almost three hours on it because we kept stopping at each of the historical spots. A half hour at the Paul Revere House, twenty minutes at the Old North Church, and I can't remember how long we meandered around the Massachusetts State House. Not to mention the rest of the sites on the tour. Besides, I don't see any cupcakes." Piper pointed to the display case as they strolled by the bakery. "But don't let me stop you if you want something else." She kissed his cheek. "You *are* the birthday boy, after all."

He flashed her the sweetest grin and her heart turned over. The man was absolutely adorable.

"Yes, I am. I've decided I want a cannoli." He turned them back the way they came and they stepped up to the counter together. "I'll have one of those, please." He pointed to the rack on the top shelf of the case. Looking at her, he asked, "Are you sure I can't interest you in one? They're really good."

Piper gazed at the tray. With all of the creamy filling stuffed in the sweet, crispy shell, they did look delicious. "Maybe we can split one?"

"That's my girl." He pulled her close and draped his arm around her shoulder.

His girl. She liked the sound of that. She'd decided not to beat herself up about what was or wasn't developing between them. She liked spending time with Cooper, and she was pretty sure he enjoyed spending time with her, too. She'd go with the flow for now.

Coop broke the shell in half. At least he tried to, but the pieces came out uneven.

"I'll take the smaller piece, please." She extended her palm to him. "I need to save at least a little room for dinner tonight."

He handed her the treat and they continued on their way.

Piper bit into the sugary confection. "You're right. It's fantastic."

"It is." Cooper cocked his head toward the exit. "We should head back to the hotel. We need to change before we meet up with my friends."

"Agreed. It was a good idea to stay here overnight tonight." They exited Faneuil Hall and headed toward the waterfront area. "That way we can relax and have a drink without having to worry about driving the forty minutes back to New Suffolk. I especially like the idea of staying in the same place we're having dinner." Piper grinned. "No car or bulky winter coat needed. We'll just take the elevator down to the main level and walk into the restaurant."

"That's why I suggested it," Cooper agreed.

The wind picked up the closer they got to the water and Piper shivered. Without saying a word, Cooper pulled her into the crook of his arm. He slanted his body to shield her.

Sweet, sweet man.

"So, tell me more about these friends we're having dinner with," she invited. He hadn't told her anything, and she had to admit she was quite curious. "How do you know them?" Why had Everett pestered Cooper to have dinner?

"Everett is one of my fraternity brothers. We met freshman year of college. He was my roommate. He's become my best friend."

"Really?" She'd assumed Tom still held that status. They'd been friends since preschool.

Cooper nodded. "We've had this connection since the first day we met. I know he'd go to the ends of the earth for me, and I'd do the same for him. Do you know what I mean?"

Piper had never experienced a relationship like that outside of her siblings. She'd never allowed anyone close enough to make such a friend. She realized it was why she hadn't exchanged phone numbers with Elle and Abby until they'd pressed the point. She'd kept all of these kind, supportive women at arm's length for the same reason she ran like hell from relationships with the opposite sex. She didn't want to get hurt.

The thing was, she liked Layla, Abby, Elle and even Zara. They had each other's backs and they'd have hers, too, if she allowed it. All she needed to do was take down the walls she'd erected around her heart and let them in.

Piper slanted her gaze to Cooper. Could she let him in, too?

"Annalise is Ev's fiancée. They met at work about three years ago. She's a great person. Kind, supportive, and a heart of gold." He smiled at her. "She's a lot like you."

Her heart turned over. Yes, this man was the sweetest.

"She's become a close friend, too," he said.

"They both sound like great people."

Cooper nodded. "They are. I think you'll like them a lot. I know I do."

Piper shot him a curious glance. "Can I ask you a question?"

"Sure. What is it?"

"Why are we having dinner with them? I'm not complaining. I'm just curious as to why."

A hesitant expression crossed his handsome face. He stayed silent for a moment as if deciding what to say.

"Do you remember the other night when I told you about Rachel?" he asked.

She nodded. "Your ex, right?" The woman he'd wanted to marry. Piper swallowed past the painful lump in her throat. Lord, what was wrong with her tonight? Who cared if he'd loved the woman enough to want to marry her? Not her.

Liar.

"Yes. That's her. Rachel and I met through Annalise. She's Annalise's cousin." Cooper shook his head. "I don't want either her or Everett feeling sorry for me."

Piper nodded. "So we're having dinner with them to show them that you've moved on."

"Exactly. I also don't want them worrying about any awkwardness at the wedding. Rachel and I are both in the wedding party."

No wonder Cooper had wanted a date for the wedding. She couldn't imagine having to face someone you loved, especially at a wedding, if that person chose someone else over you. "Don't worry. I've got you covered. We'll make her sorry she ever dumped you."

Piper wasn't sure why he turned silent again. His stony expression sent a wave of unease coursing through her. What was going on with him? What wasn't he telling her?

They reached the hotel a few minutes later. The stunning lobby with its shining marble and glittering vintage chandeliers awed her as they crossed to the elevator bank. "This really is a spectacular place for a wedding, if grand opulence is your thing."

Cooper peered over at her. "But it's not your thing." It was a statement, not a question. "You're more of an intimate gathering of family and close friends at a small but classy venue person."

She looked at him. He knew her well. Not that she would be getting married any time soon. But if she was...

They rode the elevator to the second floor. When they reached their room, Coop opened the door and gestured for her to precede him in.

Piper gazed around the space. She hadn't had the opportunity to check out the room earlier. When they'd checked in, they'd dropped their luggage and headed out right away. She walked to the floor-to-ceiling windows that offered spectacular sweeping views of the city skyline.

Cooper came up behind her. He wrapped his arms around her waist and pressed her against him. "I had a great day today. It means a lot to me that you went out of your way to make my birthday special."

He turned her to face him. His tender gaze sent a rush of warmth flooding through her system. Her heart beat a rapid tattoo. "I'm glad you had fun."

"I did because I was with you." He grasped her chin with his fingers and brushed his lips over hers and...there it was again. That warmth that rushed through her and made her feel all tingly inside when he came near.

Cooper tucked a loose strand of her hair behind her ear. "Thank you. I can't remember the last time I enjoyed myself this much."

Piper smiled. "You're welcome."

He released her, reluctantly, if the look on his face was anything to go by. "We should get ready." Glancing at his watch, he added, "We need to be downstairs in twenty minutes."

"It won't take me long. I just have to change my clothes and throw my hair up."

He eyed her skeptically.

Piper burst out laughing. "Don't worry. I promise I'll be ready on time." She walked to the closet and grabbed her suitcase.

Cooper's brows furrowed. "Where are you going?"

She dropped a quick kiss on his lips as she passed by him. "To the bathroom. To get changed."

"You could get changed out here, with me." He sent her a wolfish smile.

Piper grinned and made a tsking sound. "Not if you want to be on time. Don't worry, I won't be long."

She hurried into the spacious bathroom and shut the door. Stripping out of her clothes, she shimmied into her short, black knit dress with a drop shoulder and loose, long sleeves. Gathering up her long hair, she twisted it into a haphazard bun and secured it with an elastic band.

She added a touch of blush and raspberry-colored lipstick. Stepping into her strappy heels, she surveyed herself in the mirror. "Not bad," she murmured.

Piper closed up her suitcase, opened the bathroom door and wheeled it out. Cooper stood in front of the bedroom mirror straightening his collar. Dressed in a pair of navy dress pants and matching jacket with a white button-down shirt, the man looked sexy as all get-out.

She let out a wolf whistle. "You clean up nice, Mr. Turner."

He looked at her. His eyes turned smoky, and a little thrill of excitement ran through her. "So do you, Ms. Kavanaugh." He snaked his arm around her, pulled her against him and kissed her senseless. "So do you."

Piper sucked in some much-needed air when he released her. "Let's go meet your friends." She eyed the massive king-size bed with its plush comforter. "Now. Before I change my mind."

"By all means." He let out a deep, rumbly chuckle and crooked his arm.

She looped her arm through his and grabbed her purse on the way to the door.

They rode the elevator down to the ground floor and crossed the lobby to the restaurant's etched-glass double doors with gold metal frames.

"After you." Cooper pulled the right door open and gestured for her to precede him.

Piper peered around. "I love the ambience of this place." The low lighting and floor-to-ceiling windows gave diners an unobstructed view of the Boston harbor while they ate. "The long tables make it a great venue for a large gathering."

Cooper nodded. "There are a lot of people coming to the rehearsal dinner. We have twelve people in the wedding party alone, and that doesn't include the bride and groom. Oh, there's Ev and Annalise." He pointed to a couple seated at a table in front of the windows sipping a glass of wine.

"Are you ready?" Cooper gave a nervous chuckle.

She nodded. "I told you. I've got your back." He was counting on her, and she wouldn't let him down. She clasped his hand in hers.

He walked with purpose to where the couple sat. "Hi, guys."

Everett stood and clapped Cooper on the shoulder. "Hey, man. It's good to see you. Happy birthday, buddy."

Annalise rose. "I'm so glad you could join us this evening." She hugged Cooper and kissed his cheek.

Cooper put his arm around her. "Everett, Annalise, I'd like you to meet Piper. Honey, these are my friends, Everett and Annalise."

"It's so nice to meet you." Annalise grinned and shook Piper's outstretched hand.

"You, too," she agreed.

Annalise and Everett returned to their chairs.

"Have we met before? You look familiar." Everett scrutinized her face.

Cooper pulled out her chair for her and she sat. "I don't think so," she said. "I've been living in Los Angeles for the last ten years."

"Then how did you two meet?" Annalise asked.

Cooper sat in the empty chair beside her. He grasped her hand in his and gave it a gentle squeeze. "Actually, Piper and I have known each other pretty much since birth."

She nodded. "Our fathers opened a construction firm together about thirty-five years ago."

"That's it." Everett snapped his fingers. "I knew your last name sounded familiar when we spoke on the phone this morning. I do know you, er, your family," he corrected. "I've met your brother. Shane, right? You also have a sister, but I can't remember her name."

"Mia," Piper said.

Everett nodded. "You look like her. That's why I thought we'd met before."

"You know my sister?" Piper's brows drew together.

Everett grinned. "I spent a lot of time at Coop's house during the summer when we were in college. Your brother used to hang out with us. Sometimes your sister would join us, too."

"I forgot about that," Cooper said.

"Wait a minute. You live in LA?" Everett asked her.

"I did until a few weeks ago. I moved back to New Suffolk in early January."

"So you just started seeing each other?" Annalise asked.

She shook her head. "We started dating last summer." That was the cover story they'd agreed on when they'd made their deal.

Was that only a couple of weeks ago? So much had changed between them in such a short amount of time. She was happy they'd cleared up the misunderstandings between them, because the man sitting beside her was an incredible person and she was lucky to have him in her life.

"You old devil, you. You never said a word. Here I was thinking you'd spent the last ten months pining over Rach—" Everett yelped. He glared at Annalise. "Why'd you kick me?"

She gave him a do-you-have-to-ask look and then gestured to Piper.

"Oh, ah…sorry." Everett flashed her a contrite expression.

"It's okay," she said. "Cooper is just fine now."

"That's right." Cooper snaked an arm around her and pulled her close. He beamed a happy smile. "As a matter of fact, Rachel did me a favor. If she hadn't left me, I would never have reconnected with Piper." He lowered his lips to hers.

His sweet, tender kiss was almost her undoing. She blinked and drew in a deep, steadying breath.

If she wasn't careful, she might start believing that this thing between them was real. It felt genuine, true. It felt… right.

"Aww," Annalise cooed.

Piper jerked her head away from Cooper and faced the couple sitting across from her. Heat scorched her cheeks. Once again, she'd lost sight of everything and everyone else when Cooper came near.

"That's so cute." Annalise went all dreamy-eyed. "You guys make such a great couple."

Real, or not. Annalise was convinced. That was what mattered tonight.

"I know." She flashed a 1000-watt smile. "Isn't he

great?" Piper gave Cooper a peck on his cheek. "I've never been happier." *That's the truth.*

Everett grinned and nodded. "I'm happy for you, buddy." To Piper, he said, "You're a lucky woman."

She leaned her head against Cooper's shoulder. "I know I am."

Later in the evening, Cooper laid his fork and knife across his empty plate and leaned against the chairback. "That was a fantastic meal."

Piper nodded. "Annalise, your guests at the rehearsal dinner are going to love the choices you've selected."

"I hope so. I can't believe the wedding is a week from tomorrow." Annalise turned to Everett. Glancing at her watch, she said, "Eight days from now, we'll be married."

"I can't wait, my love." Everett kissed Annalise.

Cooper cleared his throat. "I think that's our cue to leave."

Everett and Annalise jerked apart.

"Sorry." Annalise wiped her lipstick off Everett's mouth. "Sometimes I forget..." Her whole face turned fire-engine red.

Trust me, I know the feeling. Piper grinned. "It's not a problem."

"Don't leave yet." Everett straightened in his chair. "Stick around for a while. The night is young, and it's your birthday. Let's celebrate with a drink in the bar. You two are staying here at the hotel tonight, right?"

"We are," she agreed.

"Us, too," Everett said. "We don't live that far away, but I didn't want to have to drive after a couple of glasses of wine."

Cooper nodded. "Same goes for us."

"This way we can relax and enjoy ourselves. There's

supposed to be a live musician in the bar tonight. Do you like jazz?" Annalise asked.

Piper smiled. "I love it."

"Let's grab a table now," Cooper said.

Piper gestured toward the restaurant exit. "I'll meet you over there. I need to make a stop in the ladies' room first."

Annalise giggled and stood. "That makes two of us. You guys go ahead."

Piper walked with Annalise toward the restaurant exit and into the hotel lobby.

"The restrooms are around the corner." Annalise pointed to her right.

They started walking.

Annalise turned her head toward Piper. "I'm really happy for you and Cooper. He's such a great guy."

She nodded. "He is." Cooper was one of the best guys she knew.

Annalise flashed a brilliant smile. "I'm just thrilled that Cooper has found someone." She turned serious. "I was worried about him and so was Everett. It's been almost a year since...well, you know." She gave a little twirl of her wrist.

"Since Rachel ended things," Piper supplied.

Annalise's brows furrowed. "Um...yes."

Something in Annalise's expression told Piper there was more to the story than she was letting on.

Piper arched a brow. "You don't sound convinced."

Annalise let out a soft chuckle and waved away Piper's concern. "It all worked out. Cooper has you, and Rachel has Tom."

Tom? No. It couldn't be. Piper stared at Annalise. "Cooper's friend Tom?"

Annalise gasped. "You didn't know?"

"I didn't." *Cooper forgot to mention that little detail.*

"I assumed Cooper had told you." Annalise shook her head
Nope again. Why hadn't he?

An image of his face floated into her mind from earlier when they were walking back to the hotel. His stony
expression when she'd told him she'd make Rachel regret
dumping him. It didn't make any sense unless… Could
Cooper still want Rachel?

Piper's stomach plummeted.

Chapter Twenty-Three

Piper peered around the partitioned section of the ball-room at the hotel in Boston. Everett and Annalise's guests milled about the space, noshing on oysters and littleneck clams on the half shell, jumbo shrimp cocktail, short rib dumplings and a whole lot more while they sipped wine and mixed drinks. They all waited with bated breath for the wedding party to finish the picture-taking portion of the evening so they could move on to the main event. Dinner and dancing.

With its ornate columns and elegant chandeliers, she supposed the space was nice enough, although this space did not offer spectacular views of the harbor. That was reserved for the dining room, which they'd move to as soon as the photographer completed his mission.

Still, Piper couldn't help but remember Layla's restaurant and the gorgeous patio that overlooked the Atlantic Ocean.

Now that she'd envisioned that fantasy, nothing else compared. Damn Mom and Debby for making her think about weddings and receptions.

Tom waved at her from across the room as he made his way to where she stood.

She still couldn't believe he and Cooper's ex were a thing.

Why hadn't Cooper told her? She was obviously going to find it out today. It wasn't like she couldn't put two and two together when she saw them.

Her mind kept circling round and round the events of the last couple of weeks. Cooper's caveman actions when he saw her talking with Tom in Layla's restaurant. His stony expression the night they had dinner with Annalise and Everett, when she promised to make Rachel pay for dumping him. Not to mention the look on Annalise's face when she'd mentioned Rachel leaving Cooper.

None of it made any sense.

Could Cooper still have a thing for Rachel?

Her stomach churned at the idea. Which meant what?

You care about him. A lot.

"Hi, Piper." Tom pulled her into his arms and gave her a big bear hug. "How are you?"

Okay, the touchy-feely thing from him was driving her a little crazy. He acted like they were long-lost friends. The truth was, they were casual acquaintances at best. "I'm fine." She stepped back when he released her. "And you?"

"Doing okay. Hey, would you like to grab a drink?" He gave her a winsome smile. "We can finally catch up with each other."

Why? They'd never truly been friends. Not even when she'd had that crush on him in high school—for all of five minutes—and certainly not after the way he treated her after the skunk incident.

"Thanks, but—" She was about to turn him down when her phone started broadcasting, "Your sister is calling, your sister is calling. What are you waiting for? Pick up the phone already."

Son of a gun. She thought she'd turned her phone off before Everett and Annalise had exchanged vows, but she'd only turned the volume down. Good thing Mia hadn't called during the ceremony.

"Please excuse me," she said.

"Rain check?" he called to her retreating form.

Piper shook her head as she headed toward the exit.

"Hello." She stepped into the large hall that connected the banquet rooms to the main lobby.

Throngs of people milled about out here as well.

"Hey, got any plans for tonight? Elle and Abby are coming over," Mia said.

"I can't. I won't be home until sometime tomorrow afternoon." She and Cooper planned on having a leisurely breakfast in the morning and indulging in a couples massage at the hotel spa before heading back to New Suffolk.

"Where are you? I can hardly hear you. There's a lot of background noise."

She laughed. "That's because there's a lot of people here." Over two hundred guests were attending this event. "I'm in Boston at a wedding with Cooper. One of his fraternity brothers just got married."

"Interesting." Mia snickered. "Maybe you can get some ideas for your own wedding. I hear Cooper's been looking at rings. According to Mom, a proposal is imminent."

Piper snorted. "Didn't Mom already tell you? She and Debby already have the whole wedding planned."

"Yeah, I heard about that. I almost feel sorry for you." Mia chuckled.

"You don't sound it." Piper spotted Tom heading her way. *The man won't take no for an answer.*

"Who won't take no for an answer?" Mia asked.

She hadn't meant to say that out loud. "Tom Anderson. He wants to have a drink and catch up."

"I can't believe it." Mia huffed out a breath. "He's got a lot of nerve after what he did to Cooper."

Piper knew there was more to the story than Annalise had let on. "What happened?"

"He slept with Rachel. While Rachel was still going out with Cooper. For like a couple of months."

Piper's jaw dropped. She couldn't believe what she was hearing.

Tom strode toward her like a heat-seeking missile flying toward its target. Her hands clenched into fists.

"Piper? You still there?" Mia asked.

"Yeah, but I've got to go. I'll call you tomorrow." She disconnected the call.

"Here you are." Tom waved at her as he approached.

Piper gritted her teeth. *Damn it.* She didn't want to talk to him. Not after what he'd done. The guy was a class A jerk.

She opened her mouth to tell him as much and closed it without uttering a word. She wouldn't cause a scene. Not on Annalise and Everett's wedding day. They didn't deserve that.

"Hey, we need to be getting back inside." Tom draped his arm around her shoulder and propelled them forward. "They're about to introduce the wedding party."

Piper stopped short. "I'm capable of walking to my table alone. You don't have to escort me there."

Tom held up his hands as if he were surrendering. "I was just trying to be nice, that's all." He gave her an affable smile. "What kind of friend would I be if I left you alone with over two hundred people you don't even know?"

"Friend?" Piper rolled her eyes. "Do you even know what that word means?"

"Of course I do." Tom stared at her as if she'd sprouted another head.

"Oh, so you were being a *friend* when you started seeing Rachel behind Cooper's back?"

Tom shook his head. "Okay, I didn't mean for that to happen."

She gawked at him. How could he say such a thing? "And yet it did, because you did nothing to stop it."

Tom crossed his arms over his chest. "Don't go all judgmental on me. You have no idea what was going on at the time. I was going through a really tough time and Rachel was there for me. We didn't mean to hurt anyone."

Piper shook her head. "Yeah, but you did."

"You think Cooper's such a great guy? Well, let me tell you…"

"No." Piper held up her hand to stop Tom from saying anything further. "Let *me* tell you. Cooper is the kindest, sweetest, most loving man I know." He made her laugh, and she was happier when he was around. Her life would be empty without him in it.

"Oh, please. You're not fooling me." Tom's features twisted into a sneer. "You and Cooper hate each other. Everyone knows that."

"You're wrong." Piper shook her head. "We—"

"*Love* each other?" Tom gave a disparaging laugh. "You've got to be kidding me. I'm not buying that you're in love with Cooper for a single second."

Of course, she wasn't, but she liked him. A lot. *A lot, a lot.*

Piper caught a glimpse of Cooper standing with the other groomsmen. Her heart turned over and everything went all soft and mushy inside.

Oh dear Lord in heaven. It was true.

Piper's jaw nearly hit the ground. Somehow, some way, she'd fallen head over heels for Cooper Turner.

No, no, no. That wasn't the plan. Love didn't last. She knew that.

He smiled and waved at her, and her chest filled to bursting point.

She *loved* Cooper Turner. With all her heart and soul. What the hell was she supposed to do now?

Coop stood by the door to the groomsmen's suite, people-watching while he waited for the photographer to finish photographing the bride and groom.

Piper walked out into the hall with her cell glued to her ear. God, she looked amazing in her long navy gown that clung to her in all the right places. He couldn't wait to dance with her later and touch all of the smooth, creamy skin on display.

She grinned a mischievous smile and he wondered who she was talking to.

"Checking out the scenery?" His fraternity brother and fellow groomsman, Jack, handed him a glass of Scotch on the rocks. "Mind if I check out the scenery, too?" He winked and stood beside him.

They stood in silence for a few moments.

"Hey, guys." Everett clapped both men on the shoulder. "The DJ just asked our guests to take their seats. Five minutes and then we head in."

Coop nodded but he never moved his gaze from Piper. What was he going to do about her? Was he ready for something more? Things were pretty good right now. Why mess up what they had by getting feelings involved? Then again, things were slated to end between them sooner rather than later. Piper's grand opening was a week away, and he still hadn't asked her if she'd be interested in extending their deal indefinitely. The words got stuck in his throat every time he started to bring it up.

"Now, there's a sight to behold." Jack gestured to where Piper stood.

"Hands off," he growled. "She's taken."

"Ah…" Jack gave a sage nod. "So that's how it is. Another one bites the dust."

He jerked his gaze to the man standing beside him. "What are you talking about?"

"You. You're a goner for the short, blonde chick standing by the door. I was wondering when I saw you with her before the ceremony started. I can understand why. She's gorgeous." Jack snorted and shook his head. "Won't be long until we're all gathered together again for another walk down the aisle."

"Speak for yourself." Coop wouldn't be getting married anytime soon.

"You're funny." Jack chuckled.

Tom appeared by Piper's side.

Every muscle inside him stiffened. What the hell was he doing? Why wouldn't he just leave Piper alone? He started into the hall, ready to put a stop to Tom's meddling once and for all but froze when she smiled at him. His stomach jumped and jittered.

Coop loved her smile. It made him feel like he was everything she could ever want. Everything she'd ever need. All was right with his world again.

Except…

She wasn't smiling at him. She was smiling at Tom.

His stomach plummeted.

"Hey, loverboy," Jack called. "There'll be time for her later. Right now, we gotta go. It's showtime."

He turned to see the bridal party lining up.

"Come on, Cooper." Rachel gestured for him to join her.

It was the last thing on earth he wanted to do, but he had no choice. He trudged over to where she stood at the back of the line.

The announcements began. Coop gritted his teeth.

"We're up next." Rachel extended her hand to him.

Coop fastened his palm to hers, albeit reluctantly.

"Would it kill you to smile? I don't want to do this any-more than you do, but I'm at least making a show of it for Annalise and Everett."

He wanted to bare his teeth and growl, but she was right. He needed to pretend for a little while longer. For Everett and Annalise.

"And the maid of honor and best man—" the DJ shouted "—Rachel McCarthy and Cooper Turner."

Upbeat music started playing and he and Rachel en-tered the room. They joined the rest of the wedding party and waited as Annalise and Everett made their entrance.

Coop slanted his gaze toward Piper's table. He spotted Tom seated next to her.

Son of a bitch. The two of them were laughing together and having a grand old time.

His hands clenched into tight fists.

Coop wasn't sure how much time had passed by the time the waitstaff cleared the dishes. Most of the evening was a blur.

"Hey, man." Everett clapped him on the shoulder. "Your duties as best man are done." His expression turned seri-ous. "Thanks for everything. I know the past few hours with Rachel have been less than pleasurable for you, and I—*we*," he corrected, "because I need to include Annal-ise, too—appreciate you toughing it out for us. You're a true friend."

The sound that came from his mouth was a cross be-tween a snort and a laugh. "I'm just glad I'm done."

"Obligation fulfilled." Ev gave him a thumbs-up. "Time for you to have some fun. Go find Piper and get her out on the dance floor."

"I'll do that." He needed to talk to Piper. He'd overreacted earlier when he'd seen her and Tom together. Not that she knew that—thank God for small miracles. Seeing her with Tom… Bile churned in his gut.

No, damnit. Piper wasn't Rachel. She wouldn't do to him what Rachel had. She'd been nothing but honest with him since the beginning. So why was he creating trouble where none existed?

Coop walked over to her table. "Excuse me," he said because one of the other women sitting with her was talking. "I was hoping I could steal you away for a dance?"

She looked at him, uncertainty in her gaze.

Had she picked up on the bad vibes he'd been putting out lately?

She gave him a hesitant smile and nodded. Standing, she joined her hand with his.

Coop guided them through the maze of couples to an empty spot on the dance floor.

The DJ announced they were going to slow things down and a romantic ballad came through the speakers.

Coop drew her in close and she melted against him. He blew out the breath he'd been holding.

They danced together to the slow, sensual beat, and he couldn't help remembering the day they'd danced together in her gallery. Coop grinned. He'd wanted to show her how much better the adult version of him was compared to his thirteen-year-old self.

"This is nice." He liked holding her close like this.

She didn't respond.

"Are you having a good time?" he asked.

She nodded, but never uttered a word.

"You're awfully quiet. Is everything okay?"

"Yes. Sorry. Just thinking." Her voice held an odd tone that set his nerves on edge.

He eased away from her to see her face. She looked… "Are you sure you're all right? You're white as a ghost."

Her face turned stricken. "I need some air." Piper bolted from the room.

He raced after her and found her in the hall, pacing back and forth. Color had returned to her features. At least that was a good thing. "Hey, what's going on?"

She peered up at him. "Nothing. I'm tired, that's all. Plus, I've got a splitting headache. I'm going to call it a night." She started to walk away from him.

A muscle in his neck jerked. "Oh, sure. You were fine earlier when you were with Tom. All smiles and full of energy, but now you have a headache. Is there something going on with you two I should know about?"

Piper rounded on him. "You've *got* to be kidding me."

He crossed his hands over his chest. "I call it like I see it."

She stared at him as if he'd lost his mind. Maybe he had. "You're one to talk. You think I didn't notice how chummy you've been with your ex all night? Well, I did. And so did everyone at our table, including Tom."

"You can't be serious." Although he couldn't deny that a tiny part of him was cheering because Tom was pissed. "Come on, Piper. What's really going on here?"

Her whole face turned beet red. "You know what? I'm done with this whole charade. It's over. Our deal is done."

"Fine by me," he spat.

She turned and started to leave.

Stop her. Don't let her go.

Coop couldn't move. His stomach churned as he watched her walk away.

Chapter Twenty-Four

Piper rubbed her bleary eyes and snuggled up under her favorite blanket, a gift from her father for her tenth birthday. She ignored the knocking on her apartment door. Maybe they'd go away if she stayed silent. No one knew she was here.

"I know you're home." Mia's voice was muffled. "I can hear your TV."

Damn it. That's what she got for binge-watching…wait for it…*romance* movies all night long.

Piper shook her head. She'd started channel surfing and stopped on the channel playing *Falling for My Brother's Best Friend.* Out of curiosity, of course.

That was five movies ago. And yes, she'd liked each and every one of them.

"You might as well let us in, because we're not going away," Elle called.

Piper heaved out a sigh. Grabbing the remote, she flicked off the television and tossed the blanket aside. She rose from the couch. "Hold your horses. I'm coming."

She trudged to the door and opened it. Mia, Layla, Abby and Elle stood in the hall.

"Why did you dodge all my calls?" Mia asked.

She'd turned off her cell after leaving the wedding reception last night. She didn't want to speak to anyone. Still didn't, but it appeared she didn't have much choice in the matter.

Not true. She could ask them to leave, but she didn't want to. She wanted the love and support these wonderful, funny women had offered from the start. "Come in, ladies. I hope you brought chocolate." Piper yawned. "And coffee. Lots and lots of coffee."

Piper tried, but failed to stifle another yawn. She hadn't slept. Too many things running through her mind. Like how she'd gone from enjoying being held in Cooper's arms as they moved to the slow beat of the music to, "I can't do this anymore," five minutes later.

Okay, yes. She was being quiet. She'd needed to come to terms with the fact that she'd fallen in love with him—her insides were still jumping all over the place at that revelation—because that was the last thing she'd ever wanted. One way or another, love didn't last. Mom. Mia. Even Shane because he'd gotten divorced, too. He might have Layla now, but who knew if it would last?

And Cooper... Why was he acting all kinds of crazy? He'd practically accused her of cheating on him.

Piper mentally smacked the palm of her hand on her forehead. Of course it was because Rachel had cheated on Cooper with Tom. Which meant what, exactly? He didn't trust her not to do the same?

A heavy weight settled in her chest.

Doesn't matter. Their deal was done. They'd ended their charade.

Her heart gave a painful thud. Not because they'd ended it. It was the fact that Cooper couldn't trust her. She'd thought they'd become friends. It was the one good thing that had come out of all this.

The idea of going back to the way they used to be... Her stomach twisted. She couldn't bear that.

Piper closed the door when the last of her friends walked in.

"Coffee. The way you like it." Abby handed her a large to-go cup.

"Chocolate." Elle handed her a cupcake. "With extra frosting, because I have a feeling you need it."

Her chest filled to bursting point. How lucky was she to have such compassionate friends? Fortunate was an understatement.

"Thank you so much." She glanced at the sugary treat. *No conversation hearts.* Why moisture pricked at the corners of her eyes, she couldn't say. She didn't even like the candies that much.

Oh, who was she trying to fool? Not the sisterhood, if the expressions on Abby's, Elle's, Layla's and Mia's faces were anything to go by. That just left herself.

"What's wrong?" Mia draped an arm around her shoulder and guided her to the couch and sat beside her.

"Nothing. Everything's fine," Piper insisted. She tried to smile. She really did.

"Then why are there tears streaming down your face?" Layla sat on the other side of Piper.

"Did you and Cooper have a fight?" Abby grabbed one of the club chairs in the living room.

"Is that why you changed your plans and came home last night?" Elle plopped down in the other chair.

"We broke up." Piper scraped the back of her hand across her face. Lord, why was she crying? She never shed tears when a relationship ended. She never moped around lamenting what might have been.

"Oh, honey. What happened?" Mia hugged her tight.

"He said stupid stuff. I said stupid stuff." Why had she done that? *I was jealous, that's why.* She should have explained. Instead, she'd lashed out. She couldn't stand to see Cooper with Rachel. Not for one minute. Every smile he flashed at Rachel was like a dagger through her heart.

Piper blinked because, damn it, more tears were starting to fall.

"It's okay." Layla patted her arm. "You can fix this. Talk to him. He's probably thinking the same thing."

Apologizing wouldn't solve anything. It was not like they were a real couple and could get back together.

A loud wail escaped from her parted lips. It sounded like a wounded animal. What was wrong with her? Tears wouldn't solve anything.

"It won't help," Piper insisted. "You don't understand."

"You had a silly fight." Abby acted as if it were no big deal. "You can kiss and make up. It's allowed."

"You've never done that before." Mia gave a sage nod of her head. "You end things and it's over. It's okay to care enough to want to fix things between you and Cooper. I'm sure he wants that, too. You two are great together. He loves you. I know how much that scares you, but it's a good thing." She smiled. "Trust me."

She shook her head. "It's not like that between us." *Ah, hell.* The waterworks were in full force again.

"What do you mean?" Elle asked. "Anyone can see you two are crazy for each other."

She swiped a hand across her face. "It was all for show."

Layla's brows drew together in a deep V. "Come again?"

Piper slumped back against the couch. "We were acting." She explained about the deal she and Cooper made.

Elle burst out laughing. "I wasn't serious when I told you to do that."

"Maybe not, but I was desperate." Piper's lips quirked into a small smile. "My mother wouldn't stop fixing me up. And Cooper..." She wasn't going to explain further. "Let's just say he had his own reasons for making the deal.

"Everything was perfect until..." Piper heaved out a sigh.

"Until you fell in love with him," Mia finished.

She nodded. "That wasn't supposed to happen." She still didn't want a serious relationship. This thing… Cooper… It was hard enough.

"Does Mom know about any of this?" Mia asked.

Piper shook her head. "She certainly doesn't know about our deal, and I don't want her to know about the breakup until after the gallery opens. I have too much on my plate to deal with right now. The last thing I need is for her to go into fix-up mode again."

The idea of dating anyone other than Cooper… Piper shuddered.

An image of Cooper holding his gorgeous ex in his arms as they whirled around the dance floor last night slammed into her head. No, damn it. She wasn't going to think about him with her.

She straightened her shoulders and lifted her chin. Enough was enough. It was time to move on. She wouldn't spend the rest of her life pining over a man because he was gone.

Mom's face appeared in her mind.

The loneliness… The devastation etched in her beautiful features after Dad's death…

No way. She wouldn't end up like her.

She couldn't go through that. Wouldn't.

"You're still here." Levi propped his tall frame against the open door of Coop's office at TK Construction. "It's after eight p.m."

"I'm working." Coop kept staring at the computer monitor sitting on his desk.

"You said the same thing every night this week."

Coop glared at his brother. So what if he'd worked late the last four days? "I've got things to do."

"Ah." His brother gave a sage nod. "That must be why you've locked yourself in this office for more than sixteen hours a day since you came back from Everett and Annalise's wedding."

He nodded. "That's right. I need to catch up after being out of the office for five weeks."

"While you renovated Piper's gallery," Levi stated.

Coop stiffened. Leave it to his brother to bring her up. Not that he'd been able to get her off his mind. The truth was, she'd consumed his thoughts 24/7 since she walked out on him during the reception.

Coop gritted his teeth. She'd acted as if everything they'd shared during the last few weeks meant nothing to her.

He wouldn't think about her anymore. "Is there a reason why you're here?"

"Yes. Are you still participating in the ice art competition on Friday?" Levi asked. "You haven't told the committee what you're planning to sculpt yet."

"I don't know what I'm going to do yet."

"Remember it's a love theme this year, since the festival lands on Valentine's Day."

Coop groaned. Talk about a kick in the teeth. This was going to be the worst Valentine's Day ever. "I've changed my mind. I'm going to pass this year."

"You're not entering?" Levi's brows knit together.

Coop blew out a breath. "That's what I said."

"But you enter every year," his brother insisted.

"I don't have time this year. These quotes need to go out in the next two days." Coop gestured to the stack of paperwork piled on the right corner of his desk.

Levi sauntered in and dropped into the chair in front of Coop's desk. He grabbed a handful of the quotes and thumbed through them. "These have already been reviewed. By me." He pointed to his signature at the bottom of each page.

Okay. Fine. Levi was right. He'd already reviewed all the quotes that needed to go out. Coop just...needed to keep busy.

He didn't want to go home.

Everything there reminded him of Piper. Which was crazy. It was his house. He'd lived there all his life.

Without her.

So why did he wake each morning and reach for her, and why was he disappointed to find her side of the bed empty? Why did he set out two plates for dinner before realizing he'd dine alone? And why couldn't he bear to look at his favorite comfy T shirt, the one Piper had commandeered to sleep in?

Coop scrubbed his hands over his face. He knew why. He missed her smile. Her laugh. He missed the way she snuggled against him while they sat on the couch in front of a roaring fire, or when they watched TV. He missed the way her body fit with his.

He missed...her.

His brother crossed his arms over his chest and narrowed his gaze. "Okay. What's going on?"

"Nothing. Why would you think something is going on?" He hadn't told anyone he and Piper were no more. They'd agreed to break up after her gallery opened and he was going to stick to the plan, even if she hadn't.

She must not have said anything either. Otherwise, Shane would have paid him a visit. Coop remembered Shane's reaction when he'd first found them together. He could only imagine what would happen when he learned about the breakup.

"You won't enter the love-themed ice art competition." Levi's voice boomed in the otherwise silent room. "And you're making excuses to work late, like you did when you and Rachel split.

"Did something happen between you and Piper?" Levi asked.

"I don't know what you're talking about." Coop lowered his gaze to the quote sitting in front of him.

Levi let loose a loud snort. "What'd you do to make her dump your sorry ass?"

His lips tightened into a thin line. "Oh, sure, take her side."

Levi rolled his gaze skyward. "What happened?"

Coop looked his brother in the eye. "It's none of your business."

"Hate to break it to you, but I'm the least of your troubles. When Mom finds out…"

His shoulders slumped. She was going to be on his case for sure. Mom adored Piper. Mia, too. "It's none of her business either. Piper and I broke up. End of story."

"You really think that's going to fly, given how close our families are?" his brother asked.

Neither of them had thought about that little complication when they'd come up with this deal. How could they have believed for a second that a fake relationship would work?

"Why don't you tell me what happened. Maybe there's a way to fix this before Mom finds out."

Was that even possible at this point? Lord, he wanted that more than he could say, but he couldn't see how it was possible. "Okay." Coop slumped back against the back of his leather chair. He told his brother everything.

Levi doubled over with laughter. "A fake relationship. Now, that's one for the books."

"I needed to save face at the wedding," he insisted.

Levi laughed even harder. "You actually believe that, don't you?"

Coop scowled. "It's the truth."

"You could have chosen anyone to take to the wedding. Hell, Fiona from the Homes for Humanity crew would have jumped at the chance. She's had the hots for you for months now. But you chose Piper. Why do you think that is?"

Coop closed his eyes and prayed for patience. "I told you. She needed this as much as I did."

Levi grinned. "You still won't admit it, will you?"

"Admit what?" he growled.

"You've had a thing for her since you were in the eighth grade. Ask Mom, she's been saying you belong together for years."

Damn it. He wished Mom would keep her thoughts to herself when it came to Piper and him. "Mom has no idea what she's talking about. Piper and I didn't even like each other until recently."

Levi's smile widened. "That doesn't mean you haven't been crushing on her all this time. Now why don't you tell me why Piper ended your deal early? It doesn't make sense."

"I don't know." He knew he sounded like an obstinate child, but he couldn't help it.

Levi burst out laughing again. "Man, you really have it bad."

He had it bad for her all right. Too bad his feelings weren't reciprocated.

An image of her standing with Tom at the wedding burst into his head. The smile on her face… *His* smile. That was how he thought of it, because she only flashed it for him. He told his brother what happened with Tom.

Levi shook his head. "Boy, you really are a moron."

"What?" he cried. "Did you even listen to me?"

"You saw her talking with Tom," Levi stated.

"Yes." He nodded.

"And she was smiling."

"Yes," he repeated.

"I understand that Tom's a sore spot with you."

Sore spot was an understatement. The guy was supposed to be his friend and he'd turned around and slept with *his girlfriend*. Coop didn't trust Tom, or Rachel, for that matter.

"The whole thing sounds pretty innocent to me," his brother said. "Did you ask her about it?"

"No," he admitted. He'd…reacted without any thought. Which was pretty damned stupid when he thought about it now.

Coop exhaled a heavy sigh. He couldn't trust Tom, but Piper… *Ah, hell.* She'd never lied to him. Not once in all the years they'd known each other.

"Please tell me you didn't accuse her of cheating—" Levi broke off and shook his head. "*No.* You wouldn't be that stupid."

Coop looked away. He couldn't meet his brother's gaze. He might not have said the words, but yes, that was exactly what he'd done.

"What is wrong with you?" His brother jumped up from his seat and thwacked him in the head, like he used to do when they were kids.

Coop recoiled. "What the *hell*?"

"This is Piper we're talking about, not Rachel," Levi said. "Piper would never do anything like that to you. Or anyone else, for that matter. You should damned well know that."

His brother was right. He'd allowed his anger, his fear of losing her and his insecurities—because that was what it really boiled down to—to get the better of him.

He loved Piper. He wanted her to love him, too, but he'd never plucked up the courage to ask her to turn their fake relationship into something real. Something that would last.

Stupid, stupid, stupid. "I know. I know. I screwed up. Big-time." He couldn't have made a bigger mess of things if he'd tried. "The question is, how do I fix things?"

Levi arched a brow. "Is that what you want?"

"Yes." He wanted a life with Piper. More than anything else in the world.

Chapter Twenty-Five

Piper stood in the middle of her gallery on Saturday morning and peered around the space. The wood floors gleamed. LED lights highlighted Jax Rawlins's wildlife photos that hung on her freshly painted white walls.

In less than six hours, the rooms would be filled with patrons milling about the space, commenting on the displayed pieces. Servers would discreetly serve trays of delicious hors d'oeuvres provided by Layla. A bartender would serve beer and wine in fluted glasses from behind the beautiful new bar.

In less than six hours, her lifelong dream would become a reality.

She should be beyond excited. She should be floating on cloud nine. She should be doing a happy dance.

So why was she standing here with a heavy weight in her chest?

Tears gathered in the corners of her eyes. Cooper wouldn't be here to share this with her, that was why.

She swallowed hard. How could she miss someone so much it physically hurt? Instead of getting better each day, the pain in her chest grew worse and worse. How was that even possible after such a short time together?

Piper dragged the back of her hand over each eye to stop the tears from falling.

It wasn't supposed to be this way. She wasn't supposed to fall in love. Love wouldn't last, and when it ended…

She couldn't handle the despair. Couldn't relive the all-consuming grief she'd experienced when her father died.

Piper drew in a deep, steadying breath. Life without Cooper…

She rubbed at the center of her chest. She couldn't think about that reality.

"Piper, honey?" Mom's muffled voice came from the first floor. "Are you here? The door is open."

Right. She'd propped it open when she'd arrived because she needed to unload the contents of her car. Toilet paper for the restrooms, paper towels for the kitchen. Cleaning supplies, coffee from the Coffee Palace, boxes of tea she'd ordered online. Piper had forgotten to close it behind her after the last trip.

She opened the doors to the gallery and stepped out on the landing. "I'm up here."

Mom hurried up the stairs and presented a beautifully wrapped box to her.

"What's this?" Piper asked.

"It's something for good luck on your new adventure." Mom kissed her cheek. "I'm so proud of you, sweetie."

A rush of warmth filled her and she smiled. "That's so nice. Thank you. Do you want to see inside?"

Mom grinned. "Are you kidding me? I thought you'd never ask, but first, I want you to open the gift."

Her brows drew together. She'd planned to wait until they walked inside but now was as good a time as any. "Okay." Piper removed the wrapping paper and lid. Inside lay three-inch tall, baby-pink-colored wood letters that spelled out her first and last name.

"Do you remember those?" Mom asked.

"Yes. They used to hang on my bedroom wall when I was little." Piper had removed them when she'd entered middle school and Mom had remodeled her room.

"Your father carved them for you the day you were born. I know you already have a sign on the wall that says Kavanaugh Art Gallery." Mom pointed to the block letters that stood to the right of the gallery door. "But I thought you might like to have those—" she gestured to the letters in the box "—to hang in your studio."

"Dad made these?" She touched the letters reverently. "I never knew that." Piper swallowed hard. She wasn't going to cry, damn it, but the tears started falling nonetheless. Happy tears. To receive such an unexpected treasure made her day. "I'm so glad you saved them." She hugged her mother hard. "These are perfect for my studio."

"I'm so glad you like them," Mom said.

Piper wiped her eyes and grinned. "I love them. It's such a thoughtful gift." One of the most thoughtful gifts she'd ever received. "Come on." Piper opened the door to her gallery and gestured for Mom to precede her. "I can't wait to see what you think."

Mom stepped inside. "Oh, Piper." Her gaze darted around the room. "This is fantastic. The space looks amazing. I love the mix of old and new," Mom said, gesturing from the wood floors and ornately carved crown molding that surrounded the ceilings to the industrial metal shelves behind the bar.

Piper beamed a mile-wide smile. "I'm so glad you like it."

"Where's Cooper?" Mom peered around the room. "I saw his truck in the parking lot and assumed he was up here helping you."

"Cooper's here?" She raced to the windows. Yes. His truck was indeed parked in the parking lot.

Piper spotted him. Happiness bubbled up inside her.

He walked toward the building and…into Layla's restaurant.

He wasn't here to see her.

Her heart clenched. The painful thud making it hard to breathe.

She turned away from the window.

"What's wrong, honey?" Mom rushed to her side.

"Nothing." Piper couldn't look her mother in the eye.

Her mom draped an arm around her shoulder. "You look like you've lost your best friend. What's going on with you and Cooper?"

"Don't worry about Cooper and me." Piper marched over to the bar and grabbed her coat from where she'd draped it over the chair back. The last thing she wanted was to tell her mother she and Cooper were finished. "I need to head out. I have a few more errands to do before the grand opening this afternoon."

"You broke things off with him, didn't you?" She couldn't miss the accusation in Mom's voice.

Piper stiffened. Of course her mother thought Piper had ended the relationship. Why had she ever believed she could fool her?

Idiot, idiot, idiot. Her plan would never have worked, because Mom knew her too well.

Piper turned and faced her mother. "Yes. I ended things with Cooper."

"But why? I don't understand. You seemed so happy together."

She was happy with him. Happier than she'd been in years. Piper drew in a deep breath and released it. "It didn't work out, so I ended things."

"You didn't give it a chance," Mom countered. "You've never given any relationship a chance."

Piper folded her arms over her chest. It appeared that they were going to have this out once and for all. "I don't want a relationship. I keep telling you that, but you never seem to listen. You keep setting me up with guy after guy."

"I want you to find love, sweetheart."

"Why? So I can end up like you? Distraught and devastated for the rest of my life? Or divorced like Mia and Shane? That's a hard no. I'll skip the heartbreak, thank you very much."

Her mother gawked at her. "Is that really what you think?"

Piper's eyes bugged out. Why would she think otherwise? "Mom. It's been more than fifteen years since Dad passed and you haven't so much as *looked* at another man."

"Oh, Piper." Mom laid her head in her hands. "I thought I was protecting you all these years, but I've done you a huge disservice."

"What are you talking about?"

Her mother lifted her head and looked Piper in the eyes. "I thought you and Mia and Shane would be upset if you knew. You loved your father so much."

Piper rubbed at her temples. "I don't understand. What would we be upset about?"

"I've had other relationships," Mom said.

Piper blinked. She couldn't have heard her right. "Say that again."

Mom dragged her fingers through her hair. "I've dated other men over the years. I just haven't told you about them."

Piper shook her head. "Do you really expect me to believe that? Why wouldn't you tell any of us?"

"At first, you were young and I didn't want to expose you to someone if things didn't work out, and then..." Her mother shrugged. "I thought you'd be mad. You loved your father so much."

There was some truth to what Mom believed. As a teen, Piper would have seen it as a betrayal against her father.

"There is someone I'd like you to meet if you'd be open

to the idea." Mom gave her a tentative smile. "His name is Chris."

Piper's jaw dropped. "Book club Chris?" The person Mom had gone away with last summer?

Red color crept up Mom's neck and flooded her cheeks. "Yes. We hit it off when he joined our group last year."

"Oh my God. All this time I believed Chris was a female friend of yours."

Her butt-in-ski mother, who'd made it her life's mission to find Piper a husband, had a secret boyfriend. Talk about the hypocrisy of it...

Although... Given Mom's perceptions of how she thought Piper would react to that news, she understood why Mom never said anything.

"I'm so happy for you." She hugged her mother. "Are things serious between you?"

Her mother's smile broadened. "I think he's going to propose soon."

Piper gasped. "And you're going to accept if he does?"

"I will." Mom grasped Piper's hands in hers. "I loved your father with all my heart, and it's taken me a long time to find someone who I can love again. I can't... I won't allow this opportunity to slip away."

She'd been wrong about her mother. On so many levels. Mom might have been grief-stricken when Dad died, but she hadn't stopped living. She wasn't wasting away, pining for something that could no longer be. She wasn't trying to live vicariously through Piper, or anyone else. Just the opposite. She'd found the courage to move on with her life, and had never given up on finding love again.

"Chris is a wonderful man," her mother continued. "He's kind and loving. He makes me laugh." Her mother glowed with happiness. "I can't wait for you and your brother and sister to meet him."

"I'm thrilled for you, Mom." Piper hugged her again. "You deserve to be happy and I can't wait to meet him. He's a lucky man to have you."

"You deserve to be happy, too." Her mother's words shook with conviction.

"Mom…" Piper began.

"Do you love Cooper?"

Piper closed her eyes. She couldn't lie anymore. Not to Mom, and not to herself. "With all of my heart."

Mom kissed her cheek. "Take a chance. Turn your fake relationship with Cooper into something real. Something lasting."

Piper stiffened. "You knew?"

"Of course I did." Mom planted her hands on her hips, but she was smiling. "Did you really think Debby and I would believe that story the two of you concocted?"

Yes. She'd 100 percent believed Mom had bought their tale hook, line and sinker. But once again, Mom was one step ahead of her. Piper snorted. "I can't believe both of you knew all this time and never said anything."

"It almost killed me. Debby too, but we went along with it. Actually, we did everything we could to encourage the idea.

"She's right you know. Debby," Mom added when Piper's brows knitted together. "You two belong together. We all saw your budding romance start that summer between seventh and eighth grade. Ron and Debby. Dad and me. Then your father died and whatever was starting to grow between you and Cooper died, too. Don't make that mistake twice."

"Oh, Mom." Piper sniffed and wiped the moisture gathering in the corners of her eyes.

Her mother winked. "Layla's place *would* make a great wedding venue."

"Mom!" Piper gasped. "I don't even know if Cooper feels the same way about me as I do about him." He'd been so angry with her at the wedding.

"There's only one way to find out." Mom flashed a wide grin. "Ask him."

Piper's mind spun faster than a Tilt-A-Whirl ride at an amusement park.

"Make peace with the past, Piper, and choose a life worth living.

"Choose love, darling. I'll see you later. And I'll bring Chris to the opening, if that's okay." Mom giggled like a schoolgirl.

Could she take the risk and open her heart? Could she be brave, like her mother?

"Yo, Coop." Levi stuck his head through the tarp that surrounded his ice sculpture on the front lawn of the co-lonial mansion. "You've got thirty minutes until the dead-line."

Thank goodness he'd convinced Layla to sponsor his exhibit at the last minute. He would have been excluded from the contest if she hadn't.

"I'll be done. I'll be done." He chiseled a piece of ice away from his sculpture. No way could he not be. His en-tire future with Piper was riding on this.

Levi peered at Coop's work. His brows knitted into a deep V. "How is this supposed to win Piper back?"

"She'll understand." At least he hoped she would.

Levi shook his head. "Tell me again why you didn't just talk to her. Why couldn't you just apologize for being a butthead and beg for forgiveness?"

That was plan B, if this didn't work. He could and would grovel if the situation called for it. "Actions speak louder than words. I want to show her how I feel."

Levi shrugged. "If you say so."

"I do." Coop glanced at his brother. "How's it going in there?" He gestured to the second story of the old mansion that housed Piper's gallery. He wished he could be there with her. To support her and cheer her on. If he hadn't been such a... What had Levi called him? A butthead. He'd been called much worse by his brothers for less offensive behavior.

What if Piper couldn't forgive him? What was he going to do then? *No, damn it.* He couldn't think that way. He'd fix this. He had to.

"The place is packed. I'm pretty sure she sold every print."

Coop smiled. "That's great."

"Yeah. Her customers are crying for more. Jax says he can't wait to come back."

I'll just bet he can't. Coop's lips tightened.

"What was that?" Levi asked. "I didn't catch what you said."

Great, now he was grumbling out loud. "Nothing. You should get going. I need to finish this up and I need every second I have left."

"Good luck." His brother waved and stepped outside.

"Thanks." He was going to need it.

Chapter Twenty-Six

"Congratulations, little sister." Mia walked up and slung an arm around her shoulder. "You did it. Day one of your new business was a resounding success."

Piper peered around the now-empty room. A wide grin spread across her face. "Yes, it was." A good portion of today's achievement could be credited to Jax Rawlins, because many of the people who attended her grand opening today came because of him. But a lot of those people seemed interested in returning to see works from the artists she'd booked over the next few months.

Mom walked into the main space with Chris at her side. "We had a wonderful time, dear. I'm so proud of you."

Piper smiled, and yes, a touch of heat flooded her cheeks. "Thanks. I'm proud of me, too."

"A job well done," Chris said. "It was a pleasure to finally meet you." He extended his hand to Piper.

"The pleasure is all mine." Standing on her tiptoes, she hugged the tall man.

"Mine, too." Mia copied Piper.

"We're going to head down to the ice art festival now. The judges are going to announce the winner in a few minutes." Mom narrowed her gaze. "Will we see you there?"

Piper chuckled. "Yes." She couldn't wait to find Cooper. "That reminds me, I need to grab something from the kitchen before I lock up."

"Good luck." Mom gave her a quick hug, and headed toward the elevator with Chris by her side.

"I'm going to head out, too." Mia turned to leave.

"It was nice that Kyle stopped by with the girls," Piper called. "I know you wanted them to be here."

Mia whirled around. Her expression was… Well, Piper couldn't tell if Mia was ticked off or happy about Kyle's appearance this evening. "Yeah. I guess it was."

"Piper?" Jax stepped off the elevator and into the hall. "Thank goodness you're still here. I dropped my cell phone and…" He stared at her sister. His gaze locked with hers. "Hey, Mia."

"Hi." Mia's cheeks flamed fire-engine red.

Jax's gaze jerked to Piper. "Okay if I look around for my phone?"

"Sure, but make it quick." She needed to find Cooper.

"Maybe Mia can help me?" His gaze landed on her sister again. "If you're not busy, that is."

Mia's lips parted and her eyes went wide. "Um…okay."

The air sizzled between the two of them.

One and done, huh? I don't think so. Oh, yes. This was getting more interesting by the second.

"Lock up for me." Piper grinned. "I've got to find Cooper."

"He's set up in front of the mansion." Jax shook his head. "I'll be honest. I don't think he's going to win this year. His sculpture… I mean it's cute, but…" He gestured to the front of the building. "You should judge for yourself."

Truth be told. Jax's opinion didn't matter. Nothing was more important than finding Cooper and telling him how she felt about him. She walked into the kitchen and grabbed the small cupcake box from the fridge where Elle had placed it earlier.

After Mom left this morning, Piper had called the Coffee Palace and asked Elle to prepare a very special, very personal chocolate cupcake with extra chocolate frosting. She and Abby had dropped it off during Jax's show. They couldn't stay long. With the ice art festival underway, the Coffee Palace was packed with customers. The same was true for Layla. If the parking lot was anything to go by, her restaurant was slammed.

How lucky was she to have such great friends that they'd take time out of their busy schedules to stop by and support her?

It wasn't luck. She'd opened her heart and received a wonderful gift in return.

Cooper's smiling face popped into her mind. Piper crossed her fingers. *Here's hoping.*

She exited the kitchen. Mia and Jax were nowhere to be found.

Piper grinned and exited the gallery. Once downstairs, she hurried around to the front of the mansion.

A throng of people milled about the area, but Cooper was nowhere to be found. Piper rushed into the crowd. Where was he? Had she missed him? "Excuse me." She turned sideways to pass through a swarm of humanity. "Pardon me." She squeezed by others. Her gaze darted around the mob, searching for Cooper's face.

"Cooper," she called, but there was so much noise she doubted anyone heard her. "Where are you, Cooper?" she yelled. How was she going to find him with all of these people clustered around her?

Her heart hammered as she continued weaving her way through the multitude of people and shouting Cooper's name. Where was he? She needed to find him.

Piper wasn't sure how much time passed when a pair of

strong hands grabbed her waist from behind and hauled her out of the crowd. She whirled around.

"Cooper." She threw her arms around him and planted kisses all over his face. "I've been looking all over for you."

He grinned. Wrapping his arms around her, he held her tight. "I've been looking for you, too."

"You were?" She luxuriated in the press of his body against her and the warm, minty scent of his breath on her face.

"I ran into your mom and she said you were here." Worry creased his brow. "I thought maybe she was wrong when I couldn't find you."

"I'm right here." She brushed her lips against his. She wanted to linger and savor his sweetness, but she needed to set the record straight first.

Piper grabbed his hand with her free one and led him to a spot a few feet away that was less congested. "I love you, Cooper Turner. With everything that I am and everything that I will be. I want to turn our fake relationship into something real and something lasting.

"I never dreamed that I could love someone as much as I love you." She shook her head. "I didn't want to. When I lost my father…" Piper swallowed hard. "I was afraid. Loving hurt too much."

"But you've changed your mind."

She beamed a mile-wide smile at him. "Yes. I've been miserable without you this past week. I've learned a life without love isn't living at all. It's just existing. That's what I've been doing for the last fifteen years. Then you came along. You broke through all of my defenses without even trying."

Coop grinned and kissed her hard.

"I want to play in the snow with you. Cuddle on the couch and watch sappy romance movies with you. I want to argue with you when we don't agree—we'll keep that to a minimum—and make mad, passionate love with you." She grinned. "As often as possible. I want to make a life with you by my side, and I'm hoping you want that, too."

Her insides jumped and jittered as she waited for his response.

This brilliant, thoughtful, giving woman loved *him*. What had he done in this life to become so lucky?

"Yes. I want it all, as long as I'm with you." Coop was pretty sure he was sporting a goofy grin. He didn't care. Piper loved him. "I love you, too, Piper. More than words can say." He stroked his palm over her cheek.

"I screwed up, sweetheart, and I'm sorry. I saw you with Tom and… I was jealous. Plain and simple. I couldn't stand him being anywhere near you." Coop dragged his fingers through his hair. "There's something I never told you about Tom and Rachel."

"I know. Mia told me the night of Everett and Annalise's wedding. My question is, why didn't you? I thought maybe you were still in love with Rachel."

All his tension eased away. "No. No. I am not in love with Rachel. Any love I felt for her disappeared when I found out about her and Tom. As for why I didn't tell you about them…" Coop shook his head. "I felt like such a fool. They were together right under my nose for two months and I couldn't see it. What does that say about me?"

"It says you are a kind, loving man who chose to trust his partner and his best friend. They didn't deserve that honor."

He pulled her against him so that every inch of her touched every part of him. "Can you forgive me for being such a jackass to you at the wedding? I should never have implied…"

"You're right. You shouldn't have," she admonished. "I would never do that to you."

"I know." He kissed her because he needed the contact. "You're as honest as they come." Coop shook his head. "I knew I was in love with you, but I couldn't pluck up the courage to see if you felt the same way. I thought maybe you still liked Tom." There. He'd admitted the truth.

Piper eased back. "You thought I had a thing for *Tom*?"

He cringed. "You admitted you liked him in high school. It's why you were so upset the night of the Valentine's dance."

Piper shuddered. "That was before he acted like such a colossal jerk to me." She brushed her lips against his. "So we're clear, I have no interest in Tom Anderson. Now, you…" Piper nipped the corner of his mouth "…are another story. I have *immense* interest in you." She cupped his face with her palms.

A thud sounded behind her.

"Oh, no. Crap." She jerked away from him and bent to pick up something from the ground.

"What's that?" he asked.

Piper handed him the deformed cardboard container. "It's for you." She shook her head. "I'm sorry. It's a little smushed. I forgot I was holding it."

He lifted the top and smiled. A cupcake topper that said Happy Valentine's Day sat in the middle of a huge, now-flat, mound of chocolate frosting flagged by two candy hearts that sat slightly askew. The words *Luv U* were written on one heart and *Forever* on the other. Coop burst out laughing.

Piper sighed. "That's definitely not the reaction I was expecting."

"No. I love it." He dropped a quick kiss on her pursed lips. "Looks like we're both on the same wavelength."

"What are you talking about?" she asked.

He grabbed her hand with his free one and walked her around to the front of his exhibit. Most of the people had moved on to view other sculptures. Only a few stragglers stood in front of his piece.

"Love Conversations?" She glanced at the name on the plaque as they passed by.

"You'll understand why I chose that name for my sculpture in a moment." Coop stopped in a spot that gave Piper the best view of his work.

She flashed a happy grin in his direction. "You made giant candy hearts carved out of ice. Oh my gosh. You even colored them." She touched the light orange and yellow hearts. "And etched words on the face. *Be mine. Always.*" Piper grinned and clapped her hands. "That's so sweet."

Coop handed the cupcake to his father who stood a short distance away with his mother, Jane, and a man he didn't know.

He reached inside his pocket and pulled out the small box he'd stored there for the last two days. The ring she'd spotted in the jewelry store window the day they'd made their deal.

His palms turned sweaty. His heart hammered faster than a racehorse galloping toward the finish line.

"Piper." Dropping to one knee, he cleared his throat.

Mom gasped. He was pretty sure Jane did, too.

Piper gawked at him. "What are you doing, Cooper?"

He sucked in a deep, steadying breath. A few short weeks ago he couldn't imagine doing this ever again, let alone five weeks into a fake relationship. Now he'd never been so sure of anything in his life.

"Will you be mine always? I fell for you when I was thirteen years old." It was the truth. His brother was right about that. "But fate had other plans for us. Then, a few short weeks ago you walked into my life again, and turned my world upside down. I haven't been the same since. I love you with all my heart." He flipped open the top on the ring box and presented the diamond solitaire to her. "Will you make me the happiest man alive and marry me?"

"Yes." She gave him a watery smile. "I would love to marry you. I can't think of anything I'd like more."

Coop rose and smiled a mile-wide grin. "Love you so much, sweetheart." He lifted Piper into his arms and twirled her around.

"I love you, too. Now put the ring on my finger. Please." She bounced up and down.

"Bossy." He grinned.

"Euphoric. Ecstatic. And head over heels in love with you," she corrected.

She was as honest as they came. He'd never doubt that again.

Coop slid the ring on her finger.

"It's perfect. I love it." Piper grinned and raised her left hand in the air and waved.

Mom and Jane rushed over and hugged both of them.

"I always knew you two belonged together." Mom kissed his cheek.

"A Valentine's proposal." Jane clapped her hand to her heart. "How romantic. I'm so happy for you."

Piper twined her arms around his neck and brushed her sweet lips over his. "Best Valentine's Day ever, and it's all because of you."

He grinned. "It's definitely an improvement over that fateful night all those years ago."

"No skunk, for one thing." She waggled her brows.

He chuffed out a laugh. "Ha ha. You're funny."

"It's the new me." Piper chuckled. "Happy and in love. What do you think?"

He winked. "I'm liking it very much."

Piper smiled. "I can't wait to start our new life together. You and me. Forever."

He nodded. "Always. Through good times or bad."

"I love you, Cooper."

His heart filled to bursting point. "I love you, too." Best Valentine's Day. Ever!

* * * * *

Special EDITION

Believe in love. Overcome obstacles. Find happiness.

Available Next Month

The Cowboy's Road Trip Stella Bagwell
Flirting With Disaster Elizabeth Hrib

....

The Pilot's Secret Allison Leigh
Twenty-Eight Dates Michelle Lindo-Rice

Keep reading for an excerpt of a new title
from the Western Romance series,
FORTUNE'S BABY CLAIM by Michelle Major

PROLOGUE

ESME FORTUNE DIDN'T allow herself to believe in karma because that would mean she'd done something acutely awful to wind up in her current situation.

"You're doing fine," the nurse told her with a gentle pat to her arm before rushing out of the makeshift delivery room that wasn't a room at all—just a tiny alcove on the first floor of County Hospital outside of Chatelaine, Texas.

Another contraction started, bringing a surging wave of pain. At the same time, a flash of lightning followed by a booming clap of thunder shook the window next to her hospital bed.

The lights flickered again, something they'd been doing off and on for the past hour despite the various nurses who popped in and out to monitor the progress of Esme's labor and assure her that the hospital's backup generator was reliable.

At this point, she didn't trust anything—or anyone—other than her sister, Bea, who wasn't here yet. A fallen tree and downed power lines blocked the two-lane highway that led from Chatelaine to the hospital.

But she couldn't worry about her sister right now and instead concentrated on breathing through the pain that ripped through her. One, two, three, four. One, two, three, four…

The first thing she'd done after moving from Houston to Chatelaine a month earlier was to sign up for birthing classes with Bea as her coach. Esme, who'd spent her childhood dreaming of the sort of fairy-tale love that filled the romance novels she devoured, had failed at love and marriage, but she was determined to be the best mother she could.

Her baby would have a wonderful life full of laughter, happiness and no uncertainty about whether they were cherished and adored.

As the contraction subsided, a cold droplet hit her smack dab in the forehead, and she looked up to see water dripping from the ceiling above her. Esme sighed. Clearly, motherhood was not off to an auspicious start.

Who could have predicted that her water breaking would coincide with the late-October storm ravaging the region? It was the kind of storm that happened once in a lifetime—a hundred-year storm, the older neighbor who'd driven her to the hospital ominously reported, glancing at Esme like her situation had somehow predicated the lashing wind and pounding rain.

As it turned out, Esme wasn't the only soon-to-be mother whose baby seemed eager to meet the world in the middle of a torrential downpour. The frantic young woman at the admissions desk reported that four other women were already on the labor and delivery floor of the small hospital—a veritable baby boom in this sleepy region of Texas.

But now they were all crowded into a section of the hospital's OR with hastily constructed fabric partitions separating them after a burst pipe flooded the floor above them.

Esme cradled her stomach and tried to calm her nerves. It would work out. She could handle this. Her late husband might have believed she was weak and ordinary, but she was made of stronger stuff than Seth Watson had claimed.

And she'd do anything for the baby she already loved with her whole heart.

A woman's cries from the other side of the divider made Esme's anxiety ratchet up a few levels. But at least she could take solace in the fact that she was managing this unexpected turn of events with more calm than her neighbor, who had been swearing and screeching at staff and the man she kept calling "you big oaf" since Esme had been wheeled in.

"I don't want this," she heard the woman complain in a fierce whisper. "Make it stop. This is your fault, you big oaf! I'll never forgive you."

Esme couldn't hear the guy's response, but his tone was low and calm, especially given the venom being spewed his way. His words might not be comforting to her neighbor, but they had an oddly soothing effect on Esme, and she was grateful to the stranger.

Another contraction roared through her, so she concentrated on activating her own coping techniques once again. As the night drew on, the waves of pain came faster and more intensely, although the woman's shouting and cries drowned out Esme's soft moans.

She hated making any noise. It made her feel like she was losing the battle for control, but the pain slamming through her over and over felt relentless.

A new nurse checked her progress, assuring Esme it was all going according to plan, and she'd be ready to push soon.

No, she wanted to answer. *None of this was part of the plan*. Having a baby alone and raising her child as a single mother was not how she'd envisioned her life.

Was she as ill-equipped to welcome her son or daughter into the world as her neighbor loudly claimed about herself? The difference was the woman next to her had a big oaf at her side.

Esme imagined him broad, hairy and bearing a striking resemblance to the troll under the bridge from the classic children's tale.

How sad was it that even a potentially mean and hungry troll could comfort her now? Clearly, the fairy-tale life she'd imagined had gone very, very sideways.

She lost track of how much time had elapsed, but it felt like hours or days later when the curtain was yanked back to reveal another nurse and an older man who had the commanding air of a doctor.

As they entered the cramped space, tears sprung to Esme's eyes unbidden, but not in response to the pain or the exhaustion that threatened to pull her under like a riptide. She was simply so relieved not to be alone.

For an instant, her gaze was drawn to something over the doctor's shoulder, and she found herself looking into the most piercing set of green eyes she'd ever seen. Esme's eyes were green or hazel, depending on her mood, but the man staring at her had eyes the color of spring grass, vibrant and full of promise.

She had just enough time to register the handsome face surrounding those green eyes, a strong jaw and a full mouth that curved into the barest hint of a smile as he nodded and mouthed, "You've got this." He couldn't possibly be the oaf, or else Esme was delirious with fatigue.

But those three little words spoken silently by a stranger bolstered her resolve in a way that defied logic.

As the nurse pulled the curtain shut, Esme drew in the steadiest breath she could manage.

"Are you ready to meet your baby?" the doctor asked in a reassuring tone, then simultaneously winced and chuckled as another crack of thunder reverberated around them. "Because a child born on a night like this is bound to be special."

Esme swallowed around the emotion clogging her throat, then nodded. "I'm ready," she whispered.

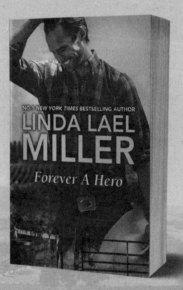

Subscribe and fall in love with a Mills & Boon series today!

You'll be among the first to read stories delivered to your door monthly and enjoy great savings.

MILLS & BOON

JOIN US

Sign up to our newsletter to stay up to date with...

- Exclusive member discount codes
- Competitions
- New release book information
- All the latest news on your favourite authors

Sign up at **millsandboon.com.au/newsletter**